Second Hand Smoke

Also by Thane Rosenbaum

Elijah Visible: Stories

Second Hand Smoke

A novel

Thane Rosenbaum

ST. MARTIN'S PRESS
NEW YORK

Library of Congress Cataloging-in-Publication Data

Rosenbaum, Thane.
    Second hand smoke / Thane Rosenbaum.
       p.   cm.
     ISBN 0-312-19954-6
     I. Title.
     PS3568.0782S43 1999
     813'.54—dc21   98-43787
                                         CIP

Book design by Ellen R. Sasahara

First Edition: April 1999

10 9 8 7 6 5 4 3 2 1

Note to Reader

In memory of Sam Rosenbaum,
a true patriot in the service of memory.

And for Basia Tess Rosenbaum,
with faith and soul.

For how much longer can I howl into this wind?

—Robert Smith, *The Cure*

Second Hand Smoke

Prologue

H<small>E WAS A CHILD</small> of trauma. Not of love, or happiness, or exceptional wealth. Just trauma. And nightmare, too. Wouldn't want to leave that out. As a young man he seemed to have come equipped with all the right credentials: primed for loss, consigned to his fate. But what kind of career exploits such talents? And who would want such a job?

He certainly wasn't pleased by the hand dealt to him, the straw that he nervously drew from the lot of random legacies—only to wish that he could immediately pick again. This wasn't a badge of honor, not the sort of thing that registered—even in his own morbid vision of the world—as a source of personal pride. But the circumstances of his birth were much like everyone else's: he hadn't been given much choice in the matter. He couldn't help who his parents were, where they had been, what they had seen, what they might have done . . .

Without the workings of a will or a bequest, he had received an inheritance that he would have rather done without, the kind of legacy he'd just as soon give back. But it doesn't work that way. What his parents gave him, he couldn't pass off on someone else. He couldn't even explain or understand what it was that he had. Splintered, disembodied memories that once belonged to them were now his alone, as though their two lives couldn't exhaust the outrage. The pain lived on as a family heirloom of unknown origins. What he saw he couldn't exactly identify; what he remembered was not something he actually ever knew. It was all interior—like a prison, like a cage.

Duncan had not been a witness to the Holocaust, only to its aftermath. His testimony was merely secondhand. Yet the staggering reality of the cattle cars, the gas chambers, and the crematoria did not feel remote to him, either, even though a half century of years and an ocean of water separated him from the actual crime. But crimes don't just end with the immediate injuries. The mind, alas, does not allow for that. And this was a special crime. The dreams of his parents—actually, their nightmares—kept it all alive.

What he saw firsthand was the damage that could never be undone. The true legacy of the *Shoah*. Lives that were supposed to start all over but couldn't. Halting first steps, then the stumbles. The inexhaustible sorrow of the parents; the imminent recognition of the children. A father rendered impotent by the violence done to his life; a mother who would not, could not, mother . . .

What to expect from such pedigrees, such misbreeds? Children of smoke and skeletons, the heirs of those who once had shaved heads and still had numbered arms. What chance did their parents have? What chance did they?

The Holocaust shaped those who were survivors of survivors. Inexorably, cruelly, and unfairly so. The choices and compromises made, the relationships cultivated and broken, the psychic demons and grotesque muses that mockingly interfered with everyday life.

$\mathcal{C}hapter\ One$

I T WASN'T SO MUCH that as a family they were strange, or that from the very beginning they had been estranged—although each in its own way was true. It was that they were damaged. Irreversibly ruined. The Katz family of Miami Beach came assembled that way, without manuals or operating instructions or reassuring warranties. Everything was already broken. Nothing worked right; nothing ever would. The damage is what defined them best.

It was the way they functioned or, as psychologists now call it, dysfunctioned. A state of mind in civil war with itself. And there were no defenses or cures for this condition. Whatever predator was out there would have little difficulty tracking them down. That was the world as they saw it. They were experts in survival, and yet at the same time they were rank amateurs in recognizing the languid, solitary, untroubled moment.

For them, the scarring ran deep and, in fact, had traded places with the surrounding skin. But the Katzes weren't visibly disfigured. There wasn't anything particularly hideous about them. A family portrait hung in the living room of their apartment, taken in 1964 by that German photographer used by everyone on Miami Beach's Arthur Godfrey Road. Framed and suspended on a stark white wall. Each day the sun plunged through the window of their high-rise apartment and faded the photograph, reducing the assorted hues to a blunt, burnt yellow. The Katzes aged better than the images around them. The three of them posing: mother and son sitting beside one another, tight-lipped, stone-faced; the father standing behind, as though a referee in waiting. No smiles, but no apparent signs of deformity, either. The camouflage was both convincing and inviolable.

The name Duncan, however, revealed the first sign of disguise. That was the name in 1953 that Mila and Yankee Katz had given their first and only child on the day of his *bris*.

"What kind of a name is that for a Jewish boy?" an old man remarked, bits of whitefish precarious at the end of a long fork. The old man speared the air, making his point, beating back any rebuttal.

"Maybe they can't spell," a younger women, armed with a more upstream appetizer—a carp or sable—whispered. "They are refugees, after all. Their English can't be so good. Maybe they wanted David but got it wrong when they looked it up in the baby-naming book. It's an understandable mistake, no?"

"What's the matter with you?" another old man joined in. He was wearing a pair of all-occasion green polyester slacks and a white shirt with a golf emblem. An outfit equally suitable for both afternoon tee-offs and the severing of Jewish foreskin. He was late for a foursome at Normandy Isle Golf Course, and had hoped that Duncan's rite of passage would have begun by now. Instead, the newborn was still waiting to have the work done on his genitals, while the golfer was forcibly delayed from the *tsuris* with his own clubs. Agitated, he said, "Yankee graduated from Heidelberg. You mean to tell me a man of such learning couldn't tell the difference between a David and a Duncan? Listen to me," he urged as the nibblers of nosh inched forward, "one thing is for sure: the boy's name isn't a mistake. These people are trying to tell us something."

"They were both kings," a young college coed interjected. She was slender with sleepy brown eyes. The daughter of a neighbor. Until now she had been sitting demurely on a soft, velvet, floral club chair in the Katz apartment, all the while wishing to be elsewhere, her mind not so much wandering as in a dull state of perpetual park.

"Who?" the golfer wondered. "Yankee and Mila? Of what kingdom? Auschwitz?"

"No, I mean Duncan and David," she spoke up proudly, offering an insight that—for the moment, at least—justified her tuition at Miami-Dade Community College. "Maybe Mila and Yankee want to give their son a royal name. Maybe they have great things planned for him."

"Where? In Glasgow?" The man with the whitefish rejoined the conversation, having just returned with more provisions—potato salad, some tongue, a smear of mustard on two slices of naked rye.

This ancient ritual of Jewish tribal commitment had suddenly taken on less importance than the mystery behind the infant's name. The girl was right: Duncan was the name of a Scottish king, the recipient of a tragic Shakespearean end. With such a name, and finale, what were the parents hoping for?

Despite their best efforts, Mila and Yankee hadn't really fooled anyone. They were trying to have it both ways, and their guests knew it. In giving birth to a son, they were holding up their end of the sacred covenant with God—laughably, the same god who was now even harder to trust than before. Nonetheless, they showed their obedience and good faith, the *bris* forever branding their child as a Jew. But in naming him Duncan, they were also not taking any chances, either. He had to have goy papers as well, something that would allow him to blend in on the other side, to survive unharmed and completely adaptable in the larger ghettos of the outside world.

This strategic obsession with names was a fact of life for the Katzes. Everything was in the service of deception. Like secret agents, they preferred to have aliases, but they rotated them in case anyone caught on. Names were easily disposable—interchangeable with numbers, in fact. Such were the lessons of the Nazis. Upon liberation, however, the refugees all learned that, unlike everything else about their former lives, their names could be reclaimed—if they could be remembered, if they wanted to remember them.

For some, the recovery of a name was not enough. Why have that when all else was lost? For others, the memory of zebra costumes and branded arms had forever soiled their attachment to anything that was once personal, precious, and intimate. Like the costumes and the arms, their pasts could never be washed cleaned. Perhaps it was better to walk away from the camps, and the nauseating mess, with nothing at all.

So some renounced their original names, changing them, clipping off a syllable, or escaping entirely into a new language. In Israel the Jews of the new Exodus became Hebrews all over again; in America they adopted the king's English, seasoned with *shtetl* spices that refused to be shaken loose in the New World. The Gentiles of America had long known that Jews could be named Brown or Smith or Wilk or Harris. Ploys to protect the innocent. Or maybe to conceal the guilty?

Yankee had changed his name, too. No real mystery there. The guests at Duncan's *bris* all imagined that his father had once been known as something else. He couldn't possibly have been born a Yankee—not in Germany and not as a Jew. Sure, there were Jews named Yankel, but they weren't German Jews. Too lowbrow for them; too peasant-sounding. But Yankee? Still didn't sound right. Something must have gotten lost in translation.

Arriving as a refugee in New York, Herschel Katz took on the name of a baseball team. He had never played the game in his life, and Mickey Mantle was more likely to conjure up an image of a mouse than a slugger. But he was looking to lose himself in something foreign—not just in a country, but also the indelibility of its ways. The Yankees were good at world wars, and even better with the World Series. As a former German intellectual, Herschel Katz strived for quality in all things, whenever possible. But what was perhaps most important of all was that, as a Yankee, Herschel Katz would be virtually untraceable and unknowable—even to himself.

A few years before his arrival in New York, the Americans had liberated him and his wretchedness from Bergen-Belsen; now he needed to be free from Herschel as well. His entire family had been slaughtered in the camps. Vanished faces and shrieking souls. A family tree chopped down, the handiwork of ax-wielding, maniacal Nazis. The world had mistaken a forest fire for a spectator sport while a holocaust consumed the best of European Jewry.

Unlike her husband, however, the Mila of Warsaw was still Mila in Miami. A name change alone would not have been enough, at least not in her case. Not sufficiently clever. More artful maneuvers would become necessary.

And so it wasn't simply a matter of assumed or contrived or wholly improvised names. The Katzes had constructed an entire vocabulary around the mixed message, the obscure reference. Suspicions lurked everywhere: concealed within the darkness of Miami's moonlit nights, floating like a bottle along its emerald bays, cast in the shadows of its towering sun. Few anticipated such terror in the tropics. But the Katzes, of all people, were not blinded by the sun. They were not mere tourists in Miami, fleeing from hurricanes or coating themselves to prevent sunburns. Their obsessions were real; their fears, although somewhat twisted, were certainly not imagined. The family radar bleeped at frequencies that were out of range for most people. High-pitched warnings, like tocsins, that came often and hummed throughout the day; the sirens announcing the end of the world, heard only by those blessed with madness.

Among strangers they spoke in an almost flawless code. And since most people were regarded as strangers, the code was commonly slipped in between sentences like a necessary pause or a deliberate stutter. Mila and Yankee's English may have been mangled, but the code spewed from their lips with the honeyed fluency of the family tongue.

Often they alternated and recycled the code.

"Keep them guessing," Mila always said.

"About what?" Duncan often wondered. "What secrets do we have that anyone would want to know? The sale items at Publix are already listed in the *Herald*."

Duncan carried around a crib sheet in order to keep the code straight in his head. The flavor of the week in the Katz home had nothing to do with ice cream.

For years, the parents would discreetly say the word *keller* whenever a member of the family had, in his speech, strayed too far and revealed too much.

"My mother can't pick us up at the park until after she goes to the store and then gets my father at the bank," Duncan would tell a friend over the phone.

"Keller," Mila, from the kitchen, would steer her son.

"Oh, yeah . . . no, I forgot, my father isn't at the bank. He's waiting at the corner by the drugstore."

When Duncan hung up the phone, he cringed and then turned around slowly to hear Mila's decree.

"Now we have to change the bank from Federal to Jefferson. You see, we can't depend on you for anything."

Banking was a desperately private affair. But then again, what wasn't? Dealings at the post office acquired an air of secrecy that rivaled the Paris peace talks. A stock certificate was never put into street name, but rather in a safe-deposit box—or safer yet, in a shoe box under the bed. *Safe* was always a relative term. The receipt of a reparations check was a bittersweet moment. The grocery bill was naturally confidential. The meter reader from Florida Power and Light was not allowed inside the apartment to do his job. Similarly, the Katzes refused home delivery of the *Miami Herald*. Everything was paid for in cash. And only God knew what Yankee did for a living. His own son certainly didn't. One minute Mila would tell neighbors that her husband was a manufacturer, at other times an importer, sometimes a lawyer, once a builder.

And who, or what, was *keller*, anyway? Yes, it was a mantra, invoked all throughout Duncan's childhood that became an exotic conversation killer. But what else? Although curious, Duncan never bothered to ask, or maybe he was just afraid. In this classified, rarefied, survivalist home, Duncan understood that even the derivations of certain words were household secrets. He may have been born into the family, but he was never accepted into its inner circle. Maybe it was for his own protection, his own good. Or, as Mila so often claimed, maybe they just didn't trust him. Perhaps it was simply that Mila and Yankee kept some passwords just for themselves.

Now back to the *bris*. And what a *bris* it was. While embracing God's covenant with Abraham, Mila and Yankee were at the same time also breaking promises, smashing tablets, stepping outside the faith, scavenging around, and bringing back pagan souvenirs. The *bris* was unkosher in ways that violated not just the menu.

There was a rabbi in the apartment, a modern, athletic-looking clergyman who wore a fabulous tan but forgot to bring his yarmulke. And there was also a *mohel*—an expert in putting razor to penis—the one Jewish cosmetic surgeon who nobody brags about as being the ideal son or son-in-law. But circumcision was merely a sideline for this mohel, who, when not slicing foreskin, was shaving points. Around town he was known as Morty the Mohel, and this was no joke, because Morty was a well-known Miami bookie with his own table—and phone, no less—at the Jewish Nostra, a deli on Alton Road that catered to fringe mobsters and small-time Jewish hoods.

The Jewish Nostra brought a curious moose-lodge decor to Miami Beach. It had maple-paneled walls and lopsided steel tables. A stuffed marlin hung near the front entrance, its spear covering the door like a pistol. There was a gallery of black-and-white photos taken of drunken mobsters gone fishing. What caught the eye most in these pictures was not the catch-of-the-day, but that the party boat had as many machine guns as fishing rods on board. The lights at the Nostra were always dimmed, and the room combined the unusual smell of cigarettes and chicken-fat vapors scaling the walls in search of a diet.

Although the nature of the business conducted at the Nostra—other than serving the obvious corned beef and a knish—was not in keeping with any of God's commandments, these were, indeed, all men of the tribe. Perhaps still lost, as well as being faithless and corrupted, they were Jews nonetheless, convinced that the Diaspora had taken many different paths in exile, and this one was no less honorable simply because of a few sordid connections with families who confused kreplach with ravioli. A Jew in Washington, after all, had been behind Senator Joseph McCarthy's persecution of other Jews, and years later there would be a Jewish Secretary of State serving a disgraced president. How bad did the Nostra men actually look in comparison?

Sometimes, when the lunch crowd was heavy at the Jewish Nostra, Morty the Mohel would be asked to help out behind the counter.

"I only cut small pieces," he would remind the patrons, jokingly, "not enough for a sandwich, but at least when the brisket turns thirteen, he'll be able to have a bar mitzvah."

Happily, the mohel would waddle behind the counter and strap an apron onto his waist. The phone at his reserved table invariably rang throughout his shift. "He's cutting again," someone nearby would pick up and reply. "No, not *pipiks*, just regular meat. Call back. You got over an hour until post time."

This was all happening in the days before Fidel Castro had expelled the capitalists—and the mob—from Cuba, during the time when Miami was still the port of call for racketeers with business in Hallandale and Havana. But on the day of Duncan's *bris*, the Nostra was largely empty. Most of the food and the clientele had temporarily relocated a few blocks north. Minyans of mobsters gathered at the Katz apartment, savoring the smoked fish and succulent meats and celebrating the birth of perhaps the only Jew in the room whose record was still clean. Sitting around the Katz living room, they pored over racetrack betting forms, waiting restlessly for the eight-day-old Duncan to make an appearance.

The moment finally arrived.

"Hey everybody, here they come," the coed announced.

"It's about time," the golfer added, edgily. Immediately he received a jarring elbow to his ribs from a Nostra regular who didn't much care for golf, or whiny Jews.

With Yankee holding Duncan in his arms, Mila and Yankee walked from their bedroom through the hallway and then stood before their guests. Yankee, his face soft, unlined, radiated a father's pride, and yet he appeared guarded and restrained. His eyes were a bloodshot blue, like a wounded sunset. He had brown hair that was thinning at the top, and a round, bulging forehead. Fatherhood had visited him late in life. Already fifty, he was showing the wear and tear not so much of age, but of circumstance and bad luck. Smiling and gesturing, even these faint motions seemed to be wearing him out.

Mila was another matter, however. Her strength was apparent in all her movements, in everything she said and did. Although she was short, her back was always straight, which made her seem taller than she actually was. She walked with quick and determined paces, the movement in her arms abrupt and often dangerous. Her face was rugged with a doubled-up chin and sagging jowls; her hands, large and coarse. Unlike Yankee, she was a young parent, but she came to the job with a much-abused body. Overweight, she smoked too much, and her nervous system functioned like randomly ignited firecrackers. But her deficiencies somehow came across as assets, which pleased her and which she exploited to no end.

Normally, the baby would have been brought into the room by a godmother, then handed off to a godfather, finally ending up in the lap of the *sandek*, the most coveted position at a *bris*—the person entrusted with assisting the mohel. Such divisions of Jewish labor are usually parceled out according to some combination of age and kinship and trust—in a word, to family.

But Auschwitz had shattered such time-honored traditions. Since the oldest people in the ghettos and the camps were also the most vulnerable—and generally the ones who died the soonest—there was a severe shortage of grandparents after the war. Actually, there weren't that many available uncles, aunts, nephews, nieces, or cousins, either. Black-sheep relatives, who in Europe would never have been considered for an honorarable position at a family affair, after the war, and by default, miraculously rose to the ranks of royalty.

The *Shoah* had created an improvised adoption network. All sorts of people were recruited to function as family, to "stand in" at *simchas*, to assume lifelong, ceremonial obligations for people who, in another time, would have been no better than strangers.

And this was true of the Katzes as well. In fact, for them the situation was even more dire, because none of their relatives had survived.

Which explains why Larry Breitbart, of all people, was at the Katz *bris*. The future Godfather was now about to be a godfather, and a godmother, and a *sandek*—all at the same time.

Breitbart had once been a seltzer deliveryman. Every week he had dropped off crates of wooden boxes filled with green quart bottles. On one of his delivery rounds back in 1951, he had met Mila. She was an immigrant; he wasn't. He looked like a movie star; she didn't. She had survived the grandest experiment in simulated hell; he had been providing Miami Beach with the main ingredient for an egg cream. Other than that, they had much in common.

"Lady, I never met anybody like you," he once said.

"I'll show you more," she replied. "I have many tricks to teach."

Eventually she would convince Breitbart that his true calling was not in carbonated water, but in organized crime. He was charming, with an insincere smile and a face angled like a diamond. One of his eyes was hazel, the other green; his nose was cut sharp and fine. But what intrigued Mila about Larry Breitbart was an untapped shrewdness that found no outlet in his current line of work.

"Look at you," she said. "What can you expect from a person who works all day with bubbles? How can you think?"

It wasn't his fault, really. Not everyone had spent their formative years as a poster child for Charles Darwin. That was Mila's world. Breitbart had grown up on the streets of Brooklyn. He still loved the corner drugstores with their shiny chrome soda fountains, peppermint facades, and Frisbee bar stools. But he also recognized a burgeoning market with all those Jews retiring to Miami Beach and others spending the winters there. What were they all going to drink? To quench the tropical thirst of a New York Jew, you need seltzer. It was that simple. Vitamin C in those days was still an untested theory. So Breitbart decided to move down to Florida, bringing the native drink of New York with him.

A few months after he met Mila, blood became the only fluid that mattered.

She directed him to a man she had met at a poker game two years earlier: Meyer Lansky, the head of the syndicate in New York, New Jersey, and Florida. Lansky was colonizing South Florida as the new home for organized crime. Like the retirees and the refugees, the Mafia was moving to Miami as well. Lucky and Bugsy were dead. Dutch they took care of years earlier. Arnold Rothstein, may he rest in peace, would have been proud of Meyer. A Jew was still in charge.

For someone in such a violent business, Lansky was a small man with delicate features. The public associated the mob with machine guns and brass knuckles. But that kind of work he delegated to the gorillas. Lansky was better with numbers than he was with murder. Even when it came to the syndicate, the Jewish brain supplied all the necessary muscle.

Lansky always respected a hustle, as long as it was an honest one. Mila Katz was always honest, and she nearly always collected. And Lansky had an eye for talent. He summoned her to play in other games, unleashing her to turn the tables on players who had been a little too lucky at one of his casinos.

"You'll owe me for this," Mila reminded the Jewish don, fearlessly.

"People don't usually threaten a man like me," Lansky replied.

With Mila's help and advice, Breitbart, the former seltzerman, proved himself to be one of Lansky's chief Miami operatives. Soon he was put in charge of one hotel in Havana, another in Hallandale, and given a piece of the parimutuel action in Florida.

His task today was quite different, however. Now he was sitting next to Morty the Mohel. There was a pillow on his lap, and Duncan rested comfortably on top. Breitbart was participating in his first *bris*— other than his own—and it was on the occasion of the birth of his first and only godson.

Another regular from the Nostra, an Italian from New York who worked with Larry Breitbart, was loitering around the room in a crouched position, holding an eight-millimeter movie camera against his face. Larry thought it would be nice if Mila and Yankee could have a film made of Duncan's *bris*—for posterity, for the family's archives. So he arranged for his friend, Carlo Costello, to bring his equipment and make a short about a family that had already had its fill of epics.

Mila and Yankee, however, were a little uncomfortable with Larry's idea. For one thing, they preferred the anonymity of an unrecorded life. But they were also cynical about the idea of preserving anything for the future.

"Tell your man to go home, Larry," Mila insisted, as Costello, his legs indistinguishable from tripods, boom sticks, and dolly tracks, stumbled into the apartment.

"Why? You'll be sorry one day when Duncan wants to see what happened at his *bris*," Breitbart warned.

"And what if there is a fire?" she asked.

"Where, here? Today? Now?" Larry wondered.

"No, some other time."

"I don't get what you mean."

Blood rushed to Mila's face as though she was about to put out a different kind of fire. "If the film one day goes up in smoke, Duncan will lose something he wanted to keep forever. Better that he not have it at all."

Mila and Yankee had no mementos of their former lives. No baby pictures or family albums. Forget home movies; they didn't even have their prewar passports. When it came to the sentimental attachment to things past, memory had to do all the work. But memories are so often faulty, or selective, or savagely mischievous. The mind tends to forget exactly what would have been so nice to recall: the innocent days of pre-atrocity, when anti-Semitism was more ideological than lethal. Instead, the wrong set of memories kept coming back, a glorification of the tragic and dreadful rest—the nightmares that would become permanent installations in the museum of the mind. Which master does memory serve?

From the very beginning, Mila rejected the possibility that Duncan's life would be any different. Things that he wanted to keep he would lose; the people around him would leave. He would be betrayed. Why should he have had it any better than them?

But as to the home movie, eventually Mila and Yankee relented. Larry Breitbart had argued too passionately on behalf of a Carlo Costello Production.

"This is a great moment for the family," he said.

Mila wondered which family he was talking about.

Yankee started to warm up to the idea of a film that captured the Katz experience in America—in Miami Beach, with a baby boy, and a possible new beginning.

"Maybe not so bad," he concluded, "although maybe we should wear masks?"

Mila continued to see the film as an abomination, a sure ticket to disaster down the road. But Yankee wanted the baby, and the *bris*. Mila would throw in the film as well.

Given the green light, the Mafia cinematographer eagerly went to work. Carlo Costello was a professional killer who was bored with his life in the rackets and dreamed of one day shooting a feature film. Until that moment arrived, he was grateful for any opportunity to make movies. On this day, his artistic vision inspired him to super-impose an art-house setting onto the Katz *bris*.

"Okay everyone, I need to see more energy from my actors!" he said, rolling his eyes as he checked the lighting. "Try to find your motivations . . ."

He faded in and out among the guests, dollied, and panned the room—freeze frames locking in on the crowded bookshelves and the Rosenthal china. He created a dramatic tension between the rabbi and the mohel that otherwise would not have been there. As he continued to make a nuisance of himself, Costello shot one scene while lying on the floor and filming upward through a glass coffee table. Finally, to every-one's relief, it came time for the rabbi to take over the proceedings.

"Now gather around everyone," the rabbi said. A crescent of creamy onion, separated from its friend, the herring, smiled coyly from the center of a soiled napkin, which the rabbi had placed on top of his head in lieu of a skullcap. "I think we can begin now. But before we do any cutting," he said, while a number of guests who, already knowing this rabbi, imagined that he was doing everything all out of order and slapped their heads in unison, "I'd like to start by asking Mila and Yankee to tell us something about the boy's name. Where does it come from?"

"Yeah, what about the name?" an older woman joined in.

"It's been driving us crazy." The man with the whitefish—once more restocked—demanded an answer.

"What does it mean?" the slender coed pleaded.

"Come on, I'd like to tee off before tomorrow," the golfer said sheepishly, mindful of the gangster behind him.

But the parents remained silent. At one point they looked at each other for support, then returned their gaze to their guests.

Moments later, Yankee blinked. "It's from the Bible," he said.

"It is?" the coed asked. "How interesting . . ."

"No kidding," Larry Breitbart said, nervously taking his eyes off the sleeping lump on his lap.

"Which book?" the dubious golfer asked. "New or Old Testament?"

"Yeah," the man with the whitefish joined in. "I don't remember any characters named Duncan."

"Rabbi, what do you think?" a flirting woman asked.

"Well, it's hard to know . . . ," he replied, hesitatingly, but nobody in the room expected him to come up with the right answer anyway.

Mila then blurted out, "He is named for my Uncle Keller in Poland. They killed him in the camps."

The family cue. Yankee knew not to go any further; Mila would handle things from here.

"Wait a minute," the golfer began, skeptically. "You mean to tell me there were Jews named Duncan Keller in Poland?"

"Yes, many," Mila replied curtly.

Sufficiently stumped, all those in the room quieted down and prepared for the main event: the sacrificial guillotine that celebrates Jewish life and continuity.

The rabbi mumbled briskly through some prayers that may have actually been his grocery list for the day, took a long swig of wine without saying the blessing, and then turned over the remaining portion of the festivities to Morty the Mohel.

"Okay, what I do first is give the baby some wine like so," Morty announced as though he was Julia Child. He dipped his ringless pinkie into a glass of wine, and just as he was about to insert it into Duncan's mouth, Mila shouted, "No!"

Larry Breitbart, who was collecting perspiration all around his face, clutched the pillow and the baby, while Morty withdrew his hand. "Mila, just a few drops of schnapps—as an anesthetic, to numb the pain," Morty reassured her. "I do it all the time. It's very common. The baby won't get drunk."

"He won't need it," she announced. "And I want him to feel it."

Yankee looked on helplessly. "Please, Mila," he said, "don't be foolish. Let Morty do his job."

"No, without wine or no *bris*."

Larry Breitbart glanced upward for direction. The rabbi had already wandered away from the fracas, having spotted a blond moll who had been batting her eyes at him from the moment he arrived. Morty stroked his chin and pondered now doing this procedure in the absence of a painkiller. He searched Yankee's face for advice, and received none. He glanced down at Breitbart, whose eyes were now especially large and whose hands were drenched from all the suspense in the room. Mila, by contrast, was calm and resolute; the trace of a smile seemed to cross her usual poker face. Meanwhile, Costello the Sicilian captured all the tension and drama in these Jewish faces with the cinematic eye of a Fellini.

"Ah, what the heck," Morty concluded. "Let's just do it . . ."

The rabbi gave the order; the camera swerved into position. In the finality of a split second, the mohel cut; the child never cried. The father flinched; the mother didn't. The gangster, Breitbart, fainted at the first sight of blood. Mila reached out and rescued Duncan from Breitbart's arms before the ill-chosen *sandek* collapsed to the floor, almost taking the baby with him.

Mila held Duncan up in the air, at an angle, away from her body. Beads of blood dripped from his circumcised penis as if he were a stone cherub in a Florentine fountain. Morty hadn't had a chance to dress Duncan yet. And because Mila wasn't holding Duncan close, the wound was open, the mark of Duncan's manhood and the fresh bond with his God there for all to see.

Suddenly, Mila turned her face away, too, recoiling as though something about Duncan—whether it be the blood, or his newborn smell, or perhaps because the rest of the room smelled like lox—was giving off a terrible, odious stench. But it wasn't Duncan's circumcision that repelled her, but rather the birthmark of another child, from another time, that now made it necessary for her to look away from her own son.

"*Out, damned spot! out, I say! . . . what's done cannot be undone. . . .*"

Chapter Two

A JEWISH MOTHER was about to die. Cancer, what else? Another life claimed, a victory for the forces of an underachieving anatomy. Such news came as no shock to anyone from Miami Beach—the epicenter of fading grandparents and terminal senior citizens. Death happened many times throughout the day, as routine an occurrence as liver spots or hemorrhoids. Ambulances would race up and down Collins Avenue like souped-up jalopies on a drag strip. Sirens piercing the evening calm, red lights spinning and flashing, the casualties so endless, it would have been quieter—and certainly more understandable—if a war were going on.

The tantalizing tropics. Exiled Cubans playing dominoes along Miami's Southwest Eighth Street. Black tiles clicking. The pulsing rhythm of Latin soul. The gasping gargle of ancient espresso machines. Across Biscayne Bay, the tourists had spread out along the sand like shipwrecked castaways. Foolish enough to sweat through the interrogation of Miami's third-degree sunburns. The powerful rays magnified by fan-shaped reflectors. These visitors from the north would baste themselves with repeated coats of baby oil, baking until they were well done.

It was, after all, the allure of the sun that brought them to Miami in the first place. Home of the parched fountain of youth. The illusion of paradise. But in reality, Miami was like Mahler's Fifth, a death march. Tourists returned each year for vacations, but retirees came just once—to die. Not immediately, but eventually, and without real conflict or protest. It was all part of the migratory pattern of elderly Jews. Not unlike a salmon's upstream swim or a bear's winter nap. Old

Jews in America knew in which direction the compass pointed, where the true feasts of early-bird specials could be found, and where to settle on a family plot.

Some, the refugees from Europe in the days before they called them survivors, were already dead, but they came anyway. Ironically, they sought refuge in a city that they lovingly described as being as hot as an oven. A bunch of poker players with beaten faces that betrayed their hands, and their ages. Eyes that had seen too much, now hiding behind glasses. Their movements slow, an ordeal no matter what the distance. They possessed minds that had been erased of all vital information. For others, it was even worse. The mind was too good, working overtime in memory—becoming even more vivid and unrelenting with age. The flashbacks were the ultimate prisons, the true assassins. Daily reminders of loss and regret. Sins that could never be—perhaps should never be—pardoned.

Mila, who was somewhat younger than the others, nevertheless suffered as well. But she didn't show it. More than anything else, silence was the bitter syntax of survivors. The secret codes that could never be cracked. Torture would not work, because worse had already been tried.

The world had been reborn with Auschwitz. The Big Bang that doubled as a Second Coming. The Burning Bush that this time consumed whatever was within its flame. God spoke; the ovens of Auschwitz swallowed. Whatever happened before no longer mattered. Whatever happened during was stored away as life lessons. Whatever happened in the immediate after didn't count, as though it were all a false start. The hope was just to be forgiven.

DESPITE ALL ITS open, tropical vistas, the Miami that festered in Duncan's memory was limited to one image—that of his mother, Mila. Forgotten was the sun and the sand, those seasonal football games where he had become a local legend, even his exploits in radical student politics. Those distantly recalled flashes were gone, relegated to a shapeless blur of moments neglected. Mila had crowded them out. In life, she was pushy, demanding, and overbearing; in his memory of her she was no more patient or pleasant. Duncan would need to locate a high-school yearbook in order to patch together the necessary proof that he once existed in some way other than as Mila's son.

But things might now be different. It was 1982, and everything was about to change. That's what happens when children grow up and suddenly became the oldest people in their family.

The doctor told Duncan that Mila had only a few more days to live. Perhaps, with Mila almost gone, Duncan could finally return to his own home without the journey feeling like an act of trespass.

All of this was wishful thinking, of course. He doubted that Miami could ever be rehabilitated in his head. That would be expecting too much, and he was, if anything, a creature of reduced expectations. For Duncan, Miami would always remain a forbidden place. He was haunted by the memories that awaited him there, the very same memories that had traveled with him the entire time he had been away. The ghosts of a robbed childhood. The clock that sprinted without regard to actual time. Duncan had skipped many steps from birth to manhood, his family life having much in common with basic training during time of war. Adolescence was a luxury that the Katzes could ill afford. You had to be ready to move at a moment's notice.

And what complicated matters worse about returning to Miami was that Duncan hadn't been a particularly loyal or devoted son. All those years that he had been away—at college, then law school, and now finally living in Washington, D.C., working for the government. His last official appearance in the Sunshine State was at Yankee's funeral. After that, Duncan became a virtual no-show in Miami. The fact that his mother still lived there—*particularly* that she lived there—didn't make his reappearance likely. Nor, for that matter, did it change the force, or sting, of his absence.

And he hadn't even said goodbye—to his hometown or to his mother. For over ten years since graduating from high school in 1971, he simply never returned, and he rarely called to speak with Mila while he was away. All that time they communicated with messages and cryptic, impersonal notes, as though they feared detection, as if a simultaneous exchange of voices was far too intimate an experience for either of them to chance. A silent war raged between them. Although the exact cause of the conflict was unknown, it had always been this way. It wasn't so much that the maternal bond had been severed, but rather that the fibers had never quite taken hold. It was as though Mila had delivered him into this world, and once that was done—once the umbilical cord went the way of fluids and placenta and all the other lifeless litter of birth—there was nothing linking them together other than the coincidence of a common address. When Duncan left, they no longer had that anymore, either.

LATE NIGHTS WERE not unusual for Duncan. As a child he had never slept well—too much painful noise coming from his parents' room—and so he learned to keep himself busy when the outside world was asleep. Now, as an adult—and a lawyer, no less—the nights had another purpose: he worked through the darkness, like a vampire. A bachelor in his late twenties, he was far too young to live life this way, but he did.

Duncan had a handsome but rugged face. The nose small, as though stunted, perhaps forcibly moved around over the years. Compact body. A full head of thick, dirty blond hair. Deep, exaggerated blue eyes, like the murky dye that swirls around a fish tank. Muscular shoulders and arms that seamlessly filled in the slack in his clothes. The waistline thick but hard. A strong jaw that concealed a set of unsmiling, gritting teeth. Like a box he sat there, unopened and shut tight.

Except for Duncan, a few security guards, and janitors, no other employees at the Department of Justice in Washington, D.C., remained in the building at this late hour. It wasn't just that he was conscientious and hardworking. He was not alone in that regard. Many of his colleagues were similarly fanatical, unafraid of initiative, even on a government salary.

What set him apart was the endless procession of demons. His work at Justice was less about livelihood than about life. There was old-time religion in it, too. In the absence of a god, he took it upon himself to do God's work. His caseload featured a rogues' gallery of fugitive murderers. But for Duncan, this career—part lurid obsession, part calling—offered not merely a profession but a complete existence.

He was savage and relentless in peeling off their masks. Duncan's hands clamped the witness box, the railing nearly coming unhinged.

The accused were not safe in there. They would have to tell the truth; otherwise, they might simply not get out alive.

"Just answer the question, Mr. Federenko!"

"Just answer the question, Mr. Schellong!"

"Just answer the question, Mr. Kairys!"

"Just answer the question, Mr. Linnas!"

"You worked the gas, didn't you?"

"You fired your gun and killed . . ."

"You played target practice with their caps . . ."

"You raped . . ."

"You followed orders . . ."

"You lied . . ."

All he had to do was bring the butchers to justice. One at a time, before the clock ran out. Before the collusion of old age and natural causes proclaimed the final, unpunished sentence. But to what end? Certain wrongs could never be righted, even if he was to spend his entire life trying.

He wished to be like everyone else in the department, or so he claimed: impassioned, yet without the overwrought intensity. But the horrifying truth was that he could never be like them. He had, after all, descended from royalty of the cursed, condemned kind. His burdens were different. He was special, not because of anything he had done, but because of the bleak lessons his parents had learned.

"So tell me, Duncan, why do you want to do this kind of work?"

The man who put that question to him a few years earlier was Bernard Ross, the director of the Office of Special Investigations—the OSI—the unit charged with tracking down Nazi war criminals and bringing them to justice. Duncan would eventually work his way up to become the OSI's principal deputy director, but at the time he was merely trying to latch himself like a rider onto the Holtzman Amendment, the act of Congress that created this new investigative, prosecutorial body. As a recent law-school graduate, Duncan greeted the news about the OSI as though God had finally shown himself—late at Auschwitz, but on time in Congress. Divine Providence in the form of a perfect job.

"My parents were Holocaust survivors," he replied.

"In the camps?"

"Yes."

"Which ones?"

"Auschwitz and Bergen-Belsen."

"I see . . ."

"Is that a problem?" Duncan asked, not sure if he had just inadvertently hoisted up a red flag on a windy day.

"No, not really . . . I guess. I hadn't thought about it before," Ross replied.

"Thought about what?"

Ross was an elegant and refined man. He wore smartly tailored suits, fancy English shoes, an assortment of paisley suspenders, and a designer haircut from some salon in Dupont Circle. He was tall and athletic with a thick red mustache that seemed to completely swallow his upper lip.

"Having someone like you in the office . . . just as we're starting out. Could be risky."

"I'm not sure I understand," Duncan persisted.

"The OSI is a brand new division of the Justice Department. You realize that, don't you?"

"Of course."

"And that we've been given exclusive and extraordinary enforcement powers?"

"Absolutely."

"And with that—and the delicate nature of our job—will no doubt come a great deal of public scrutiny."

"It should. We're going after Nazis," Duncan reminded him. "The country should applaud every time we find one."

"Don't be surprised if some Americans boo."

"Excuse me?"

"Not everybody hates Nazis, Duncan. There are people out there who don't think about Nazis at all. Never give them the slightest thought. Don't even know who they were. *Hogan's Heroes* is the closest they get."

"Come on," Duncan said, half-smiling, assuming that this otherwise earnest prosecutor was putting him on.

"And what if we make a mistake?" Ross continued.

"A mistake?"

"Yes. For instance, what if we prosecute the wrong man? You know, some senior citizen with an accent and a suspicious last name and an unexplained past."

"We won't make mistakes," Duncan assured the director.

"Fine, have it your way. I'll ask the question differently. Let's say the guy we catch is actually guilty. What happens then? You realize we're going to have to be able to make our case without any doubt?"

"You mean reasonable doubt."

"No. I mean *any* doubt. We're not dealing with those ordinary crimes you studied in law school. The murderers here were special; the way we expose and punish them has to be special, too. Too much time has passed; the burden is on us to show that these men were who we say they were. The proof must be unassailable, and as you can imagine, proof in these matters is going to be hard to come by."

Bernard Ross stood up from behind his desk and walked over to a large canvas map that covered nearly an entire wall hanging above a long, black-dimpled leather sofa. The map had a glossy green finish and an oily black matting. It was written in German; "Deutschland," the letters—wide and generous in arcs, loops, and stems—had an inflated sense of importance, even in calligraphy.

Pictured throughout this map of wartime Germany and its Nazi conquests were yellow watchtowers, each representing a concentration camp. And written alongside each tower was the number of people projected to be killed there—if the murder machines worked well, if everyone was up to the task. Ross had received the map as a gift from a retired GI, a Jew who had helped to liberate Ravensbruck and who had confiscated the map from the commandant's abandoned office as a spoil of war.

"We can't afford to appear overzealous, Duncan," Ross continued. "For some people, this whole enterprise is a waste of time and taxpayers' dollars."

"That's hard to believe."

"And that's my point. It is hard for *you* to believe. You've come here with all the right and wrong baggage."

"I'm qualified for almost any legal job. I was editor-in-chief of my law review."

"And you also have a huge chip on your shoulder. I can see it from here."

"It comes from long gym workouts."

"No, I think it comes from someplace else. You might just be a little too overdeveloped in your passion. I can't have any vigilantes—or worse, crusaders with a badge—running around here. There can't be any appearance of impropriety. Do you understand?"

"Yes."

"I need to know if you can play by the rules. Or are you here for the wrong reasons?" Ross leaned back against his chair. He stretched a thick rubber band around his large open palm and extended fingers, making a web. "I'm also a Jew, Duncan. But I'm afraid you're a different breed from me. That also might make you a different breed of prosecutor. And that's what I'm afraid of."

"You're talking as though I'm with the Jewish Defense League or something."

"Frankly, you're much more dangerous than any punk Jewish kid with a pipe bomb. Your résumé got you through these doors. You've become an insider, now. If you work for me, you'll be representing the United States government. That's a lot of power for a kid from Miami Beach, even one out of Yale Law School." Ross realized that the interview was beginning to sound more and more like a grand jury investigation. "Hey, I'm sorry; I must be coming across as way too harsh. I'm not doing a very good job of recruiting you, am I? Don't take it too personally," he said, glancing back down at Duncan's résumé and scribbling something in the right-hand margin. "I'm a career prosecutor. I make people defensive for a living; my wife tells me there is a tone to my voice that makes everything I say sound judgmental and accusatory."

Ross rubbed his eyes and then swiped the bristles of his moustache, finally ending up with his hands folded over his chin. He checked the Roman numerals on a hanging clock beside the German map. Then he continued. "I don't really know anything about you, other than what you told me and what's here on your résumé. We'll have the FBI run a character and background check on you. But from what I can already tell, it's obvious that as we move forward in this job, you and I will probably always see the mission of the OSI differently."

"Does that mean I'm hired?"

From that point on, the work of the OSI filled Duncan's nights. He paced around the office, nervously running his hand through his hair. Flipping pages from side to side, his head plunged into a library of black, three-ring binders, piled high in every direction. At this hour, 2 A.M., he was careful to steer himself clear of the outside hallways, not wanting to accidentally trip the alarm on the security system, which he would have to remember to disengage before he left. But this also made him a prisoner, confined to his office under mental lock and key. And worse yet, he was left alone with all those file folders, and the horrors and secrets buried inside.

Duncan jerked his neck, as though he were yanking against a leash. He pressed a stubby pencil hard against the lined sheets of a yellow legal pad, the eraser long gone, lopped off or savagely depleted. A thin podium faced a mirror against a wall. On any given graveyard shift, he might stand and rehearse a summation or the taking of testimony. Anchored below the lectern were two thirty-five-pound dumbbells that he would manhandle when his energy level wasn't being sufficiently exhausted elsewhere.

His large oak desk was barren of family photos. No one was waiting for him to come home. What occupied the surface instead was an electric pencil sharpener jammed tight with curly shavings, and a green bottle of Donnatal—medicine that he used to relieve stomach spasms, a malady that had plagued him since childhood.

An hour later he stopped retracing the path that he had worn thin into the maroon carpet. He looked out the window and stared intently—and curiously—at his own reflection, as though he didn't recognize himself, as though he were standing alone in a lineup and yet was still unable to make out a positive identification. Across the street, spread wide like the grid of an unascertainable code, blinked the alternating lights and darkened cubicles of neighboring office buildings. Further in the distance, the Lincoln Memorial threw a rippling shadow onto the black-water shoals of the Reflecting Pond.

Duncan would leave for Miami tomorrow, early in the morning. The very thought of it caused him to glance back at the Donnatal, just to reassure himself that the soothing elixir was close by.

He returned his face to the window, staring, searching through the glass as though it were a magic mirror threatening to bring some of Miami back into an uneasy, yet always sun-drenched, focus.

Chapter Three

KICK HIM! Go after him! What are you afraid of? Kill . . . !"

"I'm not afraid."

"Then finish him already!"

A fairly routine mother-son encounter—judged by standards known only in the Katz household.

It all started with karate. Professed self-defense. Good exercise. A builder of self-confidence. Stimulates proper breathing and enhances mental focus. A healthy way for children to interact.

Bullshit. The people of Miami Beach were smarter than that. Anyone who knew Mila Katz could well imagine dark side agendas that had nothing to do with recreation.

Duncan became a black belt at age nine. Record time for a Caucasian boy, and a Jew from Miami Beach, no less. He made an appearance on the *Tonight Show* with Johnny Carson. Carson stood back and watched Duncan chop down a stack of boards with one open-fisted, windmill strike.

"How about that, Ed?" Carson joked. "You can do that, but only with your breath."

"Wonderful," McMahon belched.

It was an impressive feat for just about anyone, but still not enough to please Mila. She couldn't believe how long it took for her son to work his way through the ascending color schemes—white for only a few weeks, blue and then yellow for nine months, a year or so at orange and green, a short half-year stint at brown, and finally black.

"The Israelis win wars in days, and look at the problem you have with belts," she reasoned. "How much longer is it going to take you?"

"I'm not in a war," Duncan defended himself.

But she was pleased. "My son the black belt," she would eventually crow with all the pride of Jewish mothers everywhere, even those who would have preferred the *naches* from a cardiologist, or even a Morty the Mohel, for that matter. "But don't let this go to your head," she warned Duncan. "You would have gotten the belt sooner if you practiced more. Too much watching the *Honeymooners*. You will end up like Jackie Gleason: fat and afraid of the bosses at the bus company. Better you should watch *Tarzan*. Now there is a man: lives in the jungle—all by himself, with the animals. Needs no one. Not afraid of anything . . ."

The black belt was important to Mila for reasons that went beyond mere childhood achievement. For her it was a symbol of strength, a trophy to be flaunted. There was even a time when she tried to incorporate it into Duncan's school wardrobe: through the belt loops of his jeans; sidelong over the shoulder and across the chest like a banner for a beauty contest; even as a headband around Duncan's long blond hair to keep the sweat out of his eyes. Whichever way it could be fashioned, Mila accessorized the black belt as a kind of buyer beware—this was not a child to be touched or trifled with. He can take care of himself.

For Duncan, martial arts was yet another obsession of Mila's that meant nothing to him. The circumstances were so unfair and unbalanced. Mila had her own recreational activities that kept her mind on the precarious safe side of sanity: the poker games, the jai alai, the dog track. But what toys did she allow him?

To begin with, he didn't like the way he looked in white pajamas. And he took no pleasure in humiliating other children. The fieldhouse smell from dojos in the days before air-conditioning provided the only reason he could think of to knock someone down, end the match quickly, and then run away. And finally, he detested all those grunting noises made at the point of attack.

"Tarzan makes a noise before he fights," Mila said, just before filling her lungs with enough oxygen to unleash the familiar jungle warble heard in those Johnny Weissmuller movies.

"Mom, please don't start pounding your chest."

From the very beginning, Duncan wanted to stop fighting, to unlearn what he had already been taught. The Reverend Martin Luther

King Jr. was preaching passive nonviolent resistance to all of America. In Miami, Mila wasn't listening.

"What about the violin?" Duncan asked. "How about if I take violin lessons and quit karate?"

"You must be joking," Mila chortled. "How will the violin prepare you for life?"

"Lots of parents like it when their kids learn how to play the violin," Duncan said with assurance but without much hope.

"True," Yankee said. "And Isaac Stern would be such a good role model for him. Better than Tarzan—in my mind, at least. Ah, wouldn't it be nice if Duncan could learn to play Mendelssohn's violin concerto?" Yankee removed one hand from a book and danced it in the air. "In this house, of all places—it would be a sweeter sound of music."

"Nonsense," Mila said, which was like a *keller* codeword meaning "end of conversation." "What are you going to do with a violin? What kind of protection is that? Such a delicate instrument, like a toothpick. It would break right in your hands."

"The violin is not a weapon," Duncan said. "It's not for swinging; it's for playing."

"You don't have time to play," Mila shot back. "Now go . . . practice your kicks!"

Duncan hesitated before saying, "How about a grand piano instead? That way, if anyone starts with me, I can run him over with my piano, and then bury him inside. No one will ever be able to find the body."

Mila considered Duncan's idea. There was a time in her life when a piano was just a piano, and not a convertible coffin.

"No pianos," she said. "Just kick!"

She never missed a karate class. She would stand alongside the perimeter of the spongy green mat, screaming, "Block! Sweep already. What's wrong with you? Stop playing. Attack!"

Mother and son were forced out of the first dojo because even after repeated warnings, Mila kept working her way onto the mat, standing right beside Duncan and his undermatched opponent—rattling Duncan, terrifying the other boy—ready and eager to finish off the challenger if her son couldn't.

"I got him, Mom. He's mine. Back off!"

One of Duncan's first karate teachers, Tony Saki, told Mila, "I am very sorry, but you're not welcome here anymore. I'm not carrying enough insurance for you. My policy doesn't cover acts of war."

Duncan moved on to judo, kung fu, jujitsu, and tae kwon do. As a Jewish boy on Miami Beach, he knew more Asians than Jews. Senseis influenced him in ways that rabbis could not. A sutra lingered in his mind far longer than anything out of the Talmud or Torah. The samurai son of survivors from Miami Beach.

In the early days, the Katz family kept many of the Miami plastic surgeons in business—not to redesign noses, but to fix broken ones.

"*Meshuggener*," Yankee would on occasion say to his wife. "Leave the boy alone, already. He has homework. What do you expect to come out of all this *narishkheit*?"

"What will come from homework?" Mila would reply mockingly. "You want for him to be a rabbi? Or a Jewish doctor? Or a professor?" Her voice was almost drunk with disdain.

"Why not? Each is fine with me."

"Because that kind of people we already have enough of. We need a few Jewish animals—*vilde khayehs*."

"The world has no use for warrior kings anymore," Yankee said, his reading glasses bulletproof-thick, liver spots beaming on his angry forehead. "You are wasting his time. Go ahead, read the papers," he insisted, holding the *Herald* up like an oracle. "The Israelis are doing just fine on their own. They don't need our son's help."

The life that began for Yankee after the camps was only a temporary life, a loaner; it was as though he was going through the motions of an existence that was no longer his own. From the moment of liberation, each day was both a blessing and a curse. Life demanded too many episodes of extreme coping. You had to resign yourself to loss.

Duncan's most lasting memory of his father was not the man's voice, or affection, or guidance, but the sounds that his fingers made when tapping against the keys of a manual typewriter. That old black box of German efficiency. The thin metal arms and small block heads, striking a greasy black ribbon and leaving jagged alphabetic impressions on watermarked paper. The clacking of words in composition, followed by the necessary right-hand slap against a lever that reset the carriage and signalled the beginning of yet another new line. At times, when the hallway was still and Yankee and his Naumann Erika were at their most conversational, it sounded as though a secretarial pool and a chorus line were locked in dueling professional engagements inside the Katz apartment.

Yankee would sit at a desk beside windows that overlooked the Atlantic.

Tap. Tap. Tap.

"Father, what are you writing?"

Tap. Tap. Tap. Tap.

"Father, who are you writing to?"

Tap. Tap. Tap. Tap. Tap.

"Father, what happened to you during the war?"

Tap. Tap. Tap. Tap. Tap. Tap.

Yankee had so much to say, but so little was said to his son. Instead, he talked only to that old machine. Confessions meant for no one to read, as though the ribbon discharged only invisible ink. The typewriter as most trusted confidant; the godless, mechanized priest for the burdened Jew. It was yet another in the infinite, deafening codes that Duncan spent a childhood hoping to one day decipher.

HAVING TOSSED SO many young Jewish boys over his shoulder, Duncan was—not surprisingly—short on playmates. No respectable parent would allow her child to visit the Katz household. As Duncan graduated from martial arts and moved on to organized kickboxing and random bouts of street fighting, he was forced to take his violent hobbies on the road—away from Miami Beach. Indeed, the city in those days was so tame, Mila was always on the lookout for bad neighborhoods.

Bring on the bullies, the persecutors, the pogromists in training.

Except there was always one sacred rule: Duncan was never allowed to pick a fight. The fights that Duncan couldn't start, Mila required him to finish. If nothing else, always be the last one left standing.

"You are not a thug, but a rescuer," Mila decreed.

Each month Yankee and Mila received pensions from the German government—*Wiedergutmachung*, which literally means "to make good or whole again." They would take the checks and deposit them in a separate account.

"A gift from the Germans that will pay for your bar mitzvah and future education," Mila would say, "but not for us."

"We don't want German money," Yankee would add. "Fancy words: reparation, restitution. But no such thing is possible. We are beyond repair."

"Instead, we invest in you," Mila said, her eyes burning a scar right onto the soul of her son. "You must avenge our deaths."

"But you're not dead."

Capeless and without a cowl, or even a phone booth, Duncan knew that what his mother really wanted was not a son, but a comic-book superhero.

When the family would travel up north to visit Larry Breitbart, whose operations and responsibilities by then had expanded to New Jersey, Mila would insist that Duncan be dropped off on some street corner in Newark or Hoboken. She was testing him out against the local competition.

"They don't fight any different up here," she said confidently. "Make me proud."

"I hear they use knives," Duncan said.

"You watch too much television. Besides, a big fist is still the best weapon," she said, closing the fingers of her large hands and throwing a right hook at some imaginary target.

Larry Breitbart and some of his gangster friends didn't approve of Mila's planned afternoon for Duncan. Gang wars were different from rumbles, the latter being too much of a gamble. And besides, even hardened killers wanted better for their own sons.

"Hey, boss, I don't think this is kosher," Carsage, a sympathetic lieutenant, said. "The kid could get killed. Worse, he could start a war with the other families."

Mila gave the thug a severe look, flashed him her forearm and he backed off. "Shut up, you monkey," she said. "What do you know about war? What you call going to the mattresses is like a nap compared to where I have been."

Breitbart, standing tall, dressed in a blue pinstriped suit with a red carnation wedged through the slit in his lapel, pondered the situation while cupping his chin. Carsage had made a good point, but how was Larry going to appease Mila? He then stepped in to break up the clash between his adopted family and his crime family.

"Mila, I got a better idea for you," he began. "Let's take Duncan to Palisades Amusement Park. They got a great big roller coaster over there. The biggest. Everyone is afraid of it. I myself would never get on that thing."

All of Breitbart's trained monkeys nodded their heads in unison.

And Larry continued, "Mila, trust me, you want to test his courage and toughen him up? We'll send him up in that roller coaster all by himself, and you'll see that one day . . ."

Mila drilled a finger into Breitbart's chest, and then said sternly, "Don't play with me, Larry. I'm no fool. You want for him to learn from a circus ride? That will prove nothing!"

Larry Breitbart and some of his best men sat quietly in a Lincoln Continental with a bag of doughnuts and cups of coffee, while Duncan was around the corner, a new kid on the block, going a few nasty, overmatched rounds with some of the local juvenile hoods.

"How'd you do, kid? Did you get any good licks in?" Carsage asked when Duncan finally stumbled back to the car. Bashfully, Carsage offered Duncan a once-white handkerchief now decorated with jelly and glaze.

Duncan's lower lip had been sliced thin like belly lox. There was a cut through his brow that bled into his eye, and one of his ribs was sore and probably cracked.

"I did okay," Duncan said. "You guys know of a Carvel around here? I could use an ice-cream cone right now."

"Hard or soft swirl?" Larry wondered, thrilled that his godson was still alive.

"Soft vanilla, with chocolate crunch sprinkles."

"How about half a doughnut until we get there?" Carsage asked, donating what was left in his hand.

"Thanks."

Then there was wilderness survival training in Jackson Hole, Wyoming. Four days of snowshoeing, cross-country skiing, and mountain climbing. The first trip was a bar mitzvah gift—from his parents, of course. All expenses paid, which included the ice picks and a flare gun.

"Have a nice time," Mila said, handing Duncan his snow skis and goose-down parka.

"Stay with the group," Yankee warned.

"Unless they are too slow and will make things dangerous for you," Mila said. "Then leave them and go on your own."

Surrounded at all times by the desolate, windswept hum from the frosted white Tetons. A pack of modern-day thrill seekers, naturalists, and searchers of one spiritual destiny or another. Testing the wilds, teasing the avalanches, pitching tents, and then undertaking improbable climbs, Duncan was perhaps the only one whose mission was genuinely about learning how to survive, and yet he was also the one who needed the least amount of instruction.

But there was one source of refuge where Duncan found true recreation. And in this case, Mila didn't disapprove. Any activity that even remotely prepared her son to do battle against real or imagined enemies could not be harmful—regardless of the separated shoulders, bruised thighs, blown-out kneecaps, and torn ligaments that routinely took place on the gridirons of organized football.

Such a curious way to unleash Jewish aggression. All that fuss over a ball slapped and laced together with the skin of that most forbidden of all Christian meat. Games were usually played on Friday night or Saturday—a time of rest and peace for Jews—in a sport that borrowed much of its rhythm and inspiration from war. The size and speed of the players were so vitally important; Jewish kids always seemed to be lacking in one or the other—or often both at the same time. The contests required all sorts of protective gear—most particularly, helmets for the head and cups for the genitals, two sacred places for Jews who no longer committed themselves to putting on tefillin or yarmulkes or to protecting that precious Jewish seed.

Mila loved the game. All the elements that challenged survival were represented on the field. The ball bounced with its own reckless, unspecified will—like the world, lopsided and unpredictable. The athletes had to be able to play in all kinds of weather, particularly on winter days when it was dreary, cold, and wet. Dropping the ball was the most unpardonable and costly of mistakes. And there was a scoreboard and clock—a big one that reminded players of how much time they had left, and whether they would live on to play another day. Time was important; timing, even more so.

And of course, there was a great deal of that therapeutic hitting and tackling.

During all those years that Duncan played, he was a middle linebacker, starting out as a seventy-five pounder in the Pop Warner leagues; continuing on in that position through high school, where he was selected to the All-Dade County first team for three consecutive years; and then eventually at Yale, where he was an All-Ivy Leaguer. He was a natural linebacker. A vicious hitter, strong in pursuit, he had excellent vision and balance and was able to push off blocks and chase down whoever had the ball—which no one wanted to carry if Duncan was in the game.

Mila picked the position for him. "This you will be good at," she said, lowering the shoulder-pad chassis around his head and then pulling on the laces of the chest flap as though trying to choke him. "Now remember what I told you. When the running back comes through the hole, you smash him; and when the tight end runs a crossing pattern in front of you, take his head off. That will teach them . . . Are you listening?"

Always Mila had great instincts to assess a person's strengths and weaknesses—whether in football or just plain life.

"A sissy," she would point.

"Wouldn't be able to make it without food and rest. Otherwise could be useful."

"One broken fingernail and when the first hair goes out of place, she would give up."

"Now that one . . . he might have a chance, but I'm not sure if he is crazy enough."

She did it ruthlessly, by process of elimination, and for no apparent end or purpose. Sizing up the harsh realities of who had the necessary physical resources and psychic equipment to survive—and who would have to be left behind. Because in the end, someone always is.

Before Duncan ever played a down, Mila did research on the game of football—specifically, on the art of how to play middle linebacker. She watched endless college and pro games, taking notes on what each player seemed to be doing at every given moment. She even attended the Miami Dolphins' training camp facility at Barry College, so she could get a close-up of the field and scout the best players in the state. One time she flagged down Don Shula. The coach thought she wanted an autograph, but what she had in mind was a private consultation.

"Whatever he wants to play, ma'am," the coach said. "At that age, it's just a game."

"For you maybe, Mr. Shula. For me, nothing is a game."

Duncan would pounce on ball carriers and turn them into divots. He would then stand over his grounded opponent, helmet and shoulder pads in backlit silhouette against the orange sun.

"He's down, Duncan," a teammate would say. "He might not ever get up again."

But Duncan, delirious from the heat or from the lunacy of his home, imagined the uniform rising, the SS armband returning to the huddle, the battle still unfinished.

Duncan's breath would become deep, sinking into that thick, cavernous torso that rumbled with the threat of thunder. The yell that he resisted in karate was roared shamelessly on the football field. A gladiator from some post-Holocaust world.

But apart from the action on the field, there was also a simultaneous war being fought over Duncan's soul. And Mila was determined to take on all challengers in defense of it. She wasn't the sort of person who backed away from a fight easily, and in this case, she had too much to lose. Duncan was being groomed. He was evolving into a very different conception of the standard Jewish prince. Not simply God's gift to Jewish women (as Jewish mothers all assume of their boys), but rather, Mila's gift to all Jews. A Frankenstein experiment gone right this time; a modern-day golem from Miami Beach who could defend any Jewish ghetto anywhere, anytime.

What Gentile would risk the damage that Duncan could inflict? It was about time that Jews grew them as big as Goliath, when they no longer had to rely on David's crafty slingshot, or the cleverness of a Solomon, or the permanence of Samson's hippie haircut. No more need for gimmicks or cunning or finesse; with Duncan it was all reducible to brute force. In the modern era the Israelis were certainly setting a good example of creating an altogether new ethos of the badass Jew, but Duncan's destiny was to finish the job. The pained history of Jewish suffering and exile had been answered with just one accidental, regrettable birth. A reluctant savior had been born to two

Holocaust survivors in south Florida. Mila's investment in this project was not merely familial. In fact, it was hardly about family at all.

But the Bible is filled with saviors and prophets who are irredeemably lonely. As Duncan got older, he searched for affection much like a pilot light craves gas, but with less success. When he finally was able to find love, it came not from his home, but in the polling booths and ballot boxes of Miami Beach Senior High School. For the entire four years that Duncan was stopping opposing offenses from scoring points, he was also receiving landslide votes on the way to becoming both the class and then, finally, the student body president.

Duncan had learned early on that becoming a leader among his peers offered at least the illusion of being connected to something other than the vise grip of his legacy.

In sixth grade, he had been elected captain of the safety patrols.

"That's a laugh," Mila said upon first hearing of his appointment, the orange belt and blue shield crisscrossing along her son's chest and waist, shrouding the black belt. "You think walking on green is all it takes?"

Curiously, Duncan's electoral popularity in high school did not please Mila. She feared that these diversions could only result in a softer body and a tenderized heart.

"Mr. Life of the Party," she would tease. "Prince Charming. One John Kennedy is not enough? The man was assassinated before he got a chance to finish his mission. It's better to work alone and not be responsible for others."

If she wasn't about to love her son, then no one else should either, nor could he ever learn to love himself. Her experience had taught her not to rely on the kindness or good will of others. The chance of deceit was always too great. Groups were bad—the propaganda of mobs and Marxists. Safety in numbers was an illusion. Just ask the crowded gassed and burned ones who never survived the camps. Or those tens of thousands who fell into the grave pits of Babi Yar, all piled on top of one another. Mobs cause riots and pogroms; they break glass and burn books. They lose their individual selves inside the savage logic of rising sounds and stomping feet, swept away by the simple seduction of a madman's thinking.

But it wasn't just that Duncan was among the herd, it was that he was leading it. He was right out in front, making him too easy a target. Leaders used to get assassinated in those days, particularly the ones who had an agenda. Unlike most politicians, Duncan was not going to be satisfied by just having the title. The desire to feel needed—whether in the middle of the crosswalk, or on the gridiron, or as student body president—created an obligation to earn that love as well. To do that on the football field was easy. Stop the run, defend against the pass, sack the quarterback—each took little energy from him. But there was a more complex responsibility that came with elective office. He had a constituency to serve, interests to identify. And figuring out just how to do that—passionately and with dedication—remained a formidable hurdle for Miami Beach's resident jock-Jew.

Then came the war in Vietnam.

The atmosphere in the Katz household always celebrated rebellion. Yankee and Mila were naturally skeptical of authority, resented people with portfolios, and sneered at those who luxuriated in badges, uniforms, and stripes. Duncan adopted these attitudes as well, which made it hard years later to rationalize what he was doing working for the Justice Department. It required that he focus entirely on the Nazi-hunting objective of his department, because in all other aspects of his life, Duncan always detested the people in charge. And while he was a high-school student, that person was Walter Frank, the high school's principal.

"I've just about had it up to here with you, Duncan," Frank heard himself say to Duncan more often than the principal liked. "First there was the student court. I told you, students can't bring formal charges against teachers. Then there was the reduced school day. That's not a decision for the students to make. They decide that kind of thing downtown. Next was the resolution banning grades under a B. Then some crazy idea about holding a Holocaust Remembrance Day. That kind of thing is never going to happen. Besides, this is a public school. Now this business with the war."

Frank was a man in his late fifties who looked as though he had played for double or nothing hundreds of times and lost each one. Miami's sun and Duncan Katz's imperious grief-giving no doubt had aged the man. His hair was a powdery white. His teeth were yellow. His skin was spotted. A pair of large, silver-rimmed glasses magnified billowy eyebrows that puffed out like cloud cover on his face. Walter Frank had the walk of someone unsure of his height, his stature, his entire purpose for living. With each step he seemed to be shrinking under the weight of his own insecurities.

When the American Legion came to visit the high school, Duncan made sure that the students boycotted the assembly. In fact, when the uniformed visitors arrived, Duncan and the entire student body walked out into the parking lot and remained there until Walter Frank followed them, carrying a bullhorn.

The vice-principal, Jaskins, a tall black man with a large forehead and sloping shoulders, assisted Frank onto the front end of someone's illegally parked car. Frank hoped that this elevation would bring him more respect.

"Students," he began, just as a flying Oreo sailed past his head. The dessert of some student's unfinished lunch had been recruited into the anti-war effort. "Who threw that?" Frank screeched into the bullhorn. Jaskins was then ordered to dive into the sea of teenage protesters and fish out at least one heckler who was armed with cookies.

"You must return to the building," Frank continued cautiously, mindful of flying food. "You are embarrassing our school. These men are here to explain our involvement in Vietnam and how necessary the war is for our national interests. Your parents all fought and lived through wars to protect our country. Now it is your turn . . ."

From the center of the parking lot, a muscled, longhaired teenager commandeered the roof of some other car, and was then handed a bullhorn of his own. Duncan placed the screeching cone to his mouth and said, "This is not our war! Our parents didn't fight for this! We don't believe in conquering another people. Leave the Vietnamese alone!"

The crowd erupted with a roar. From where Frank stood, everything was out of control. A forest of unkempt hair. Discipline trampled by a new culture that was fascinated by everything deemed counter. Postwar innocence corrupted; an Eden overrun with snakes. Duncan was a new breed of student leader, while many of his classmates represented a new wave of students, holed up in their cars, smoking dope, and blasting the Doors on Infinity speakers. The Age of Aquarius had sprung a leak.

More lunch leftovers took to the air. Some students—the politically apathetic ones—decided to go home and catch repeat episodes of *Dobie Gillis*, *Gilligan's Island*, or *Flipper*. Others stumbled around the parking lot, absorbed in the primitive dances of the sufficiently stoned. To capture all this on film for the evening news, local television cameras parked themselves like snipers around the perimeter of Prairie Avenue.

Walter Frank was getting nervous, and it showed from perspiration that was unrelated to the humidity. Professionally and publicly, he was looking like a buffoon. There were no flattering sides to his predicament. This most recent episode would no doubt give the school board proper cause to have him fired. Miami Beach Senior High, flat-roofed, spread wide with four unconnected wings, a large field in the back, was once again leading the way in student revolts.

Finally, rescue came to Frank from an unlikely source: Mila Katz, the mother of his archnemesis. Was it so strange for Mila to have been on campus at that particular moment? Not really. Maternal instincts sometimes show themselves, even in the absence of love. During the years when her son was running unopposed in studentwide elections, she was capturing equal support among the mothers of Miami Beach, winning four consecutive terms as PTA president.

"I accept this position because if I don't, our school and your children are in big trouble," she said, receiving a grateful applause.

She had to take some responsibility here. You can't just fire a gun into a crowd and then throw the weapon away, pretending to be blameless. Rabbi Loew of medieval Prague had the same problem with his creation. Mila had fashioned Duncan in her own image, and she was generally pleased with the outcome, but she also couldn't deny that in her exuberance also came excess. Son as student leader; mother as elected bulwark against son. The delicate checks and balances at Miami Beach Senior High School.

"Oh, thank heavens you are here, Mrs. Katz," Frank said, bowing down humbly toward his PTA president. "Duncan has them all out of control again. I may have to call the police this time. Is there something you can do? We may have a riot on our hands."

"Get down from there, Frank," Mila ordered. "You are a weak and pathetic man. They are just children. Give me that bullhorn, and get out of my way."

Mila didn't need Jaskins's assistance in mounting the hood of the car. She seemed to almost leap on it, her knees bent, her arms thrust forward for momentum. She placed the bullhorn near her mouth. "This is Duncan's mother. Please listen to me." Her voice was strong, almost unaccented, as it mediated the Miami air. "I know what it is like to want freedom, to feel alive. I understand what you want. But this is not the way. You are doing this all wrong."

"No more war!" Duncan returned a volley.

"Nothing good comes from angry crowds," she continued.

"Right on, Mrs. Katz," a stoned senior said just before tripping beside Mila's vehicular soapbox.

"I know how terrible it is when good people follow the ideas of a crazy man," she pleaded.

"We will not return to class!" Duncan threatened.

"This country liberated the world over twenty-five years ago," Mila said. "To fight a dictator is an honor. We should also be fighting against Castro."

Mila was now playing dirty; she understood how to manipulate a Miami audience.

"Impeach Nixon!" Duncan bellowed.

"The Communists will be no better than the Nazis!" Mila warned.

"Stop burning babies!" Duncan said. "Save the children!"

"Sometimes war is good," Mila answered. "It makes you strong and prepares you for other difficult times in life."

"Don't trust anyone over thirty!" Duncan replied, quoting another young, restless-souled Jew.

This amplified duel between bullhorns went on for some time. After a while, most of the students had gone home. The first to depart were those who had become bored, followed by the ones who could never quite deprogram themselves from responding mindlessly to the school bell, which signaled the end of yet another day. The students who remained were too wasted on pot, glue, and quaaludes to drive or even to get on the school buses. The fact that everyone now had the munchies led to a serious, although incoherent, discussion about how to order a pizza into the parking lot. As for Walter Frank and most of his administration, they had left as well. Their focus was now on revising their résumés in anticipation of incoming pink slips. But perhaps the very first to leave were the representatives of the American Legion, who had long since decided that recruitment at this high school could only jeopardize the country's chances of winning the war.

Even after the large crowd had dissipated to a curious few, and the cameras had gone off to file their reports, and the sun edged downward in the direction of Biscayne Bay, the odd exchange between mother and child continued. Civil disobedience in a domestic setting. Without shouting—but loudly nonetheless—they talked through each other, and at each other. Nothing else mattered. The afternoon was a high point in their relationship. It was, without question, the most intimate conversation they had ever had.

Chapter Four

EVERYONE IN THE chapel was accounted for: the old people from the condominium; Mila's cronies from the dog track and jai alai; those with whom she had played cards at the Caribbean and the Deauville on Collins Avenue; other refugees she had met at the beach or at local restaurants. They would all die, too. Eventually. But Mila Katz was the first to win that round, as well.

They had all come to Hermon Memorial off Normandy Drive to pay their respects. Mila was someone they would miss. Not just another neighbor, one of those *alter kockers* who shared a predictable fate. She was a unique soul. A wizened lady with a versatile disposition—one moment airy, followed by a demented laugh. And popular no matter where she went—at the cardrooms and frontons, or lounging at Bal Harbor poolsides. Mila was never the source of envy or resentment, even after she had cashed in her winnings for the night. Her gambling wasn't about money; it was about distraction, keeping her mind occupied and her demons at bay; it was about sending God a message that he would understand.

In the years before she died, there were many nights when, as a gesture of friendship and good will, she paid for her cohorts when they ate at Pumpernickel's, Wolfie's, or Rascal's House. Most of them earlier in the evening had been separated from a sizable chunk of that month's social security, the betting windows now a co-beneficiary of their retirement. In defeat, they would consume colossal corned beef sandwiches and granite wedges of strawberry cheesecake that would have murdered the organs of a less resilient bunch. Once the bill arrived, Mila would grab for it and start calculating. She was obsessed with numbers: a constellation of odds always danced in her head, while a faint row of blue digits clutched her forearm. And she didn't trust machines, or the cashier's honesty, either.

"You don't need to do this, Mila," her friend Ruthie said. Wearing an oversized floral smock and a pair of white plastic sandals that featured a prominent box-weave toe, the desperate Ruthie sifted through her purse and found a cache of useless betting tickets—unshred confetti—but no money. "We can pay for our own cheesecake."

"Nonsense," Mila admonished. "We are family, this is how we survive. It's time to enjoy. Enough with misery. One for all and all for one." She lifted an arm, naked without a sword. "What else should I spend my money on?"

The entire group of them—Sylvia, Sadie, Ruthie, Effie—looked at each other blankly.

"Besides, it's not like I deserve this money, or worked hard for it."

True enough. Mila was naturally lucky, mostly where it counted—in concentration camps, and in casinos. For her this was all just another night at the office—payday at the track, or the fronton, or at one of the hotels overrun with suckers and chumps, people who couldn't bluff no matter what the stakes. But she always could.

"Yes, but it's your money," Ruthie reminded her. The others nodded their heads in agreement. "And this is Miami Beach. We're not on a kibbutz; we don't share our losses."

No one answered, perhaps because Ruthie was wrong: some losses, at least the nongambling variety, are shared.

Mila interrupted the silence. "We are together every night, no?"

"Sure . . . ," Ruthie replied.

"What else do we have but each other?"

The years had tempered the dark past and doomsday prophesies of Mila's life. With her husband long dead and her Yale-boy son AWOL from her command, Mila underwent a wholesale shift in survival strategy. Community had now become important. Friends were not necessarily enemies in disguise. The world, with all its bleak moments, also revealed—if one chose to look—pockets of consolation, forgiveness, and, yes, even a little happiness. Why the change, a new wisdom that before now had been choked by the reflux of chimney smoke? The premonitions of a life about to end always bring forth a clarity that is unachievable when the body is young and unthreatened. Only in youth is it possible to gorge oneself on rage alone.

"We have our children," Sylvia chimed in excitedly, like a stymied game-show contestant who until then hadn't pushed the buzzer. But she soon shuddered under the weight of so many disapproving looks, as though the entire lot of them had simultaneously bitten into lemons.

Mila pretended not to notice.

Arguing was a treasured pastime, and so they argued and walked out into the warm Miami night. Gushing neon beams that spelled "Wolfie's" shadowed Mila and her friends as they wobbled to their cars.

The sky seemed endless, filled with cracks of mottled blue clouds that hung above the carnival atmosphere of Collins Avenue. The moon lay obscured, hiding in the darkness, trapped between the shifting clouds. A block away, the Atlantic gently lapped the shore, scattering driftwood, tangling seaweed.

Cadillac Sevilles and Eldorados with sharp, shiny fins cruised Collins Avenue with all the mobility of beached whales. The leather interiors were punctured with errant cigarette holes. Senior citizens were at the wheel, navigating slowly, as though in search of a docking slip. Sammy Davis Jr. headlined at the Fountainbleau; tickets to his show were being hawked by scalpers clopping around in rubber beach thongs. A Star of David was soon to swing from Sammy's neck in quarter time with his tapping feet. Dean Martin, with a self-mocking drink in his hand, was right next door at the Eden Roc. The rest of the Rat Pack would probably show up, drunk and unannounced, by the second show.

This was the predictable Miami that Mila and her friends all knew. Where the loan sharks and the card sharks outnumbered the sharks in the Atlantic. It was the Miami of Coppertone *mikvahs*, Zinc Oxide war paint, the couture of bleached white cabana shorts, the cheap souvenirs that had more to do with native Indians than transplanted Jews, and the parimutuel addictions that had served them so well in the past.

The next day the ritual would begin again. Only death could interfere. Monday nights they were off to the greyhounds at either

Biscayne or First Street on Miami Beach. Tuesday was always jai alai. Wednesday, the horses at Gulfstream. Thursday, it was usually back to the dogs, unless Tuesday's jai alai had led to such spectacular results that it was necessary to wager once more on helmeted Latin Americans with enormous straw hooks attached to their arms—only a slack net cage separating the spectators from the buzz of the hard, sizzling pelota. Friday and Saturday was seven-card poker at the hotels. There were hands being played all over Miami Beach, and in some corners, bodies were being whacked and turning up, as well.

Regardless of the game, Mila was deliberate in her betting strategies, and unreserved in her emotions.

"Run! Run! Move it! Hurry! Don't let them catch you!" she would yell, pounding on the railing that surrounded the open-air track.

The grandstand rose behind her, filled with anxious bettors and no-good losers who wasted the night away engaging in the most futile of get-rich schemes. But the one person who knew what she was doing, who instinctively could separate the true greyhounds from the mere dog—who in fact was getting richer by the day— seemed to blend right into the subculture of Jewish demimonde that surrounded her.

Mila looked so small, standing in the middle of all this roundabout motion, this habit-forming frenzy. Her hair was a darkened strawberry, like rust with ambition. She had a round face, a gap between her front teeth, a squat body that was efficient, but at times also illusive.

Rusty the Rabbit streaked by her once again, followed by the charging, lunging pack. Her dog, of course, was always out in front.

There is more to luck than just mere happenstance, because there's always something else underneath, no matter how random or unchanging it may look on the outside. And that's also true of pain, and sin.

WHEN MILA DIED, the refugees—even more so than the gangsters and gamblers—all had difficulty accepting the news. The loss of another widow should have been unalarming for a group who had watched friends succumb to all manner of biological breakdowns, while others had witnessed the unmarked European graveyard where so many had fallen or been turned to ash. But Mila's death somehow struck them as being strangely, and even intolerably, more cruel and unjust. It was as though it were all somehow a continuation of the tragedy—only the second of three acts, and still without a happy end.

They all worshipped her as a survivor among survivors, the one with the real instincts and stamina. Her death had made them feel more vulnerable to the natural perils of life, the standard risks, the outcomes that couldn't be avoided—not even by those who years before had miraculously dodged gas and sidestepped fire, who had marched out from under gates that promised freedom, but only after soul-crushing work. The gates lied. It took tanks, not work, to make them *frei*.

Many wept silently in their seats. Duncan was there, too, sitting in the front row. The youngest in an otherwise fast-decaying audience. They pointed at him without discretion, followed by loud whispering among the largely deaf. Duncan had finally come home to Miami. The lapsed son, the disgraced seed.

"He should have stayed away," Ruthie said. "The nerve of him showing his face around here."

"Why come back now?" Sylvia added. "What good does this do Mila?"

They expressed their loyalty toward Mila by taking out their fears and disgust on Duncan. Avenging her death somehow. Curiously, they held him responsible. His voluntary exile. The neglect, the distance. The Oedipal contempt.

Despite all the mounting scientific evidence, the refugees didn't necessarily buy into any of the new theories about the causes of cancer. Pollution. Toxic substances. Cigarettes. Faulty genes. The warring factions of biology. Science could produce only some of the answers. By blaming the obvious suspects, medicine had taken the easy way out and ignored abuses that were even more annihilating.

The refugees had all lived long enough to believe that cells sometimes go their own malignant ways even when the body is otherwise fine. The miseries of life. The unfulfilled promises. The murderous memories. And of course, the disappointments of children. All just as likely reasons why a body can go bad.

Trained as he was to anticipate danger, to breathe in the menace of his surroundings, to locate concealed enemies before they had a chance to strike, Duncan was certainly not unaware of Mila's scornful posse—but he didn't seem too bothered by them, either.

His attention was elsewhere. Three black women sat off to his left and one row behind. They were crying noisily. Eyes swollen from tears. Their chests visibly heaving with stammered breaths. Embroidered veils shrouded their faces. All dressed in black, except for one, who was wearing a short white dress with a sailor's hat, a lavender feather pluming from behind. The handkerchiefs in their laps had been transformed into dishcloths—dense and sopping.

Normally it would have been hard for Duncan to turn his head so far in any one direction to have even noticed them sitting there. But in this case, curiosity overpowered the strangled muscles in his neck, and aided by a shift of his body and a tilt of his hips, he managed to get a good view of the one group of mourners he would not have imagined seeing at a Jewish funeral home in Miami Beach, hysterical over the death of his own mother.

Who were they?

In 1982, Miami Beach remained a segregated community. Blacks lived in the Overtown section of Miami, as well as in a pocket of Coconut Grove and the whole of Liberty City. The arterial causeways that stretched across the calm turquoise waters of Biscayne Bay offered no promise of racial solidarity. The right of way was restricted to one direction. Black schoolchildren were bused over to Miami Beach, and black adults traveled there, as well, but with their own temporary and conditional passports—as the providers of necessary services. Maids. Nurses. Bus drivers. Gardeners. Dishwashers. Construction workers. Schoolteachers.

And now mourners.

Just a few Confederate states above, Jews and blacks had engaged in a unified struggle to integrate the Deep South of Dixie. But in Miami—about as far south as you could go, where the accents were newly flavored with the rapid-fire patter of Spanish replacing the slow drawl of the South—they lived apart. Neither had yet embraced the other as a neighbor. Even years of dedicated service in both households or hospitals failed to eliminate the word *shvartze* in Miami's unabridged, uncensored vocabulary.

But Mila never had a maid.

So who were these women?

"Oh Lord Jesus Christ, please watch over Mila . . . ," the one in white, with lips quivering, mumbled.

Another was sitting tall and stoic, looking straight ahead, fully absorbed in the moment. "Stop that! Mila was a Jewish woman. There's a rabbi up there. Don't you see him? Now pay attention and listen to the man," she said.

The third woman seemed hesitant, self-conscious, nervous, as though she alone among her friends realized how strange it was for them, and their emotions, to be on display.

Duncan's back was turned away from the rabbi and from Mila's sleek rosewood casket, which was elevated on a block of marble right beside the pulpit. The rabbi and his mother's coffin were mere distractions from what really interested him most. He stared at the three women intensely, focusing on their faces, drawing them nearer, then back. He framed them one at a time, then as a group.

Duncan envied their emotion as much as he resented them for having it. What was his mother to them? Why did they care so much? What were they feeling?

Who the hell were they?

Rabbi Vered was finishing his sermon. "Such a wonderful wo-man . . . ," he droned on, his voice—halting and unrhythmic—coming in like a badly tuned radio, "so filled with life and yet so familiar with death. This is precisely why I don't believe in God."

Most of the mourners were members of his congregation, so Vered's wacky rabbinic pronouncements about either a world without a god, or one with a deviant god, didn't faze them anymore. In fact, they half expected it. Rabbi Vered never missed an opportunity to take a cheap shot at the Almighty. Usually it was aimed below the belt, when Yahweh was looking the other way—a familiar defensive position for God. It was a sucker punch delivered by an irreverent rabbi whose only apparent calling was to piss God off whenever possible. But Vered's scornful efforts would go unrewarded. God never showed himself in Miami, either.

Rabbi Vered glanced down at the lectern to check his script, which was filled with profanities, proverbs from the New Testament, and a few choice jokes:

"Knock knock."

"Who's there?" the congregation would recite in unison.

"God."

"God who?"

"My question precisely."

Having exhausted all that he had come prepared to say, Rabbi Vered concluded, "And now let us say, Amen."

With his closing remarks, many of the women began to swoon. What the rabbi lacked as a god killer he more than made up for with the ladies—young and old alike. He was a handsome man with finely cut silver hair, a tall and lean frame, and a bronze face that was way past the point of peeling. Clasping his large hands together, he said, "But before we depart for the cemetery, is there anyone who would like to say a few words about our friend, Mila?"

One by one they rose and made their way to the pulpit. Misfits, gamblers, and convicts. Old ladies with crayon-white hair; old men with pathetically little hair. A parking lot of wheelchairs, walkers, and canes broke up and reassembled as orderly traffic in the aisles.

The mourners took their turns eulogizing Mila. Carlo Costello— a little older himself but still surprisingly spry when it came to maneuvering a camera—moved from the back of the room and positioned his tripod closer to the pulpit.

"I'll tell you what; the lady had balls, nothing scared her," said Cappy, a thin reed of a man whose entire existence almost disappeared in profile. He was one of the men of the Jewish Nostra. A hanger-on; the kind of guy who just liked being around the action—not as a hit man, or shakedown artist, or nervous bettor—but just being there, sitting, as spectator only. The vicarious thrill of palling around with the naughty Jewish boys of Miami Beach. Other retired men of Miami spent the mornings swinging rackets wildly on the tennis court, or getting sand-trapped on the golf course, or camping out in their stockbroker's office, enjoying the climate-controlled air while neon-dotted numbers whirled past them, wrapping around the room, a carousel of bids and asks.

Had they been smart enough to show up, the police in the Miami rackets bureau could have all retired on the jackpot of arrest shields that would have resulted from the bust at Mila Katz's funeral. Everyone except Larry Breitbart was there—bookies, numbers runners, and goons with ties to the protection business. Breitbart himself couldn't make it to the funeral. He was a marked man in Miami. So he sent a delegation in his place.

"She knew something about odds," Cappy continued. "Knew when to bet on Joey at jai alai. Knew when a dog or horse was running lame. Knew when to fold the deck. Morty's here, he'll tell you . . . ," Cappy said, realizing that it was best that everyone hear it straight from the horse's mouth. Cappy then pointed out into the congregation until everyone's eyes rested on Morty the Mohel, now an elderly lump of a man, round and unmovable, as lifeless as a sculpture of discarded foreskins.

The mourners nodded their heads in concert with everything that had been said so far. Duncan wondered whether he—and perhaps the three mysterious black women, as well—were the only ones in the chapel able to form a sentence without relying on casino jargon for inspiration.

The chapel at Hermon Memorial was a narrow but deep room that had two wide doors in the back and a side exit near the pulpit that later would allow for the casket's getaway. The carpet was a thick blood red. The walls were white and spare, except for a few painted by numbers Edwardian foxhunt scenes. There were no windows, but the air-conditioning blasted overhead and frosted the room, producing an extra shiver in those whose bodily thermostats were gradually being lowered anyway.

Sylvia now stood before the mourners and said, "We who knew Mila well," pausing for a moment to glare at Duncan, "realize that she was no ordinary woman. She had several lives; we were lucky to be around for the last one."

Ruthie followed her. "We know what it is like to lose a friend. But this time we lost more . . ."

The dirge continued. A man from the condo association, wearing a navy business suit that was too tight just about everywhere, said, "I loved her, but she suffered. None of us could help her. I always felt that her memories were worse than ours, which I can't even imagine. After all, we each have a story . . ."

The room fell into an even deeper silence as the mourners reviewed their own scorecards in suffering.

The condo officer continued, "I really believe she took her worst secrets and heartaches to the grave with her," he added, dropping his chin in the direction of the casket.

When there was no one else left to speak, one of the black women—the tallest of the three and the one least intimidated by the surroundings—rose and started walking toward the aisle. She wanted to have the last word on Mila Katz. But she was thwarted by her friends, one of whom grabbed her arm while the other hooked the strap of her purse and swung her back down into her seat.

"Somebody should say something," the tall one mumbled in anger.

"This is not the time, or the place," said the woman with the lavender feather sticking out from her head.

From the pulpit, Rabbi Vered noticed the commotion but didn't interfere. Instead, he just tried to keep the proceedings moving, like a plate spinner after a commercial on the *Ed Sullivan Show.*

"Well then," the rabbi continued, slapping his hands together, "if there is no one else, I understand Mila's son is here with us today. Duncan, I have not seen you since your bar mitzvah. And who can forget your *bris?* Morty certainly can't." Morty smiled passively from his seat and waved at Rabbi Vered. "And neither could Larry Breitbart, if he were here . . . a seltzerman with such butterfingers. By the way, he sends his regards to all of you. And of course, his sympathies to Duncan. So, where is Duncan?" he asked, forming a plank with his hands, squinting and searching the room. "Duncan Katz, do you have anything you would like to say about your mother?"

Duncan turned around and faced the rabbi but remained still, refusing to answer. The mourners all pressed forward. They would give him up easily. His identity wasn't safe with them.

"He's right in the front row, rabbi, all the way to the side," a heavyset numbers runner yelled from the back. "The stiff in the gray suit."

"Ah yes, Duncan, there you are," the rabbi said, his face now more serious, lips brought together, the forehead creased. Despite the spiritual emptiness of his pulpit, he was, after all, the Katzes' Miami Beach rabbi, the cleric and kook who had been with them right from the very beginning. He knew many of the truths, and some of the lies, but even he was unable to patch together the whole story. "So many years that you have been away. Our famous local sports hero. The

Miami Herald used to write about you almost every day. Our Jew with muscles. And now, our Nazi hunter. Would you like to speak?" He paused, then added, "But if you are uncomfortable, we would understand."

"No, we wouldn't!" an elderly gentleman piped up. "Make him speak. You're the rabbi. Force him!"

"Quiet!" Rabbi Vered bellowed from the *bema*. "Don't listen to that man, Duncan. We realize the strain you must be under."

A cynic coughed from the back row; schoolyard high jinks that still worked well even in old age.

Duncan didn't want to speak. More importantly, he didn't think he could. He felt more than a bit nervous—and that was even before the rabbi had unexpectedly recruited him for the keynote address. In situations such as these, he thought it best to say nothing. It was all part of a lawyer's training: knowing the pitfalls of speaking off the cuff. He wasn't required to speak; even the rabbi had said so. Duncan wasn't in Miami answering a subpoena; he was attending his mother's funeral, and other than for an occasional show of grief—which wasn't coming easily to him, nor was it particularly genuine—he had no reason to move from his seat.

Besides, as a matter of principle, he never gave information away voluntarily. It was not only a lawyer's mantra, but also a credo shared by children of Holocaust survivors. Speech should be deliberate and thoughtful. The mind must prepare before the mouth opens. Secrets are concealed for a reason. Duncan hadn't planned on speaking at his mother's funeral. He wasn't about to go ahead and improvise with either the eulogy or his emotions.

But there was more to his resistance than the Fifth Amendment. He belonged to the generation that was born in the shadow of shame, memory, and nightmare—foot soldiers conscripted into a trembling army of "Never Again!" placard holders, where no draft dodging was possible because there was little choice but to serve. He understood all that could be said by saying absolutely nothing at all.

Not all questions require an answer.

Silence not as equilibrium, but as way of life.

By attending the funeral—by even coming back to South Florida—Duncan had already delivered a silent requiem.

Anxiously, he began to wrap his tie around his fist as though it were a bandage. He stared straight ahead. He waved his arm and brushed his hand to the side as though smoothing out musty air, hoping that the rabbi would understand this gesture to mean that they just move along, go on to the next event—whatever that might be. He thought desperately about the bottle of Donnatal he had left in his hotel room at the Doral on Collins Avenue. Was it on the bed? Or on top of the nightstand? He couldn't recall. Why did it even matter? Where it actually was would do him no good now. He reached his hands into his pockets and slinked down into the pew. Unaccountably, a few awkward seconds later, he felt ready to bury his mother.

So he steeled himself, rose to his feet, and scaled the two steps that placed him upon the circular podium where Rabbi Vered had been standing all along. Duncan stood in front of the microphone—a gun metal rod topped off with a bulbous mesh surface—and said, "Thank you all for coming today. Mila would have appreciated it." He quickly slid past the microphone and back toward his seat as though he had just been pushed out of the podium's way.

That's it? they all thought. A congregation of elderly eyes blinked in unison, like a folding row of Levelor blinds. You've been away from Mila and Miami this long, and that's all you have to say for yourself, and her?

Rabbi Vered regained the abandoned *bema*. "Well, then," he said calmly, "let us now all go over to the cemetery. Please make sure to follow the lead car, and also to keep your lights on at all times."

Having just about returned to his seat, Duncan suddenly wheeled around and clumsily leapt back over the steps, returning himself to the pulpit with a heavy thud.

"Actually, just a second, rabbi. Please, forgive me," Duncan said haltingly, buttoning his jacket, straightening his tie, and trying vainly to extend his former linebacker's neck. "I think I have more . . ."

The mourners rustled in their seats. This funeral for a friend might prove exciting, yet. Better than re-runs of *Maude* or even *All in the Family*.

Naturally Duncan had more to say. All those years of estrangement would have required an oration to explain. He couldn't remain mute; his accusers, and his mother, demanded more.

He faced downward, not looking at anyone in particular, as though he were more interested in the carpet of the sanctuary than anything else. Leaning forward against the pulpit for support, he began, "I know you have all been looking at me as some evil person, like I don't belong at my own mother's funeral. I know I abandoned her. I ran away from home, and I never came back—until the other day. But I don't owe any of you an explanation for where I've been, or who I've been, or what I've been doing, or what kind of a son I was when Mila was alive. It's really between Mila and me. And believe me, you don't know the half of it. If there is a god, Mila will have to answer to him. That much I am sure of."

"She won't find him there, either," Rabbi Vered muttered under his breath.

"Does anyone here remember what it was like in my house?" Duncan pleaded. "You didn't have to actually live there to know."

If anybody did, no one was confessing. Not here, not anywhere. People kept better secrets in those days, and also had a better angle on looking the other way. Doors that were closed were that way for a reason. There was no Freedom of Information Act on someone else's privacy. Reputations mattered; revelations did not. Mila was now dead. Why allow the awful truth to surface here, at her funeral of all places? Why give Duncan the satisfaction?

"Fine. I know you all loved Mila; I'm sure you had many reasons why you did—so keep on protecting her. But that won't change my childhood. I was there. I guess there's a limit to how much neighbors can know."

The microphone screeched as though in defiance of what it was about to hear.

"So she's dead. And you all feel loss, but let me tell you something: I feel freedom. I am newly liberated. For me, today is not about mourning, but about celebration. No sitting *shivah*—at least not by me. I don't want to remember her; all I want is a fresh start."

A collective hush overtook the room.

"Shame!" someone yelled from the right side of the sanctuary.

But Duncan continued. "I am what I am today because of my mother. And let me tell you something: I don't like myself very much. I'm her creation. A creature. A machine. In those days they didn't call anything child abuse, but Mila gave the term new meaning."

A few pacemakers faltered in mid-rhythm; scattered gasps echoed throughout the chapel. Hearing aids were tapped and adjusted as though they had been tuned to the wrong frequency.

"Liar!"

"Make him stop!"

A beefy middle-aged man with a lopsided wedge for a nose and an apparent rap sheet in his past, approached the pulpit respectfully and addressed Rabbi Vered. "You want for me to trow him out, rabbi? The kid's too fresh, talking about his mudder like that. Let me take care of 'im, the old-fashioned way—wash his mout out wit soap. Come here, boychik . . ."

Rabbi Vered never got a chance to give his blessing because the self-appointed bouncer at the funeral quietly, but eagerly, climbed the steps and then lunged for Duncan's shoulders. But his hands never arrived; instead, he froze as though caught in the middle of a sleep walk.

Duncan's instincts had summoned that part of him that always remained caged until called upon. The heavy artillery was always well rested—on standby and ready alert. Ask anyone who had ever been on the receiving end of Duncan's fire. He didn't grow up with the Brown Shirts, but he was superbly trained in how to deal with them if they ever showed up. Until then, he practiced on everyone else.

First came the cement-block stare, then the crackling growl and the beaming rush of blood to the face. Finally Duncan warned, "Stay back! Don't fuck with me! I'm not through yet."

The mobster was surprised by his own fear. His legs wouldn't take him forward. Choosing survival over honor, the mobster blinked first, retreated backward, and fell off the platform, landing on his ass.

The mourners, those not giggling, feared that this was a eulogy without remorse or end. Duncan could not be stopped.

Just then, a throaty rumble, followed immediately by a blast of thunder, shook the foundations of the sanctuary. The lights inside the chapel flickered; then for a long few seconds the room went completely dark. Since there were no windows, the mourners were thrown into the blackness without warning. Everyone was silent, including Duncan. They all listened to the creaking, high-pitched sound of a door opening slowly. Some feared that the screeching hinges belonged to the coffin; perhaps Mila had somehow managed to escape from death once again—this time in Houdini-like fashion, seeking vengeance against her son.

The lights returned, and Duncan saw the three black women leaving through the rear entrance of the chapel. The one wearing the sailor hat closed the door quietly. No one would have noticed them leave had Duncan not yelled, "Hey wait! Ladies, where are you going? Come back! . . . Stop them!"

But no one in the room was about to do any of Duncan's bidding. They had had enough of him and whatever it was he had meant to accomplish with his parting words to Mila. The rows began to empty out into the aisle, and everyone, fully disgusted—including Rabbi Vered—followed the cue of the three women and rushed as best they could to the exit, leaving Duncan finally alone with his mother. All departed with their heads bowed, mournful once again not only of Mila's death, but of the auto-da-fé that, regrettably, had not taken place in their presence.

Chapter Five

A LONG, DARK BLUE LIMOUSINE—the lead car of the procession —took to the causeway and headed west, away from Miami Beach, in the direction of the Jewish cemetery. This was where all the old Jews of South Florida eventually ended up—near the airport, entombed under flat and unbearably hot ground. The supersonic roar of international jets taking off and landing could be heard in the distance. So much for resting in peace. During their twilight years the survivors had lived in deluxe condos near the ocean. Now death brought them closer to the inferno.

The limo snaked slowly through traffic. The intermittent pattern of rain clouds and dry-heat thunder continued to soak the roads. It was a typical Miami summer deluge, making Little League games— and the burial portion of funerals—impossible to attend with confidence.

Swollen darts of rain plunged into Biscayne Bay and bounced on the sizzling pavement. From his childhood Duncan remembered how these tropical episodes usually came hard, fast, and unexpected, and then almost immediately gave way to sunshine. The dark cloud cover and savage downpours were always threatening, but temporary. Miami's psychic climate may have been best suited for the tranquility of leisure and retirement, but its summer weather traded in extremes.

As Duncan sat in the lead car, he realized that he didn't have an umbrella. And he couldn't imagine that anyone who was trailing behind in that orderly line of connecting headlights would offer him one, if an extra one could be found.

He leaned forward, rapped on the plastic partition, and said to the driver, "Excuse me, do you have an umbrella in case it's still raining when we get to the cemetery?"

The man didn't reply; perhaps he knew what had gone on back there at Hermon Memorial and was appalled by what he had heard. A career-minded fellow, maybe he didn't want to risk having any association with the deceased's son.

"He can't hear you," a voice from behind Duncan spoke.

"Huh?" Duncan turned around, jittery, always mindful of the blind side. For him, Miami was congested with ghosts, and he imagined that the road to a cemetery must be their natural haunt.

"The compartment is soundproof," the voice continued, slowly. "He won't be able to hear you unless you press the buzzer, the one off to your right, against the door panel, over by the electric window lever. They make it silent in here so you can have privacy while you grieve."

"Who's that talking?"

Duncan separated a curtain that he had assumed opened out onto a flatbed where his mother's coffin would have been slipped in and clamped down. Instead, all he saw was yet another cabin of seats and the back of a man's head; the man was facing out the rear of the limousine. The body of Mila Katz must have been traveling in another car, while in the lead car—where Duncan was sitting as the sole surviving family member—a stowaway had apparently come along for the ride.

The man had a large frame. His jet-black hair was greased tight against his scalp. Even in the darkness of the cloaked interior, Duncan saw that the man's rounded jawline and the one unshaded side of his smooth face were well pampered and tan. He was wearing a light beige suit that had the look of silky pajamas. Glossy fingernail polish shimmered from a hand that rested on his thigh.

"Who are you?" Duncan repeated, grateful that at least he was speaking to a live body.

"It's just your Uncle Larry."

"Jesus Christ, Larry, you scared the crap out of me."

"I thought you were fearless?"

Duncan calmed himself. "I am. I just have a thing about dead people and coffins. Gangsters I can handle. So what are you doing here?"

"You think I wouldn't make it to your mother's funeral? Besides, you might have needed some help."

"I should have realized you'd be here somewhere. I couldn't help noticing all the wise guys inside the chapel. A real hood convention."

"I never travel alone," Larry Breitbart said while lighting the tip of an expensive, and illegal, Cuban cigar. One smoke-ring later, he added, "Those guys loved your mother; they would have come anyway."

"Is that supposed to make me feel good? My God, the company she kept. I work for the government, and my mother's funeral is jammed with criminals. I was really outnumbered in there."

"I don't know, I thought you handled yourself pretty well. You took good care of fat Schwartz," Breitbart said glibly. "But I wouldn't get too excited; the guy's on his last legs. I've got some guys with real muscle who might have made it a fair fight."

"How'd you hear what went on in the service? You were there?"

"Nah, I had the whole thing piped right here into the back—in stereo. Blaupunkt speakers. The latest thing in audio. And no more eight-track tapes, just these little cassettes. I got *Fiddler on the Roof, West Side Story*, Eddie Fisher . . . do you want to hear Eddie?"

"No thanks. I'm about to bury my mother."

"You sounded good on these speakers; very little distortion, although very much demented. Can I be honest with you?"

"Sure, go ahead."

"I'm your uncle; I only want the best for you."

"Yeah, so . . . ?"

"It's time for you to see a psychiatrist. I know you're working on a government salary, but I bet therapy is covered, and if not, I'll pay for it. This isn't the old days anymore. There's no more stigma. You go, you talk, you let things out. I'm telling you, if you had a few sessions, there's no way you would have said those things back there. Don't be mad, but you have a lot of issues to address."

"Are you finished?"

"I send some of my best people to a guy who has an office in Manhattan. I make them go because they have too much hostility. It clouds their judgment. Bad for business. This shrink in Manhattan works miracles with them. He's got them in a group—they talk from the heart; they even cry. You know my line of work is frustrating and stressful. In that way, my men are really no different from you. You're all blocked, and you all come from fucked-up childhoods. Believe me, you're not alone with this problem."

"Don't compare me to them. Weeping men of the Mafia is not the same thing, and you know it."

"You need help, that's all I have to say. I don't know whether there is a twelve-step rage recovery program, but if there is, you should be in it."

"Larry, I've never been better. You heard what I said in there. I wasn't kidding; my life now begins—for the first time."

"Personally, I think you're getting worse."

Duncan didn't respond. How would Larry know what his nephew was really like? He had been no better than a phantom uncle, dropping in from time to time bearing gifts, renting out an entire room of a restaurant, meeting clandestinely at a park bench. Now they sat with their backs to each other, no closer than before.

"When did you get in, Duncan?"

"Two nights ago. Mila's doctor called me in Washington. He said she was dying and that I should come immediately."

"I know. I told him to call you. I was afraid if I called, you'd hang up. I wanted you to say goodbye to your mother."

"I already said goodbye—a long time ago."

"Running away from home doesn't count."

"It does for me."

"Then why did you come back?"

"I don't know . . . maybe I just wanted to do the eulogy."

"Is that what that was? By the way, did you get a chance to see Mila? Did you talk to her?"

VISITING HOURS AT Mount Sinai Hospital had ended at 8 P.M., so a midnight call on a sick person was simply out of the question—unless the visitor was Duncan Katz, the former student council president of the high school down the road, and a violator of rules everywhere.

The hallways of the hospital were deserted. The lights were dimmed or, in some cases, turned off completely. Machines blinked in the darkness. Speckled tile floors had just been mopped down, leaving a filmy layer of puddles arranged like a game of Twister. Fluorescent beams, tucked away behind beds and encased within plastic moldings, generated a buzz that would have been indistinct and un-noticeable had it not been so late and otherwise quiet.

All the floors, entranceways, and elevators clearly indicated that visitors were no longer allowed inside. But Mila had readied her son—from birth, maybe even before then—not to surrender to signs or to the people who wrote them. Mount Sinai—whether the mountain with its Commandments or the sleepy Miami hospital with its cur-few—wouldn't present much of a challenge.

Duncan read the posted sign telling visitors to come back in the morning, and then he glided through the electronic doors without so much as registering a wink from the zombie at the security desk. The Hispanic receptionist, with a Cubist face, straight angular lines, an ice pick for a nose, and a trapdoor jaw, was off getting coffee. Duncan quietly leafed through a three-ring binder on the reception desk until he found the name of a patient who, nearly three decades earlier, had been admitted here for the first time—to give birth to him. "Mila Katz. Room 1016. Cancer Care."

Duncan located the entrance to the corner stairwell, which he sensed would be totally abandoned, and he scaled it one flight—and two steps—at a time. Floor after floor he ducked underneath the square portholes that were placed at eye level on each of the heavy entranceways. When he arrived on the tenth floor, he waited a mo-ment to still his breathing, and then opened the door just a crack and snuck past a massive white reception desk. A nurse was staring into the hypnotic jelly of blue light that bounced from her computer screen while she input the data of blood tests, cell counts, and urine samples. She never saw the intruder, who slipped right past her.

The door to room 1016 was wide open. As he walked in, he made sure to close it just enough to prevent anyone from noticing that Mila was not alone. Inside, a small luminous night-light, like a beacon, peered out from under a wall socket right beside Mila's bed. There was a fresh rose in a crystal flute vase resting above a ruffled linen mat, all positioned on the nightstand.

Duncan moved cautiously toward the bed. He hadn't seen his mother in years. The doctor who had called had warned that she wouldn't be recognizable, not even to someone who might have seen her just yesterday.

The wretched workings of cancer had accelerated, making time now seem irrelevant. Mila's life was racing in perpetual, unyielding forward motion. No pause button; no rewind. An hour was now measured in decades; a minute, in years. A lifetime came to an end in a matter of weeks. There was no turning back, no remission, no miraculous recovery, no government reprieve or last-ditch postponement or forestalling clemency. Not the slightest show of mercy was possible or expected.

Duncan had to reintroduce himself to a mother who was now more like a corpse. The sight of her was jarring. He wished he had brought along a few pictures to recall her more vital days. Yelling at him at the dojos. Insisting that he do more wind sprints after football practice. Pushing him in directions that he otherwise would not have gone. At this point, a picture of anything from that era would do, something to glance at in between the horror, reviving the memory of who she once was, while he sat there incredulous over who, or what, she had become.

Her body so frail, more skeletal structure than human flesh, wrapped up loosely in a translucent, bloodless skin, its texture coarse and ravaged. Her once robust cheeks had been reduced to hollow pouches, sagging below her jaw. Her hair had gone gray; almost overnight it had changed, as though the strands had been frightened by all the deterioration taking place around them. Her full lips, having been deflated the least, stood alone in overwhelming her face.

She had been weightless like this once before . . .

No doubt the Nazis had been using the wrong formula all along. Cancer was seemingly the most effective killer of all.

He pitied the life that she had lived, and yet he selfishly pitied himself for being the son who had to watch, and ignore, and in so many ways contribute to the aftermath.

The door to the bathroom was nearly closed, but a light was on, a milky beam, the kind of role given to God in a feature film. Duncan heard a sound coming from inside, the chiming of a water glass that had been tapped against a porcelain sink. It startled him, but not nearly as much as when Mila began to speak.

"MAMA! ZEIDA. YANKEE. CHECK. CHECK. KNOCK. KNOCK. HIT ME. HIT ME! HIT ME AGAIN. CALL. RAISE. RAISE AGAIN AND I'LL SEE YOU ANOTHER DOLLAR. CUT. CAROM. CHULA. JOEY. RUSTY. ASIS. PUPPY POLAND. KICK!

GET HIM, DUNCAN! ISAAC. SO SORRY. SO SORRY. ISAAC. MY BOY. MY BOYS. DUNCAN . . ."

Duncan tried to move closer, but Mila's garbled rantings froze him in place.

Her wrists had been tied down. Restrained at last. What she could possibly do to harm herself at this point, he couldn't imagine. A decrepit arm punctured blue with bruises from an assembly line of hypodermic and intravenous needles; the other arm branded blue from hot-iron prejudice.

"PHOTO FINISH. BY A LENGTH. A HAIR. RAISE. I'M IN; I'M OUT. NEVER FOLD. CALL. DEAL. LAST CARD UNDERNEATH. IN THE HOLE. CUT! CUT! BURN! BURN! SHOW YOUR CARDS. BLUFF. ROYAL FLUSH. STRAIGHT FLUSH. FOUR OF A KIND. DEALER CALLS. DEUCES ARE WILD. JACKS ARE WILD. THE QUEEN WITH THE ONE EYE."

"What are you saying?" Duncan screamed back.

It might have all been different with another son, or someone else's mother. But this was a family that thrived on secret passwords, an obsession that grossly overmatched their talents for decoding them.

"Talk to me! Stop with this already! Say something I can understand . . ."

Red hot hallucinations, mumblings from another world, gibberish for all except those lucky few with a special talent for dead languages: Latin, Yiddish, Aramaic, Sanskrit, and of course, the howling vernacular of the Holocaust. Morphine now freed her mind to translate the forgotten tongue that would both unravel and reveal her sins. Sedated lunacy would soon unchain the nightmare of Duncan's childhood, explaining its logic, taming the mystery. But how was he to make sense of this all? Duncan simply stood in front of his mother, his heart beating faster, his mind racing elsewhere, his head nodding even though he had no idea what direction or meaning or method her madness was taking.

Duncan couldn't crack the code.

"KILL! KILL! GET THEM! AVENGE ME. BOYS. SONS. FULL HOUSE. JACKS OR BETTER. TWO PAIR. JACKS OVER DEUCES. ONE-EYED JACKS. JACKS ARE WILD. WILD. WILD. WILD. MAMA! ZEIDA. YANKEE. KELLER. FORGIVENESS. SHAME. AKEDAH! AKEDAH! THERE IS NO RAM! DEAL ME BACK IN."

He ran from the room in terror and without much finesse. Various hospital personnel spotted him as he barreled into a serving cart, knocked over a tray of medicine, spun around into the waiting arms of a scowling nurse, and then vomited his airplane dinner soon after falling to his knees on the slippery, newly washed floor.

THE LIMO EXITED the ramp, yielded, then veered into local street traffic. It then turned a corner and took a sharp right, driving underneath a sandstone archway with a menacing lion gargoyle staring out from over the top, guarding the entrance.

"Lakeview Memorial," the sign read, although there was neither a lake, nor any sign of water, anywhere in sight other than rain pockets fast drying under the August sun.

Curved and bowed palm trees with ashen gray trunks lined the cement roadway. Olive green lizards scuttled along the curb. Near the gate a noiseless lawn mower posed like a statue.

The driver of the limousine was waiting for directions. In front of him stood a white, flat-roofed pavilion surrounded by thick bushes and gravel. This was presumably the office where plots were purchased, burial arrangements made, and maps given to help find a loved one. There was an open grave somewhere along this massive stretch of soggy burial ground, waiting for the snaking queue of cars to wind its way to a final stop in observance of Mila's final rest.

When no one came to meet him, the driver stepped out of the car, signaled a gesture of patience to the air-conditioned fleet behind him, and then walked over to the pavilion.

Duncan and Larry sat quietly in the car, still looking through opposite windows. Duncan tapped away at a lever that rolled down his. "You know, Yankee is buried around here, too. It's been so long since that funeral . . . ," Duncan reflected, then shuddered and hugged himself, as though gripped by a sudden chill. He thought about his father, about the death certificate that seemed to sum up the man's life: "Cause of death: heart attack from acute wartime trauma. Nightmares."

Whoever dies from nightmares? Four heart attacks over his lifetime and yet no indication of congenital disease. A nonsmoker. Low cholesterol. Not overweight. In all other respects, in perfect health. Except that nightmares played like double features in his mind, freeze-frames at the worst possible scenes, and then the inevitable fade to black.

Duncan recalled those nights of his childhood; the lullabies, never by Brahms, that his parents would sing to him; the strange serenade— in truth, the shouts that came from their bed. The sounds of his parents at their most revealing. They weren't yelling at each other, because they were both asleep. Thrashing away at low-flying ghosts, communicating with the dead by way of nocturnal smoke signals. In dreams, fears are never overcome; the tormented are always stuck in slow motion.

"Funny, I always knew that Yankee wouldn't live long," Duncan said. "In fact, it would have been much more humane if he had died even earlier. But I never imagined that Mila would die. I mean, really, I thought she'd go on forever. Who was going to stop her?"

"She hadn't planned on dying," Larry Breitbart replied. "Too much unfinished business."

"You think so? I think she had done enough. Look at me. I prosecute Nazis for a living. I dream about them in my sleep. I walk around with Nazi names in my head. I have their wartime faces memorized in case I ever bump into one. What more could she ask for?"

"A son." Breitbart was now staring impatiently out his own window. "I'm sorry to hear you didn't get a chance to make your peace with her."

The driver finally returned, glanced back at the line of cars, and hurled his arm forward in a "follow me" fashion, as though leading the flock on to Canaan.

"Were there any nurses in the room with her?" Breitbart asked.

"No, why?"

"Because I paid for them, that's why! Round-the-clock. And they want hard cash for that sort of thing."

"She was alone when I got there."

"I think I'll pay these women a little visit."

"Lucky them."

The car lurched forward and entered a maze of fictitious avenue and street names. Crespi Lane. Tatum Street. Flamingo Court. Fairway Canyon. Polo Boulevard. North Shore Avenue. Parkview Way. Whatever city life was suggested by this farce of urban planning was no doubt happening below ground only. For Mila's sake, maybe there was a working crypt for a casino, a buried Golden Nugget.

At each plot of the cemetery, the headstones were all the same, engraved copper rectangles laid flat on the ground, with just enough room for the name and life span of the deceased, and a word or two about who he or she had been. "Devoted Wife," "Loving Husband," "Caring Mother," "Joyous Son."

Nothing fancy or elaborate. An egalitarian community of dead people. No mausoleums or extravagant marble edifices. Not enough space to tell much of a story, or imprint poetry, or even leave behind a witty epitaph. Years earlier, Duncan had wanted to recycle the sentence that appeared on Yankee's death certificate and insert it onto his father's headstone, but there wasn't enough room.

After zigzagging through a few turns, Breitbart's limo reached Parkview Way and edged behind a dilapidated white pickup truck. A stone path led from the curb over to the burial plot where two laborers from the cemetery were waiting beside a gurney that would eventually lower the casket into the earth. They had just finished digging out a mound of soil and, in its place, carved into the ground a perfectly shaped rectangle. The sides smooth and damp, the soil glinted in the sun as though alloyed with crystals.

One of the laborers wore a baseball cap; the other, something that had safari origins, but which, after a few years in the tropics, now looked as if it were a relic from some early Havana exodus. The men were deeply tanned and whispered in Spanish to each other as car doors opened and mourners spilled out for the final leg of Mila's funeral.

Duncan exited the limo and slipped on a pair of sunglasses. Mourners passed by him coolly on both sides. He didn't expect Larry to join the proceedings, but his uncle's door did open and out came an umbrella handle, followed by the tethered umbrella itself. Duncan grabbed the metal-tipped rod at its point.

"Here, you might need this." The voice, like the umbrella, seemed unattached to anything.

"It's not raining anymore," Duncan replied.

"In Miami, you never know. Besides, it might come in handy—for protection. Think machete, and hack away if it boils down to that. Now go and say Kaddish. Be a son."

The mourners had all formed a large circle. Heads remained bowed. Some folded their arms; others just clutched pocketbooks or leaned against a cane or the next person.

Hurriedly, as if he were late for an appointment, Rabbi Vered uttered a few brief, closing remarks, and then recited the Kaddish, the only prayer that he ever took seriously. It was the only prayer, perhaps, that he even knew.

Duncan remained mute throughout, checking his back. Everyone else was busy reciting the Hebrew prayer for the dead. Suddenly he noticed the three women, like furies, who had departed from Hermon Memorial early. They were here, too. One of them looked at Duncan, then turned away. Finally, they each strolled over to the casket and took turns stroking the rosewood casing.

"Bye, Mila. Miss you, baby," said the one dressed in white with the sailor hat.

"Sorry we don't know this prayer," added another with a wavering breath, "but we'll get it down."

"Yeah, we'll learn it," said the third, the tall one, showing the least emotion. "And we'll see you sometime."

"Sure we will," said the one in white.

"The next world will be better," said the tall one. "It'll have to be. And you'll probably own it."

"Or win it in a poker game," said the second, her hand pressed like a sealant against her mouth to cap any leaking laughter.

"Probably bluff in that one, too," said the one in white.

A pulley lowered the casket into the ground as the two cemetery hands steadied the box, directing its descent, preventing any wild swings. When it had latched onto the metal railings below, Rabbi Vered said, "And now, as is our Jewish custom, we each take a turn with the shovel, returning the earth back into the ground and covering the casket."

Ordinarily, the first to be given the shovel would have been a member of the family, but neither Rabbi Vered, nor any of the mourners—not even the tawny, shiftless personnel from Lakeview Memorial—were about to put a heavy object in Duncan's hands. This funeral was going to end in dignity, and in order to accomplish that, it had to be made childproof. The shovel was dangerous for many reasons. Duncan would have to find his own toy.

The replacement of the dirt began. The mobsters traded off with the senior citizens, passing the shovel back and forth and then down the line. There were so many mourners, and the shovel was so heavy for most of them, that the task of filling up the grave was moving very slowly. The two laborers removed their hats and threw wet towels on their heads. There were other holes to dig and caskets to lower; this Mila Katz affair was taking far too long.

In frustration over the bottleneck with the shovel, a good number of the mourners stepped out of the line, approached the grave, and began to topple the earth on their own. Canes were used like putters; walkers became bulldozers; wheelchairs backed right up to the precipice, and tires began to spin, sending crescent streams of soil backward into the grave. Soon the mound of soil had been completely returned into the hole from where it came.

When the mourners were finished, somebody yelled out, "Okay, let's string him up!"

"Finish him off right here!" Ruthie joined in, gripping the shovel with menace as if she were storming the Bastille.

Mesmerized by the three women and oblivious to everything else, Duncan hadn't noticed that a circle of mourners had collapsed around him, closing in, fists pumping madly, rage-filled eyes out for revenge.

There was going to be a lynching right there in the cemetery. Such a convenient location. All the necessary equipment for a burial was already in place. They even had a rabbi. There were two bored laborers who could have been recruited into doing some extra digging. And while the fan-shaped shrubs from the surrounding palm trees may not have been ideally suited for tossing a noose over and supporting the weight of a dangling former linebacker, there was the pulley-and-hook apparatus, which might have worked well in hoisting and suspending Duncan until his breath gave out.

"Wait a minute," Duncan, recovering, finally said. "What's going on here? . . . Hey, you have to be kidding. You all don't have a chance . . ."

He then noticed that the mob had just diminished by three. The holy trinity wasn't about to join this battle. Instead, they cut through the Jewish cemetery and returned to their brown, wood-paneled Chevy station wagon, which was parked several lengths ahead of Breitbart's limousine. Two of them got in the car immediately, but the third—the tall one—the one who had been denied the opportunity to speak at the chapel, the one who wished to unburden herself of the awful testimony that was now their secret, turned around to find Duncan staring desperately back at her.

Although they stood at least one hundred feet apart, her eyes cut right through him, stunning him far more than the actual violence that was threatening to take place. At that moment, Duncan realized that she knew what he had long only imagined. Yet, Duncan would learn nothing more. The woman turned and folded her long frame into the backseat of the car. As the station wagon sped away, Duncan felt sickeningly empty and alone—his first true encounter as an orphan.

Breitbart had watched everything from the rear of his plush asylum from the law. Familiar with the car's advanced gadgetry and appointments, he pressed the correct button alongside the door handle and called out to the driver, "Follow that car!"

The limo quickly pushed into high gear and chased after the station wagon, swerving in reverse order through the maze of mocking streets and avenues until finally passing underneath the lion-gargoyled gate.

"Larry, goddamn it!" Duncan muttered and then added, "Thanks for the getaway."

It started to rain all over again. Duncan stood his ground against the combined forces of nature and revenge, finally knowing who the black women were, but still left wondering just what they knew.

"Action!" Costello screamed as the camera rolled.

Chapter Six

MOURNING REQUIRES THAT something deep inside the soul of those left grieving must die as well. A hole is created. A wide scar left. And yet people survive and go on. But what is the quality of that survival? What kind of a life are they expected to lead? What life can they lead once the unappeasable loss monster pays a visit and then departs without any apology for the wasteland left behind?

Duncan was not a rubbernecker at death's door. He knew to keep moving. There was nothing special or unusual to see; nothing at all lurid about loss. He was raised to be impervious to what others deemed a crisis. People die. They leave you. You are abandoned and end up alone. That's it, right? The whole story. From the very beginning Duncan was cautioned against dwelling too much on unpreventable matters. Reflection only leads to paralysis, and paralysis of any kind can only slow down getaways, cause missions to abort, thwart spontaneous decision-making.

"Always travel light," he could hear Mila say, even now, years after her death, "and leave behind what you must in order to survive."

What does that include? How is one supposed to distinguish between the disposable and the essential? Who, other than his mother, knew from such things? And are there costs to making a mistake? You take a toothbrush; you leave behind a pair of socks. That's one thing. But what if you leave behind something more precious? How did Mila get so good at this parceling out of what she could live with, and what she could live without? Or had she really been that good at this game?

Duncan didn't know the answers to any of these questions. He wasn't even sure whether they were valid questions, whether he had a right to ask them, whether he should want to know the answers—even if there were answers to give.

So Duncan traveled light at all times. He shed himself of everything. And some things—primarily people—distanced themselves from him. There are those who can sense when invisible, yet elaborate, guards go up—the movie set facades that humans use to adjust the Technicolor of life. Yet it took no special sensory skills to recognize the unconcealed and unscalable walls that always surrounded Duncan. The slightest outside overture from a friendly face would necessarily bump up against all those layers of camouflage that he had erected for his imagined protection.

This is the way he liked it. "Never get too attached to anything." Mila's voice sounded like heavy-metal music rapping against his eardrum. So he stripped himself bare, ensuring that no matter what might lie in store for him, he would never be forced to part with anything because there was nothing left to part with. He was a man naked to himself, living neither in the Garden of Eden nor the camp of Auschwitz, but still without knowledge, and with much in the way of shame.

Alas, when it came to Sharon, he slipped up. He let someone get too close. Duncan had been standing flat-footed on an Achilles heel and didn't know it. Perhaps this had always been the case. Sharon had found the spot without any real difficulty, as if she had been tipped off to the coordinates and the combination. Before then, Duncan wasn't aware that he had any vulnerabilities, other than that nervous stomach. The armor had been tested so many times in the past, stamped with Mila's own factory seal of approval. How surprised she would have been by this new discovery—a formerly undetected defect, and now too late for a recall.

Duncan had adopted the old survivor's trick of mock coping. Yankee's and Mila's deaths years earlier had made him an orphan, just as they had predicted, the shambled state of family affairs that the Katzes had oddly wished for themselves. But was he really that much more alone without them? What was the practical difference, anyway? He had been trained to be alone, and now he finally was. Mission accomplished. He felt nothing by their absence, and so he didn't miss them. A specialist in accepting loss, but a real greenhorn on the subject of grieving, he never allowed himself an opportunity, or a moment, to even try.

Until now. Duncan was living in Manhattan, on West Eighty-seventh Street, near Central Park. Twelve years had passed since Mila's funeral in Miami. He was no longer a prosecutor with the OSI. And he was no longer a husband, or much of a father, either. That's another story.

But first, there was this unfinished business with the *yohrzeit* candle. It was the first time Duncan had ever attempted to light one. Not once for his father, or his mother, but today, for no apparent reason, he picked one up on Upper Broadway—at Korean market, of all places—and planned on setting it on fire for Mila. Like a toast, a *l'chaim* for a dead person.

For twelve years he had allowed the anniversary of his mother's death to pass as though it were just any other day, as though he had no obligation to honor her memory with this curious, understated, yet dignified Jewish candle—the one with the wax stuffed into an open glass jar and the twenty-four-hour flame. This year was different somehow. He had this yearning to look back before moving forward again. A slight pause in his journey, and yet he had no idea why.

The *yohrzeit* beamed in Duncan's apartment, which was largely empty except for books. Everywhere, books, as though the walls were being invaded by a strange form of cleaving ivy. And in the center of the room, stacked from the floor to the ceiling, pillars of books, as though the very foundation of the brownstone were supported by a geologic phenomenon called Holocaust literature. Duncan owned virtually every tome ever published on the Holocaust, as if he were barricading himself in against a genocide-friendly world.

With a new century imminent, and the old one an embarrassment, death tolls had become mere abstractions, numbers more numbing than revolting. Yet the obsession to know more continued. The Holocaust had become a legitimate tourist attraction. There were now simulated visits to hell, courtesy of Disney-style museums, with all the "you are there" urgency of a Walter Cronkite docudrama. And of course there was no shortage of books for those who still favored the more modest thrill that comes from reading.

The people of the Book had become the people of Holocaust books. The canon of the *Shoah* was now a loaded cannon, the fuse eternally counting down with the firepower of memory and accusation. There was even a comic book, and a cookbook, too. What next? A special *Vogue* fashion layout? How many more books would it take? When will the world learn that the mystery of madness and atrocity can never be found in books—or even museums—because the questions themselves are unknowable, and the answers, even more so?

Duncan hadn't quite caught onto this idea. A stroll through his barren one-bedroom walk-up apartment proved it. A pale wood futon with a limp mattress gathered on the floor like an unraveled tongue. That was it for the furniture. The windows were without curtains. A card table with a Formica finish stood on wobbly legs, unoccupied except for a gray notebook computer with its white-noise hum. There was an empty birdcage left over from a prior tenant. Dust bunnies were the only domestic life. No plants. Not even any food. The con at Con Edison was all that wasted energy motoring a refrigerator that was virtually empty. Cold seltzer never deserved such privacy.

Duncan had just moved to Manhattan from Washington, D.C. He was adjusting slowly to the chaotic rhythms of extreme urban living— the raw nature of New York, where jackhammers and concrete are the percussive instruments in the daily creation of jungle music. The orchestration would not be complete without the honking horns of cars, and the locking horns of people, harmonizing fortissimo in the background. Adding to this mix of sensory irritation were those undefinable smells—from street vendors and the roving herd—intercepting one another in the never-ending competition for unattainable space. And the shared isolation. People sitting in diners and sushi bars eating alone, the opposite side of the tables empty, the menus and place settings already taken away.

None of this mattered to Duncan. His own identity wouldn't sit still; he was always in flux, looking to be found, a soul in search of an anchoring Web site. He preferred roaming the streets to sitting inside his empty apartment. So he prowled inside the perimeters of Riverside Drive and Central Park West, from Seventy-second to Ninety-sixth Streets, blending into the natural habitat of Manhattan's exotic, and neurotic, cage.

Standing on the steps of the Museum of Natural History, leaning up against the statue of Teddy Roosevelt, Duncan watched as busloads of tourists emptied out like conventioneers on their way to a camera show.

A light snow oozed as slush on the sidewalks, the performance art of trampling feet. Duncan's collar was turned up, his chocolate-brown mohair coat and large frame making him look like a stuffed bear that had just escaped from the museum. A black scarf was wrapped around his thick neck. A hot pretzel steamed in his glove-covered hand, each looping piece like a warm handle through which his large fingers could not fit.

The streets were littered with Christmas tree carcasses, the branches cut off from now naked Douglas firs and balsams, sitting curbside, awaiting the inside joke that passes for recycling in New York. Duncan headed west toward Broadway. A short woman with dark hair and a Betty Boop curl on her forehead was standing by a table, hawking information about the Kabbalah. Duncan watched little boys going off to *shul* dressed in unbuttoned coats and ill-fitting suits that made them look like Wall Street puppets. Nannies pushed strollers languidly, as if each were walking a plank with a cigarette and a blindfold. The surrounding buildings on West Eighty-first were guarded by gargoyles, their faces splashed with tears of snow.

Duncan entered and then soon left the mayhem of Zabar's. The frenzy for deli was great, an Upper West Sider's idea of essential provisions no matter what the occasion or catastrophe. On Broadway, Duncan floated into the gaggle of dodging, anxious commuters, jigsaw pieces all rushing somewhere with exaggerated purpose.

"Keep moving, white boy!" Duncan turned around. He heard the warning, his radar always sensitized to a nearby taunt.

The mohair coat, maybe the pretzel, had brushed up against someone already looking for an excuse to uncork. The man was powerfully built, an African American with a tense and twitching face. His head was shaven, but kept warm underneath a snug New York Jets ski hat.

Amidst all the congestion, bulky winter coats are bound to exchange fibers while rubbing up against one another. Yet, this all mattered little to the man. There was no remedy for the insult he felt. Duncan had invaded his space. Turf wars can occur on many different kinds of turf.

"I'm sorry," Duncan said.

"Yo, man, your sorry ass better be sorry," the offended man replied, squaring off to look directly at Duncan. "Now why don't you just take your white motherfucker ass and go home?"

In times like these, Duncan's body would normally light up like a switchboard. All the dangerous, red-hot buttons would become activated. Blood that should have been simply channeling throughout his body instead percolated like a whirlpool, overflowing rivers of rage with nowhere to drain off. The tacit body language of an accepted dare. No room for restraint. Self-control gone. The demons would take over from here.

"Hey, I said I was sorry, but I can't back off," Duncan said, frozen, his fists clenched, the pretzel in his callused hand long since mangled into something more deformed than a mere pretzel. "You see . . . forget it, it doesn't matter; you won't understand. I'm not wired to surrender. I can't let this moment pass. So do us both a favor; just walk away. We'll forget this ever happened."

"Are you listening to this shit?" Duncan's implacable neighbor said, gesturing toward an intrigued bystander on Broadway. "Motherfucker says he won't move. You *better* move if you don't want any of me."

Who can claim to have a monopoly on anger? Like all other emotions, anger plays no favorites. Duncan shook his head in pity and then took the first in yet another preemptive but entirely misdirected step—the long familiar history of vindicating the crimes committed against his parents. Yet, as always, he was seeking retribution from the wrong source.

THEY WERE ON top of one another, and it went on this way throughout the night. At times their arms were locked; at other moments it was each other's wrists that they grabbed for. Sometimes it was just the tight squeezing of hands and the interlacing of fingers. Body movements for better leverage. The mixing of their sweat had become pungent and tart. Finally they rolled over and switched positions.

Duncan had first met Monica at a party given by one of his old law-school classmates, Howard Minskoff. A tall man, handsome and prematurely balding, Howard had moved quickly from law to venture capital, finally ending up as principal investor in a formerly defunct but now, through his efforts, distinguished modeling agency known as Head Turners. During law school and, no doubt long before that, leggy and attractive women were always on Minskoff's mind; now he made them his business, too.

"This profession is perfect for me," he once boasted to Duncan while Duncan was still an OSI prosecutor and Howard was away from his Flatiron District office, scouting talent in D.C. "I come from a long line of womanizers. Think about it this way: we're both fulfilling our destinies. You belong in an office just like this, totally trapped, tracking down old German Nazis. I, on the other hand, am much better suited to chasing after young, innocent Germans, like Claudia Schiffer."

Duncan forced a half-smile and said, "The super model, the one with David Copperfield?"

"Way to go, Duncan. I thought you only keep up with the super-Nazis—the Mengeles and Eichmanns. The hip crowd for Duncan Katz. It's nice to hear that you've heard of some other Germans. Don't worry, Claudia is clean—no Nazis in her closet."

"What were you doing in her closet?"

"Duncan, you're going to have to get past this Nazi obsession. This is America. Jews have power. I run a modeling agency; Christ, your Jewish godfather is a Mafia chieftain. We're safe."

On news of Duncan's recent separation from Sharon and his arrival in New York, Minskoff threw a party for his friend, hoping to introduce him to a model who might stand in for Sharon in her absence.

Monica was from Toronto, with short red hair, green eyes, and a body so seductive and unending, it looked as though its maker was still tinkering with improvements, refusing to let go. Her face was small and her nose petite, but her eyebrows were set in an angular Nike swoosh and her smile was wraparound wide, with teeth that seemed to decline in size from right to left. She wasn't new to the modeling business; in fact, she was one of the older women on the Head Turners roster. In a business where thirty is old, she was thirty.

"So, is there a wife?" she asked the morning after the first night she and Duncan had spent together.

She was standing underneath the bathroom doorpost, wearing nothing but green bikini underwear, a toothbrush in her hand and her face flushed from a sleepless night of repeat orgasms. Duncan was still lying naked on the futon. He got up, walked over, and brought Monica near to his body. Her breasts were small, and now seemed trapped against his chest. He searched for her mouth, freshly clean, a mint aftertaste now shared between them.

"Is there a wife?" Monica repeated.

"*Keller,*" Duncan whispered, then realized that no one other than his wife, and perhaps Larry Breitbart, would know what he meant by that. With their bodies slapped together, Duncan became erect. He lifted Monica and carried her back onto the futon, the green underwear lost somewhere in transit. With one hand inside her, he lightly stroked her body, while with the other he passed freckles and goosebumped nipples and then dipped into that sinkhole of underfed flesh that so often serves as a fashion model's stomach. Duncan seemed to have no control over where his hands were moving, as if Monica's body were a Ouija board scornfully ducking all the hard questions that had haunted him all these years.

Is there a wife? Monica wanted to know. Was there a wife? Is there still a wife? Should he, of all people, even have a wife? Duncan imagined Sharon's body lying there instead of Monica's, a superimposed transparency that would have been possible only if the two women looked anything alike. Sharon was of medium height, with long blond hair, ocean-blue eyes, and a round face. Her breasts were full; her legs, muscled and thick from her collegiate years as a cross-country runner. After five years of marriage she and Duncan had now been separated for almost a year. And since that time, Duncan had been with no woman other than Monica. So, the fact that he could no longer recall the shape, the contours, even the imperfections of his own wife's body caused him great confusion as he lay there caressing the body of a beautiful stranger.

"Oh, Duncan, yes, that's it, stay right there . . . keep going . . . ," Monica stammered softly.

With each day, Duncan was losing the memory of his marriage. It was as though emotionally he was waving good-bye. Sharon had asked him to leave, and he had complied. A divorce would follow, but first there would be a separation. Milan, their four-year-old daughter, would remain with her mother.

"I can't lose this family," Duncan repeated so many times, like a mantra.

Milan was finally asleep. Duncan and Sharon started out whispering near their daughter's room, then moved into the hallway, and finally down the stairs. The house was old, nestled on a sloping embankment on Yuma Street in the American University section of

Washington, D.C. Duncan had bought the green-and-white, tree-shaded, wood-framed, two-story Colonial soon after he and Sharon were married. It was a hard purchase, but not financially.

Duncan had never lived in a house before. It wasn't the Katz way. In Miami Beach they had always lived in that high-rise apartment building with those easy escape routes, whether by land or by sea.

"I won't have anything taken away from me anymore," Mila always said. "If they come and drag me out again, there is nothing here I can't leave behind."

And that's why homeownership held no appeal for the Katzes. They were afraid not only of the responsibility, but also the emotion of being connected to something too large to stow away in a backpack. The heart rarely weeps for things that are subject to rent. You can always break a lease and leave.

But is a marriage a lease? Duncan didn't think so.

"I'm not like other people," he continued. "You can't just marry someone like me, have a baby, and then take off. It's not right. I have no one else." His voice trembled like the final yelp before the down dip on a roller coaster. "I thought we were creating a nuclear family here. Something that was safe and solid. Something that my parents never gave me."

"Nothing is forever, Duncan," Sharon said. "You of all people should know that."

"I wanted better for Milan; I wanted better for me."

Duncan recalled the day Milan was born. Despite everything that had gone wrong for them in the past, the Katzes had not yet given up. Yankee and Mila were dead, and their son was insufficiently alive, yet there was going to be a grandchild. Hopefully, she would learn how to breathe without the gas and smoke entourage. That would be such an enormous family victory, even though only Duncan was left to celebrate.

"Push Sharon, push . . . ," Duncan urged softly, holding Sharon's hand in the delivery room. "Bring her out . . . That a girl . . . I really love you." Dressed in scrubs, Duncan wore a green mask over his mouth while a hygienic cap puffed up on his head. "This is incredible," he cried.

Now he walked over to a black leather sofa that was showing the wear that comes from years of people sitting down with their troubles.

He sat and remained quiet, his elbows driven into his knees, his cheeks slipped into the palms of his hands. The living room was nicely furnished, yet lacking in empty wall space. The Holocaust books that later towered in Duncan's brownstone were once pillars of both domestic decor and dysfunction in the house that he shared with Sharon.

He looked up at his wife and continued, "My parents were right. This is how it all ends up—nobody is safe. I thought marriage and a child meant that I had finally attached myself to something that couldn't be taken away." A moment later he added, "I can't lose this family . . ."

For Duncan, fatherhood had been both a miracle and a challenge: could he break the genetic chain? Could Milan inherit what was best about him and the world of the Katzes without the nasty, toxic stuff being passed on as well?

The way to accomplish this, Duncan believed, was to raise Milan in a home that, if nothing else, felt safe. Part nest, part tree house, part sanctuary, part pouch, part cocoon—with no parts left over for fear or uncertainty. Two parents. One child. Everyone cozy and tucked in. What was the point of all those years of martial arts, street fighting, football, weight lifting, and law if it couldn't provide at least that? But now Duncan was leaving behind a new and unimagined legacy for his daughter—divorce. A different kind of brokenness, but equally unfixable.

"Oh, Duncan, I'm almost there, don't leave . . . ," Monica interrupted, her eyes closing, her voice fading. "Oh God, you smell so great . . ."

Sharon had tried to convert Duncan, not to a particular religion, but to a more even-tempered range of humanity. There were years of therapy—individually, and together as a couple. They consulted specialists who worked with the neuroses of the second generation, trying to understand their ways and exotic rhythms. It was as though Duncan and his kind had all somehow been resettled on Earth from Planet Auschwitz, a universe unknown to astronomers and beyond the sight of telescopes or NASA's curiosity. Often these children of survivors looked and acted very much like everyone else. But in their most private and desperate moments, their eyes would become vacant, their heads shaven, their skin reduced to mere bone wrappings, their cavities suddenly unfilled and goldless. They breathed in the rarefied, choking vapors of an atmosphere known only to their parents. What had killed the survivors had somehow become oxygen for their children.

Sharon had collected a library of self-help books on anger and depression, loss and mourning, coping and letting go. While Duncan was preparing briefs on the prosecution of Nazis, she was marshaling all the psychological data on what had, in actuality, become the Nazis' purest victory—unintended, inadvertent, but a stunning achievement of the Third Reich, nonetheless. There were millions of dead Jews, and then there were those who had survived but who still qualified as dead under certain measurements for living. And now the children, the next generation—paralyzed, frozen in time, unable to move forward and hauntingly afraid to look back. A recycling of the nightmares; an enduring premonition of death.

A Final Solution that had no end.

Sharon tagged pages and underlined sentences that spoke to her husband and the life that she was—vicariously—living. It was as though, by linking Duncan to the dysfunction of others, she was somehow reaching him, grounding him, penetrating the pain, making him less a statistic of generalized depression and more a wounded soldier of the *Shoah*.

But finally she gave up, reshifted her focus and strategy, and decided that the results would be better if she worked on saving Milan rather than her husband. She had underestimated her enemy. What she had battled by way of her own internecine methods was a monster of mythic proportions, one that could not be stopped. The Holocaust was too big for her. The massacre—this time of the minds—would continue, so perhaps it was just as well that she simply get out of the way.

And so she retreated, convincing herself that what she had been dealing with all along was a congenital, viral, and hopelessly incurable condition of the Katz family. A legacy that must continually mutate and rejuvenate itself through the generations until—eventually, hopefully—it ran its course and canceled itself out. By banishing Duncan and blanketing Milan, Sharon was no doubt taking desperate maternal measures. Quarantine the father; insulate the daughter. Maybe there was hope for the child, after all.

"There's a black hole inside you, Duncan," she said, "and it will eat away at anything that gets near it. I know, I've been too close for years, and I don't want Milan to get swallowed up in there."

"Come on . . ."

"No. It's like a vacuum. It sucks up Nazi war criminals, but it doesn't stop there. It saves some of its best work for the people who love you the most. It's an eating machine with an enormous appetite. Only you can turn it off, but you don't have any idea where the switch is. What's more, I don't think you want it to be shut down. That's what really scares me: I think you like what it has done to you. And it's not finished yet; it never will be. Believe me, this is what's going to kill you, nothing else. And nobody will be able to figure out the actual cause of death. The reason is too perverse. They'll come and ask me, and I'll say, 'My husband's arteries were fine and unclogged, his cholesterol count was low, but his memory was a savage killer'—even though they weren't even his memories. It will be the burden of history that kills you, Duncan, and the way you have responded to it— and nothing else. That's what should be written on your tombstone."

"But you married me. You knew what you were getting. There had to be some special handling. Why would you have married me if you couldn't stay?"

"Oh, Duncan, I really love you," Monica said, spoken so close to climax when nothing can be taken seriously. It wouldn't have mattered to Duncan anyway, because he no longer believed words of love, no matter when said or who may have said them.

"Because I loved you," Sharon said. "I still love you. But the anger, the depression, the exaggerated fears, the intensity of your reactions are all too much. The environment in this house is polluted with smoke imported all the way from those German ovens. We all need some air to breathe."

"There is no such thing as air."

"There is for us. This is a big project, Duncan, and you still haven't broken ground yet. And you're the only one who can do it. It can't be done for you. There are no rescue possibilities here—no Wallenbergs, no Schindlers—because your desire to be rescued is really all part of the same problem."

"Hey, I've been alone almost all my life," Duncan snapped back. "I don't need anyone to rescue me. And I'm not asking for it."

"Yes, you are," Sharon, her arms folded, said. "You just don't realize it." She sat down next to him and spoke slowly. "I've said this all before. It's really not your fault. Your parents did this to you, and the war did it to them. The most vicious of cycles; it's all very unfair—to everybody. Too many victims and too few people to punish," she said, resting a hand on Duncan's lap and hesitating to speak any further.

"You're making me an orphan all over again, and at the same time, you're also telling me there's nobody to blame for it?"

"It doesn't have to be anybody's fault," Sharon said. "Life is complicated sometimes."

Duncan resented the post–pop psychology, the unassailable slogans of the me-first generation. What did Sharon know from a complicated life? Raised in a middle-class home with two parents, three siblings, no abuse or alcoholism or divorce or sickness or severe shortages of money to speak of. And most of all, no genocide in her family's genes.

"I'm working on getting better." He spoke calmly, despite the mounting landslide. "I'm just overwhelmed with this Maloney case. You have to give me a chance."

A whiny but contemporary folk tune, sung by some Canadian singer who would have been totally obscure if not for the blessings of college radio, was mournfully shrieking in the background. Sharon sighed, looked intensely into Duncan's eyes, and said, "You don't even know the kind of work I'm talking about, do you?"

Duncan's mouth widened, then halted. He had nothing to say.

Monica began to moan. Her eyes rolled back inside her head like a slot machine; her jaw sent her teeth clapping against one another. "Woo, woo, almost there, oh God, Duncan, keep going, oh Christ . . ."

"Please . . . don't leave me, Sharon . . . And don't make me go . . ."

"Duncan, you have so much grief inside you," Sharon replied. "It's all impacted, buried and knotted. You have to get underneath it all—inside the place where it hurts the most. But to do so, you have to also get out from under the waves of anger and pain that you've been swimming in all of your life. It's the only world you seem to know. It's familiar and safe for you, but it's also poisonous. I've been fighting for your soul for years, and I'm losing, and I'm sick about it."

Frustrated, Duncan leapt out of the couch like a displaced cat.

" 'Get inside the grief,' " he said mockingly. "What language are you speaking?" He had heard this all before, and it never resonated as something he could do, or wanted to do, or even—as Sharon always suspected—understood. He was now standing by the window. Outside, a car slowed down for a stop sign, a solitary beam from a headlight almost creeping into the Katz household, then thinking the better of it. "What does that mean? It all sounds so abstract to me. I'd like to help myself—do what you want me to do—but I'm trapped in this head. There *is* no other space. I've gone through a shredder and all that's left is masking tape. I'm living the life of a fighting Jewish warrior. I don't have any idea how else to live."

"That's what I'm saying. There are other paths; you just won't allow yourself to see them."

"I need maps. Some signs. Give me directions. Draw me up some plays. Just show me . . ."

"It can't be done externally. You're looking for someone to swoop you up and make it all go away. You're too big, and so are your problems."

"And leaving me is the answer?"

"For now it's the answer—for Milan and me." Sharon's upper lip began to tremble, and her face shuddered as though she had seen a ghost, which perhaps she had. She plucked a loose thread from her wool, ash-colored sweater. Finally, she steadied herself and said, "We're survivors, too. Or at least we're hoping to last long enough so we can call ourselves survivors."

Finally, Monica was finished. "Woo, Duncan, that was nice, thanks," she said breathlessly, her eyes closed, her smile still open. "Now that I've been taken care of, I want to feel and hear what's inside you."

"Believe me, you don't."

"Yes, I do. But first, tell me already, is there a wife?"

MONICA HAD GONE off for a booking with *Victoria*, a fairly prim and dour magazine with a readership that favored French country inns, long leisurely hikes through winter wonder trails, big brass beds layered with clouds of goose-down quilts, and romances that are both sensible and discreet. Monica's job on this assignment was to bring a wistful, mature, and decorous image to a story on sunflower facial soap. But the camera never lies. It would now be next to impossible to conceal what she had done the night before. No matter which way they photographed her, she would end up looking sleep-deprived and carnally stimulated, neither pose having ever before been featured in the pages of this magazine.

Duncan left soon after Monica. He got dressed, searched for his keys and gym bag, passed on taking a shot of Donnatal, and instead opened a bottle of seltzer, spinning the cap too hastily. The liberated bubbles shot out from the liter like an angry geyser and cascaded over the black-and-white tiles of Duncan's kitchen. He didn't bother to wipe it down. "It should take out all the stains on the floor," he thought.

He had no appointments that morning, other than to meet Orlando Garcia at the gym near Lincoln Center. Orlando, a former lacrosse player at Princeton and now a philosophy professor at Columbia, was Duncan's latest training partner. The others—the ones not hospitalized—had decided to take up chess, instead.

To get the twenty blocks down to the gym, Duncan opted for the subway. Ordinarily he would have walked, but the winter days of New York—and the neurotic impulses that make everyone a candidate for depression—had a tendency to drive people underground.

The 1 train rocked noisily on the track as though it were a barfly staggering home at 3 A.M. Rats darted along the rails, scavenging for the remains of food that pedestrians had started out eating on the run—candy bars, corn muffins, a Whopper from those rare Burger Kings in New York—but now had become litter. Inside the subway cars, the lights flickered on and off like a strobe, drawing attention to all those faces in spasm with misery. Worn out from a day that hadn't yet even begun. They looked as though they didn't seem to know where the train was going, or if they did, they didn't much care. Sitting almost on top of one another, many were reading newspapers folded into the size of napkins, others had their ears attached to buzzing headsets, the rest stared at nothing. Those who stood clamped themselves to poles like children on monkey bars.

A young Hasidic man, with long sidelocks curling down like a Slinky, concentrated fiercely on a religious text. He was destined to miss his stop. Duncan looked up and noticed the cardboard advertisements. Low-cost divorces. Free consultations on how to obtain a green card. A dermatologist was promoting a new laser treatment for acne. The New School was seeking new students.

Duncan always arrived at the gym a half hour before Orlando. That gave him enough time to run on the treadmill before he and his partner would "attack the weights," as Duncan liked to call it. Without a warm-up, or stretching, or even a slight limbering twist, Duncan mounted the machine, pushed the flashing and beeping buttons to a setting that was more sprint than run, and then began pumping his legs and arms as if he were a marionette spinning out of control at the hands of a psychotic puppet master.

There was a mirror directly in front of him. As each minute passed, Duncan watched the buildup of his own sweat, beads multiplying on his forehead and chin, and dangling on the split ends of his hair. He prompted the machine to go faster, stabbing away at the "up" arrow key. Racing to catch himself, he was colliding into his own reflection, the merger that eluded him in real life. He imagined seeing Sharon and Milan trapped in the mirror looking back at him. Could he catch them? Would they disappear?

The gym, located on the second floor of an office building on Broadway, overlooked Lincoln Center. It had tall rectangular windows, which allowed people on Broadway to glance up and see heads bobbing up and down on simulated stair-climbers, arms flapping and legs kicking to the choreography of some aerobic maestro, weights being pushed and cables pulled and yet everyone remaining in the same place.

Orlando arrived, slowly changed in the locker room into a Columbia University T-shirt that read "Philosophers Pump Metaphysically," and then crossed himself for good luck.

"Ease up, my friend," Orlando said, tempted to pull the circuit breakers on the cardio machine that Duncan was torturing. "This is supposed to be good for our health. We're both getting older, you know. You're pushing yourself too hard; we'll be dead before the HDL levels do us any good."

"My heart has nothing to fear from fat deposits," Duncan replied in one shortened breath, "because my heart has already been attacked."

When not in his gym clothes, Orlando sported the look of an academic. Wire-rimmed glasses over a long, anvil face with a wide forehead. An elbow-patched corduroy jacket. A knit tie. But there was another side to Orlando, the one that Duncan was most interested in: the ex-jock trying to beat something back. In Orlando's case, it was the midlife clock. Duncan's goal was less clear.

"Come on, spot me, three more reps," Duncan said, his face scrunched, his breath like wind, his chest throbbing, his teeth grinding as he lay on the bench press, sending the barbell up and down like a piston. There was the clanging sounds of weights stacked together. Duncan grunted savagely with each movement. His muscles didn't tire from all the exertion; instead, they seemed to gain renewed strength. Fellow gym members working out elsewhere inched away slowly, scared off by the noise, the intensity, and . . . something else.

There was the smell. In times of crisis, or when physically engaged, Duncan would release a body odor that had no field-house origins. This was no mere glandular response to physical fitness. No deodorant or antiperspirant was of any use. Yet another coat of armor for a man already wearing too many layers.

"He's not going to make it," predicted a well-built, long-armed man working out on a deltoid-press machine, turning to his own training partner.

"He's looks pretty good to me," his friend replied.

"I'm not talking about his body."

Duncan finally ceded the bench to Orlando. As Duncan sprang to his feet, Orlando noticed a bruise on his partner's left shoulder.

"Ah, a memento from Monica, I see," Orlando said. "I saw her picture in *GQ* this month. She looks like a wild one."

"It's not from her," Duncan said impatiently. "Let's go. Start your set; I'm cooling down."

"Patience, patience, my friend," Orlando said, always welcoming a delay. "We can take a Kantian approach to our workouts, or something out of Nietzsche. I prefer Buber myself. I would love to have an I-Thou relationship with my abs. So tell me, what happened to you there with your shoulder?"

"Street scuffle."

"What, did you run into a Nazi in the diamond district, like in that scene out of *Marathon Man?*"

"No, just some guy."

"Some guy? You have to be careful in this city. This is not a suburb of D.C. 'Some guy' may be carrying a knife in New York."

"I'm not worried."

"You know, for a Yale-educated lawyer and a college professor, you sure have a barbarian's solution to most problems. You'd think that someone like you would have more faith in the written word—you know, the pen is mightier than the sword."

"What are you writing with nowadays?"

By the time Duncan returned to his apartment, the day was almost over. He ran a few errands. Checked his email at the university. Purchased a few books on the Cambodian and Armenian genocides, passing on one of those John Irving novels that looked interesting, but also too diverting. He then went to buy some food at Fairway. The gray winter of New York quickly surrendered to darkness. It was only 5 P.M., but there was enough nightfall to pass for midnight.

Duncan unlocked the door to his apartment, paused, and then listened for sounds of life. He entered, disappointed. The apartment was cold, and it felt like the heat had been off all day. He headed toward the thermostat but was derailed when the phone rang. He thought it might be Milan, and that made him excited. Sharon promised that she would call Duncan whenever Milan wanted to speak with her father.

"Hello," Duncan answered.

"Duncan, is that you?"

It wasn't a child's voice.

"Yes. Who is this?"

"It's Larry . . . your uncle, remember?"

"Larry, I meant to call you but . . ."

"What's the matter with you? You move to New York and you don't look me up? And I hear you're in trouble."

"That's not true . . ."

"Bullshit! I called your home in D.C. I spoke with Sharon. She told me everything. You're an orphan, and I'm your godfather . . ."

"And you don't have to take care of me," Duncan said while pulling a sweater down over his head, as though peering out from a bunker.

"I'm in New York all the time. I keep an apartment at the Regency. The family is getting more legitimate. The muscle jobs go to the Russians while we keep the municipal-bond work for ourselves."

"What do you mean?"

"We're into municipal bonds these days."

"Why, what do you care about tax-free interest? You people don't pay taxes."

"Let's just say our core businesses have changed a little. We now help depressed cities with their financing."

"Oh wow, that makes me feel real safe in America. First it was the unions; then cement trucks; from there gambling casinos; and now the subways. No wonder the trains don't run on time. Look Larry, let's see each other next week . . ."

"Don't be in such a hurry to get off the phone. What are you, paranoid? Don't worry, your phone isn't bugged. And besides, you don't work for the government anymore. You can speak to your uncle all you want without worrying that the FBI is tapping the call. 'Hello boys, this is Larry Breitbart here. I got my nephew on the other end. He used to be a hotshot prosecutor, but he lost his job. The government is not like a family; they don't know how to take care of their own.' "

"Larry, that's not funny. Your line probably is tapped . . ."

"Forget that, I have great news for you, and I think you could use some."

"What is it?"

"I'll tell you in person. I need to make sure you're sitting down."

"I can sit here. I'm walking over to a stack of books right now," Duncan said, but never moved his feet. "Okay, I'm sitting. Tell me . . ."

"I'll meet you in Central Park tomorrow morning—ten o'clock at Tavern on the Green. I'll buy breakfast."

"Larry . . ."

A few hours later, Duncan sat on an unopened, still unpacked box in the corner of his apartment. A smoky beam of eight-millimeter light unfolded against a scarce bare wall. Another light, the flame from the *yohrzeit* candle, tossed off a liturgical shadow against the haunted spines of looming books. Duncan's eyes were moist but unblinking as the images of his *bris* nearly forty years earlier—the gathered mobsters, the hesitant parents, the gold-plated whitefish, and the near fall from Breitbart's arms—danced wildly on the wall.

Chapter Seven

LOUISE OREY DRAGGED the curtain along its brass-plated rod and then drew the blinds. The early dawn light streamed into the hospital room as though it had been waiting outside for hours.

"Just look at that Miami sunshine, Mrs. Katz," she said. "It's going to be a fine day. Just fine."

There was much to do this morning, Mila's sheets needed to be changed, as well as her gown, which had become soiled and damp overnight. Each day Mila awoke to the crudely organic evidence that she had lost command of many of her bodily functions. Savagely, Mila Katz had been returned to the dilemma she had faced at Auschwitz, the once assured sovereignty over her bowels had been taken over by others. Imprisoned and dehumanized in the camps, she was now incontinent and equally disgraced at Mount Sinai Hospital.

A small pharmacy of new medications had been prescribed by the oncologist and noted on Mila's chart, all of various dimensions, colors and dosages—some to be taken before or during meals, others after. Louise knew that they had to be administered with precision in order for them to have the desired effect. But glancing over at her patient, the nurse wondered what outcome the doctors were expecting, and to what end?

Cancer, radiation, and chemotherapy were waging war against one another. All those daily, uninterrupted skirmishes had led to the beginning stages of cachexia. It was Louise's experience that someone in Mila's condition would doubtless have trouble eating her breakfast, so the nurse readied herself to spoon-feed her patient.

Perhaps by the end of the morning she would try to take Mila for a short walk down the hall and out onto the wide and windy terrace that faced Biscayne Bay. Of course, such a journey had a kind of Mount Everest quality about it, and so Louise didn't have high hopes that Mila would get very far. Mila might make it to the watercooler and back, if she was lucky. Or just to the door; or maybe only to the chair by the window. Perhaps after Louise bathed Mila and brushed her hair, Mila, exhausted from the entire ordeal, would just fall asleep.

Louise removed the wasted tissues from the nightstand and then wiped down the puddle that had gathered overnight from a sweaty glass of water. She filled a new glass from a plastic yellow pitcher that had been delivered earlier in the morning, and plopped in a straw. Louise brought the glass over to Mila, who sat up with difficulty and attempted a few uneasy sips.

Finally, the nurse carried in a large vase pluming with fresh violets, lilacs, and delphiniums, all surrounded by small patches of baby's breath. She primped the bouquet with one hand and rearranged it with the other. Then she sat the vase down upon a dresser against the wall.

"How did you sleep?" she asked Mila.

"Not so good," Mila replied quietly, inaudibly, the first words of the day.

"Pain?"

"Nightmares."

"Don't worry, it comes from the drugs. You'll get used to it."

"No, not from the drugs, from the camps, from Auschwitz. And I won't get used to it. I never have. You can't . . . you see."

Louise didn't understand, but said, "These flowers came for you this morning. They're from a Mr. Breitbart. Aren't they just beautiful, Mrs. Katz?"

Mila no longer had much perception for beauty. It was as though she had been robbed of a vital sense, or maybe it had just disappeared in disgust. She remembered the Old Town Square in Warsaw, with its four-storied, seventeenth-century buildings painted in pastels and crowned with jagged, ornate rooftops. That was beautiful. And the elegant palaces along Miodowa Street—the great big mansions of the Polish aristocracy with those wide, finely cut lawns and abundant flowers that poked through shimmering gates and teasingly scented all who passed by. They were quite beautiful, too. And the grand Tlomackie Synagogue, where her grandfather, the Rabbi Chaim Lewinstein, studied and taught. He was one of Warsaw's most acclaimed Talmudic scholars. Mila remembered with fondness the gardens at Lazienki Park and the promenade lined with oak trees that led to the lake and over toward the grand neoclassical palace where King Stanislaw once lived. Such a picture of beauty. And of course she was able to recall the gleaming baby grand piano—the one of German design and Polish pitch—that stood in the middle of her parents' home, the ivory keys smooth, the strings golden like fine hair. All equally beautiful.

But these artifacts of memory that Mila could recall with great tenderness and accuracy all shared one thing in common: their moments of beauty existed in that unreturned echo of history known as "prewar." In the years between 1939 and 1945, everything took on different, often contradictory, meanings. Beauty came with a conspicuous scar. Friendship and trust carried the seeds of betrayal. God was a creator cowering in the darkness. Love and loss became interchangeable commodities.

For many survivors, the postwar period required a new comprehension of the world. Columbus was wrong; the planet was flat, after all. It was also sinister. Whatever once had luster had now been stripped down to its gruesome core. Distortions were everywhere, as though the windows of the new world were plated with funhouse mirrors. Almost everyone suffered from a freakish strain of color blindness that produced a kaleidoscope of sunless, concentration-camp grays. Smoke and fire were seen even in places where there was warmth and kindness. And fueling every impulse was anger. A survivor's world was generally divided into black, off-black, more black, and still blacker perceptions—with no other color combinations left on the palette.

The flowers must have been beautiful. Why would the nurse have lied about such a thing? But Mila had no way to see for herself.

"What is your name?" she asked.

"Louise."

"Are you new?"

"Yes. First day, ma'am. From now on they got you down for private nurses—twenty-four hours, all day. You have me in the morning, Cynthia in the afternoon and early evening, and Judy at night. We're all good nurses."

"A present from Larry," Mila said, gazing out the window. "He should save his money for more important things—like paying off judges."

Again Louise didn't understand.

"Is there anything you need, Mrs. Katz?"

"Call me Mila. How about a priest?"

Louise peered down at Mila's chart, which had been hooked onto a steel railing at the foot of Mila's bed, and checked once more whether she had been pronouncing Mila's last name correctly.

"Katz. That's a Jewish name, isn't it?"

"Of course," Mila replied, then, after a halting breath, she continued, "What else could it be?"

"But you want a priest?" Louise asked, the puzzle on her face still in pieces.

"Yes, please call one."

"But why?"

"Dr. Grant, he came to see me last night."

"And he'll be here today again, I'm sure."

"He told me there is no hope. Nothing is working anymore. I will be dead by next week."

Louise quickly put on her game face and tried to remember her lines. She had done this act many times before, performing on the road at various hospitals, in front of so many different kinds of patients, all of whom were surrendering to one fatal illness or another.

Private nurses are often brought in at the most dire of moments. The terminal cases are their usual trade. Louise's patients tended to die—sooner rather than later—the hospital usually being their last stop. Not a pleasant assignment for someone in the healing profession. But Louise never concerned herself with the side effects of matters that were beyond her control. In fact, she preferred hospice work. She could handle the bedpans, but she would leave the existential dilemmas to others, having long reconciled herself to the fact that not all patients recover. Why God treats some more harshly than others was simply not a subject covered in nursing school.

"You can't give up hope, Mila. Life has a funny way of fixing things.

Lots of people have been in worse shape than you and walked out of here alive. I've seen them."

"So have I. I was one of them—but not in a hospital. I escaped death once. I don't think life gives people so many chances. This time God is really calling my number."

It was then that Louise Orey noticed the row of blue digits that lined Mila's forearm. The sunlight cast it with an inky glow, as if the numbers had smeared overnight, disappearing like the rest of her. Once an indelible, oddly unifying brand was now, like her breath, fading, finally saying goodbye.

Mila closed her eyes, and Louise could tell that her patient had transported herself to a place much farther away than the hospital corridor.

"If you need to talk to someone, let me know. We have us a chaplain who's a rabbi. What about your family? It says here you have a son . . ."

AUGUST IN WARSAW. Unbearably hot. The air quality was so poor from years of widespread pollution, it made the temperature feel even hotter. Now that Communism was finished, perhaps one day the country would have air conditioning—no doubt, the greatest of all capitalist goods. Better than blue jeans, or soft drinks, or camcorders, or Toyotas. But now, even water was a scarce commodity. And on this day, it was the most valuable of all.

During the war the landscape of the city had been leveled by bombings. There were mounds of rubble where it had once been flat. Buildings formerly blocking the sun would never again see sky. And a good number of Warsaw's once lush trees had long become separated from the ground. Shade was now impossible to find, because with the exception of the Sony Tower on Marszalkowska Avenue—Warsaw's one, eerie skyscraper—the gray, dismal buildings of the former Eastern bloc were not tall enough to provide much relief from the torrid sun.

The one place that was still rich with shade, however, was the Jewish Cemetery on Okopowa Street, located in the northwest corner of the city, not far from the site of the Warsaw Ghetto. Nearly two hundred years old. Over one hundred and fifty thousand graves deep. Eighty-two decomposing acres, poignant testimony of a former Jewish existence in a nation now largely bereft of Jews and Jewish memory. Before the war, there were three and a half million Jews in Poland, four hundred thousand in Warsaw alone. Once Poland had the largest concentration of Jews in the world. Over ninety percent were killed. Today the remnants of Jewish life in Poland consisted of, maybe, ten thousand people. A once vibrant culture had disappeared, never to be reclaimed. Left behind was an eerie sense of ghostly inhabitance, an inaudible whimper amidst all the amnesia.

The outrage that comes with eradication. A monument of graves buried within a wild, overgrown forest. Soft breezes shuffled the branches of thick, gangly trees. The trees themselves were ancient, their roots swelling, gnarled, ossified—pushing up caskets, toppling headstones, creating barricades. Scattered everywhere were crumbled tombstones, serving as topsoil.

There were dirt trails overrun with moss and weeds, and divided stone walkways that were wobbly and unsteady, refusing to grip the haunted earth. An obstacle course both above and below ground.

One trail led to a clearing that appeared sunken. It was the site of a mass grave filled with thousands of Jews murdered by the Nazis during the Warsaw Ghetto Uprising in 1943. Near the entrance to the cemetery was a section of grand marble tombs and lavish mausoleums, a place of honor reserved for the great rabbis of Polish Jewish history. A massive red brick wall surrounded the entire cemetery. There was a wrought-iron gate entrance that pointed directly to a small pavilion made of brick, no bigger than the size of a woodshed. It was the office of the caretaker, Isaac Borowski, a man in his mid-forties. His thick red hair was covered at the top with a tiny white embroidered yarmulke trying to cling on to something more dependable than a bald spot. His teeth were rotting and unevenly spaced, and he had sagging cheeks and a squat nose, and round fleshy lips, all above a short and anchored body.

Despite his appearance, Isaac moved around the cemetery quite gracefully, hurdling over fallen headstones and landing squarely on otherwise treacherous patches of earth. He could hang from the limbs of large banyan trees to remove branches that were knocking up against mausoleum walls.

The ghosts of Jews past were lost inside this jungle of brush and foliage and cool breezes that seemed to exist nowhere else in Warsaw. Isaac circled the grounds and continued with his unending job of tending to the graves and registering the names of all those forgotten Jews whose headstones were slowly becoming erased. Victims of decay, a different fate from the culture and its people, who vanished also, but far more quickly.

He took out a handkerchief and wiped his brow. As always, he wore long pants and a long-sleeved shirt. The cemetery was too raw a terrain for skin to be left uncovered. But his clothing only worsened the already unmerciful heat.

He surveyed his kingdom of the dead, this haunted archeological dig, the irrefutable acreage of lives forever lost—the only proof that they had ever existed.

Isaac recited the Kaddish for them, for all of them, and then prayed for rain.

THE OLD MAN sat down on a clean but faded park bench in St. Mark's Square, took out his Ukrainian newspaper, and stared for a brief moment at the Second Avenue Deli across the street. His bones ached. He suffered from arthritis and a bad back. It didn't help that he had been living in the same building on East Seventh Street for the past forty-six years, a five-flight walk-up, with his apartment, most inconveniently, on the top floor. At least the building was rent-controlled, which was a small consolation for the suffering he endured in climbing those stairs, punishing his body with each step.

He was tall with a round moon face and only the slightest hint of white hair along the sides and back of his head—with an empty stretch on the top. His eyebrows, however, were blessed in ways that his scalp was not. Thick tufts of white growth clutched his forehead as though he had just stepped out of a freezer. A brown knob of a mole protruded from his left cheek. He had eyes that returned a cold, ice-blue stare, overwhelming a pair of doltish reading glasses. His frame was large and clumsy, with a body language that did nothing but trip and stutter. And his clothes were rumpled as though he, and they, had been together far too long.

As on most summer days in New York City, the streets were particularly oppressive. There was the baking heat and the swirling grime. Add to that the frayed nerves and the taunting words, the coughing fumes and the churning exhausts. Where else but in New York could park benches face out onto vistas that signalled civilization's very decline?

Soon another man sat down on the bench beside him. Much younger and no doubt an American, with a kind of self-assured native presence and decidedly Protestant features. Yet, he was unshaven, his hair was somewhat wild and long, and he was dressed in faded blue jeans and a white T-shirt.

The old man raised his canopied eyebrows but otherwise didn't blink at the stranger. The East Village had undergone many changes over the years, and all sorts of people had, at one time or another, occupied a space on this park bench. In between the two great wars, the East Village had been a place of Yiddish Theater on Second Avenue, and outdoor cafés where young Jewish artists and intellectuals would smoke cigarettes and argue over Socialism and the other progressive movements that alienated them—even back then—from their immigrant pasts. Then came the Ukrainians after World War II, followed by the beatniks dressed in black, with their goatees and their Camus and their Camels. Later, tie-dyed hippies settled in at the Fillmore East, followed by Indians and East Indians and squatters in buildings along Avenue C, and then the homeless in Tompkins Square Park, and now a new generation of young East Europeans hanging out at restaurants deceptively called Odessa and Kiev, but which served hamburgers, french fries, and apple pie throughout the day.

The old man was a veteran, but not of a war. He had seen strange things in his life. So he wasn't surprised that a stranger would park right beside him when all the other benches were vacant. The younger man reached into a black attaché made of ballistic nylon fabric, and pulled out the *New York Times*.

Rifling through the first few pages of the Metro Section, he said, "Oh boy, crime is up, but the mayor says here that law enforcement is making progress in catching the criminals. Good for him."

The old man turned to respond, but then caught the penetrating blue eyes of the stranger, set above a smug half-smile. The Ukrainian froze as though he had suddenly recalled the Russian winters of his youth. At first it was difficult for him to speak, so he looked away nervously. He could hear himself swallow, could hear the silence of his thinking. Finally, he said, "What are you doing here? What do you want from me?"

"What do you think?"

"Go away. Leave me alone."

"This is a free country. I can sit where I want." Stretching his legs, the stranger continued, "Nice day, isn't it, Maloney? You know, since we're here on your Ukrainian goose-stomping grounds, why be so formal? We've known each other for some time. Your real name is Malyshko, let's not forget that. Maloney may be your stage name, but you kill under Malyshko."

"I didn't recognize you," Maloney said. "Your hair is longer, and these clothes," he looked on disapprovingly. "You have changed."

"You haven't, but I would have found you anyway."

"You are not allowed to follow me around like this."

"Why not? I'm a private citizen."

"You no longer work for the government?"

"No, I retired with you. You no longer gas; I no longer prosecute. Now we can spend some quality time together."

"Thank you, but I have other friends."

"Really . . . well, I'm anxious to meet them."

A teenager with hair spiked like rooftop antennas streaked by the two men on a skateboard and then hurdled over an empty park bench. Maloney looked on enviously.

"When I was in that courtroom," Maloney said, "I always wondered why you went after me with such passion. You have a Jewish name, but you don't look like a Jew to me—particularly now."

"The horns are retractable, Malyshko; people are rarely what they seem. Hell, the court treated you like a kindly old man."

"So what do you want from me? I will call the police if you don't leave me alone."

"What kind of police, Malyshko?" Duncan asked cynically. "The SS? The Arrow Cross? The Death's Head Regiment? The 101 Police Battalion? The Lithuanian Security Police? The *Einsatzguppe*? The *Einsatzkommando*? Which police did you have in mind? I'll just sit here and read the paper until one of your former units shows up. I'd love to meet them, too."

Maloney hadn't seen Duncan in well over a year, since the conclusion of Maloney's denaturalization rehearing. They were sitting at opposite tables in the courtroom. Even then, as a defendant facing possible deportation, Maloney looked disheveled; but Duncan was, in those days at least, a clean-shaven, starch-shirted, wing-tipped, cocksure federal prosecutor. Obviously, much had happened to the both of them since that day. One had become a free man; the other now languished in an even deeper prison.

"I will just walk away from you," Maloney said fitfully. He rose and then lunged a few steps forward. Duncan calmly returned his newspaper inside his bag and started to follow Maloney down Second Avenue.

The former guard turned around to check on his pursuer, but found Duncan standing right beside him. "What do you want? I am an old man. Let me live in peace."

Duncan started to laugh like some homeless kook. It started out as a slight giggle, gradually escalating into a series of hoots; finally he was doubled over, clutching his sides and howling, wiping tears from his eyes.

"Malyshko, you kill me. What is it with you camp guards? Where's the irony with you people?" Maloney looked on impassively. "How stupid did you have to be to qualify for the job of human butcher? Let's see . . . ," Duncan began, counting off on his fingers, "you ran the gas chamber in Maidanek; you shot at least fifty Jews who were working in rock quarries because they couldn't climb out fast enough by your stopwatch; you strangled an infant you found hidden in the prisoner barracks. Now you tell me you want to 'live in peace.' We call that *chutzpah*, Malyshko. What do they call it in Ukrainian?"

"The court said I was innocent."

"No, wrong again, they said I was too aggressive. That doesn't make you innocent. It just makes me look stupid, but you're still a mass murderer no matter how you look at it."

"Again I ask you: what do you want?"

"Difficult question, Malyshko. There is so much I want. The question is, can I count on you?"

"To do what?"

"To make the nightmares go away."

"I don't know what you mean," Maloney said angrily. "Take sleeping pills. It will help you; it works for me."

"You have trouble sleeping, Malyshko? I'm surprised, though I'm happy to hear it. Please, tell me about your dreams."

"Leave me alone. I'll scream."

"And I'll watch you scream. You've done that before, haven't you?"

Maloney tried once again to free himself from Duncan. Hurriedly, he shuffled a few, wobbly steps, his feet spread wide apart as though Second Avenue were lined with hot coals. One step to Maloney's five, Duncan was still in front of the man he was hunting, this time without government approval.

"What do I have to do to make you go away?"

"A confession, just between us—between friends."

"Are you wearing a tape recorder like the last time?"

"No, go ahead and frisk me. I'm clean."

"I can't confess to something I didn't do. I have already had my day in court. I can't be punished again—by you or anyone else. I have suffered enough."

An M15—not a machine gun—pulled alongside the curb at a designated stop. Maloney saw his chance, ran awkwardly toward the DKNY ad plastered on the side of the canopy, and pushed to the front of the line.

"Excuse me, please . . . I must get on this bus. Sorry. Pardon. Forgive me."

Duncan watched as the old man shouldered and elbowed others aside in a struggle to save himself. Women. Children. People even older than him. The scene was familiar; whether in Lublin or the East Village, nothing had changed.

Then Duncan announced, "Ladies and gentleman, please be careful. There is a killer among you. A Nazi is getting on that bus. He knows a great deal about fumes, and fire, and overcrowded trains. Keep an eye on him at all times. He is very dangerous. Check the air you breathe. Whatever you do, don't let him light up a match."

Maloney didn't hear any of Duncan's warnings. He had been the first to board the bus, flashing his senior citizen's pass and then sitting down in the seat closest to the driver. He wiped his forehead anxiously. Then he peered out the tinted window to see whether Duncan had followed him. Duncan was still on the street. All the other passengers had by now paid their fares and boarded, as well.

None of them, however, seemed alarmed by what Duncan had

said. Even if true, the shady affiliations in the old man's past were none of their concern. Many people in New York have some kind of unseemly, unspoken history. That's why they lived there. The city was like an overcrowded, dry *mikvah*, with sinners splashing up against one another, and yet nothing got washed away. A daily dose of strange encounters was the price of admission for living on the island. What would a day in the city be like without them? So a Nazi is on the M15? Big deal. He'll blend in well with the transvestite, the crack addict, the welfare mother, the proverbial midnight cowboy, the alcoholic banker, the Hasidic embezzler, the Mafia bagman, the grandmother addicted to Percodan, and the bus driver himself, who no doubt has his own secrets, all unknown to his passengers and often hidden from himself, as well.

Duncan had not moved, still at the same corner from where the Ukrainian had escaped. As the bus started to pull away, Maloncy felt relieved. An attempt to breathe heavily was thwarted by a wheezing lung. He dusted off his glasses and settled back into the hard shell of the bus seat.

But just before he did, he turned once again to make certain that Duncan was indeed getting smaller with distance. Standing on Second Avenue was the former prosecutor, the one who had hounded Maloney for four years, the dirty Jew who nearly had him deported back to Ukraine. Maloney squinted his eyes in disbelief as Duncan clicked his right heel to his left and raised his right hand in the gesture of a Nazi salute.

The new world was truly without irony, and what had remained in its place was madness.

A LARGE WHITE Mercedes Benz slowed to a stop outside the Jewish Cemetery on Okopowa Street. There were two men inside. The one sitting in the passenger's seat stepped out of the car and approached the gate. He was dressed in an elegant beige suit, a black tie, and a milky white panama with a maroon band wrapped around its crown. Once at the gate he rapped against a rusty panel with an open palm.

The man had dark hair, deep-set eyes, and a strong face. He was solidly built, and the lightly colored suit made him look even more so. Getting no response, he looked back at the driver, shrugged, and then, more loudly this time, resumed his rapping until Isaac Borowski hurriedly came out of his office in the pavilion to meet his unannounced visitor.

"Can I help you?" Isaac asked, peering through the slats in the gate.

"My name is Nathan Silver. I am an American Jew. I would like to come inside."

"Yes, of course."

Isaac yanked on a latch and pulled, and then swung the mangled wrought-iron gate backward, allowing Nathan Silver to enter.

"Thank you, Mr. . . . ?" Silver said.

"Borowski. Isaac Borowski. Shalom. And you are welcome. What about your friend? Would he like to come inside also?"

"No, thanks. He'll just wait in the car. He always waits in the car."

"Oh, I see," Isaac said, but didn't. "So, how can I help you? Do you want a tour of the cemetery?"

Silver took off his hat, then tilted his head downward, using the hat to somewhat shield his face. He said, "Actually, I'm looking to trace some of my family history. My relatives were here before the war. Our family name was Lieblich. Many were killed at Treblinka, but our side made it over to America in the early part of the century."

"Yes, of course, I see," Isaac said, nodding sympathetically. He had heard many such stories of death and timely desertion before.

"Do you think we can find some graves of my relatives? I would like to pay my respects."

"That may be difficult," Isaac said resignedly. "Tens of thousands of graves. I have been walking around this cemetery for many years, writing down names. But we have no computers. I do it all by hand, and I am alone here. The registry is not organized. And you must know that Lieblich was a very common name in those days. We might find Lieblichs, but of course we will not know if they are your relatives. Please wait here . . ."

Isaac darted back inside the pavilion, while Silver waited patiently for him to return. Silver glanced over at the black forest, and came to the following conclusion: People are neither wholly courageous nor complete cowards—in fact, courage is entirely situational. For instance, there were many acts of bravery that he had been asked or had volunteered to perform during his professional life, and he had done so unflinchingly and with honor. But yet he had no desire, under any circumstance, to enter the hollow of that cemetery alone. Simply put, he was afraid. It was not something he would admit readily to anyone in his line of work, but here, alone with Jewish ghosts—with the ancestral history that had perhaps contributed in some ways to who Nathan Silver had become—he felt humbled and weak.

So to distract himself from his fear, he smoothed down his jacket, took out a toothpick from his vest pocket, and started to remove a piece of herring that had been lodged in his teeth since breakfast that morning. He was the kind of man who liked to look at himself in a mirror whenever the occasion presented itself, but in this case there was no mirror to be found. In fact, the place didn't seem to even have a bathroom. Instead, he began to polish his lizard-skin shoes. But what for, he thought? The search for the Lieblichs was going to be messy, and he wasn't properly dressed for the adventure. That forest called for hiking boots, and perhaps a safari suit. And no matter what he wore, his family—whether here or in America—was so ashamed of his present line of work, they wouldn't acknowledge him, anyway.

Moments later Isaac returned with a few possible names that may have been Lieblich, but may have also been Liebkin or Liebstein or Lipsky or Liebman. In that Jewish jungle, with its decay and fading epitaphs, who knows what their search might turn up?

Isaac Borowski and Nathan Silver entered the forest through an artery tangled with moss and vines. From the outside it looked as though it could have been a cave. Silver hesitated before taking his first step. Isaac was already well inside, each of his spry movements like a moonwalk glide. In the darkness, Silver heard a laugh.

"Isaac, is that you?"

"Yes."

"What's so funny? And don't go so fast," Silver said nervously.

"I'm sorry. I will move slower."

"Christ, this place is a disaster," Silver observed. "And look at that: there's a Nazi swastika painted on that stone."

"Vandals," Isaac replied. "It happens sometimes. I'll remember to wash it off later," he said. Then he slid a pencil from his ear as though it were a dart, removed a small spiral pad from his back pocket, and made a note to himself about yet something else to do in this gridless, mapless, bottomless pit of thankless work.

"Do you have problems protecting the graves from vandals? Because I know some people who could help out here with security."

"It is not so much the vandals I worry about, but the trees; they are much worse. The roots smash headstones, claw through caskets, and dig up the bones."

Silver shuddered and stepped closer to Isaac.

Trudging through the cemetery grounds with Silver close behind, Isaac pointed out a few noteworthy graves: L. L. Zamenhof, the creator of the language Esperanto; the director of the orphanage in the Warsaw Ghetto, Janusz Korczak, who died with his children at Treblinka; the head of the Warsaw Ghetto Jewish Council, Dr. Adam Czerniakow, who committed suicide rather than continue to serve the Nazis by organizing the deportation of Jews to the death camps.

Over the past several years, in addition to his other duties, Isaac had become a sort of unofficial tour guide of the cemetery. He didn't really mind the added responsibilities, because there was no other choice. Jews—living ones, tourists—kept coming, which more than compensated for the fact that he hardly ever had to bury anyone in this otherwise Jewless Poland. The cemetery had become Poland's answer to the Magic Kingdom—a never-never land minus the songs and the costumes.

When democracy came to Poland, so did the seductions of foreign currency. Tourism was the first and most obvious choice of a hook to reel them in. The bait of course was landmarks; those that had survived the war and the shameful neglects of Communism. A nation poor in Jews, but rich in Jewish ruins. And the fish in this case were the Jews themselves—particularly the sentimental and affluent American Jews, tearfully seeking every opportunity to retrace their family origins. All sorts of package tours had been created, which included the major sites: the concentration camps, the ghettos, the markets, the monuments, the synagogues (some now being used as movie theaters), the cemeteries—even the location shots for *Schindler's List*.

Suddenly, Poles who hated Jews found a way to cash in on the absence of Jewish life. A cottage industry of shtetl revivalism. As Silver had done, the ancestors of this vanished breed were returning, carrying American dollars and American Express. The only risk—small, but nonetheless real—was that the Diaspora would once again fall in love with Eastern Europe, sell all their possessions in Brooklyn, West Hollywood, and Shaker Heights, and make *aliyah* to Warsaw, Lodz, and Kraków. The Poles didn't want that; what they wanted was for the Jews to visit, take some Polaroids, stay in a hotel, and buy a hat. Maybe that's why Poland had been left a little primitive: to keep out those looking for luxury.

"I think we are coming close to where we will find Lieblichs," Isaac announced cheerfully. Isaac was comfortable with the bumpy terrain; he traveled on roots like a sandstone skipping along the water. Every so often he spun around to make sure that his guest was able to manage on his own.

Isaac stopped suddenly and leaned forward with his ear, like an Indian scout.

"Shsh."

"What is it?" Silver asked.

"I hear something."

"I don't hear anything . . ."

"Shah. We are not alone. There are other people here."

"Are they vandals?"

"Shsh . . ."

Quietly and nimbly, Isaac moved over behind a headstone as though it were an eight ball, and peered out from the side. Then he stood up, wheeled around, and returned to Silver.

Silver opened his jacket and slipped a hand inside. "Do you want me to take care of them?" he asked.

"What? No, no, I know who they are," Isaac said, giggling. "There is no reason to write down their names. They are not vandals; I have seen them before. Also, reporting them to the Warsaw Police will do no good."

"Who said anything about reporting them . . . ?"

A young couple carrying a small bouquet of flowers circled the monuments and graves. Occasionally they would perform the balance beam on some especially thick roots. At one point the woman lost her footing, but the young man reached out, caught her and pulled her close to his body. They kissed on arrival.

"They look like vandals to me," Silver said.

"No, they're just Polish Catholics."

"Are they lost?"

"No, they come to leave flowers on Jewish graves."

"Why? These people finally got what they wanted—no more Jews. The joke's on them, of course, because they also got no money, no culture, no highways, no trains, no decent fruits and vegetables, no major industry, not even air-conditioning. But they don't even get the joke, which itself is a Polish joke. Dumb fucking Polish peasants. I don't trust any of them. Maybe they leave flowers to celebrate having the country all to themselves."

"No, some are sorry."

The young lovers noticed Isaac, bowed, and waved. Isaac smiled and waved back at them.

"These are good people," Isaac said. "There are many decent Poles, and the two over there are young; they were not here for the Holocaust."

"I imagine you are Polish."

"Yes, I am," Isaac replied neutrally.

"You were born here?"

"Yes, right here in Warsaw."

"Are your parents still alive?"

"No, my father died when I was a small boy. My mother left me before I had time to know her."

Silver paused before asking, "Any other relatives?"

"No. I was an orphan."

"I'm sorry."

"It's okay. I managed," Isaac replied, his voice assured, his eyes undiverted.

"Child of the streets."

"No, the cemetery."

"You grew up *here*? In this dump?"

"When I was thirteen, I came here for the first time to visit my great-grandfather's grave. My father once told me that my mother's grandfather was a famous rabbi. His name was Chaim Lewinstein. So, because I did not have a bar mitzvah, when I became a man, I climbed over the walls of this cemetery and started to look around—to find this man Lewinstein, another one of my dead, or missing, relatives."

Isaac leaned up against the scaly bark of a massive tree and then twisted his hips to the side and bent his torso toward the ground so that he ended up with his left arm over his left ankle and his right arm—with an open palm—pointed skyward. After a few seconds holding this position, he returned to a normal, upright stance, closed his eyes, and inhaled deeply, but also noiselessly. Silver looked on, wondering whether this tour also included a demonstration of cemetery calisthenics.

Soon Isaac resumed his tale. "Nobody ever worked here before me. The cemetery was abandoned after the war. People came to steal marble and stone, but that was it. When I first came, I searched for my great-grandfather a long time—just like what we do now with your family—and then finally I found Lewinstein's grave. It is back in the front where we started. He was an important man."

Silver was taking notes, but without pen or paper.

"I see his tomb," Isaac continued, "which is all broken. There was a hole in the top. Inside, I see beer bottles and a broken wooden rake. The next day I came back with new stones, some cement and tools, and I worked until I fixed the tomb. I even found a machine that writes on stone, and I engraved the same Hebrew words that were on the old tomb. When I finished, I cried. Even when my father died, even when I was a little boy wanting my mother, I never cried. But here, with Lewinstein—on my bar mitzvah—I cried for the first time. So I decided to stay here and take care of my great-grandfather, and everyone else's family, too."

"Some story," Silver said without emotion, even though this was Poland, and he would be forgiven for breaking old habits.

A few yards further, Isaac announced, "Ah, yes, here we are. We have Lieblichs, after all."

Covered by moss and cobwebs was a series of graves all bearing the name, written in Hebrew, "Lieblich"—Nathan Silver's maternal family name.

"Of course, I can't tell you this is definitely your family, but . . ."

Silver didn't care; it was enough of a bloodline for now. He fell to his knees, the suit becoming fatally soiled, and then brushed off each of the graves with his hand. Soon he gave up on the cleaning. Silver closed his eyes and prayed softly in Hebrew.

Rising to his feet, Silver said, "Isaac, thank you. I got what I came for."

They shook hands.

"I'm happy this was a good visit for you," Isaac beamed.

"It really was. Now, could you please get me to my car?"

Isaac led his visitor back, retracing their steps without detour or delay.

When they returned to the gate and Silver signaled to his driver that all was well, he said, "Isaac, I'm happy to have found you." Then he reached into his jacket and drew out a fat wad of rolled-up American dollar bills. Holding it right in front of Isaac's face, he explained, "There's two thousand bucks in here." Then he stuffed it inside Isaac's shirt pocket, and dusted around the seams.

"You are kind," Isaac said, sounding uncomfortable, "but . . . this is so much and . . ."

"Don't mention it. We are in the same business, you and me."

"You work in an American cemetery?"

"No, but I know about the underworld. So enjoy the money. Do what you want with it. Maybe, for me, you could clean up the Lieblich plots a little. I don't know . . . maybe plant something nice around the area." Then, recalling his visit, he added, "On second thought, don't plant anything." Jabbing a finger into Isaac's pudgy chest, Nathan Silver said, "And definitely buy yourself a computer. I'm sure I'll see you again sometime."

The gate opened. Silver checked both ends of the sidewalk, then wiped off his pants once more before getting back into the car. Without exchanging any words with his boss, the driver started the engine, and the Mercedes purred down Okopowa Street, the only sign of Western industry in all of Warsaw that day.

Chapter Eight

"WE'RE READY FOR you now, Mr. Katz," the young woman beckoned.

Duncan had been sitting patiently in the Green Room of the Craven Studios on West Fifty-seventh Street, a block away from the West Side Highway. The room was, in fact, green, with a 1960s green shag carpet that probably hadn't seen a shampoo since the unkempt decade of its birth. There were four green, sunken swivel chairs made of a hard plastic shell, and a small green leather sofa that, with age, had begun to show cracks of white varicose veins. The coffee table was green, too; so were the mugs. Obviously the green-room concept at the Craven Studios had become a design motif without shame.

Duncan occupied one of the chairs, swiveling back and forth, his feet changing direction, stepping over one another cha-cha style. He was flipping through an issue of *Elle*, staring at cosmetic ads and the long conga line of designer clothing that Seventh Avenue was showing well in advance of the upcoming season.

"Can I get you a drink to take on the set with you, Mr. Katz? Coffee? Mineral water?" she asked.

The young woman, dressed in a green designer suit, had come to escort Duncan over to Studio A for the *Molly Rubin Show*.

"No, thank you. I'm fine," Duncan replied.

"We'll be ready to tape in about ten minutes, but I'll bring you over now so you can meet Molly and we can get you all set up."

The woman was tall and slender with brown, shoulder-length curly hair. Her lips were thin; the same could be said about her nose, which tilted slightly to the left. She had eager brown eyes and deep, un-creasable grooves planted in her forehead. Overall she was quite young, and displayed the kind of deference of someone just out of college. Duncan assumed that she was the producer, since she was the only one in the studio carrying around a clipboard.

"This is the first segment I ever produced on my own," she con-fessed to Duncan as they walked down a green-paneled hallway. "I've been an assistant producer for a while, but Molly dumped my boss and put me in charge. I've got to bring the ratings up, and . . . well, I'm a little nervous."

"Don't worry," Duncan assured her, "it'll be great. I'm a professional. I've been on a million of these programs."

That was true. Throughout most of his career with the OSI, Dun-can had been a frequent guest on a great many news and information programs, both on television and on radio. Many of them were low-budget cable operations like the *Molly Rubin Show*. But he had also appeared on *Nightline with Ted Koppel*, *60 Minutes*, *20/20*, *Dateline*, and *48 Hours*, as well as on *Charlie Rose*, *Geraldo*, *Court TV*, *Larry King Live*, Na-tional Public Radio's *Fresh Air*, and as a guest on local news stations across the country.

Those were in the days before the Maloney debacle, when Duncan was still very much in demand. The *Shoah* had long doubled as part catastrophe, part curiosity. The media relentlessly competed with one another to carve out a unique corner of the Holocaust kingdom. Duncan, a Jewish golden boy who was gridiron tested, Ivy League educated, telegenically suitable, and best of all, a Nazi hunter, was the perfect spokesman to offer a lurid quick fix to an always atrocity-hungry America.

Now living as a civilian in New York, without either purpose or portfolio, Duncan was surprised to receive a call to appear on this or any other television program. Since his OSI ouster, the public eye had developed an astigmatism when it came to his opinions.

But Molly Rubin and her young producer had other ideas. With the show's ratings sagging and with Duncan Katz probably eager to tell his side of the story, they imagined an incendiary program that might bring a new audience to their rescue.

Sitting around a walnut table in Studio A was the host herself, Molly Rubin. She had the look of a well-dressed Jewish grandmother:

the hair pulled back tight in a bolted bun; the fingernails layered with lacquered red polish; the lipstick as thick as tar on macadam; and of course, the outfit, a cheap Loehmann's Donna Karan knockoff. She was short. Her neck was a vine of dangling skin. A flock of crow's-feet fanned out from the corners of her eyes. With a kazoo for a voice, she had been on the air in New York for many years, and before that on radio on Long Island. Her audience consisted mostly of Jews, and her commercial sponsors reflected the tribal buying habits of such viewers, with products ranging from matzos and bagels, to indigestion tablets and creamed herring.

Molly rose to greet Duncan. "Mr. Katz, it's so nice to finally meet you," she said, clasping his outstretched arm firmly with both of her hands as though she were trapping a butterfly. "You know, I tried to get you on my program several years ago, but you wouldn't come."

"I was probably busy."

"No, it probably was that you didn't think my show was important enough. You were such a big shot in those days. But let me tell you something, I've had my share of celebrity guests over the years: Golda Meir, Elie Wiesel, Albert Einstein, Henry Kissinger, the young Barbra Streisand, even Sandy Koufax."

Duncan looked dubious, then said, "All of Mount Rushmore, I see. An impressive list. What happened, Brandeis was busy?"

"No, he died before I could get him."

"It's a good thing I got here while I'm still alive."

"Well . . . yes . . . but, with all due respect, you're not exactly in their league. Now of course who knows what would have happened if you had kept going? With a name like Duncan and your position in the government, you might have wound up as a United States senator. Maybe even the first Jewish president. Your parents would have been very proud. But what with this Maloney business and all, things are now different," she said, sizing Duncan up critically, "and so are you. What, you come on my show wearing a motorcycle jacket? And your hair, it's too long. You should cut it; you look like a *sheygits*."

"I wear the jacket for the padding, and the rest is just a fashion statement."

"What, to be the Jewish Terminator? I got a tip for you," Molly Rubin said, sliding closer to Duncan, her hand pressed on his elbow. "Elie Wiesel wears a suit—Perry Ellis, I think. Go get yourself one. If you want to work your way back to prime time, get a new suit, a haircut, and a shave; then call Mike Wallace. Who knows, we live in an age of second chances. Only Nixon couldn't make a comeback. There seems to be forgiveness for everyone else. Now, enough about your career; let's talk about your personal life. I see you're wearing a wedding band—on your right hand."

"I do everything differently."

"That strategy has done wonders for you, I can see," Molly Rubin said with a smirk. "Anyway, let me tell you, my young producer over there is single. She's a terrific girl. Jewish, too. *Nu*, so tell me, is there a wife?"

Just then the producer returned to the set, smiled at Duncan, and said, "Mr. Katz, I'll hook you up to the microphone now." Fumbling with a long thin cord, she eventually managed to clip it onto a side-long zipper on Duncan's motorcycle jacket. A wire trailed underneath his arm and traveled behind his back until it connected him to a large camera. Black cables crisscrossed the hard rubber floor. The front of the camera registered first a dim white light, then a bright red re-cording light the size of a clown's nose. Duncan half expected Carlo Costello to peer out from behind the machine, but instead a much younger cameraman, a young Hispanic teenager on leave from his high-school AV club, removed his head from the camera and an-nounced with a crack in his voice, "We're ready, Mrs. Rubin."

The producer counted down for Molly with a precise cadence: "Three-two-one, okay, clear the set everyone, we're filming," she said, but Duncan noticed that there was no one else on the set, except for a teenage boy standing off to the side, leaning up against a green wall. The young man looked no older than the kid behind the camera. At first Duncan thought that the boy might have been an alternate in case the cameraman needed a break; but then the former prose-cutor's intuition placed the young man with other company. Perhaps it was the lemon blond hair mowed down to a buzz cut. Or the gaunt face, dominated by a pair of Arctic-blue eyes. Or the Midwestern origin that showed itself in Manhattan with the conspicuousness of a Macy's Thanksgiving Day balloon.

In other respects he looked like any ordinary teenager. He had the dazed, zombie expression of misdirected, unguided adolescence. A casualty of yet another broken American home—the most prevalent, and perverse, achievement of American culture. A nation rich in real estate but poor in the mortar that binds families together. He was wearing a long, dirty white T-shirt decorated with the emblem of a postpunk rock band. There was a time when this kind of John Glenn innocence was shot into orbit; now people wonder what planet some of these kids actually come from.

An oddly shaped tattoo encircled the boy's unmuscled right bicep. From where he was sitting, Duncan couldn't quite make out the image, although he sensed it was the mark of something that he would be better off not seeing at all.

"Welcome to the *Molly Rubin Show,*" Molly began, pausing to treat her viewers to an uncommonly large dentured smile. "Our guest today is Duncan Katz, formerly with the Office of Special Investigations in Washington, D.C. Mr. Katz was once this country's chief prosecutor of Nazi war criminals. Now he lives in New York City, no longer affiliated with the government, no longer a Nazi hunter. Instead, he works as a college professor teaching courses on the Holocaust. To-night we'll find out what has happened to him, and how the case of Feodor Malyshko, alias Fred Maloney, ended his promising career. We'll get to those questions in a moment, but first, a word from our sponsor, Philadelphia Brand Cream Cheese . . ."

An off-camera, prerecorded silky voice eased into a segment on the unending miracles of cream cheese. "And with only a few extra ingredients, you can make a delicious and simple cheesecake just in time for Rosh Hashanah . . ."

Annoyed, Duncan asked, "Are we off the air?"

"Yes," Molly replied, "but right after this clip there will be a short segment from Streitz's Matzos . . ."

"I don't care about the matzos," Duncan interrupted. "What were you trying to do with that introduction?"

Molly Rubin began to fidget with her left earring; then she looked over at her producer. "Don't worry Mr. Katz," she replied awkwardly, but Duncan had already figured out the ratings-enhancing agenda be-hind his appearance on the *Molly Rubin Show.*

"We're back now with Duncan Katz," Molly Rubin continued. "So tell me, what do you think of Philadelphia Brand Cream Cheese?"

"I take it with me wherever I go," Duncan replied, imagining yet another use for the cream cheese, one involving Molly Rubin's rectum.

"You are a charming man." Shifting abruptly, Molly asked, "Mr. Katz, was Fred Maloney a Nazi murderer?"

"Without a doubt."

"Then why is he living in a rent-controlled apartment in the East Village free from the law while you lost your job?"

"That's a complicated question."

Taking her cue from prime-time journalists who had nothing to fear from her, Molly Rubin quickly put on her reading glasses and peered down at a legal pad, reviewing her notes. "A federal appeals court ruled that you behaved unethically and that your conduct cast doubt on whether Feodor Malyshko was indeed the notorious Butcher of Maidanek that you claimed he was."

"Malyshko, or Maloney, as he has been known in the United States since 1948, was Boris the Butcher, a concentration-camp guard who carried a gun and followed orders and sent thousands of people to their deaths. There is no question of that."

"Then why is he still in this country?"

Painfully, Duncan replied, "Due process sometimes allows killers to go free. They walk the streets even though they are guilty. It has always been this way in America. It's the price we pay for democracy. Maloney is now one of the few mass murderers who has ever benefited from a legal technicality."

At that moment, the loitering teenager joined the proceedings. The producer slipped a chair right beside Duncan. She had already taken care of the microphone.

Molly Rubin announced, "With us now is Arthur Schweigert, who is the leader of the White Aryan Militia, a neo-Nazi youth group headquartered in Nebraska. Welcome Mr. Schweigert, and thank you for coming all the way from Omaha to join us."

"Thank you for inviting me," the young man said politely.

Duncan braced himself. He was now sharing his interview with an adolescent Nazi wanna-be. The tattoo was no longer a mystery. Painted in hunter-green around Schweigert's bicep was what might have been a Crown of Thorns, but to Duncan it was unmistakably the coiled barbed wire of a concentration camp.

"What do you have to say about the Maloney incident?" Molly Rubin asked her young guest.

"It is yet another example of the Auschwitz lie," Schweigert replied calmly. "Maloney is obviously an innocent man who was persecuted by Mr. Katz and his Jewish friends—the same ones who control the banks and the media. For once and for all, let's remember the most important fact: a man like Maloney must be innocent because there were no killings at the concentration camps. The Six Million is a vicious Jewish lie, told to manipulate world public opinion . . ."

Molly Rubin squirmed in her chair. The producer's forehead became even more furrowed. Nervously she placed a braid of her hair inside her mouth. Seconds later she returned to her clipboard as though it were in need of some last-minute jotting. The cameraman moved his head away from the machine to get a better look, as though the lens was picking something up that wasn't really there.

Duncan was now being held captive on a daytime talk show. The only escape would come from inside himself. He recalled the last conversation he had had with Bernard Ross on the day he was fired from the OSI—the event that left him jobless and marooned to answer the Schweigerts of the world all by himself.

He had been sitting in his office, reciting—no, more like memorizing—the court's fateful words: "The prosecutor acted with a reckless disregard for ethics and truth-seeking."

Without Duncan noticing, Bernard Ross entered and shut the door. Ross sat on the corner edge of the desk and said, "Duncan, I want you to take some time."

"What does that mean?" Duncan looked up, suspiciously.

"You need a rest."

"Like a nap?"

"No, like a sabbatical. Call it leave."

"You're firing me?"

"No, just making sure you get some distance from this place."

"I don't need distance, unless you need distance from me. What I need, Bernard, is another case. What about that guy in Tampa?" he asked, fumbling through papers. "What's his name again? I think it's time we got going on that investigation . . ."

"You're not listening to me," Ross interrupted.

Schweigert continued, his voice a mixture of delirium and deranged puberty. "The government has spent millions of taxpayers' dollars punishing old men simply because the Jews of the world will never be satisfied until their blood libel—this Holocaust hoax—is burned into the mind of every last human being on earth. They say 'never again,' but I say 'enough already'! . . ."

There was so much collective cringing on the set of the *Molly Rubin Show* that nobody quite knew how to derail Schweigert in order to pause for a commercial.

"You'll come back during the next administration," Ross said, half-heartedly. "Right now the political situation around here is too inflamed."

"Fuck off, Bernard!" Duncan shouted. "Don't patronize me. What do you mean, next administration? That's three years from now. You know how many more Nazis will be dead by then? Who knows if the OSI will even be around?"

"That's my point, Duncan. I want us to be around as long as there is work to be done here. You've read Bucholz's editorials. Did you see today's paper?" Duncan of course had. He *was* the editorial. Bernard Ross removed the *Washington Post* from Duncan's desk and began reading: " 'The OSI has become thoroughly corrupted by malice and obsession.' Do you want me to read on?"

But Schweigert wouldn't stop. "Where are all these alleged dead bodies that Mr. Katz claims were killed by Germans? Where are the death certificates? There is no proof of these killings. The camps were merely work camps—in some cases, spas, sanatoriums. Why won't the Jews leave us all alone? Don't they have enough already? They are turning America into one big synagogue. They used the Holocaust to get Israel, now they want America, too . . ."

The camera swung in Molly Rubin's direction for a reaction shot. She didn't know whether to nod or wince, so she stared into the camera as if pretending to introduce some other guest.

With his mind still elsewhere, Duncan recalled saying, "I don't care about Bucholz; don't quote him to me. The guy's a Jew hater and a Nazi lover. We should be checking into *his* past."

"Duncan, I promise we'll bring you back."

"When? The clock is ticking. They'll all be dead. Who will I go after then?"

Duncan slipped out of his trance for a moment and thought about young Schweigert. This child of a foreclosed family farm in the Nebraska breadbasket was for the most part, unlike the Nazis whom he now came to adore and emulate, innocent—crazy, destructive, misfired, deluded, and delusional—but innocent, nonetheless. He was a bored, unemployed kid faced with too much idle time and not enough of an inner life to resist the most unoriginal of hatreds. The Nazis always had a thing about Jews, but Schweigert had never even met one until his appearance on the *Molly Rubin Show*.

The real culprit here from Duncan's point of view was Molly Rubin and people like her, who, in the name of ratings points and advertising dollars, provided forums for maniacs to ventilate stupidity on the open airwaves.

"You need me, Bernard," Duncan pleaded.

"There is nothing I can do. Just lay low for a while and . . ."

Molly Rubin realized she had made a terrible mistake. Schweigert was even worse than she and her producer had predicted. This kid made Farrakhan sound like a cantor. No one at her synagogue out on Long Island—and none of her pals from the local Hadassah chapter—would ever forgive her for this. Streitz's Matzos would doubtless now be gone as a sponsor. So too would the cream-cheese company.

When this was all over, she would have to remember to fire her young producer. Somebody had to be blamed for this mess. Sure, having Lorna Luft or Linda Lavin as guests didn't exactly draw huge audiences, but at least those programs were family-oriented. Nobody was ever offended. But this segment was a moral trespass, which sadly, in America, passed for quality entertainment

And on top of everything else, Schweigert showed himself to be an ungrateful son of a bitch. He had gorged himself on lox and cream cheese in the Green Room and now here he was, a kid who hadn't even finished high school, on television for the first time, being given a platform to rail against Jews, and then suddenly, without provocation, he turned on his benefactor, Molly Rubin, herself.

"And you, you Jewess kike, cunt, with your money and fancy clothes," Schweigert seethed, pointing his finger at Molly, "you think you can buy me? We don't need people like you to get our message out. True Americans know what kinds of Jewish vermin and scum you people are. I can't wait until the day when we build our own concentration camps. Then the Aryans of the world will be able to live without the racial filth and disease that you bring wherever you go!"

The young producer was doing a mental count of how many censuring bleeps needed to be inserted into the tape before this segment could air. Meanwhile, Molly leaned over the round walnut table and whispered to Duncan, "Are you going to kick his butt, or am I going to have to do it for you?"

Duncan rose from his chair, towering over Schweigert. He then faced the camera and asked, "Is everybody bananas here? What kind of an X-rated show is this?" Then turning to Molly, "What is this kid even doing here? What if he was saying that there had never been any slavery in America? That the plantations were really summer camps for vacationing African Americans? That the whole idea of slavery was made up, a clever conspiracy by blacks to extort welfare payments from guilt-ridden white Americans whose ancestors never actually owned slaves?"

"He would never be permitted to speak on my show," Molly replied assuredly, facing the camera. "That would be totally ridiculous."

"What's more ridiculous than Holocaust denial?" Duncan shot back. "There aren't any living witnesses to slavery. No documentary footage. No photographs. The scholarship isn't as comprehensive. And yet you gave this idiot a chance to share his nonsense with your audience. He might as well have said that the world was flat." Again staring directly into the camera, Duncan said, "The Holocaust is not a debate; it's not a matter of opinion. It's not like whether you believe the Yankees will win the World Series or not. Six million Jews may sound like an abstraction, but it was as real as the weather, except that the storm clouds that gathered over Poland were filled with smoke."

"You make a good case, Katz, but . . ." Schweigert began to say.

"Shut the fuck up! *Romper Room* is now officially over . . ." The hot overhead lights had beamed down on Duncan far too long. He was now dehydrated, and his stomach was beginning to go into spasm. He felt dizzy. Schweigert's barbed-wire tattoo flashed and swelled in Duncan's spinning head. "Isn't there any public education in Nebraska? Where are your parents? Why can't you just join a 4-H Club or Young Farmers of America? I hate fucking cream cheese! Is there a wife? . . ."

With knees bent and his long, scruffy hair tickling the walnut wood, Duncan clamped his large hands around Molly Rubin's solid circular table and lifted it directly over his head. Schweigert trembled. Molly Rubin, quite ably for someone of her age, hid underneath a chair. The producer prayed that the camera was still filming. Somewhere an absent Carlo Costello lamented missing this exquisite Katz photo opportunity. Gripping the table tightly, Duncan hurled it like an oversized discus right at the camera, which the cameraman had already abandoned in fear for his life. The boy's last prophetic words before sprinting back to Bronx Science were: "Wow, this is going to make great TV . . ."

And with that he was right. The entire shoddy circus act of tabloid lunacy produced the highest rated episode in the long history of the *Molly Rubin Show*.

Chapter Nine

THE DOCTORS HAD been wrong; Mila would last longer than a week. In fact, she would ultimately set the longevity record for late-stage pancreatic cancer at Mount Sinai. Cynical orderlies and cafeteria attendants had started to take bets on when Mila would finally die. Fools. What a mistake it was to wager against her. A scrapper to the end, she would hang on simply for the satisfaction of upsetting the odds. Tenacity and luck had never failed her in the past. Yet, even she realized that this time was different. There was no hope for a final victory with such an implacable enemy.

At moments when it seemed that the disease would claim her, she would somehow rally. She still needed the extra time. Some secrets would not fit snugly in the grave. They had to be left behind—remembered, even if not atoned.

Over thirty-five years after Auschwitz, she finally began to talk. And talk. She didn't want a priest or a rabbi. What she wanted were her round-the-clock nurses. They would become the perfect confessors to her sins. They were, as she saw it, perfect—great-granddaughters of slaves, former welfare mothers who were unashamed of their own sacrifices. Perhaps they would be able to understand her failings in a way that her own people could not.

"I have more to tell you today," Mila said.

This did not come as much of a surprise to Cynthia Perkins. The past few weeks Louise Orey and Judy Stokes had overdosed on Mila's testimony. In fact, even one shift at a time, the evolving story was becoming too much to take. Each day produced something new. The three nurses made it a point to confer with one another in order to piece together all the details. There was little time left over for nursing. But medical neglect didn't matter much to Mila, because it wasn't nursing that she needed.

"When I was a child, I loved to play the piano," Mila announced weakly. "Have I told you that yet?"

"No, you haven't," Cynthia replied, propping up a pillow, wrapping her arms around Mila's chest and back, and lifting her patient into a seated position on the bed. This looked to be one of Mila's better days. She had had only a few shriek-producing nightmares: blurted-out names, the head tossed back from side to side, a kickboxing clinic with swinging arms and pedaling feet. Otherwise, she had slept well.

"I was good at the piano," she said, coughing flatly. "When my parents had guests, they would ask me to come into the parlor and entertain. My father was very proud of my playing. My grandfathers were both rabbis, and my father was a bit of a rebel for not following in the family business. He loved music, and I played mostly for him. Usually it was classical, but sometimes I would sneak in some American jazz."

Cynthia walked over to close the vertical blinds. The low-lying western rays had turned each metal strip into a sizzling skillet. The darkening sun had filled the room with streaks of smoky, sepia grays. A radio tuned to a Spanish call-in program buzzed from a nearby, semiprivate room. The contents of Mila's lunch tray waited by her bed, cooled and uneaten.

"I also loved to sing," Mila continued. "When my son was a baby, I would sing lullabies to him to help him go to sleep." Mila looked away, catching a tear before it escaped from her eye.

"What would you sing to him?"

Mila sighed lightly. "Oh, music from the Gershwin brothers. Do you know them?"

"*Porgy and Bess?*"

"Yes, of course, the opera—a nice tribute to your people. But after the war, when I still lived in Poland, I fell in love with the Gershwins' popular music."

"I know some of those songs. 'Embraceable You,' 'I Got Rhythm' . . ."

"My favorite was 'Someone to Watch Over Me,' " Mila offered.

"Sweet song." Cynthia began to hum the melody for the chorus.

Mila joined her. They both finished by singing a final refrain: "Someone to watch over me." Mila's voice was faint, but also sandpaper rough, her vocal cords shredded from years spent not singing, but screaming.

The nurse and the patient laughed. Cynthia gently touched Mila's patchy hair.

"You have good pipes, Mila. You should keep singing."

"Enough for today," Mila replied.

"What about the piano? You still play? You know they have one downstairs in the entertainment room."

"No, I won't be playing. When I came to this country in 1950, the music stopped for me."

"Why?"

"Music is a luxury; you don't have to have it."

"But it sounds like it was your life, or a good part of it, at least."

"I lost more than music to the Germans," Mila hesitated, the memories flooding and fatiguing. "I learned to do without everything. Music was just the smallest sacrifice."

"But you didn't give it all up. No ma'am. How about those lullabies to your son? You sang that sweet Gershwin song to Duncan . . ."

"No, Isaac. My son's name is Isaac."

DUNCAN LEFT HIS brownstone and headed east toward Central Park for his meeting with Larry Breitbart. All of Eighty-seventh Street appeared to be unbalanced, with double-parked cars lined up on the north side. As for the south side of the street, it was naked of vehicles yet shamefully littered. Along the way Duncan passed a few dog walkers, their hands gloved in Ziploc bags.

Once inside Central Park, he stared at the reservoir; ducks mingled on the water's algae-skimmed surface. Shadows of light sliced through the surrounding chain-link fence and warmed the damp, dirt path. The sky was washed white with an early morning haze. He continued south, down the hills, past the Belvedere Castle and the Ramble, winding around Strawberry Fields. A smooth December frosting of snow caked the former grazing field of the Sheep Meadow.

As Duncan approached Tavern on the Green, it occurred to him that the restaurant was not open for breakfast on weekdays. Larry obviously had made a mistake. They would have to change their plans and try a coffee shop on Columbus Avenue instead. But as Duncan got nearer, he realized that there was no mistake. Tavern on the Green was already open, but seemingly for a private party.

Two navy blue limousines were parked out front. At the entrance stood three men. One was large with a fat face that was biting down hard on a cigar. His wrists and fingers were outfitted with so much garish gold that he looked like a display case for a tacky Forty-seventh Street jeweler. He was dressed in an oversized red sweat suit as though he was a Soviet sumo wrestler. The other two men were smaller in size and had sunken cheeks. They were dressed in sport coats from Moe Ginsburg. All three were wearing standard-issue FBI sunglasses, even though they worked for the other side.

From where he was standing, Duncan could see that the trees in the restaurant's backyard, which during winter evenings were lit up by long strings of white lights, had already been turned on, giving the restaurant—at this time of day—the twinkling facade of a movie set. Before Duncan reached the long, canopied entrance, a family of tourists carrying videocameras approached the front, thinking perhaps that the limousines and exaggerated lighting might mean that Princess Di was in town.

One of the men immediately waved them away. "Sorry, private party, closed for the day," he said in a gruff voice. "Come back tomorrow."

As they walked away disappointedly, Duncan arrived. The goon was about to recite his script once more when a voice from inside one of the limousines said, "It's okay, boys. Let him through." The window was down; Larry leaned his head out before opening the door. "This is Duncan, my godson."

"Sorry, Mr. Breitbart," one of them said shyly. Then turning to Duncan, he said, "You're okay, my man."

Larry Breitbart emerged from the rear limousine, took a step toward Duncan, and embraced him warmly. "Lost some weight, kid," Larry said, brushing Duncan's cheek with his knuckles. "Sorry about the problems at home."

Larry's jowls drooped from his face. His once-slick black hair had thinned to the point where styling mousse no longer made any sense. His wardrobe, however, remained smart and flamboyant in a way that suggested money but betrayed a lack of taste.

Yet despite the fancy duds, Breitbart suffered from the same plight of most once-handsome, but now elderly, Jewish men. Age ultimately unveils the once convincing masquerades. The thin coating of surface gentility eventually wears off, and what is left is something far less glamorous: the remnants of a former immigrant whose first words of the morning might as well be, "Oy, my back."

"I love this park," Breitbart began as his men pulled open the heavy wooden doors at Tavern on the Green. "And this restaurant is great. Did you see the lights in the back?"

"I didn't know it was open for breakfast," Duncan said.

"It never is. I bought the place out for a private party—just you and me," Larry explained.

"Do they know who you are? I don't think they would want to be known as a catering hall for gangsters."

"What are you talking about, Duncan? You don't know nothing about anything unless it has to do with Nazis, do you? This is America, cash is king, money talks; that's all that matters. What do you think, the mob is that easy to spot? I got M.B.A.'s working for me now. My law firm is pure blue chip. My money is as clean as the day it came out of the Treasury. A far as this place is concerned, I'm throwing you a belated bar mitzvah celebration."

The restaurant was empty, although tablecloths and place settings crowned every table in case Larry Breitbart wanted to rotate with each course. A full complement of waiters stood around idly, like matadors at a dance hall. The maître d' walked over and greeted Larry and his nephew, and then took away Duncan's brown mohair coat and Larry's soft blue Ralph Lauren.

"Thank you, Matthew," Larry said to the maître d' when he returned. Larry nodded to one of his henchmen, who handed Matthew a white envelope stuffed with green bills. Matthew bowed in gratitude and then escorted Larry and Duncan to their table.

Before sitting down, Duncan couldn't resist commenting, "Larry, I'm surprised there are no violinists from Juilliard to serenade us while we have our eggs."

"Do you want me to get a few?" Larry asked earnestly. "Lincoln Center is just down the street. For the right price . . ."

"No, just kidding."

"You sure? I can have it done. Just say the word."

They sat down at a table beside a tall window overlooking the artificially lit garden.

Larry ordered eggs over easy with bacon and muffins that were specially baked in his honor. "I want the eggs soft but the yolk intact, you got that?" Larry reminded the terrified waiter. "And make sure you bring the ketchup." Duncan ordered orange juice, an eggwhite omelette, and seven-grain toast. Larry scoffed and lifted his eyebrows disdainfully. He never trusted anyone who shied away from cholesterol.

"Terrible thing this divorce business. The sickness of the modern world," Larry observed. "Milan will always be scarred—nothing you can do about it. I hate to tell you this, but I'm sure you already know."

"I'm not divorced yet, Larry."

"I wouldn't call what you have a marriage, or a family, either. I see this kind of thing all the time with my young people. There's no loyalty anymore," he said wistfully, "not in marriages, and not in the Mafia. In the old days, nobody ever ratted on anybody, and the guys stayed with one family all their lives. Today we're like baseball teams. I gotta keep my free agents happy just as Steinbrenner does; otherwise they bounce around looking for a better deal. The same thing with regular families—husbands and wives don't think twice about switching teams."

"It may be more complicated . . ."

"Bullshit. Families stay together; that's the whole point of getting married and having kids. And that's why they make you say vows. It's a promise, for God's sake. Doesn't anything matter anymore? Nothing's binding; people are always trying to weasel out of something. Sharon's not saving Milan from you; she's just running away from herself. In my book, they call that selfish, and I told her so."

"I'm sure you won't get a Hanukkah card from her next year."

"Tell her to save it. The real problem is that your generation values freedom above anything else. You think everything is supposed to go your way all the time. Autonomy and perfection—no matter what!" Larry said excitedly with his arm in the air, which prompted a waiter to sprint over to the table, only to be dismissed until further notice. "Where was I? Oh yeah, your generation can't tolerate even the slightest down moment. And what's even worse is that you can't tol-

erate any intolerance. Everyone is supposed to accept people no matter what they do, no matter how selfish they are, no matter how many
mistakes they make. Everybody gets away with murder nowadays.
There's no stigma, no shame. Fuck that!

"What happened to the days when judgment kept people in line?
Today, God forbid, anyone says an opinion that sounds too judgmental, or steps on somebody else's idea of morality, and they treat you
like you just whacked somebody. Let me tell you something," Larry
said, his knife now pointing at Duncan, "the answer is public stoning.
You stick someone's head and arms in one of those town-square torture contraptions . . . What do you call those things?"

"A pillory."

"Yeah, that's right, a pillory, and you throw a few rocks at their
face, and you'll see—no more adultery, no more cheating, tax evasion,
bankruptcy, sexual perversion, drug addiction, no more crime. The
world would be a better place. The Puritans had the right answer all
along."

"Larry, you're Mafia."

"That's a different story. I'm in it for business, not pleasure. I still
respect people's feelings. So anyway, about this Maloney character.
You should have let me take care of things for you. You have a godfather who wears two hats, and you never call me for either."

"What would you have taken care of?" Duncan asked curiously.

"I could have finished him off years ago, and nobody would have
noticed him missing." Larry made a gun sculpture with his hand and
pressed down on his thumb. "I got special guys who handle this type
of work. They use silencers, and of course nobody talks. It always
takes too long with the government. And nobody's really ever punished. With me, everything is nice, clean, and fast. And we get the
job done."

"Whatever happened to the municipal-bond work you were telling
me about last night? I thought you were into more legitimate businesses these days."

"We are, but that doesn't mean we don't fall back on our bread
and butter from time to time—especially when we're helping out a
member of the family."

"Larry, I'm not a member of your family," Duncan said, twirling his silverware between his fingers. "And I'm hoping to return to the Justice Department someday, so let's just forget we ever had this conversation. Where's the food already? . . ."

"Duncan, you're not going back there."

"What do you mean?"

"You're finished at OSI. You have to face that fact. What's done is done," Larry said emphatically, as though washing his hands of the conversation. His eggs had just arrived. Before continuing to speak, he drained a half bottle of ketchup onto his plate, followed by a snowstorm of salt and pepper. Larry began to eat, stabbing his eggs in the heart, one at a time, which caused massive, high-cholesterol bleeding into the bacon and home fried potatoes. With each bite, he produced nose-snorting and lip-smacking sounds of pleasure. Duncan's mouth turned up a partial smile. A swallow later, Larry continued, "You've been blackballed, branded—the Jew who knew too much. They gave you the keys to the kingdom, the chance to hunt down Nazis. A real privilege for a Jew, not to mention a child of Holocaust survivors. From their point of view, you went over the top. They'll never trust you again with the franchise."

"Larry, I have a long, stellar record of achievement with the government. This isn't the mob underworld we're talking about here. They don't just whack you and then pretend that you never existed."

"The hell they don't!" Larry jumped back in loudly, moistening his lips as he passed on another blood-red forkful. "You know from your parents not to trust the government. Don't get me wrong. You're a hero in my eyes, and probably with most Jews in this country—at least the ones who have a conscience and a memory, those who read the papers and know what the fuck is going on. That Nazi had no constitutional rights. What due process did they show us? It would only be right for him to rot away in the back of one of my Lincolns— his fuckin' legs sawed off—then dumped off somewhere along the Northern State Parkway. But that's not how the goys see it. To them, Maloney's a senior citizen, and you know how Americans just forget about old people. And then there's that other thing they say: that Jews don't know when to stop and let go, that all we care about is the Holocaust. Like that piece-of-shit kid on TV with you the other night. I was watching. What an embarrassment. You should have just shot him. Instead, he and that Maloney clown are alive, and they've turned *you* into the bad guy. You're just another version of Leo Frank, the Rosenbergs, Jonathan Pollard, Ivan Boesky, Michael Milken, and now Duncan Katz."

"My situation is different," Duncan said. "I'm too valuable to them."

"A Jew is never too valuable. Read your history. We're as welcome as we're useful. Step over the line, and you're finished. What's a Jew? Jew-pointing has been around for two thousand years, maybe even longer, Duncan. No Jew is safe, including me."

Breitbart lifted the final piece of egg-soaked bacon into his mouth, the pearl polish on his fingernails now recoated with the splattered orange guts of a dried-up yolk.

"You've seen too many movies, Larry."

"And you've seen too few."

Resignedly, Duncan downed the last gulp of orange juice, picked at a carob banana muffin, and said, "Larry, what did you want to see me about?"

"You're right, we need to get down to business." Breitbart patted his hands on a napkin, then snapped a finger and motioned to one of his men, the one in the red sweat suit who was stationed at the front door. The guy jiggled over with a brown folder and handed it to his boss. Breitbart gently placed it on his lap, and then sent the man back to hang out with the waiters. "Before your mother died, she asked me to do something for her. A deathbed wish, so to speak."

Duncan waited without emotion.

"How do I say this . . . ," Larry began tentatively, folded his arms, took a deep breath, unfolded his arms, then started again. "Okay, here it goes: Duncan, you have a brother."

"What do you mean? I'm an only child."

"You *were* an only child; now you have a brother."

"How did that happen? My parents are still having children even though they're dead?"

Slowly, Larry said, "Listen to me. Mila had a son, in Warsaw, right after the war. When he was six months old, she smuggled herself out of the country, and she left the baby behind. She went to Germany. There she met Herschel, before he became Yankee. They got married; then they came here. It's all in this file. I had one of my lawyers write up a memo."

Duncan digested, and a few chilled seconds later said, "Wait, are you telling me she abandoned a child in a Communist country?"

"Unbelievable, isn't it? Who would have figured? You have a brother."

"Impossible."

"Flesh and blood."

"No, she wouldn't have done that. It must be a mistake. Whoever told you this is wrong."

"Mila told me herself, the last time I spoke with her in the hospital. I think she was going to finally tell you, but by the time you got there, she was pumped with too many drugs to say anything."

A waiter darted over with a shiny, brass pitcher of water. The glasses at Breitbart's table were nearly empty, but there were so many hand gestures and earnest, bobbing heads exchanged between uncle and nephew that the waiter backed away shyly.

"If it's true, then how come you didn't tell me years ago?"

"I didn't want you running off by yourself trying to find him," Larry explained, his palms facing upward. "Poland was a jungle when the Russians were in charge. It wasn't safe, not even for a Jewish Rambo like you. When the wall came down, and capitalism crept in, so did the Mafia—mostly the Russians and Poles. I put some of my best people in there to set up new business opportunities and to help find your brother. It took several years to finally track him down. One of my men, Nathan Silver, had his own family reasons for doing the job. What Jew doesn't have some unfinished business with Poland? It also helped that we have a good working relationship with the Russian-Jewish Mafia that operates here out of Brighton Beach. They trust me because I'm Jewish. Also, they know from the Holocaust. I told them what I needed in Poland, and they were more than happy to lend a hand. It was like a United Nations rescue mission comprised mostly of felons, all because of you . . ."

"Larry," Duncan interrupted, "I don't care what Mila told you. She wouldn't have abandoned a child." Duncan shook his head with no hint of stopping. "I can see torturing a child . . . I *was* such a child. But not abandoning; she wouldn't have so easily given up the sadistic pleasure of raising him her way."

"Say or believe what you want, Duncan, but you're no longer alone in this world. Somebody shares Mila with you."

The shock of this news continued to tumble whatever words Duncan had in his head. He now wished that he hadn't eaten, or that he had brought along some Donnatal to this five-star restaurant. "Okay, so tell me about him," Duncan asked.

"His name is Isaac Borowski. He runs the Jewish Cemetery in Warsaw. He's an undertaker."

Slowly, Duncan repeated the name Isaac Borowski. Then he said it again, even more slowly and silently to himself. Then once more—out loud this time—as if by acknowledging the name, some unconsciously deep sibling connection might register somewhere. If he had a brother, surely he should be able to feel it, to know it somehow . . . But it was no use. Nothing about the name Isaac Borowski—or the very idea of having an older brother—felt real to him. Finally, he said, "I just can't believe it . . . What else do you know about him?"

"Silver told me he's a yoga teacher, and that he's also some kind of a spiritual mystic. He might even be a healer. People from all over Poland treat him as a holy man." Larry looked down at Duncan's plate and observed, "Duncan, you hardly touched your eggs."

Duncan was silent.

"I know this is all too much, kid, but you have to admit, the news couldn't have come at a better time. You lose a wife, you find a brother . . ."

"Does Isaac Borowski have anything to do with Nazis?"

"No, like what do you mean?" Larry wondered.

"He lives in Poland. He's a Jew. What else can I mean? Is he fixated on revenge?"

"I don't think so. I'm sure Silver would have mentioned something like that. Hey, do you want some dessert? They have great walnut chocolate mousse here."

"What about Polish anti-Semites? There's a lot of them still there. How does he deal with that?"

"Silver said that your brother is some kind of passivist. There doesn't seem to be any hate in his heart. That must explain the fact that you're only half brothers."

"Yeah, but the hate part in me, that comes from Mila, and so does he." A beat later, Duncan continued, "How can I have a brother who lives in Poland—of all places—and he isn't obsessed with what happened over there? That alone makes me doubt that he's for real."

"At least have a cappuccino, Duncan. You can't leave hungry. But I was thinking the same thing myself. Maybe you're just complete opposites. That happens sometimes with siblings. I have a younger brother who works in a pet shop. I bet you didn't know that."

Duncan didn't reply, but rather stared out the window at the necklace of tiny lightbulbs all clinging tightly to the branches like ivy.

"So what are you going to do?" Larry asked.

"I don't know; maybe I should go to Poland and look him up."

"I was afraid you'd say that. You know, it's not that much safer over there now. For one thing, the Russian Mafia is virtually running the country. I think it would be better if I got Silver to arrange to bring Isaac over here."

"Like a kidnapping?"

"We do it all the time."

"I'm not having my older brother kidnapped. Besides, does he even know about me?"

"No, he just knows that his mother left him when he was an infant. He doesn't know anything about what happened after that."

"Tell your man in Warsaw to bring my brother up to date about the family history. I'll leave for Poland as soon as I can."

"I don't think this is such a good idea, Duncan."

"How can I not go, Larry? What would you do if you were me?"

"There are not that many people like you, Duncan; it's hard to say. Listen, I'm your godfather," Larry pleaded. "I'm here to protect you. You know I dropped you once—at your *bris*. I still can't forgive myself. From that point on I promised myself—and your mother—that I'd have better hands with you . . . Oh Mila, what a mess you left back here." Larry's eyes turned to another side of the restaurant and noticed the sparkling ivory keys and smooth, black wood finish of a baby grand piano. "You know, your mother could really play."

"The piano? Please, she wouldn't even let me have a toy one when I was a kid. Music lessons were for sissies."

"She may have said that, but believe me, the lady could play. When I first met her, soon after she came to this country, we were walking through the lobby of the Delano Hotel down on South Beach. Big lobby, white couches, a portrait of FDR by the elevator, an open mezzanine. We went to get a drink at the bar, a lounge with flamingos and zodiac signs carved into the walls. I remember the day exactly:

she had a screwdriver; I was drinking Chivas. Anyway, there was this piano, just like that one over there. She walked over, sat down, and then banged out a whole medley of Gershwin tunes. Without sheet music, all by ear. I swear . . . I'm talking *emmes*. It was amazing."

"Larry, I'm overloading here . . . Who was this lady?"

"You're right, never mind. I'll save it for another time."

They rose and moved toward the entrance. A generous outpouring of tips the size of Christmas bonuses was handed out to a concatenation of waiters standing nearby. Matthew, the maître d,' waited by the door. He was holding onto the cashmere and mohair coats, which he had been guarding. He walked his guests out into the cold air, and watched as Larry embraced his godson before stepping back into the rear of the second car.

Duncan and Matthew faced the two Lincolns with the beaming wax jobs and the black-tinted windows that could have shielded Larry from nuclear fallout. The engines warmed up.

"You really know how to roll out the red carpet for my uncle," Duncan said. "You even turned the garden lights on for him."

"We didn't turn the lights on for him," Matthew said assuredly. "We would have, if he had requested it, and paid for it, but he didn't. In fact, I thought he was annoyed that they were on."

"Then why are they lit?"

"I don't know. A few minutes before you got here, they went on all by themselves. We've been trying to shut them down ever since."

Shivering, the maître d' went back inside the restaurant. Duncan remained outside, reflecting on the sibling who now anchored him somehow, but not knowing to what end. The two limousines circled the open driveway in front of Tavern on the Green, scaring a few horses with NYPD on their backs. Larry waved to a spellbound Duncan, who missed the gesture entirely. A few tourists, overly impressed by the unexplained early morning sideshow, pointed a camera in Duncan's direction and snapped a picture. For all they knew, they might have been in the presence of a celebrity, and it was worth wasting a frame for the memory. Just then the long trail of lights that had blanketed all the trees at Tavern on the Green flicked off—one at a time, like fallen dominoes—as Breitbart's limousines turned the corner and headed down Central Park West.

Chapter Ten

TOMORROW IS ANOTHER DAY. Duncan had heard that one before. So had Mila and Yankee. Most people need to believe in such things. But the Katzes didn't put much faith in the healing power of time. Tomorrow was just as treacherous and uncertain as the day before, and two days from tomorrow would be pretty much the same, if not worse. The wounds that puncture the heart are unhealable. Time is of no help or consequence; it is no anodyne. If anything, time is a transient narcotic, a prison that compels another day of memory. More time is just buying time, as if clocks and calendars can bring about a rose-colored glasses effect. Nightmares come for a reason. The sun passes overhead; eventually, snow melts and leaves fall as if there were no grassy cushion below. And then it starts all over again.

Secretly, Duncan had always rebelled against these familial prerecorded tocsins, sirens piped into his head like elevator music. In many ways he functioned as a double agent: a memory artist in some hastily assembled post-*Shoah* army; yet, there was also a side of him that wished to sabotage all the warped premises that his parents lived by.

Now there was news of a brother, a brother who came from the same womb but who had been nursed on life lessons from somewhere else. With the mystery of Isaac Borowski more dream than nightmare, Duncan wondered whether tomorrow could possibly be different after all.

THE HOUSE ON Yuma Street always looked as though it was about to fall down—but it never did, nor would it ever. When the realtor first showed it to Duncan and Sharon many years earlier, Duncan's reaction was, "I already come from a lopsided home. Why should we tempt fate?" But Sharon's response was, "We should buy this house as an act of defiance. You have to learn to see things through a different lens. Just because something looks like it's going to fall doesn't mean that it will. Positive thinking sometimes helps, too."

Duncan bought the house, tilt and all, despite all the doubts that came with it. He did it mostly for Sharon. For him, outlasting this house wouldn't prove a thing. No amount of positive thinking could change certain realities. For instance, pure and peaceful thoughts would have done little to repel the Nazis. The power of the mind was insanely overrated. Sure, there were people who claimed to be able to bend a spoon by the use of some telepathic force. But so what? How often is someone attacked by a spoon? Duncan stood no better chance of defying his legacy than this house did in overcoming gravity.

Besides, what did a blond *shiksa* like Sharon know about the curses that attached themselves to some people? She was not a daughter of Holocaust survivors—only the wife of their son. That gave her some insights into a certain surreal mind-set, but the design plans for the whole operation were subject to much tighter security. Some truths can never be shared, not even among family. There was a limit to how close she could get without being scorched by the whole damn tragedy. But in the end, perhaps she did get too close.

When Duncan first bought the house on Yuma Street, he prayed that the white-and-green, picket-fenced, Pisa-inspired structure wouldn't one day collapse and take with it all of Sharon's faith in a safe world.

It was winter in Washington, D.C., just days after Duncan's breakfast meeting with Larry Breitbart. Soft patches of snow had gathered on the Yuma lawn. The large birch tree in the Katz backyard was bare but beautiful in its nakedness. The sun threw down an enveloping blanket of warmth and light.

Still dressed in her pajamas—a white thermal two-piece with baby-blue arabesque designs—Milan was playing in the parlor. The parlor had been a late addition to the house, built for reasons having as much to do with a need for more space as with Duncan's idea that additional reinforcement was necessary to prevent the entire homestead from capsizing. The sun had overtaken the room, brightening Milan's blond curls, which varied with each strand. Her teeth were small and unevenly spread apart, with some having already fallen out. Her cheeks were pink and dimpled; her eyes, round and enchantingly blue. She was talking to herself, jabbering away, moving the dolls around, perhaps pretending that her parents were still together. The family dog, a large, floppy-eared golden retriever, barreled into her, knocking over the gossiping dolls. It was the first of many tackles of the morning.

"Go away, Keller," Milan said. "Go away."

Sharon was watching silently, standing beside an upright island that occupied the center of the kitchen. She was on her second cup of mint tea. Her blond hair fell to the center of her back. She was wearing a green sweater above a long, white wool skirt.

Adjacent to the kitchen and off to her side was a small bookcase, no longer filled with Duncan's Holocaust books. Instead, Sharon had replaced them with lighter fare: feminist poetry, gender studies, books on meditation and yoga, organic cookbooks. On the very top of the bookcase rested a clay bust of Moses, clutching the Ten Commandments. There was also a brass-plated Elijah cup, a pair of opaque Shabbat candles, and a spice box for *Havdalah*. A laser cone of sunlight seemed to be drinking from the cup. Framed on the wall was a fully breached and hopelessly loopholed *Ketubah*, which for Sharon now symbolized a declaration of independence.

Despite the past year of Duncan living in New York, estranged from his family, Sharon and Milan carried on as Jews. The rituals continued as always, largely because it was Sharon who had been responsible for maintaining a Jewish household. She was a convert to Judaism. Originally from a small town in North Carolina, where there were absolutely no Jews, she ended up marrying into the granddaddy of all Jewish lineages. She had hit the Jewish jackpot. It wasn't simply that Duncan descended from Polish rabbinic royalty; it was that his family had survived the most lofty of Jewish tragedies.

In many ways this marital alliance made sense. As a child, Sharon had always felt a certain peculiar kinship with the Jewish people. She read *The Diary of Anne Frank* and tried to imagine herself surviving in an attic. After finishing the book, she climbed into her family's own attic, and in solidarity with her heroine, stayed for days, insisting that her meals be brought up to her. Sharon read *The Chosen* and wondered what it would be like to live in an American Hasidic shtetl. She danced the hora in gym class, favoring it over all the other folk dances of the world. In ninth grade she won North Carolina's statewide essay contest on the Holocaust. Her parents never quite understood her obsession with Jews.

"Honestly, dear," Sharon's mother would say, "these are not your people. You're acting like you have a Holocaust ghost inside you."

In light of all this anomalous personal history, and perhaps to appease the ghosts, as well, Sharon was simply fated to marry a son of survivors.

Soon after she had met Duncan, she discovered that he slept with his eyes nearly open. For a while, Sharon took great pride in the fact that on some nights, when she held him a certain way—one arm over his chest and the other with fingers gently pressing against his temples—his lids remained closed. But was he at rest? Sharon knew not to buy into any false hopes. Her husband had spent virtually all the nights of his life in a state of nonsleep. He would awaken, but first there would be a scream and a river of sweat that soaked right through the center of the mattress.

"Ahhh! Ahhh! . . . No!"

"It's okay, shsh, shsh, shsh," Sharon would say, grabbing Duncan around his waist and shoulders and trying to pull him back into bed.

It was never clear to Sharon—or to Duncan, for that matter—whether he was having actual nightmares. He never remembered anything, and whatever foggy, vanishing story line lingered in his head the morning after was not something he recognized as his own. The bad dreams, like everything else about his life, had already been decided for him. They had been preselected, like the menu in *TV Guide*. The fact that he didn't know what they were, or what they may have meant, or whether they depicted anything real, didn't matter. He may have actually had nothing to fear from them. But he was required to receive them, nonetheless, because they were commanded to come. Duncan was powerless to do anything other than play the good host and patiently sit through to the end.

Duncan and Sharon filed joint tax returns, but their dreams would forever remain separate. Her tranquil, nocturnal memories were filled with visions of vegetable gardens, nature trails, and blue forests; his unsettled, spasmodic sleep was haunted by the open ditches and smoking chimneys of a Europe that he had neither visited nor known. In their dreams they had always lived apart; now they were separated in life, as well.

Actually, it was more than just separation. It was abandonment, then exile. How was she supposed to explain this to herself? Knowing what she knew about him and the demons that trailed him, how could she do this? She had married a man who had come from a place of total brokenness. And he had joined with her in the hope of defeating the dire omens of his parents, of restoring a lost world, and in the process, rebuilding one for himself. What he wanted most of all was to find sanctuary, something that would always be there. And now that had been taken, too; the nuclear family was gone—atomized, nuked, vanished so soon after the roots of a new family tree had taken hold.

But what could Sharon do? She no longer loved Duncan. Bitter words, but in the modern world, the only ones that mattered. Her happiness would come first; their vows, his woes, ultimately counted for less. Larry Breitbart was right: "till death do us part," "in sickness and in health," "for richer or for poorer" were fatuous phrases repeated by millions with two fingers crossed behind their backs. They were mechanical but unfelt slogans, like the pledge of allegiance, uttered casually in advance of an even less earnest "I do."

For Sharon, what had once been an exotic and attractive feature of Duncan's life had now become a revolting turnoff, a legacy that no longer appealed to her. But in her own disgust, and under the pretense of overprotection, she was prepared to deprive her daughter of not only the legacy, but also the father who came with it.

Now standing in the kitchen, she recalled their conversation from the night before.

"I'm coming for a visit," he announced. "I have something important to tell you. I'll see you tomorrow."

She was afraid of him, not because he was ever physically abusive, but because he was emotionally overwhelming. Her breath tightened, and her stomach dropped.

"What is it about?" she asked. "Maybe we can do it in a few weeks. I think we all need some time to prepare."

"Come on . . . prepare for what? I haven't seen my daughter in several months. And I'm leaving the country in a couple of days."

"Where are you going?"

"I don't want to talk about it over the phone. I'll be there in the morning."

"Should we meet you at the train?"

"No, I'll come right to the house."

Where was he going, Sharon wondered? She forgot to put down the receiver, and the phone reminded her by squawking like an inhaling trumpet. Almost a year earlier, when Duncan left for New York, she and Milan had gone to Union Station to see him off. Milan fidgeted on a bench with a naked doll sitting beside her as her parents said goodbye.

"Why are you even taking the train?" Sharon asked while they waited for the Amtrak Northeast Corridor line to pull into track 18. "You hate trains. Why not the shuttle?"

"You've exiled me to New York, so I'm going to start out fresh, try out new things," Duncan said. "Maybe this will be a whole new way to see the world."

"On a train?"

"Without the Holocaust lens. Maybe then you'll take me back."

Sharon frowned, as if to say that one train ride—even if it brought clearer vision—wasn't going to be nearly enough.

Duncan dropped a carry-on bag, which grazed his heel, and said, "I don't understand. How can you do this to us? How can you do this to Milan?"

"I'm not going over it again . . . not here."

"Why can't we go over it here? This is the perfect spot. Look where we're standing. It's a train station. And we're Jews. This is where all the grief begins for our people. If trains were invented when the Bible was written, Job would have been sitting on a train, and train tracks would have run right through the Red Sea. My daughter is soon going to be taken out of my arms. The only difference is that instead of a Nazi taking my child, it's going to be my wife."

"That's sick and unfair, Duncan," Sharon retorted, squaring around to check on Milan. "These are modern trains, not cattle cars. And I'm not a Nazi, although you'd never know the difference because you're a one-man walking *yohrzeit;* the flame never goes out."

"You don't know the first thing about the Holocaust," Duncan snapped back. "The fact that we're here, saying goodbye, is proof of it. This shouldn't happen to me and my daughter. This family has seen enough separation for one century. Even Yankee and Mila would have been shocked by this; it's a good thing they're dead. How can you lose a family this way?"

"It's not that simple," Sharon said.

"Sadness is not grounds for divorce."

"Who said anything about a divorce? I just need some space . . ."

"I'll give you your space. I'll even move to New York, or to outer space—if that's what it takes to get my family back. But while I'm honoring what you need, do you have any idea how big a hole there is inside me now?"

"I didn't put it there, Duncan."

"Maybe not. But you pulled off the unthinkable: you made it larger."

"I understand why you feel that way, but . . ."

Duncan was now screaming. "Stop making me feel like this is only about me! Like I'm some contaminated person. Like there is a genetic defect in the Katz DNA. I'm a good husband and father . . ."

"You are . . . but *there,*" she said, pointing right back at him.

"What?"

"There it is. That look . . . ," Sharon said, shrinking backward. "It's like you're possessed. Your eyes are burning with rage. It's the look of the Six Million in one fragile, but very frightening, face."

Milan hopped off the bench and ran toward her father, leaping into his arms.

"That a girl," Duncan said, drawing her body against his chest, tucking her head underneath his jaw. Her arms reached around his neck. Duncan then pressed his face up close to his daughter's. Their noses touched. For a moment they shared the same air; their breaths warmed the small corner of space between them. He stared intensely into her eyes.

"Tatty, what?" she asked; it was the name she always called him.

Duncan didn't speak. He just continued to inhale the face and eyes—so identical to his own—of his child, like totem poles of the same family leaning up against one another. Perhaps the longer he looked the more it would be impossible for her to forget him. Memory was the only anchor that he knew, all that he could rely on. Maybe it would work for Milan, as well. By staring long enough, maybe he could burn his presence into Milan—an absent father, and yet known. The separation would no doubt kill him, but perhaps there was a way for him to survive in some other form—inside his daughter, the selfish wish of every parent.

Milan squeezed her thighs into her father's hips, and she tightened the hug around his neck. Finally, she placed her hands on Duncan's temples and caressed his face, like her mother used to do, holding his soul while helping him go to sleep. Duncan cried into his daughter's tiny hands.

"We'll see you soon, Tatty. You won't go away for long. You said you'll be back, right?"

Recovering slightly, he said, "Make sure Mommy sings our song to you when you go to sleep." Duncan turned to Sharon and said, "If you need me, all you have to do is call New York and . . ."

"I know, code word: 'keller.' We've been rehearsing for years. Let's hope it never comes to that. I'd rather just say 'Duncan.' "

The New Englander seemed to groan as it turned the final bend and pulled into Union Station on track 18. A loud whistle blew, sounding more like a frightened cry, as the train came to a stop. Yuppies wearing designer suits and swinging buttery leather attaché cases boarded and exited, purposefully trading places on the train. Baltimore, Philadelphia, New York, and Boston would be the next stops. But these passengers all knew where they were going. They were holding tickets for either a coach or club car with windows and plenty of ventilated air. Duncan, however, imagined himself on a different kind of journey.

Handing Milan to his wife Duncan stepped into the train. He took a seat by a window and held his arm out to his daughter, but he couldn't reach her. Milan waved back, and as the New Englander pulled out, heading north and east, Duncan watched his family shrink before him while his mind framed the image—the dark clothes, the gray colors, the calamitous fear, the foreboding of nightmares to come—as if it were all happening in Warsaw in 1941.

·   ·   ·

TYING HER WRISTS down accomplished nothing. When the nightmares came, she was no longer a cancer patient, but rather a warrior who refused to be confined.

"AHH! ISAAC! KELLER! THE NUMBERS! THE NUMBERS! . . ."

The leather straps broke once again. Would the orderlies ever learn? Next time try steel. Judy Stokes, the night nurse, with her own pained face, reached over to comfort her patient. But a human touch was not going to be enough this time. Judy accelerated the slow drip of morphine that traveled down from hanging tubes and into Mila's veins.

"Easy, baby," Judy said, applying a cold washcloth to Mila's drenched forehead. "It was just another one of those nasty nightmares."

"I am alive?" Mila asked.

"Oh yeah, you're a battler, all right," the nurse said with admiration. "There's still more fight in you."

"Lucky me." After a sip of water, Mila asked, "Please, a cigarette."

"No way, Mila," Judy replied. "They're going to fire me. How many cigarettes have I given these past few months?"

"You've been good to me," Mila conceded quietly. "But it's the middle of the night. What harm can it do? Nobody will know, and what difference is more cancer going to make? I already know the risks of smoking. The doctor told me this is what is now killing me. But he's wrong. It was the chimneys that killed me, not the chimney smoking."

Judy walked over to the window where a hot, creamy white moon illuminated the Miami night sky. She searched for her purse on the windowsill. It was alligator skin, laid flat, the snout snapped shut. Mila was awake, coherent but needing to connect to an old habit. Thoughtfully, but also guardedly, the nurse removed a cigarette from her bag and brought it over to the bed.

"Just one," Judy warned, holding the cigarette back. "Do you hear me?"

"You are an angel."

"Don't bullshit me. I got kids to support. I need this job."

Despite the protest, she wasn't overly concerned about putting her job in jeopardy. She, Louise, and Cynthia were too caught up in Mila's confessions to worry much about anything else. Officially, they were now addicts: totally high and wasted on concentration-camp gas and crematorium vapors. Yet another cigarette was more than worth the risk—to both patient and nurse—if Mila truly needed it, and if it brought out more of the tale.

Before Mila, not one of these nurses had ever heard of Auschwitz or Birkenau. And why should they have? Even most American Jews thought of camps only as places to send children during the summer. But now, weeks into her care, the nurses would forever know the words. It was more than just that death had occurred there. It was, at least for their patient, the place where life became twisted and deviant. After liberation, from that point forward, every decision Mila made was shadowed by Auschwitz.

At the age of fifteen, Mila had been taken from the Warsaw Ghetto and brought to Birkenau. Her parents were sent to Treblinka, and she never saw them again. One died from starvation; the other gas. Once the privileged child of a prosperous Jewish family, she became almost overnight an orphan and—after her experience in the ghetto and the camp—a seasoned scavenger. Survival came to her naturally; the same fingers that once tapped piano keys now learned the sleight of a grabbing hand. She made the right allies in the camp, avoided the harshest work detail, got hold of essential provisions, made her cheeks appear more robust with contraband rouge, enabling her to pass through selections and live another day.

She returned home knowing that no other member of her family had survived. A new set of drastic measures was necessary. She would now live without moderation. Not quite seventeen years old, she began to smoke and drink heavily, as if she were both Lotte Lenya and Marlene Dietrich. She spent many nights in makeshift Polish night-clubs, listening to American jazz, dancing to American bebop and swing, seduced by life in whatever imperfect form the world after Auschwitz could offer.

And there were many men. Their names were unimportant. So were their pasts, which had been obliterated anyway. Only the syntax on the forearms was unerasable. They could look to no one but to each other, and when they looked at each other, they knew that nothing further had to be said. Nobody else was waiting, and their confiscated homes did not expect their return, nor would such home-comings have been welcome by those who now occupied them.

What they shared in common was the poisonous knowledge of the camps, and that was more than enough. All other dating rituals were superfluous. Conversation was itself a waste of time; silence was the most reliable language of all. Foreplay was foolish. Cheap thrills were precious. Attractions had little to do with love. Mila's circle fucked wildly, with total abandon, and sometimes silently with orgasms of anguish, mournful and true.

Mila's hair had barely grown in. It would also take years for her period to return. Or so she thought. Mila had never learned much about menstruation. Puberty had been placed in a deep freezer. There were other matters of far more consequence that had to come first. As a child of the Warsaw Ghetto and then Birkenau, she stepped back into the free but shell-shocked world without a basic working knowledge of her own body. Biology seemed to work despite the surrounding indignity. But suddenly she was a young woman who had never had a chance to be a teenager. Within a few months she had made up for lost time, sacrificing nothing to memory-numbing pleasure.

What difference would one more smoke make? Her nurse spun the grooved wheel on the silver lighter, which put an orange flame on the tip of Mila's cigarette. A cloud of smoke drifted into the soft blue light of the room.

"Don't forget to exhale," the nurse reminded her patient.

Mila took a drag and caressed the guardrail on the bed. "The smoke or my story? Which do you want out? I should tell you that the smoke never leaves me." Mila's eyes trailed off toward the window. She could see the mop tops of palm trees peeking in as if standing on tiptoes. "Did I tell you that even when he was an infant, Duncan favored his father more than me? He knew I didn't want him. A child knows when his mother is without love. I didn't want to be his mother. I was not able to be anybody's mother."

"You feel guilty about that, don't you?" Judy asked.

"No . . . the guilt is over the other one."

"Isaac?"

"Yes, Isaac. Poor little Isaac. He was such a frail baby. Very sickly. Duncan can take care of himself. Isaac," she said, and then sighed, followed by a faint cough, "only God knows what happened to him all these years. I asked Larry Breitbart to find out, but he told me that with the Communists, we will never know. The Iron Curtain covers more than just politics. It is also hiding my son."

"Why did you leave Isaac behind?"

"It is late. Let me enjoy my cigarette, my Lucky Strike."

"Please tell me. I want to know."

"*Ach*, I am only entertainment to you. Go see a movie, and leave me to die."

"You wanted to clear your conscience. You said that . . ."

"But what good will that do without forgiveness? You can't pardon me. You don't have the power, and you wouldn't do it if you knew the whole truth."

"Tell me about Isaac."

"You won't understand."

"Try."

"Do you know what a *pogrom* is?"

"No."

"It's when a mob of people kill Jews."

"Like a lynching."

"Yes, that is true—a big lynching, but for Jews only."

"So? What does that have to do with your son?"

"In 1946, in Poland, even after liberation, we had such a *pogrom*. It started in Kielce. So soon after the Nazis had killed three million Polish Jews, the Poles decided there were still too many Jews around."

With sad, sympathetic eyes, Judy reached for Mila's hand. "First a Holocaust . . . then a program." A few tears broke from Mila's eyes, and then simply taxied on her face. "In 1947, I was a young mother. My only education was Auschwitz. I had no family. I had nothing. I wanted more. I was trapped in Poland when the Nazis came. I wasn't going to have it happen to me again with the Russians. I had to leave the country—to save myself . . ."

"And Isaac?"

A cart carrying sanitized towels and toiletries rolled down the corridor. Quickly Mila threw the cigarette down beside her bed near

Judy's foot. The nurse knew the proper choreography and immediately stepped on the stem. She then waved her arms around madly to clear the smoke.

When it was silent again in the hallway, Mila continued. "What could I do? Poland was not a free country. Some time later they let Jews go, but not then. The only way to leave was to escape. And escape was not possible with an infant. It was too dangerous to try—even alone." She paused, waiting for some sign of sympathy. Judy offered none. Finally, Mila said, "Please, another cigarette."

Judy obliged, her tall frame—a black body uniformed in white—glided confidently across the room and over toward her purse. She unsnapped the latch and returned with what had become for Mila both nerve relaxer and truth serum.

"I had to leave him," Mila repeated, the second cigarette now lit and passed on to the patient like a torch. "I had no choice. There was nothing I could do." Glancing up at her nurse, she said, "I remembered what happened to the women in the camps who tried to hide their children."

"What happened to them?"

"The children were taken and killed, and sometimes the mothers, too. I wanted to live, and I wanted my son to live."

"But you weren't in the camp anymore?"

Mila hesitated; then she said, "You never leave the camp. I survived, but I am still there."

Judy seemed puzzled. "And so what happened to Isaac?"

"I left him."

"With who?"

"His father. He was a jeweler. We were not married."

"At least he had his father."

The patient stared at her nurse, her eyes unblinking in the darkness of the room, and asked, "But what kind of mother would do such a thing?"

"We have young girls in Liberty City who do it all the time. Unwanted teenage pregnancies. The newborns go to foster homes, hospitals, grandmothers, and sometimes . . . you know, garbage dumps, empty stairwells, even somebody's front door. You had a lot more reason to be selfish than any of them have."

"You aren't making me feel better by telling me that I am not alone. Nothing will fix my sins."

"We all sin, Mila."

"Yes, but I didn't finish telling you about Isaac. What I did . . ." Sighing, Mila added, "Yes, we all sin, but mine is what they mean by the original."

Chapter Eleven

C HILDREN WITHOUT SIBLINGS learn to live a certain way. They don't have to take others into account. Sharing is not an important part of their household experiences. The cookies and toys are all theirs—provided there are cookies and toys. But what happens later in life when they find out they are not alone? That there was a brother or sister all the time, living somewhere else, with other people?

That said, Duncan still saw no reason to change simply because he had been spooked by the news of a phantom brother. If anything, now was the time to carry on as usual.

Duncan had spent five days a week for more than half a lifetime pushing weights up and down. With the trip only a few days away, he feared what Poland would do to his body. For one thing, he couldn't imagine the country having a decent health club. What could Poland offer him physically, other than perhaps street fights and property repossessions?

Although it was still winter in Manhattan, the day was warm and pleasant. The western light of the afternoon gave a golden cast to those endless rows of brownstones. Duncan and Orlando decided to walk down Columbus Avenue on their way to the gym. Their sunglasses were drawn over their eyes, their unbuttoned coats flapped in the wind. Duncan remained quiet throughout most of the walk. Orlando assumed that his friend, and training partner, was preparing himself mentally for either the workout or the trip, and didn't want to be disturbed. They walked without exchanging a word.

"I usually don't like to go outside on weekends," Duncan said.

"Why not?"

"That's when the families come out, like little parades up and down Columbus and Broadway. Mothers, fathers, kids—too painful to watch."

Near Lincoln Square, parked on a side street beside the Sony Theater, was a large, late-model black Mercedes with a "For Sale" sign posted on the windshield.

"You don't see that very often in New York," Orlando commented. "A new Mercedes parked at a meter like that."

Duncan didn't respond, but nodded in agreement.

"Sweet and shiny," Orlando said. "Ah, the Germans. They made the best philosophers, and they still make the best automobiles."

When they reached the car, Orlando peered into the driver's side, admiring the dashboard and the leather appointments. Duncan cupped his hand around the outside rearview mirror, and with one powerful yank, tore off the contraption as if it were a piece of fruit.

"Duncan, what the fuck are you doing?" Orlando straightened himself quickly.

But Duncan wasn't through. He stepped back from the car, and obviously recalling some episode from his childhood mastery of martial arts, wheeled his leg around like a whip and thrust it into the driver's door, crushing the steel as if it were no more durable than papier-mâché.

"We're not working legs today," Orlando said.

Duncan leaped onto the front hood, then raised himself up into the air one more time, crashing down on the front end with all the buoyancy of a wrecking ball.

"You planning on buying this car?" Orlando asked. "Because this is a little more than kicking around the tires."

Orlando made a mistake in mentioning the tires.

Before too long, the Mercedes had been reduced to a Schwinn.

"Now go sell it," Duncan sneered, his voice concealed within an inflamed breath.

Two admiring young women on furlough from New Jersey threw Duncan a few flirty smiles as he returned to the pavement.

"Rage is sexy, don't you think?" one of them asked the other.

"Yes . . . but I think he's way past rage," the other observed.

Orlando wasn't all that surprised by Duncan's manic response to what for many people would have simply been an alluring symbol of German wealth and excellence. Put simply, Duncan was not impressed by German engineering. Yes, they made great cars, but their mechanical, cold-blooded genius was more present in their ovens. With all due disrespect to the German philosophers whom Orlando revered and taught to his undergraduates at Columbia, Duncan believed that the great ideas and inventions of the German people would forever be overshadowed by the smoke stacks and Red Sea skies, the train tracks and human fossil remains of unburied Eastern Europe. The truest memory of the Master Race. For him, the grotesque landmarks of death were far more emblematic of Teutonic taste and virtue than was all the Gothic architecture of Dresden, Munich, Heidelberg combined. Germany was a nation rightfully stuck with a stigma, like Jews indelibly scarred by the knowledge of once having been an endangered species.

The Mercedes couldn't help getting into an accident with Duncan. His rage was magnetized for such moments. A collision was inevitable.

But Orlando realized that it was even more complicated than that. Being Duncan's training partner was hard work, but being his friend was no less exhausting. No matter what the circumstances, there were no slow speeds or gentle cycles to Duncan's reactions. He was easily disappointed, and from there it was only a small step to feeling betrayed. And although his body was thick, his skin was not. He wounded without resistance, as if his flesh was far too exposed to human pain to defend itself properly.

The incident with the car was frankly beside the point. Over time Orlando had witnessed many such aspects of Duncan's crazed *weltanschauung*. Just last summer they were headed uptown on the east side of Broadway. Duncan stopped on the sidewalk near a pasta restaurant that offered outside table service. He stared strategically at the busboy station, which was up against the corner wall of the building. When no one was watching, he walked over to a pileup of dirty dishes and uneaten food and grabbed a few pieces of bread.

"Do you want some?" he asked Orlando.

"It's from someone else's plate!" Orlando replied. "They got rid of it already."

"So what? It's going to go to waste if we don't eat it."

"Come on, I'll buy you fresh bread at Columbus Bakery."

But Duncan didn't want any other bread. What he had in his hand was just fine. Orlando slithered away as Duncan chewed savagely a few steps behind.

That's why, after the bodywork with the Mercedes, Orlando couldn't help himself when he said, "You know, I've been thinking about this Poland trip."

"So have I," Duncan said. "Lots."

"Maybe I should come with you. What do you say?"

Surprised, Duncan replied, "Why would you want to come?"

"Because I'm a patriotic American citizen of Cuban descent. I'm afraid if I allow you to go alone, you might set off an international incident. I owe it to my country."

Duncan laughed.

"I'm not kidding," Orlando continued. "I think you should be turned back at the border. Your picture should be up at all checkpoints. It's obvious to me that if you go, you need an escort. No good can come of you being a tourist in Poland. The whole idea is unkosher. The only thing I can imagine being worse is you in Germany . . ."

"As a matter of fact, I'm flying into Germany," Duncan interrupted. "I'm renting a car in East Berlin, and I'm going to drive through the East German border right into Poland."

"God help us all—a Jewish kamikaze. I can set my watch and listen for the explosion across the Atlantic."

Just then a group of three undersized young men, all wearing yarmulkes, sidelocks, and *tzitzits* dropping from underneath their shirts, approached Duncan.

"Excuse me," one of them, heavyset with overactive sweat glands churning even in winter, said, "are you Duncan Katz?"

Duncan didn't answer.

One of the others, balding, his yarmulke having no ground to grip, added, "We saw you on the Molly Rubin program the other night. She is a Jewish traitor, but we like what you stand for."

"Who are you?" Orlando asked.

"We're speaking to Mr. Katz; mind your own business," the third one replied, wincing, unsure of his strength.

Orlando scoffed, but didn't respond.

"I'm sure Mr. Katz knows who we are," said the one who spoke first, showing himself to be the leader of the gang.

"I have no idea who you are," Duncan finally said. "What do you want?"

"We're members of the Jewish Defense League. We can use a man like you. We hear that Rabbi Meir Kahane was trying to recruit you back in the seventies."

"That man was a lunatic," Duncan said.

"Oh, and you're well adjusted?" Orlando blurted out.

The three men of the JDL would forgive Duncan Katz for the insult to their martyred hero, mostly because they needed him—all of him, his muscle, his passion, his public profile, his *goyishe* good looks, and most significantly, his insanity.

"We have meetings every week in Brooklyn, on Saturday after Shabbat," the third one said. "We go to a kosher pizza shop in Borough Park and discuss strategy—you know, which anti-Semites we should strike. Why don't you join us this week?"

"Please get away from me. I work alone," Duncan said, pushing all three aside as if they were the connecting wings of a revolving door.

Duncan hastily, and silently, continued on. A few blocks later he stopped, turned to Orlando, and said, "And by the way, you're *not* coming with me. Now let's go up and train."

A similar caution about going to Poland was issued by Howard Minskoff. Minskoff had invited Duncan over to his home, a red brick, four-story landmark building on West Twelfth Street. It had a backyard with a covered gazebo in the shape of an open parachute, a long, interior spiral staircase, and expensive artwork that wallpapered almost every wall.

"Duncan, I need a favor," Howard began, as they sat around a titanium table, having lunch in Minskoff's entertainment room. Duncan had just finished admiring a large painting by Anselm Kiefer. The canvas competed for space with several big-screen TVs.

"What is it?" Duncan replied.

"Can you do some scouting for me while you're over there in Poland?"

"Scouting for what?"

"Models."

"You have to be kidding."

"No, I'm serious."

"I'm going over there to see my brother."

"So? You won't have time for other things? Some of my best girls have come from Eastern Europe. Don't worry about their smiles. East Europeans all have bad teeth. We can fix that here. Just make sure they're tall and sensational. You know the look, like Monica, only younger."

Duncan returned his grilled chicken sandwich back onto his plate, wiped his mouth with a black Zorro mask of a napkin, and said, "I'm not scouting for you."

"Look, it's not just about scouting. I have to confess: I'm a little worried about this trip you're going on."

"I know, the free world as we know it will never be the same," Duncan said. He noticed that the salt and pepper shakers on the table doubled as remote-control switches.

"I'll tell you what, let me make it financially rewarding. Call it an inducement. I'll give you a percentage of the first-year bookings of every girl you find—anything to keep you out of trouble."

Howard then rang for his housekeeper to bring in the desserts.

"I have important work to do in Poland, Howard. I'm not going there to check out Eastern bloc babes."

"What's so important over there? You'll find your brother, and you'll bring him back. Over and done with. You should be there for only a couple of days, tops. But I don't trust you. You're planning something, aren't you? You'll rope your brother into hunting down Nazis and Poles. The two of you will be chasing windmills, or better yet, watch-towers."

"My brother is a yoga teacher," Duncan said. "He's different from me."

"Good, maybe *he* knows some potential models. Fashion models love yoga."

"I'll mention it to him."

"Find your brother, make peace, and just come home," Howard said, raising a chilled bottle of beer into the air. "That's all I'm saying."

Before Duncan left New York, he said goodbye to those who would miss him the most. First there was Monica. When Duncan told her where he was going, she immediately asked, "Should I wait for you to come back, or are you still waiting for your wife?"

"What I'm waiting for isn't something that can be fixed, not even by my wife," he replied. "How much waiting can you stand?"

Monica didn't know. They made love one last time, neither of them certain whether the past few months were enough to sustain a wait on either side. Angry sex, forceful thrusts, choke-hold caresses, kisses more swallowing than tender—it was as if this final act of intimacy were fueled as much by resentment as passion.

It had already been a relationship founded mostly on not knowing—was there a wife? was Monica merely a distraction? was Duncan even alive? Duncan wanted his family back. If he couldn't have that, he wanted his brother near him. Where was Monica on this list? No better than a gym workout, she supposed. Duncan was emotionally elsewhere, and now he was taking himself physically out of the picture, as well. In the morning, with Duncan still asleep, she kissed him on the back and silently left his brownstone, imagining that for him there was now no longer a Monica, either.

And there was also Maloney. The stalking had continued for a full six months after Maloney's getaway on Second Avenue. Sometimes it happened every day; then Duncan would lie low for a few days to keep Maloney off guard. It was a cat-and-mouse situation, designed solely for psychological torture, in which the participants merely squared off against one another, as though neither cared much for victory. No checkmate, just a lot of checking and silent trash talking.

Duncan himself didn't know exactly what he was trying to accomplish by following Maloney around. He just wanted him to know that he was always near. But in some ways it was having the opposite effect of what he had intended. Maloney no longer feared him. Without the badge, Duncan had been reduced to a self-appointed chaperone.

On a recent early Sunday morning, Duncan had been leaning up against the sidewall of the Ukrainian Orthodox Church on Seventh Street, off Third Avenue. It was a large tan stone building with a wide archway entrance, turrets on the roof, and an attached school in the back. Duncan was dressed in his mohair coat, and on his feet were a pair of grease-black motorcycle jackboots. Sunday Mass had just ended. Maloney appeared, wearing a thick green coat that was more appropriate for survival in Siberia. He was the last to leave Mass that morning.

"Ah, I knew you would be here," Maloney said, craning his neck to the side of the building, knowing that Duncan was more likely to be lurking than waiting directly out front. "I was expecting you today."

"You were?"

"Yes, I am no longer surprised by your visits. It's like having the same dream every night. I come to depend on it. That's how I am starting to think about you."

"That's not my purpose. I'm looking to be your worst nightmare."

"That will never happen. You have too much competition. And sometimes life doesn't give us the choices we want."

"Now you're teaching me about life?" Duncan asked, angrily, as it began to snow.

"You could learn something about living, but . . . as you wish."

"I came here to tell you something, Malyshko."

"What is it?" Maloney replied, concerned that Duncan still had deportation on his mind. "There is nothing you can do to me . . ."

"It's not about you," Duncan interrupted. "It's about me."

"Are you not well?" Maloney asked with surprising concern.

"I am leaving the country for a few weeks. You'll have to do without me for a while. I assume you can handle it?"

"I will miss you," Maloney said relievedly, "but I think I can manage. Where are you going?"

"Poland."

"Why did I even bother to ask? Still obsessed with the war, I see."

"Not the war, the massacre."

Laughing, Maloney said, "You are still looking for people like me?"

"No, I have scaled down my practice to focus entirely on you."

"Then why are you leaving?"

"Because I know you'll still be here when I get back."

"You are so sure. I am old. I have no family. It is only you who cares that I still live."

"No, I just want to see you die in a certain way."

Flakes of gossamer-like snow were beginning to collect all over Maloney's head and body.

"And what then? How will that help either of us? Whatever is eating away at you will not be satisfied by my death—no matter how much pain I feel when it happens."

A priest dressed in a long, Darth Vader robe emerged from the building, smiled, and took Maloney's hand. He then noticed Duncan standing there. The priest squinted at him suspiciously. Duncan virtually growled in return.

"Is everything all right here, Feodor?" the priest asked.

Maloney answered back in Ukrainian, which drove Duncan nuts. Then Maloney added, "He is harmless, Father. Don't worry."

"What did you tell him?" Duncan asked, as the priest descended the steps.

"That you are a Jew. A child of the Holocaust. That you have come here to grieve for the dead."

"That's not funny!" Duncan fired back. "It is you and your kind who should be doing the grieving. Instead, all there is for you is amnesia."

"Even if I wanted to forget," Maloney said, "I couldn't."

"Is that an admission?"

"No, a fact."

"Is that why you come here, to atone?"

"What I share with Jesus Christ is my business."

"Not when it comes to killing Jews. Then it becomes my business . . ."

"You don't say? I didn't know they made you the savior of the Jewish people. My Ukrainian newspapers must have missed the story." Maloney laughed loudly, like an amused grandfather, shaking some of the snowflakes onto the stone steps. "So you think you have something in common with Christ? Maybe that explains the long hair. But I should tell you: the hair is not enough." Maloney surveyed his former tormentor as if Duncan was an abstract painting. "You are so hard on yourself. Now I know I chose the right gift for you."

"Gift?"

"Yes, I brought something for you. And I didn't even know you were leaving. Now we can call it a going-away present . . . for luck."

"Why would you want to wish me luck?"

"Because you need it." Then Maloney reached inside the deep, wide pocket of his polar-bear coat and removed a small light brown object. It was a wood carving. A trinket. A *pysanka*—a Ukrainian Easter egg. "For you," Maloney said, giving it to Duncan. "It is made by hand. Painted and decorated. Beautiful, no?"

Duncan removed one of his gloves and examined the egg, the

falling flakes making the world seem like a glass snow globe. He brought it closer to his face. The wood carving looked familiar. It was the same barbed-wire design that was tattooed on the young neo-Nazi Arthur Schweigert's arm.

"Is this a joke?"

"No, it is a gift."

"But there are barbed wires from a concentration camp all around this egg. I should kill you right here . . ."

"That's not barbed wire. I should know. Look here," Maloney said, pointing with a stumpy index finger. "It is a crown of thorns, what they made Christ wear at the Crucifixion."

Duncan held the oval in his palm, rolling it with his fingers. He felt both its smooth and uneven surface. A cold, stiff wind flushed the deserted street like a cresting river, scattering the snow like dust. Duncan placed the egg in his pocket and finally glanced up to acknowledge Maloney. But the guard had already gone.

SHARON ANSWERED THE knock on the Yuma house door knowing it was her husband. She was nervous, as though she were playing a tense game of "mystery date." Duncan had the keys to the house, but he must have assumed that they weren't his to use. Instead, he knocked on his own door, and then rested his head on the wood where his knuckles had just been. Sharon opened the door and, without first having taken in the sight of her husband, said, "Hey Dunkers, come on in."

She was wearing a long blue skirt with white polka dots and a black turtleneck. Her hair was pulled back; silver earrings in the shape of salmons dangled alongside her face.

Stiffly, awkwardly, Duncan hugged his wife. They had been separated for almost a year, and now he was unsure how tight she wanted to be held.

"How was the train?" she asked, stepping back bashfully with her head down when he finally let go. "I'm amazed that you're working this train phobia out of your system."

"One of many things I'm trying to change," he said.

"I'm proud of you, Duncan," she said, smiling.

"Where's Milan?"

"Upstairs. She's dying to see you."

"That's great to hear. I really miss her." Duncan removed his coat and threw it down on the sofa. He then strolled around the living room, his eyes first adjusting to, then aching for, his former home. "How's the house?"

"Still standing."

"And you?"

"Same as the house," she said defiantly. Duncan understood this to mean that she was actually standing sturdier than the house.

"And Milan?"

"She's fine."

"Does she ask about me?"

"Come on, Duncan, you're her father. She talks about you constantly."

"But she never sees me. What kind of a father is that? It's like I abandoned her . . ."

"She knows our separation was my decision, and that I've asked you to stay away."

"Where does she think I am?"

"On a secret mission," Sharon laughed. "Fighting dragons."

"Better than hunting Nazis."

"God forbid." Sharon stared into her husband's blue eyes. She wanted to lose herself somewhere in there, so she wouldn't have to face him or speak anymore. But Duncan wouldn't let her in. He wanted her to say something. Finally, she spoke. "So what's all the mystery about? Where are you going?"

"Po-land," Duncan announced, the two syllables divided with an exaggerated pause.

"Wow, I see why you couldn't tell me over the phone. This is serious. Does the pope know?"

"Why does everybody react this way? How do you know I'm not interested in just being a tourist? I own a camera, you know. Am I that predictable?"

"I think the word you mean is *dangerous*. Why are you going there?"

"I'll tell you why. But first, I think you should sit down. It's that kind of news."

"Fine." Sharon walked over and slid into a rocking chair that didn't rock but instead glided. The chair hadn't been used much since she stopped nursing Milan. "Okay, I'm ready."

"Brace yourself . . . I have a brother in Poland."

"Huh?"

"You heard it right; a real brother, *echt*, Sharon. Mila had a son after she got out of the camp. She abandoned him and never told anyone until just before she died. Larry Breitbart is the one who finally found him. That's pretty much all I know. I'm going over there in a few days to find out the rest, and maybe bring him back here."

Not a word followed. Although she never met Duncan's parents, Sharon always assumed that she had married into a booby-trapped family. She had escaped before stepping on any land mines or bomb-shells.

Duncan continued, "If he's for real, then he's the Holy Grail—the missing link. I have to connect myself to him somehow, dock into the mother ship. Who knows, when this is all over, maybe I'll come back a new person."

"He may be your brother, Duncan, but he's not the missing link. If anything is missing, it's not in Poland; it's in you."

SHARON AGREED THAT Duncan should spend as much time as he could with Milan. Duncan was eager for the chance, and had been thinking about it for days. Before he left New York, he had already planned out what they would do.

And so the day began at the zoo. Milan loved to watch the panda bears, but like her father, she had trouble with the sight of entrap-ment. Cages began to look like double mirrors.

"Let's go, Tatty," Milan finally said. "I think the animals want to be outside. They look sad. Maybe one day we can free them."

"You're right, Milan," Duncan said, his hand cradling the back of his daughter's head. "We'll come back one day with tanks."

In the afternoon they went to a local park. Milan, her blond curls flapping underneath a blue Yankees cap, bravely coasted down the big slide. And on the swing, she rocketed into orbit with each of her father's determined launchings.

"Higher!" she said.

"Very proud of you, Milany babes. No fear, just like your grand-mother."

Sharon had asked Duncan to take Milan for a haircut in George-town. But he wanted to forget that particular errand. In truth, he wished that Milan's hair would grow out long, like his own. Yet he did what Sharon had asked. But before leaving the salon, he scooped up a clutch of Milan's curls from the floor and shoved it inside his pocket.

The day ended with a visit to the Holocaust Memorial Museum. Not surprisingly, even though she was only five years old, this was not Milan's first visit. She had been to the place at its inauguration, sleeping in her stroller while her father, an honorary guest, sat and seethed. For the Katzes, the brick foundational wall—a remnant from some concentration camp—was as holy as any wailing edifice in Je-rusalem.

"Your mommy and Tatty were here, right?" Milan asked, her tiny hand secure in Duncan's tight grip. He was always ambivalent about letting her in on the family tragedy. Perhaps the legacy, like a jumping gene, might charitably skip a generation. Leave Milan alone. Pick on someone else's child. But if she wasn't going to know, who would? And could he prevent her from finding out simply by not telling her? She would know anyway, just like he did, despite the barricading codes, the clouded smoke signals, and the toxic silences. He brought Milan to the museum, but always held her close, not wanting to lose her. She had to be reassured—and he had to reassure himself—that she wouldn't slip through his hand.

"No, they were in real concentration camps," Duncan answered. "This is only a museum."

"Mommy says you're going away again. And it's far."

"But it's also home. It's where your grandmother once lived when she was your age. And there's a surprise waiting for me there. And for you, too."

Father and daughter passed through a cattle car, and then simul-taneously tilted their heads at an exhibit about Mengele's genetic ex-periments.

"A surprise? Is it a present?"

"Maybe." Duncan bent down on one knee and held Milan's face in his hands. "Tatty is going on an adventure to find his brother. You have an uncle, Milan. He lives in Poland. Tatty is going to bring him here, if he'll come. We have more family. Isn't that great?"

Milan hesitated and then said, "What's his name?"

"Isaac."

"Uncle Isaac?"

"Yeah, Uncle Isaac."

"Is he like you?"

"I don't know. I never met him before."

"I hope he's like you, Tatty." She thought about this uncle, and his brother, her father, and wondered how it was even possible that they didn't know each other. "Tatty, one day am I going to find a brother?"

"No, Milan, if you have a brother or a sister, you'll know about it. The world is different now. There aren't any bad people who keep families away from each other."

"I want a brother, or maybe a sister."

"I know. You should have one."

That night, before returning to New York, Duncan put Milan down to sleep. There was a time, when he still lived in the Yuma house, that giving his daughter a bath and then putting her to bed was the highlight of his day. Like all parents, he would reflect on his own childhood and hope that the same sins would not be repeated. Had Mila wished the same for him?

"Sweet dreams," he would say, thinking of his own nightmares.

"Pleasant thoughts," he would say, having so few of his own.

"Mommy and Tatty will always be right here, in the next room," he would say. But now that was no longer true. And what good had it done him to have his parents right next door?

Maybe the difference between Milan's childhood and his own was that he sang to her. Softly and tenderly, he would sing the chorus of "Someone to Watch over Me." It never failed to close her eyes and launch her off into a sound sleep. And he would continue singing the bars for some time after, just to make sure that her sleep was deep, inviolate, and filled with dreams worth remembering. When it came time for the final verse, he would repeat one line—the title of the song itself—over and over again, more softly and with even more tenderness, as if the lullaby for his daughter had become a broken record.

"Someone to watch over me . . ."
"Someone to watch over me . . ."
"Someone to watch over me . . ."

SOMEWHERE IN A small, cold-water flat in the center of Warsaw, a short, Buddha-like man wearing a skullcap sat in his familiar lotus position on a gray hooked rug of Brillo-pad appearance and texture. Despite the winter weather, his feet were bare, while his hands rested on his knees with the thumb and center finger of each hand touching lightly. His eyes were closed, and his breath was steady and full. Every so often he would chant, quietly, as mantra: "one-oh-one-six-eight-two, one-oh-one-six-eight-two, one-oh-one-six-eight-two . . ."

But in his mind, he was transporting himself elsewhere, to a blissful state of consciousness where he was no longer just the caretaker of the Warsaw Jewish Cemetery, or Poland's most sought-after yoga master and spiritual mystic. He had achieved a transcendent peace, a spiritually safe place of his own making. At moments like these, he was neither a half brother, nor a longed-for uncle, nor even a bastard and abandoned son.

$\mathcal{C}$hapter Twelve

*T*HEY OFFERED HER a ride in the wheelchair, but she refused.
"I never liked public transportation," Mila said. "I'm still
alive, so let me walk."

The morning was over, and the shifts were changing. Sentry duty
in a death ward. The nurses were like guards, except that Mila trusted
them, uniforms and all. Perhaps it was because they knew what Mila
needed, and they wanted her to have it.

"Why don't we all go down to the entertainment room?" Cynthia
asked enthusiastically. "They play cards down there. How about it,
Mila?"

Mila didn't respond.

"Now that's a fine idea," Louise said. Only moments earlier she had
gone into the bathroom and stripped herself of her uniform. "We
should have thought of this before."

"We've been too busy listening to Mila's story," Cynthia said.

"It's not your fault," Mila said. "I have much to tell. And I'm not
finished, not by a long shot. The worst is still yet to come."

Louise and Cynthia stared in unison. Should they have been intimidated or tantalized by what Mila had just said? There was a limit
to their stamina, and how much more they could stomach. Maybe it
was time to call in reinforcements, a fresh troop of round-the-clock
nurses who could relieve them of the custodial care that Mila's saga
required.

"You've been telling us how great you are with cards," Louise said.

"And all those bookies and cardsharks have been in and out of
here treating you as some kind of queen," Cynthia added. "Asking you

for tips, trying out card combinations. They say you're a Miami gambling legend. You must have been something, girl."

"Well, I don't know about that . . . ," Mila blushed. "They are my friends and I am dying. I'm sure they are just trying to be nice."

"What do you say we all go down there, and you can show us what you got?" Louise asked.

"But you are already finished with your shift," Mila said to Louise. "You should go home."

"The soaps can wait, honey," Louise said. "Don't worry, I won't be charging Mr. Breitbart for my time."

"I'm not worried. Larry has *gelt,* and gambling is still his bread and butter. He would be happy to know that you took an interest in his line of work."

"Okay, so let's go then," Cynthia said cheerfully.

Even though she had never backed down from a challenge before, Mila said, "I'm officially retired; I'll stay here." But then either her bettor's instincts or bedridden boredom took over, and while her nurses looked at her pleadingly, she reconsidered their proposal. "Well . . . I suppose we could go see what kind of action is down there. Maybe it could be interesting."

With each nurse taking one arm and reaching around her back, then hoisting her forward, Mila was lifted out of her bed. By now, her bones were brittle and largely exposed through the gauzy scrim of human flesh that was all that prevented her from becoming a skeleton. But the nurses were loving and extracautious with her. Soon Mila was dressed in her blue robe and beige sandals, the special ones with the red rose on the toe. The nurses combed what was left of her silver-streaked hair. And, as she had insisted, her face received several dabs of blush, along with a few uneven smears of bright red lipstick. The makeup only exaggerated all that was lacking in her gaunt face. She appeared like a ghost dressed up for the Grand Guignol.

All three walked to the elevator slowly. Mila was self-conscious about her progress. Everything was now nearly impossible to do. Eating. Walking. Sleeping. Breathing. Urinating. Defecating. Each in its own way was as challenging as a moon voyage. As a teenager in the camps, she had been reduced to a near cadaver, but a resourceful and vigorous one. Now she was no longer hopeful that defiance on such a grand scale was possible a second time. Making it to the elevator and then down to the recreation room, and after a few rounds of poker, making it back to her private room, seemed like an incredibly bold statement.

What's more, it didn't start out as one of Mila's better days. Several vomiting episodes had already marred the morning. Earlier Judy tried to pacify Mila's nightmares, but the demons would show no mercy. Mila was not going to get the night off.

Watching the slow countdown of blinking numbers in the elevator, they all hoped that the final eight hours of the day would bring Mila some peace, whether it came from cards, God, or just plain luck. Once out of the elevator, they reached the door to the entertainment room. Mila stopped suddenly and held on tight to her nurses' arms, as though pulling on reins.

"Wait," Mila said.

"Don't be nervous," Cynthia said.

"I'm not nervous," Mila responded, sounding insulted. "I just want to see who's in there first."

"You mean, scope it out?" Louise asked.

"Of course," Mila replied. "Who would play a game without knowing the competition?"

The nurses hadn't considered that before.

"So, do you know any of these people?" Mila asked.

The two nurses peeked inside the room. There were three round tables and two square ones. One of the round tables was encircled by card players. A square table seemed to be reserved for mah-jongg. At another square table several patients feebly collaborated on a jigsaw puzzle. The picture on the box showed an ocean vista: sailboats inflated by wind, and blue marlins diving out of the water, pricking the air. All they had put together so far was a shadow of sky there, a glimpse of water here, a piece of a sail completely rudderless from a boat, and a scale or two of a fin. On the opposite side of the room, two patients were tapping Ping-Pong balls on a green, white-lined, regulation-sized table. Against a wall by the window, facing the bay, stood a brown, upright piano that no one seemed interested in playing.

"I know some of the people playing cards," Cynthia said.

"So do I," Louise joined in.

"Is anyone terminal?" Mila asked.

"What do you mean?" Cynthia wondered.

"You know, like me . . . about to die any second," Mila replied.

The nurses stuck their heads in the room again.

"The guy over there just had his gallbladder removed," Cynthia said. "I know because he's on your floor. I've seen his chart."

"The two men over there had heart attacks," Louise said. "But they're fine."

Pointing to a teenager who was also sitting at the card table, Cynthia said, "The kid over there lost an arm in a waterskiing accident. The propeller on the motor got tangled up in the line and sliced his forearm off below the elbow. They couldn't save it."

"How horrible," Mila said, her eyes like a frozen computer screen.

"I don't know any of the women playing mah-jongg, or the people with the puzzle, or the two at the Ping-Pong table," Louise said apologetically.

"I don't play mah-jongg or Ping-Pong," Mila said. "And puzzles I don't waste my time with." She pointed to the remaining two men at the card table. "And who are they?"

"Orderlies." Cynthia said. "They must be on their break."

"Fine," Mila said, "now let's go over and take some money from these people. A person who's dying I won't take advantage of, but this bunch is fair game. But I will remember to be gentle with the boy."

"Wait a second," Cynthia said, just as Mila trundled into the recreation room, "I don't think they're playing for real money . . ."

"We'll raise the stakes," Mila replied, leaving her nurses to shrug at each other.

Mila made it over to the table just as a hand had ended. She steadied herself by leaning against the back of a vacant chair. The young amputee gathered his chips with his right arm and began stacking them methodically as though he were building a fortress.

"Do you have room for another player?" Mila asked.

"Depends on who it is," the teenager said, barely glancing up as he awkwardly dealt out another hand.

"Me."

"You play poker, lady?" said one of the orderlies, a middle-aged black man with wide, open pores on his face, as he lifted up the first card of his hand.

"I can learn," Mila answered in a thick Polish accent that accentuated the naive sound of her response. "How hard can it be?"

The nurses giggled from the corner.

One of the cardiac patients—overweight and dying for a cigarette and a brisket sandwich—was already disgusted by the two cards dealt to him. "Maybe you can change my luck. What's your name?"

"Mila Katz."

"Have a seat, Millie," said the other cardiac patient, a man so chinless that his mouth could have been mistaken for a hole in his neck.

"You might as well," said the other orderly. "The kid here is whipping our ass."

"Okay, then deal me in," Mila said. "That's how they say it, right?" she added shyly.

The men at the table now looked at one another suspiciously, wondering perhaps if it would have been better to keep this a private game.

As she closed the door to the apartment, a hall light flickered in lockstep with her indecision. She wanted to run away, but she was stilled by the sounds that came from inside. Finally, she let go of the knob, hurriedly walked down the two flights of stairs, passed underneath a rusty, triangular street lamp, and then disappeared into the darkness. A black shawl was wrapped around her head. She was carrying a brown leather satchel, weathered and faded, but stuffed with what she needed to make this journey.

From behind her she could hear the wrenching cries of her infant son. He was lying in his crib. Mila had called Keller Borowski, who was working late at his shop, and told him that she needed him immediately, that there was an emergency with the baby. Keller was a good and decent man. Yes, he drank too much, but why shouldn't he? And yes, he was no genius, but the geniuses had all died in the camps, and what good did it do to be smart, anyway? It was also true that he was a failure in business, but wasn't surviving the only business that mattered? He had asked Mila several times to marry him, but she refused.

"I don't need to be made an honest woman," she reasoned. "The world cares little for such things."

Isaac was an accident. And no good could come from a marriage that begins with an accident. Yet, being Isaac's father was somehow enough for Keller. Regardless of his own future, he had left irrefutable evidence of himself that his life mattered, that he would live on in some way. The Nazis had tried to end the Borowski line, but his seed broke through. Now Mila was leaving him with far more evidence than he bargained for—the full responsibility for raising their son.

When he arrived to the sounds of Isaac's screaming, he would see the note that she had left. In it she explained what she had done—everything she had done—and where she was going, and the wishes and hopes that she had for them in this forsaken Poland.

Leaving an infant alone in a house was child abuse, even under the desperate circumstances of postwar Poland, a country in shambles, where the standards of decency and civility had only recently been rewritten by the Nazis. But earlier in the day Mila had done something to her son that was far more heinous, something for which he could never again be soothed. The abandonment was only a cruel coda to the sinful act that preceded it.

Mila had stopped at the corner of Twarda Street to gather herself. She knew that if she succeeded, she would never see Isaac, or these streets, or this or any other neighborhood of Warsaw again. Getting out of Warsaw was going to be hard. She was a woman traveling alone, and there were curfews. Escaping from Poland would be even more difficult. She was likely to get thwarted at the border and never make it into Germany. But it would have been worse with Isaac; she couldn't possibly have escaped with a screaming baby. They would have both been killed. She had to save herself, and then pray for the next best thing for her son.

But why did she have to burn him? That was the question that would forever now haunt her, no matter how far away she could get from that old building on Twarda Street. This was where her son was born, where he lived with his mother up until his sixth month, and finally, where he became scarred. For her, the burning would become the last and most imprinting memory of her motherhood. An act of disfigurement—not quite infanticide, but far from love—that defined her parenthood: more umbilical than a cord, more sustaining than a breast.

After what she had done, she could not stop him from crying. Cold water made him scream even more. So did cold cream, lotions, even butter. She hugged him as close to her body as she could. She tried to get him drunk, but that didn't work, either. There was no calming of this crime. All that was left was the mark, the brand, the memory that in many ways was the very essence of her—what she had become, the very digits that defined her.

THE LINEUP OF cars was long, almost like a tailgate party at a Harvard-Yale football game. But this was the German side of the border shared by Germany and Poland, near Frankfurt. What was the fire to get into Poland, Duncan wondered? A graveyard for Jews can't be that interesting. Were there others who shared in his obsessions? He thought he had been all alone.

Duncan tried to stretch his neck outside the window of his car to see if the line was moving at all. But he was never limber enough for that kind of maneuver. From where he was sitting, everything was at a standstill. He glanced up at his rearview mirror and saw no one else behind him. He was at the back of the line. That he didn't like. Duncan mistrusted lines. He generally never got in one, and when a line formed around him, he instinctively thought to step aside and scuttle away. Like a linebacker, he was always behind the line, roaming free.

So he opened the door and stood away from the white Opel, hoping to see how far he actually was from the border station. It was still morning. The day was cold, but the sky was clear. Bunkers of snow surrounded him. Soon it would be dark all over again. During the winter months this part of the world had only a few hours of daylight. That's why Duncan started out early—so he could get through Germany while there was still light. Most of all he wanted to avoid the lines at the border, to make a seamless reentry into the land that had forever haunted him, even though he had never been there before.

Duncan stared up into the horizon, beyond the Polish landscape. To him, the clouds were nothing but a chorus of Jewish apparitions—silky, restless, as though slipped through the fingers of the sky. He took a long breath, and then felt the familiar beginning rumblings of his stomach, the place where his nerves collected in preparation for a mutiny.

Duncan had arrived in West Berlin from New York the morning before. His European homecoming back into the future had just begun. He had flown Sabena because all the other national airlines seemed tainted to him. He sat in first class, a bonus from all those years traveling in the service of his government without ever cashing in his frequent-flier miles for himself. After collecting his luggage and breezing through customs, ignoring the many signs written in German that forbade virtually any act of improvisation, Duncan rented a car at Tegel Airport.

"We have a nice Mercedes parked right out front for you, Mr. Katz," a tall, young Aryan said. He spoke deferentially, and yet somehow officiously, the way Germans, so enamored of bureaucracy, always do. He had a straight back, light blue eyes, short blond hair, and the features—and gestures—of cut stone.

"Not a Mercedes," Duncan said.

"Why not?"

"I find them hard to drive. I was just in a terrible accident with one."

"I am sorry to hear that. I hope you were not hurt?"

"I made out fine, but the Mercedes looks like shit. What other cars do you have here?"

With eyes darting back and forth across the computer screen, the attendant said, "We still have some BMWs left."

"Do you have anything *not* German?"

"Mr. Katz, this *is* Deutschland . . ."

"Yeah, I know, I know. Look, *über alles* my ass."

The attendant leaned backward from behind the counter as though the terminal had just released a squall.

Duncan continued, "Listen, you seem like a well-meaning guy, but do you have any American cars? How about Japanese? I'll even drive a Citroen if you have one."

"We have a Merkur. It's made by Ford and Opel."

"Just great . . . Do you know that Henry Ford was a major Jew hater?"

The attendant shook his head no.

"It figures his company would team up with you guys."

The German remained polite, if not totally confused. "So would you like the Mercedes, or the Merkur?"

Duncan thought it over for a moment. Ultimately, his destination was Poland; that's what the car was for. Larry Breitbart had warned him that the country was an unsafe place, that while Duncan was in Poland, his nightmares might finally have a reality to them.

The concentration camps had been converted into museums, but there were now other dangers—for both Jew and Gentile. There was mob violence. Corruption and chaos. Organized crime had become Poland's latest import, another garden-variety vice of capitalism. There was a seedy underside to a country that for so many years had been occupied by one despot or another. Now the population had the mind-set of street-side hustlers. In such an environment, did Duncan really want to rely on a Soviet Lada for his transportation? Or for that matter, even a car made in Detroit? What if a getaway was necessary? Orlando was right: the Germans were big on dark, philosophic speculations, but they were equally superior in the design of turbocharged engines. Their cars were fast, dependable, and built like tanks. Unfortunately for Duncan, they were built by Germans. His legacy was now in conflict with itself: he didn't want to honor the successors to the Nazis by driving their cars, but he also needed to be safe, to survive in Poland until his mission was completed.

"What's the least German car you have?" he finally asked.

"I'm sorry, I still don't know what you mean."

"Do you know if Opel makes ovens on the side? You know, the Mercedes people helped the Nazis, back in the good old days before you were born. Ask your parents; maybe they'll come clean and tell you about it."

The humorless, irony-deficient German blinked his eyes and then said, "Now you want an oven? We don't rent them here. Check at the hotel . . ."

"Forget it," Duncan said, "just give me an Opel."

From Tegel Airport, Duncan slipped into the Opel and drove straight for a pension located off the Kurfurstendamm—known more simply as the Ku'damm—in the Wilmersdorf District, near the new Jewish section of the city. There was a new Jewish center in the district, complete with a kosher kitchen, a Judaica shop, a Holocaust library, and a staff of German Jews who, despite being even more of a minority than they were during Weimar, nonetheless still felt proud to be Berliners. The contagion of German superiority and entitlement inflicts even those who otherwise should know better.

West Berlin had been rebuilt entirely after the Allied bombings. Architecturally, it displayed a preference for white concrete over red brick, and the Ku'damm had all the neon commercial tourist trappings of a Miami strip mall.

Duncan planned to stay only overnight. He parked the Opel across the street from the hotel and took the U-Bahn to the Kreuzberg District for dinner. He remembered a health-food restaurant on Lausitzer Platz where he had once eaten with Bernard Ross. This time he ate alone, ordering a pseudo-schnitzel and a side of wheat berries with brown rice, his eyes scanning the restaurant while he chewed. After dinner he walked some of the way back to the Ku'damm, strolling along the banks of the Landwehrkanal, and then over one of the short, low-slung bridges that dotted points along the channel. A slice of moon, as if it had been laid flat on its back, trailed each of his movements.

Stopping by a small park, Duncan watched a few jugglers toss small, flaming torches back and forth under the umbrella shadow of a street lamp. One of the jugglers was wearing a red, handlebar mustache that flipped downward in the cold wind, while the other had a beard that was busy on the cheeks but mere whiskers on the chin. A circus colleague on a unicycle wobbled in the darkness. A clown, not wearing makeup but with his mouth still downturned, sulked underneath a tree.

By early morning, Duncan was gone. He drove east through the center of the Tiergarten, the large forest of a park that would eventually lead him to the Brandenburg Gate, down Alexanderplatz, and then into East Berlin. Before getting on the Autobahn, he drove to Scheueviertel, the former Jewish ghetto of prewar Berlin, got out of his car on Oranienburger Strasse, and stared up at the burned-out shell that was once Berlin's Grand Synagogue. Several tourists snapped pictures of the front gate, while a posted guard looked back in their direction, mindful of terrorists.

This part of Berlin had somehow been spared being completely leveled during World War II, but each old building still showed the signature bullet holes of both the Communists and the Nazis who once roamed these parts like predator creatures.

Within minutes Duncan would be on a highway that cut through the entire length of the former East Germany. A few hours later he would reach the border with Poland, at the Polish town of Stubice.

Duncan had been to Germany several times in the past. In his official capacity with the OSI, there were many occasions when he needed to collect evidence, or interview witnesses, or examine records—and all of this would take him back to the land of the Third Reich. None of these visits were pleasant, largely because they required what was for him an abundance of self-restraint. Whenever in Germany, Duncan's lips remained involuntarily buttoned and his fists forcefully unclenched. He had no choice. He was acting on behalf of the United States government. His best behavior was necessary. Before Maloney, Duncan had always made sure that his actions never compromised the mission of the department. And so each visit to Germany ended without incident.

But on this latest journey, no longer bound by the diplomatic imperatives of his career, Duncan could have unleashed a wave of terrorist strikes that would have rivaled the exploits of the neo-Nazi skinheads, or the Anti-Fa anarchists, or the soccer hooligans, or even the Baader-Meinhoff gang. And yet, other than the benign bantering with that rental-car attendant, Duncan had shown himself to be remarkably self-contained and fully disarmed. He even ate a decidedly unsavage macrobiotic meal. Why was he so subdued among the murderers he so despised?

Why? Because his mind was on Poland, and he was saving his strength for that even more special visit. The Germans may have committed most of the crimes, but the soil, and the soul, of Jewish loss was a Polish affair. Now sitting uncomfortably in his plush Opel, waiting in a long, unmoving lineup of cars at the border, he realized that across the other side loomed the forbidden motherland. The place where his family roots slipped out of the earth. The land of Jewish death and detour. If not for the Nazis, Duncan, like his brother Isaac, might have been born right there in Poland.

And for that reason, the crossing of this border was not going to be a simple matter. The passport that he kept safely guarded inside his mohair coat was less crucial to his passage than the psychic docking that would have to take place first before any reentry was possible. Going over the line was not just a matter of changing time zones. In this case, Duncan would be shifting into a different twilight. Poland was Krypton; he was familiar with the paralyzing fragments of this imploded land—the accents, the nightmares, the abducted memories. But now before him was the thing itself, *terra unfirma*, the blackest hole in the Jewish galaxy.

He waited and he sat. And he couldn't stop himself from thinking. Mindlessly thinking. *They won't let me in; they won't let me out . . . I am walking into a trap . . . What if everything looks familiar, but I don't recognize anything? I'll go blind . . . I'll get food poisoning. Is there enough Donnatal in here? I won't be able to control my rage once I'm inside. And why should I have to?*

Everyone was right: no good could come of this trip. He should have met his brother on some neutral territory. This of all countries was too loaded a land for the reunion of a Jewish family. Poland was not the ideal place to become purged. On the contrary, it might ultimately swallow him up, too.

The cars began to press forward a little. Duncan reached for the Donnatal, which he had slipped into a soft-drink receptacle that extended out like a ledge from the dashboard. Before he left New York, he remembered to refill his prescription for an especially large bottle of the green potion. Such visits to the pharmacy normally embarrassed him. He would shamefully skulk up to the counter as though he were under age and clutching a supply of condoms. Mila had always been disappointed by Duncan's tender stomach.

"I got news for you," Mila would say while her son's intestinal organs waged revolutionary battle against one another. "You can't stop to take Donnatal when you're running from the Nazis. You will have to learn to do without it."

The exact diagnosis for what ailed him was never clear. Some doctors thought it was spastic colon. Others felt that it was acute, ulcerative colitis, or Crohn's disease. One internist was sure that it was irritable bowel syndrome, because he saw the problem as being directly related to Duncan's nervous system. After the examination, when the doctor met Mila in the waiting room, he was even more confident that he had made the right diagnosis.

"Is he fixed?" Mila asked in a tone that was more command than question. "A boy his age shouldn't have such problems with his health. Did I tell you that he is a football star?"

"Yes, you did, Mrs. Katz."

"So what's going on?"

"I'd like to take some more tests, but before I do, I thought I'd find out a little more about his home life."

Mila immediately suspected that when the doctor said "Stick out your tongue," and Duncan replied, "Ahh . . . ," some of the family secrets came out, as well. She was furious. Perhaps before her son went in to see the doctor, she should have blurted out "keller" as a reminder for him to relay information only on a need to know basis.

"What about his home life?" she asked guardedly.

"Well, is he under any apparent stress?"

"What do you mean?"

"I don't know . . . ," the doctor mused. "For instance, maybe you or your husband are putting too much pressure on him to succeed? Or maybe something else is going on? Could either be the case?"

"Nonsense," Mila shot back, "our son is perfectly normal. What are you accusing us of?"

"Nothing . . . I'm just suggesting . . ."

"Don't suggest, just fix. I didn't ask you to look inside his head, or my head, or my family's business. You are not a psychiatrist, and even if you were, you are out of your league. We are not like regular people. You can't understand who we are and what we do by looking at what's written in your medical books. Don't waste your time. Just find out what's wrong with his stomach; then send me the bill!"

Mila shoved Duncan's shoulder and marched her son out of the doctor's office, leaving the internist alone in his waiting room with a rumble inside his own stomach that wasn't there before.

But whatever it was that so easily inflamed Duncan's insides, it was beginning to do so again—this time in Poland. Feeling the familiar warning signs, Duncan took another precautionary, preemptive swig of Donnatal, wiping his mouth with his mohair sleeve. He then re- moved his wallet and flipped through the credit-card pouches until he came across a picture of Milan, which he yanked out and held up to his face, lovingly and longingly. She was sitting on the lawn of his former home. She gave a shy Chicklet-toothed smile; her arms were curled up in front of her body, her cheeks round and pink. She was wearing a sleeveless blue sundress with patches of yellow sunflowers. The picture was taken during summer. He recalled that day with tenderness, but now with separation there also came resentment and anger.

The cars began to move more swiftly. Between sips of Donnatal and jerky movements on the Opel's clutch, Duncan hadn't noticed that he was soon about to reach the border station. Nerves were gradually hastening the madness that had owned him since childhood. With the border now only a car length away, he suddenly wanted to turn around. But he was sandwiched in—by both cars and whatever mental roadblocks wouldn't, under any circumstance, allow him to exit. Duncan began to sweat, even though the inside of the Opel was near freezing. His palms collected water like cups.

Anxiously, he turned around in all directions, and then ran both hands through his long hair, flattening the uncombed, disheveled curls. He emptied the Donnatal with the gurgling intensity of an alcoholic; all of his credit and bank cards tumbled from his wallet as he searched again for Milan's picture. Anything to calm him, although he was now long gone. Duncan started to hear voices—shrieking ones. It sounded as though they were coming from the back of the car, as well as the glove compartment, through the air-conditioning vents, even inside the trunk. Perhaps he shouldn't have rented a German car, after all. But the voices were in Polish, a language he did not speak. He couldn't understand what they were telling him, or whether they were saying anything at all. Was this a warning, or a welcome?

Finally he heard a rapping on the hood of the car, a solid thump without a follow-up echo. A stocky man dressed in a gray uniform, his beet-red cheeks dry and swollen, motioned to Duncan to roll down the window.

After a few, failed tries in Polish, the man roared, "Passport! Papers!"

THE BALANCE OF power at the card table soon shifted from amputee to refugee. At first Mila blew a few bum hands. This was how she always started a game when playing with strangers for the first time.

Her pigeons never realized that she was laying the foundation for a hustle.

"Oh, how stupid of me, I needed that black four with the flowers on it." At another moment she yelled out, "Bingo!"

The men threw down their cards in disgust. "Wrong game, Millie," said the chinless cardiac patient.

A few rounds later Mila asked, "What's a straight again?"

When it was her turn to deal, one of the orderlies said, "Millie, you don't have to do it if you don't want to. It's a harder job than it looks."

That was her cue. It was time for the diamonds, hearts, spades, and clubs to realign themselves and fortunes to change. In her universe, the dealer always ruled. And in poker, as in life, as long as the dealer keeps winning, she keeps control of the cards. With power came new vitality. The blush on her face reddened; the lipstick looked as though it had been freshened up with Day-Glo. She had gone from bloodless to clownish in a matter of seconds.

"Let me try," she replied. "We'll see how I do. But first, why do we have to play for such chicken feed? Can we make the game more interesting? What do you say, boys?"

The teenager who had already lost an arm but still had both of his legs was way ahead in this game and therefore had the most to lose. He balked at Mila's proposition.

"Ma'am," he said politely, "maybe you should just fold . . . you know, call it quits?"

One of the other orderlies added teasingly, "The people with the puzzle over there look like they could use some help."

"Fuck the puzzle," Mila replied, shocking her card mates. "I say we raise the stakes to fifty cents. Are you all in or not?"

The men remained silent, examining one another with second-rate poker faces.

Mila turned to the overweight cardiac patient sitting off to her right, slid the deck of cards in front of him, and said, "Cut!"

"Gladly," he replied.

So he cut, and from then on, the men at the table bled. The atmosphere of a hospital filled with surgeons no doubt provided Mila with all the inspiration she needed to take the heart out of her victims.

With each succeeding hand, stacks of chips migrated over to her side as though the table were tilted in her direction.

The men soon realized that they were being conned. The lady was a ringer; maybe she wasn't even a patient, just a shark making the rounds at the hospitals and hotels of Miami Beach. Mila shuffled the deck as though she were Vegas-born. With one hand she arched the cards, and looked away as they flew out of one hand and into the other like a flock of birds. She then spread the cards out on the table in the shape of an S, lifted one at the outermost edge, and watched as the remaining fifty-one followed suit like Ziegfeld dancers.

"Call!" she insisted after pushing the cardiac patient and the teenager to bet into an unwinnable hand.

"A pair of sixes?" she mocked the cardiac patient who was carrying too much weight but too little luck. "You have to be kidding? Where did you learn to play this game?"

"Hey, lady, easy does it," the cardiac patient said. "We're among family here. I thought this was a friendly game, not a massacre. You're having way too much fun for my blood."

Ignoring him, Mila turned to the teenager's cards. "Two pair—fours and jacks," she announced. "If you were paying attention, you'd know you couldn't win with that. See, look what I have," she said, and then proceeded to fan her cards with the faces up. "Gentlemen, they call this a bicycle straight flush—five, four, three, two, ace, with the lucky diamond."

It was one of the rarest hands in poker. The two cardiac patients feared the onset of palpitations. The teenager rolled his eyes and slapped the edge of the table with the only hand that he had. The orderlies were thinking about taking the bus back to Coconut Grove earlier than usual. Cynthia and Louise playfully jabbed one another, giggling from their chairs along the back wall.

Mila noticed neither the admiration of her nurses nor the frustration of her victims. While she was indeed playing cards at Mount Sinai Hospital, in other ways she was lost. She flawlessly memorized the location of cards, while her memory locked into an altogether different game—one played thirty-five years earlier, and for much larger stakes.

SHE HAD GONE from Twarda Street directly to the train station. There she would board a train that would take her from Warsaw to Poznan. The sound of the train's whistle barely registered in her mind. Nothing from now on could block out the farewell wail that came from the infant lungs of her son. All she heard was the empty white noise of guilt.

On the train she stared at a picture of Isaac. He was a mere eight days old, wrapped in a white fleece blanket. His face scrunched up. His eyes unseeing, but tearful. He had been drugged with wine and was resting in his mother's arms. The picture was taken at his bris. With the circumcision over, Mila looked happy. Keller asked that she smile for the camera. But even then she mistrusted smiles. The emotions of a proud parent were defenseless against the darker impulses that pulled on her more fiercely. She was trapped by Poland, and now by Isaac. Confinement, of any kind, was now her most dreaded nemesis. Nothing, including her son, could force her to live in bondage all over again.

She held Isaac's picture to her chest, then returned it back inside a hidden pocket sewn into her ragged coat. As the prewar train—stripped down to nothing but scrap metal, looking as though it had been hijacked from a junkyard—rocked steadily, she glanced out the window and noted the shaggy weeping willows that stood out like green mammoths along the Polish landscape. They seemed to have grown larger and more numerous since the last time she had given them much thought, when she was a child traveling with her parents by chauffeured car from Warsaw to Kraków.

As Mila tried to think about something other than Isaac, she recalled that other train ride, the one in that stench-filled cattle car taken almost four years earlier. It was a journey without a view—or a prayer. She boarded the cattle car at Umschlagplatz in the Warsaw Ghetto. There was barely enough light to see. The wooden boards creaked under the weight of so many condemned Jews, who had no room to move or to even sit down. Smoke from burning coal trailed the engine like a kite. The locomotive coughed and whistled, but these sounds were drowned out by the moans and sobs that came from children and adults alike.

Most of these trains were headed for Treblinka, but her car somehow was re-routed to Auschwitz-Birkenau. Which memory was now worse—the ride to the camps or this one, in a direction unknown, without her son, and with the slimmest of hopes that the gods and the demons would permit her safe passage?

Mila had already plotted out her escape. From Poznan she would travel by foot to the border at Stubice. If she moved quickly, it would take her two days. This was the only way out. The border guards who worked the trains were more strict. They couldn't be bribed. She would be sent back, even arrested. Her passport remained that of a Polish Jew. She needed to smuggle herself into Germany, and the only chance to do that was to slip through the Polish border and work her way to Frankfurt. From there perhaps she could get herself to Stuttgart or even Munich. Although she was without family, Auschwitz had supplied her with ready friends. She knew some refugees who left the DP camps and found permanent residence in what would later become West Germany. These were the people she would eventually see when it was time to emigrate to America.

She passed through the wide, cobblestoned promenade and steepled buildings of the Old Town Square in Poznan. The magnificent, neo-classical architecture was jagged like chipped teeth. Mila now had two days and nights of constant travel in front of her. She drifted out of the city and into the countryside. It was early spring. Although cold at night, she would be able to survive sleeping in the forests of Poland. After Auschwitz, the imaginary bar that measured the degree of difficulty in all survivals had been lowered considerably. She trudged through Polish villages, hoarding supplies, finding commodities that could be used as articles of barter and bribe. A silent ghost. Mila observed that these towns hadn't quite recovered from the war. People living in a time warp. Who was in charge now? The Nazis? The Communists? It would be no different years later. Who could be sure what was underneath Walesa's Solidarity credentials? Maybe he was a Jew?

Mila finally reached the border at Stubice and was surprised by what she saw. Crouching down behind a tree off the side of the road, she noticed that the border station was deserted. No lineup of cars, or people. It was the middle of the night. Was she the only one trying to escape from Poland, or enter it? Was everyone else too scared? All that now separated her from her freedom were a few sawhorse barricades and a dilapidated barbed-wire fence. If she were smaller, she could probably crawl underneath a slat and be done with it. It was dark. The lighting was poor. Even the sky was cooperating; there were no stars, just a thin, faint sliver of a moon and a flotilla of jet-black clouds.

Mila also noticed that the border patrol itself—consisting of four plump, portly uniformed men—was taking advantage of the slow night. She would have preferred it if they were asleep, but what they were doing instead was the next best thing. Rather than being on the alert for illegal border crossings, they were sitting outside on crates, playing cards on a makeshift table, built from other adjoining crates. She could hear the muffled sounds of drunken Polish men slurring the Slavic, native language that, until the war, she was proud to speak. Now Polish sickened her. German was even worse. A steel kerosene lantern, and the flaming ashes from cigarettes, provided the only spotlight that kept the cards visible.

Mila surveyed the area. Could she slip by without the idiots even realizing it? Just then, the butt of a rifle was wedged into her spine, and she heard someone say, "You, stand up and move!"

With her hands raised above her head, Mila was marched out of the forest and into a patch of clearing that would become an interrogation cell.

"Look what we have here," her captor said to the others. Presumably, this game was always one shy. They must have alternated with each other: one guard given the job to patrol the area, while the others guzzled vodka and gambled worthless zlotys into the night.

Glancing up from the table, the men put their cards and cigarettes down. Mila was now more interesting than the hands they had been playing.

"I think she was trying to sneak across," the man with the rifle said. Mila never saw his face, but she could still feel his weapon pressed against her back, cold and hard, as though she had fallen asleep on the root of a tree.

"Papers!" one of the guards demanded. He was fat with a wide, red nose lined like a surveillance map. Mila slowly put her hands down and reached into the lining of her coat to remove her passport. Isaac's picture slipped out and floated to the ground. Mila tried to kneel down to retrieve it, but the guard behind her said, "Stay where you are!" He then carefully leaned over and lifted the photograph off the chilled, damp earth.

"You are Polish?" the heavyset guard asked.

"Yes."

"Lewinstein," he said, reading from her passport.

"Yes."

"And you are a Jew?"

"Yes. I survived the camps."

"I see." The guard examined Mila carefully. Then he said, "And you don't look worse for it. You are pretty, for a Jew."

Such was the perverse relationship between the Poles and the Jews, that a compliment was equally nuanced with insult. Mila said nothing in return.

"What are you doing here? And at this time of night?"

"She was carrying bags with her," the smug patrolman standing behind her said, holding up Mila's purse and the brown satchel.

"You are trying to leave this country?" the guard asked, his red nose brightening with each deduction.

"Let me pass," Mila pleaded. "I want out of Poland."

"Why?" one of the other guards asked with a toothless smile on his face. "Jews have always been welcome here." He guffawed and nudged the guard standing beside him.

"Especially in Kielce," one of the others, with blond hair and a tombstone face, said.

"I have already seen too much of Poland," Mila said. "Let me try somewhere else . . ."

"Who is this?" the guard behind her asked while placing Isaac's picture in front of her face.

Mila didn't answer, largely because she couldn't imagine what the right answer would be. Was the truth acceptable to these barbarians? Would they assist a mother who was abandoning a baby, even a Jewish one? It was hard for Mila to know. Now she would have to wear the stone-cold, poker face of maternal denial. There would be no better place to start than this.

"I don't know . . . ," she finally said. "I found the picture on the train. I brought it with me for luck."

"You will need luck," the blond-haired guard said. He rose from his box and then opened Mila's coat as though he were about to step inside.

"What are you doing?" Mila asked, although she already knew.

"We could have you for our refreshment after supper and then kill you and nobody would ever know," the final player—his hair black, his eyelids hooded—said, standing up from his box, the smell of vodka rising with him.

"Nobody misses the Jews," the guard with the rifle added.

"I am carrying vodka, chocolates, and cigarettes," Mila pleaded. "I will give them to you. Please, just let me go!"

"Ah, good," the blond guard said, "you brought provisions for a party. That will make the evening more enjoyable."

"Better than poker," the one with the black-matted hair laughed. "I have been losing all night. Maybe now my luck will change," he said, eyeing Mila luridly.

"Poker," Mila said, almost in a whisper.

"What did you say?" the heavyset guard asked. He was obviously the man in charge. Older than the others. Mila wondered how his age might play into his desires.

"I said poker," Mila replied meekly.

"You play?"

"I learned in the DP camps."

"I see," the leader said.

"Who cares?" said the guard whose rifle was now horizontally in line with his still clothed, although outstretched, penis.

"Maybe we can make this a sport?" the leader pondered, stroking a chin that was surrounded by much dangling flesh. "We are not animals. We will give you a chance to get what you came for."

"What must I do?" Mila asked.

"You say you can play poker? Well then, let's see you play for your life." The men then opened Mila's backpack and searched through her coat, uncovering zlotys, marks, and dollars that Mila had planned to use to smuggle herself out of the country. Now it would become the stakes for her survival. The guard continued, "When you run out of money, you can use the vodka, chocolates, and cigarettes that you brought with you. And if you should win at the end of the night, we will look the other way and you can run to the other side of the border and tell your story to the Germans."

"And what if I lose?"

"If you lose, you stay with us here in Poland. You will spend the night with me and my comrades, and enjoy the cool night air. In the morning, we'll decide what to do with you."

"How do I know I can trust you? I could win and you could still do what you want with me."

"True," the guard conceded, "but I am a man of my word. If you win, you are free to go. I swear on the Holy Mother and her son, Jesus Christ."

The comrades must have known that their leader was a religious man, because Mila noticed that their faces had suddenly grown more serious, as though they sensed it was possible that they could wind up losing more tonight than mere zlotys.

The guard took Mila's hand and led her to the ersatz table. He then kicked a box over against Mila's heels and motioned that she sit down. The guard then sat down on his own box and said, "Five-card poker. You know how to play?"

"Yes."

"I will deal."

"No," Mila said, "it is my life. I will deal."

The guards all took their seats around the combined crates. Mila shuffled the deck evenly, without finesse or bravado, the tricks that would come to her later.

In less than three hours and after four aces, a full house (king high), a royal flush, and several convincingly bluffed hands, Mila had wiped out all the worldly possessions that the patrolmen had brought with them to work. As the first strands of dawn light appeared, it looked as though they had just finished a game of strip poker. Now the men were no longer drunk, but angry. Mila stood up from her box timidly. The guard who had earlier carried the rifle put his arm on her shoulder and forced her back down.

"You are not going anywhere," he said.

The others agreed, except for the leader, who had gambled away all of his money—and the certainty of sex—on a foolish crapshoot.

"No," he bellowed, "we made a deal. We keep our word. She is free to go."

Mila looked into the man's eyes and saw a twinkle disguised as a wink, a sure sign that they had met before. In fact, Mila then realized that she had even seen him play poker—not in the forest, but in the camp. Ironically, before patrolling the fringes of Poland's border, this man had once been a perimeter guard at Birkenau. A few years ago he was much thinner—the food at Auschwitz was not very rich or flavorful, not even for the guards. Mila remembered him as one of the kind ones, which placed him in very rare company, indeed. He never beat any Jews. Perhaps it was because he was saving his energy for poker. Each night, at a certain hour, he and a few Ukrainians would play cards to divert themselves from the business of the death camps. On warm nights, they would play outside, sitting on boxes not unlike the furniture for this game in the forest. And on nights when Mila couldn't sleep, she would look out the window of the barracks and watch them shuffle and draw and check and call. The guard who now had become her liberator was once a better poker player.

Mila searched for her backpack to collect her winnings and retrieve her valuables. But when she found the bag, the leader said, "You can go, but the vodka, the cigarettes, and of course, all of your money stay with us—including what you won."

What she had suspected came true. "What about the picture?"

Surprised by her interest in the photo of an infant who was presumably also a stranger, the guard replied, "It stays here, too. The baby is Polish. This is where he belongs, not with those German swine. You go! Find a better world."

Mila knew not to argue. She would leave them with souvenirs of her victory and a memento of her escape. She turned around and headed toward the gate that was cut into the fence. The blond-haired guard was unlatching the door. With each step she feared that a gun would fire and a bullet would find a place inside her back. But there were no sounds other than the usual crickets and raccoons and foxes that prowled the Polish forests with more patriotism and purpose than the slothful men of the border patrol. Mila's pace speeded up, and she soon vanished into the cover of the German forest, never to see Poland, or her son, or even his picture, again.

WITH THE POKER game at Mount Sinai Hospital now over, Mila faced the one-armed teenager who kept his cards close to his vest and whispered, "What is your name?"

"Ricky."

"Ricky, don't worry, I give you your money back. The others can lick their wounds."

"I don't want my money; I want my arm."

"This I cannot do, Ricky. But I do have something I can show you."

"What is it?"

"My arm—the left one."

"What for?"

"Because it too is damaged." She began to roll up the sleeve of her robe as though about to give blood, and then pointed to the numbers on her forearm.

"Do you know what this means?" she asked, staring at him rather than at her own flesh.

"You were in a concentration camp."

"Yes, so you know from such things?"

"Just what's on TV."

"Today is a special day then; you see it live and in person."

"I'm sorry that happened to you," the boy said.

"Don't be sorry. You can be sorry that I am now dying, but not for what happened back then. You learn to live with whatever life shows you. That is the struggle that we all face—to carry our own packages. This arm is a curse: the worst reminder of what happened to me, and . . . other things that I had to do. I wish I could cut it off. I also know another boy who lives far away who probably would wish to be in your shoes rather than with what happened to him."

"I would rather have your arm than the one I am missing."

"I know. It would be better. You are young; this should not have happened to you. Come with me," she said, rising and taking his right hand. Mila led him over to the upright piano near the window. Cynthia and Louise looked on with interest. The puzzle players were still coping with more unattached pieces than they knew what to do with. The Ping-Pong players had taken a rest from the singsong monotony of the bouncing ball. The other poker players had returned from getting coffee in the downstairs cafeteria. "You sit there," Mila said, pointing at the seat next to her on the bench. "I am rusty; I haven't played in years."

But she didn't sound at all rusty. The beginning chords were full and resonant. Her hands dropped on the keys gently, then gained confidence as the rhythm required. She played from memory, which is how she did everything—it was the true curse of her life. Mila started with "Someone to Watch over Me," then moved on to "They Can't Take That Away from Me" and then "Embraceable You." Ricky's head bobbed, and he snapped the fingers on his right hand shyly. The music brought many into the recreation room. Old people—some sick, others just visiting—hospital staff and doctors all began finding partners. A room once reserved for parlor games had now been converted into a dance hall. Mila wasn't aware of the commotion behind her. She just continued playing. Tears fell onto the black-and-white ivory keys, then settled into the warm wood of the piano. Cynthia and Louise swayed to "I Got Rhythm," their forefingers waving in the air as though testing the direction of the wind. They nodded at Mila, but she didn't see them. She was lost in music, the faraway luxury that eluded her in everyday life.

"PASSPORT!" THE GUARD in the gray uniform with the beet-red cheeks repeated once again.

Duncan had lost the ability to roll down the window. He was unforcibly trapped in the Opel. His breath became short and labored, as though the Opel were an iron lung without oxygen. The voices and screams from before were now getting louder. Fitfully, he circled his head in all directions. At each window, at the front hood, and at the rear of the car stood yet another Polish border guard.

The one in front pointed a rifle at Duncan, while the one at Duncan's door opened the latch and aggressively yanked Duncan out into the cold Polish morning air. He then ordered Duncan to place his hands on top of his head. The four guards whispered to one another, forgetting that Duncan couldn't understand them, anyway. The air had somehow revived Duncan's senses. The panic was over. A moment earlier he had forgotten that he was even in the dead zone between Poland and Germany. He went blank, and his body went limp. Was it his stomach, his nerves, or something else, entirely?

Struggling to get to his feet, he reached into his coat pocket, took out his passport, and handed it to the head guard.

Duncan didn't speak the language, but the guard asked disdainfully, "What is your business in Poland?"

He then opened the passport jacket, moved it closer to his face, then further away, finally passing it around to his fellow men of the border patrol. The guard then grabbed the back of Duncan's head, took a firm hold of a clutch of his hair, and pressed Duncan's face up against the face on the passport photo. The guard then muttered something in Polish. Soon Duncan realized what was behind this harsh welcome home. The passport picture from his days as a lawyer with the OSI no longer matched the person he had become since his dismissal from both his job and home. This was a picture of the old Duncan Katz. His hair was now longer, and he shaved far less frequently. Duncan now looked more the part of a terrorist, while the passport picture suggested a person of respectability and reputation. The men of the border patrol didn't see the resemblance. The only thing about him that hadn't changed was his anger, an unphotogenic emotion that is usually camera shy.

"Look," Duncan began, "I think I know what you're worried about, but that's me," he said, pointing at the passport photo and then at his own live face. "Come on, use your imagination. It's not that good a disguise. My name is Duncan Katz; Duncan Katz, I'm an American. My mother was Polish. My great-grandfather was a famous rabbi in Warsaw. My half-brother still lives here! You all watched gleefully as the Germans murdered my family. Why am I even explaining myself to you? You should be apologizing to me! . . ."

The guards didn't understand him, nor would they have been persuaded even if they had. Their suspicions led to other suspicions. One of the other patrolmen frisked Duncan's coat pocket and removed his wallet. Out fell Milan's picture, which glided unnoticeably down to the Polish earth. Another guard kept a rifle to Duncan's back, while the remaining three removed his car keys and opened up the hatchback to the rented Opel.

"Hey, you can't do that . . . !" Duncan moaned. "There are Fourth Amendment issues here . . ."

Constitutional law did not impress these men. Normally, at a time like this, Duncan would have resorted to other measures. There were only four guards. They weren't that big—in fact, they seemed lethargic and slovenly—and the weapons they were packing were mere rifles, not bazookas. They wouldn't have stood a chance. Before they knew what had hit them, Duncan would have smashed their heads in like piñatas. But this day, and this moment, was strangely different. No Mercedes in need of bodywork fired his imagination. There was going to be no show of force. For one thing, Duncan felt as though his strength had somehow left him, as though the nerve endings that were responsible for closing his fists had suddenly taken up new assignments. Duncan watched helplessly as the border patrol ransacked his car and luggage.

After wading through essential objects of Duncan's travel—maps, flashlights, clean underwear, a month's supply of Donnatal—the men finally found something that interested them. There was some muffled, excited talk, followed by nodding heads. The border patrolmen then approached Duncan, opened the palm of his hand, and placed inside it the *pysanka* that Maloney had given him as a good luck charm and going away present. The egg toppled over, and Duncan quickly collapsed his fingers into a nest. Surprised, he looked up at the Polish guards. The former flat expressions of the border patrol had now given way to smiles. Even the patrolman who was standing behind Duncan suddenly let down his guard, his rifle now pointing in another direction.

For some superstitious reason known only to Poles and to Russians, whoever was carrying around a *pysanka*—especially one as handsome as this handcarved, exotic oval—couldn't be all that bad. Inexplicably, the *pysanka* seemed to be a better passport to Poland than any official document with a deficient photographic ID.

The guards all joined in to repack Duncan's belongings. When they were through, they vigorously shook his hand, patted him on the back, and with dopey smiles wished him a pleasant trip inside their country. Duncan didn't return the affection or well-wishes. He simply got back inside his car, threw the suitcase into the hatchback, turned on the ignition, and slipped the clutch into fast motion.

He never looked back into the rearview mirror. If he had, he would have seen one of the guards waving at him to return. The guard was holding Milan's picture high in the air. Amidst all the checkpoint chaos, the photo had gotten stuck underneath the patrolman's boot like a piece of gum.

The Opel raced through the dirt road of the Polish countryside, which on the map appeared deceptively as Route 30, a major highway. Duncan honked at farmers moving too slowly in nineteenth-century horse-and-buggy contraptions. Red Christmas gnomes the size of fire hydrants were being sold at roadside stands, folkloric dwarfs that fed Poland's appetite for both superstition and Catholicism. On either side of him Duncan noticed shaggy weeping willows swaying in the wind, as though urging him on. A mass of shrieking crows as black as crude oil clung to straw men. Obviously, they had nothing to fear from stuffed hay. This was Poland, after all. Flying over the chimneys and crematoria of Auschwitz, Treblinka, and Maidanek, the crows had already seen far worse.

With his window now completely rolled down, the cold air thundering inside the car, and the sky laid out before him in gun-metal gray, Duncan placed a cassette tape into the dashboard of the Opel. Pushing the play button, he waited until the raucous clarinets, violins, and drums of a modern-day klezmer band boomed out in stereo. And with a malevolent laugh, the kind of glee only the Grinch would revel in, Duncan said, "We're baaaack . . ."

Chapter Thirteen

*L*IFE IS AN uncooperative companion. Those who know that learn to make other friends. Isaac Borowski had lived this way, expecting less, imagining more. The tools of an orphan's trade, the unmagical tricks of survival. His childhood was painted by abandonment, the coat so thick, the doors and hinges might as well have been sealed tight.

There are those who are destined for difficulty. You can see them coming. They are naturals for suffering, magnets for bad luck. Some people just appear to be unsafe. They are without armor, or guardian angels, or peace. Theirs is the face of persecution, and they don't even have the decency to look the other way.

THE CLASS WAS about to end. A room full of Poles seated squat in the child's pose, eyes closed, their breathing tempered but deep. Most were lanky thin. Their hair was straight and flattened by sweat. Their faces were frozen with the stunned white complexion of people who looked as though they had spent too much time under interrogation lamps.

All throughout the room, sit bones were being aligned, backs lengthened, meridians extended wide and made open. Moments earlier the students had all been lying flat-faced, noses wedged into spongy, mildewy mats. From that position they limbered into the grasshopper pose, then the bow, seamlessly moving into the cobra, from there slipping into the down dog. At times they looked as though they were pulling imaginary rickshaws; at other moments they were pods of origami sculptures.

"Hold the positions," Isaac would chant. "Keep breathing . . . deep . . . Listen to the sound of your breaths . . . Feel it going through your body . . . Channel the energy, open the chakras . . . Find your life force and center it. Ease into the posture. Don't force it, just feel it . . . Open yourself up . . . Stay connected no matter what is happening around you . . ."

Although the room was freezing cold, the students didn't seem to mind. Isaac's spiritual energy generated all the heat that anyone seemed to need.

"The navel chakra is the center of your spiritual power. Do you have fire in your bellies?" he asked laughingly, caressing the pregnant dome that passed for his own stomach. "Always be aware of your breath. Breathe into the posture . . . hold it . . . Breathe into the emotion, then release it . . . Always keep breathing and tuning into your energy. What we do here will help you cope with all the tension and trauma that life throws at us . . . Open up . . . Unleash the physical and emotional poison that is trapped inside you . . ."

At the end of the yoga postures, Isaac would lead the class through their meditation work. The lights in the studio would be turned off. Some students sat in the lotus position; others simply collapsed flat on their backs, lifeless in the dead man's pose.

"Spirituality is the only way to deal with life," he would say. "Those who are on the path get hit with the stick, and those who are not on the path also get hit with the stick," he would continue, repeating one of his favorite Zen expressions, "so you might as well choose to follow teachings that place you on the path to coping.

"Use the tension that life dumps on you, and rechannel the energy into your spiritual world. Turn this tension into spiritual fuel . . . The spiritual system is just like any other muscle: you must work it. Pump the life force . . . It's all about living and surviving. The whole point of spiritual work is not to achieve a transcendent moment. That is fantasy yoga—all make-believe. Yoga and meditation are not drugs; they are the only ways to live a less stressful, more satisfying life . . ."

Bodies were being manipulated and minds transported. The return trip would leave them alternately flushed and ecstatic.

When the class ended, the students found their shoes and exited, bowing to Isaac in respect and gratitude. For them he was more than a mere yoga teacher; in ways that no one could quite understand (even if such things are capable of being understood), he was a healer, a shaman, a mystic, a holy man. That's why they came, from so many different Polish cities, in fact. Right in the old Jewish center of War-saw lived one of the few remaining Jews, and unaccountably, he had the power to heal. His past was unexplained; his laughter, a perversion in the face of so much suffering and sadness; his forearm, more riddle than limb.

Up until recently, when the Communists lost control of the coun-try, these Polish Catholics were forced to live without a god, which many of them refused to do. They were still a nation of believers—mostly in Christ. They also venerated the Polish Catholic saints: Stan-islaw, Wojciech, Jadwiga, and most recently Maximilian Kolbe, the priest who died at Auschwitz-Birkenau in order to save another life, but that sacrifice was not for a Jew.

Others looked elsewhere. Some transferred their faith to Isaac Bo-rowski. There was something unusual about him. There are some peo-ple whose personalities are so strong that while you are in their presence, only one of two things is possible: either you become blinded or you wind up with better vision. Isaac had turned his own pain around; maybe he could do the same for them, as well.

He wasn't particularly athletic looking, not even compared to other forty-seven-year-old men. For this reason alone, he wouldn't have been anyone's first choice for a yoga instructor, much less a messiah. How could this short, overweight, double-chinned man, with feet pointed out in reverse Vee formation, contort and balance his body without regard to the laws of physics, or common sense? But isn't a big belly the center of the internal universe? That's what he used to tell them. Real power comes from the stomach, where the spiritual energy is stored. The best excuse a Buddhist ever needs not to go on a diet.

Isaac could stand on his head for hours. And he could twist his spine as though it were a sopping dishrag that needed wringing. His bone structure was almost like the interchangeable pieces of a model kit.

"And have a super wonderful day," Isaac would say at the end of each class, clasping his hands together and closing his eyes in benediction.

This was the typical daily morning routine with Isaac Borowski. They came to hear his words, receive his blessing, stretch and strangulate their limbs, and be mentored by his meditations and guided into the same spiritual space from which he drew his own peace. These sessions had become a necessary prelude to their days as machinists, tellers, teachers, clerks, drivers, and bureaucrats. No longer Communists, they now timed their daily rhythms to a different kind of clock.

The studio was a spacious loft on the second floor of an old building on Twarda Street in Warsaw. Although people referred to it as the old Jewish section, so few Jews lived there now that the distinction was absurd. The neighborhood with its long, treeless streets, stunted prewar buildings, and decrepit entranceways, had long ago changed, and not by the free will of those who left. The ghosts who now returned did so only out of obligation. They were not drawn by Isaac's yoga; they haunted for other reasons.

The rough, faded-wood floors, the chipped wall paint, the hissing radiator, the rattling windows of Isaac's studio all added to the Gothic emptiness of Jewish life. It was the Poland that I. B. Singer never saw, and never wrote about. As a once-abandoned child, and as the caretaker of the Jewish Cemetery, Isaac knew how to decorate for loss. His yoga credentials were in constant conflict with his flair for the morbid. And yet, he was an expert at breathing through the pain, and through the surroundings and the silence of all those slaughtered and absent voices.

One by one his students walked down the narrow, creaking stairwell. Like a chorus line they shifted over against the railing in order to make room for a man who was climbing up without regard to the right of way. He was wearing a white suit, and his head was covered with a tilted panama. Isaac was busy rolling up mats as the stranger entered the studio. Looking up for an instant, Isaac realized who it was.

"Ah, the man in search of the Lieblichs," Isaac said. "I see you have found my other hiding spot."

"When I find someone once, I can always find him again. That's what I do," Nathan Silver said confidently, shaking Isaac's hand.

"How can I help you?" Isaac asked, his face tender, willing. "Are you here for a yoga class? I would be flattered if you stayed. The next one will be at twelve o'clock."

"No, I'm not here for yoga, or the Lieblichs this time."

"I see," Isaac said quietly.

"How's the computer? I assume you bought one."

"Yes, I did. Thank you again. It will be easier for me to find relatives from now on."

Isaac peered to the side, looked over his benefactor's shoulder, and noticed that the studio was now empty except for Silver and someone who was lurking at the door. The man had an even larger presence than Silver. He had an all-weather face. Unblinking eyes. Aluminum-siding skin. A welded nose. His thick arms were folded against a burnt-gray suit; a black hat had trouble fitting on his oversized head.

"Don't worry about him," Silver said. "He's just my driver, stretching his legs."

"I'm not worried," Isaac replied, returning his gaze to Silver. "I don't believe you or your friend are here to harm me. So what can I do for you?"

Silver placed his hand against Isaac's back, as though escorting him somewhere, and said, "Actually, I'm here to do something for you . . ."

And then Silver proceeded to tell Isaac what Larry Breitbart had sent him to reveal. Isaac Borowski had an American brother. Mila Lewinstein may have abandoned Isaac to the world, but not without company. Someone else had been damaged, too. The day had finally come to compare scars.

Silver continued speaking, while Isaac's mind went its own way. Orphans—and the survivors of broken families—dream better than the rest of us. Isaac's childhood was spent in psychic search of a mother. Mila left him and then went off to live somewhere else. That was all he had to go on for all these years. The rest was his job—filling in the blanks, his responsibility alone.

At times he wondered whether, after leaving him, his mother had became a queen.

Or perhaps she had married a millionaire.

Maybe she had never survived her escape. How else could anyone explain why she never came back for him—unless she had spent a lifetime trying, without success?

But wondering is simply the mischief of imagination. The answers are no more knowable than the questions.

Silver spoke softly, despite the fact that his voice was nearly always hoarse. He gestured with the left arm, while the right rested on Isaac in case the yogi needed support. Mila had gone to Germany, married Herschel Katz, and then moved to America. But the story didn't end there. She had given birth to another child—another son, in fact—Duncan was his name. Strange name for a Jewish boy. But that wasn't the main thing. What Isaac cared about most was that Mila had stayed put in Miami—past the *bris* and the bar mitzvah, Duncan's street fights, and his school graduations. For that she would stick around, the life that his mother chose to live without her oldest son.

"She wanted happiness, but she never found it," Silver said matter-of-factly. "Not with Herschel Katz, or by becoming an American, or by hanging around with guys like Larry Breitbart . . .

"I know you can't take this all in right now, Isaac. But you have a brother, and he's coming to see you. I don't know the guy, can't tell you much more. Geez, this whole story is so weird. Only Poland could do this to a Jewish family. Not the kind of thing you hear about in Great Neck, I'll tell you that."

There was so much more that Isaac wanted to know. He plied Silver with questions. Had Mila ever worried about him? Had she lain awake at night, tormented over what she had done? She may have wanted her freedom—indeed, she deserved it—but at what cost to her soul?

With each question, Silver simply shrugged his large shoulders.

Didn't all children have to have a mother? Isaac had wondered as a child. If so, where was his?

"She had to leave," Keller Borowski would try to explain. He would then cough, the cancer making his lungs sound like a detached muffler scraping against the road.

"Why?" Isaac would ask again and again.

"Because Poland was too much for her. She needed to run away," Keller would say, glancing at his son's frail forearm, the monstrous calling card that Mila had left behind.

Keller Borowski died eight years after Mila had gone. Heart failure and grief; the grief that never goes away. Long before the time Isaac reached the age of Jewish manhood, he was all alone. First came the orphanages, then a short stay with a foster family who had odd, Tibetan attachments; then he went off to live by himself. He unloaded fish at the docks along the Wisla River, living in a small cold-water flat on the outskirts of Warsaw. Poland was a new Communist nation in those days, and so, as a matter of ideological principle, even the homeless had homes; a shelter of some sort; a roof with paper walls; a ceiling that made standing up a hazard; a shared toilet without toilet paper; rations for food. At night Isaac would stare out the window into the black Warsaw sky. The stars had turned their backs on Poland. Scattered weeping willows were weighted down with snow. Other trees were simply barren, no better than sticks. Clouds moved swiftly in the polluted darkness, tearing up the sky, giving chase or being chased.

As Isaac became older, he searched the faces of women on the street, even the ones who appeared on propaganda television, in newspapers and magazines. If he looked into their eyes, perhaps he would find the one who was looking for him, searching in the same way he was, trying to reclaim her son.

Someone did eventually come. A week after Silver's visit, Isaac once more stood in his studio, waiting for his younger brother. His classes were over for the day. And he had just returned from his work at the cemetery. The bones and headstones and surrounding moss and weeds were tucked in for the night. Poland was shutting down, while Duncan was arriving.

The white Opel, its right front tire pinched against the curb, straightened itself and eased underneath a street lamp. In the sky a lopsided half-moon dangled in the darkness. The dense mist of a Prague fog rose from the pavement. Duncan stepped out of the car, glanced up to locate the Twarda address, checked to see if anyone was watching, and then entered the building. He had driven all day, stopping only once since crossing the border. In Poznan he searched vainly for an American Express office. He was without zlotys, but flush with dollars and marks, and he needed to change money. No one seemed interested or impressed with his traveler's checks or credit cards. When he stopped at a gas station, the attendant scoffed at

Duncan's poor excuse for currency. The man wasn't going to be fooled by this American.

"The money's good," Duncan said. "Welcome to the twentieth century."

The attendant waved him on, slurring some insult that Duncan stored away as fuel for later.

He returned to the Opel and continued east on the main highway. He had more than enough gas to make it safely to Warsaw. There was no need to stop. He had done so only because a full tank would make him feel better. The old Katz caution.

Now with the tank nearly empty, Duncan was finally at his brother's home. The building was painted red with a rounded archway entrance and wide rectangular windows. It had been a factory before the war, manufacturing *yohrzeit* candles, mezuzahs, dreidels, and spice and charity boxes. Duncan climbed the stairs. The hallway felt no warmer than the air outside. A single, exposed lightbulb was near burnout, and flickered as a warning. He reached the top of the stairs and hesitated before opening the tall wooden door that led inside Isaac's studio. Duncan removed his coat and dragged it from behind. The floorboards were warped, bending far too generously with each of his steps. His eyes roamed the quiet, darkened room.

"Hello," he said. "Is anyone here?"

A noiseless shadow, jagged like a candelabra, moved against a long white wall.

"Isaac Borowski?" Duncan asked.

The shadow remained silent. Duncan took a few steps back and stood still for several anxious seconds when the mind can't buy a diversion.

Finally, he heard a voice. "You are Duncan Katz?"

The shadow was now flesh.

"Welcome. I am Isaac Borowski, your brother."

It was at that moment—with the distance between them now so close, with *yohrzeit* candles burning in the corner, bringing light to their faces—that Duncan recoiled as though he had just seen a ghost. The ghost of his mother, the sight of Mila in drag.

·   ·   ·

"I always kept Duncan's hair long," Mila repeated between sips of water and long pauses, while catching her breath.

It was raining outside. Hard drops that suggested a sun shower, but the sun was concealed behind dark clouds, and an enraged wind pounded against windows, tossing coconuts around as though they were mere beachballs.

"Why?" Louise asked.

"The world I know is one of shaved heads. Everyone in the camps was without hair. The Nazis weren't worried about lice; that's what they said, but it wasn't true. We didn't have lice; what we had was pride. That was what they wanted to take from us. That's what the showers were for. The Nazis were experts in shame."

"And so Duncan's hair was . . ."

"Never cut short . . . a trim here and there, but always left long. All the strong men—Samson, Tarzan, Hercules—had long hair."

Louise contemplated the domed Afros that the men and women of Liberty City had worn, those Jiffy Pops of Jehri Curled black coils, and wondered how much strength could come from a hairdo.

"At least it was the sixties," Louise chuckled. "Everybody was wearing their hair that way."

"But he didn't know that I kept it," Mila confessed.

"Kept what?"

"His hair. I have bunches of it—from when he was a baby all the way through high school. I would go to the barbershop when Duncan would leave, and ask them to let me sweep up his hair."

Louise seemed puzzled. "And you never told him?"

"No, of course not."

"Why?"

"I didn't want to show that I loved him."

"Why not? You were his mother. Who else would want to keep boxes of his hair?"

"Why should he have what his brother could not? You can't love one and not the other. Isaac didn't have a mother; why should Duncan?"

"But Duncan had a mother; you raised him. That's the difference right there . . ."

A television suddenly blared from another room. The volume was mistakenly jacked up. A soap opera sounding as though the scene called for a soprano.

"I never breast-fed him," Mila said, then tiredly closed her eyes. "I couldn't. I was able to nurse Isaac, but not Duncan. I couldn't produce milk for him, and I'm ashamed to say, I didn't want to. I wanted him to be strong. I didn't want him to need a mother. A mother is like a teddy bear, a rabbit's foot, a pacifier. Mothers make mama's boys."

"But when he wasn't looking, you kept his hair. That's a mother's love for you."

Mila pondered the logic behind her parenting while listening to the storm outside—the rattling wind, the drowning drizzle, the up-ending of all that was once battened down.

"Louise, the thing is . . . Duncan was what they now call a mistake," Mila said. "I didn't want more children. I felt I owed it to Isaac not to love another son, not even to have one. When I was pregnant, Yankee fought with me to keep the baby. He said it would be a sin—a *schande*—for people like us to have an abortion. 'We survived a death factory,' he told me. 'We cannot be killers ourselves.' Duncan was born, but not loved, at least not by me. I drove him away. All I have of him are the things he outgrew: old shoes, football cleats, karate dogis, even his baby teeth."

Mila began to cry. Louise reached over to touch her patient's hair, but hesitated as though fearing a static shock. Mila's left arm, with its canvas of numbers, was now almost entirely blue. Too many needles had been poked into her trapeze-wire veins. Outside, a flash of lightning lit up the gray sky but produced no thunder.

"Mila, come on now, baby, you are not a bad person," Louise said calmly. "The war made you this way. Your sons never had no chance to know their real mother—the person you would have been if there was no Auschwitz."

Ah, the Auschwitz interlude. Louise had become familiar with the idioms of atrocity. The same was true of Cynthia and Judy. All three nurses now knew the essential landmarks, the forks in the road, the rubble of the mind. They learned to speak Mila's language. All part of their nursing assignment. Listening was just as important as care-taking; it fact, it was all that mattered. Mila didn't expect miracles, just an audience. The nurses were free to screw up with the chemo, which was going to kill her anyway. But the story must continue. Her confessions needed witnesses. While Mila's body surrendered to the ultimate truth, her memory showed no shame in revealing others. For the nurses, the Holocaust wasn't some twentieth-century mythology. It was real. It happened. They were caring for its consequences.

"I could die easier if I knew my sons would meet someday . . . Who knows? . . . Maybe they could watch over each other."

THEY STOOD BEFORE each other, both unable to move. Stunned by the sight of one another, they were without any family history for knowing how to interact. These were brothers who had never walked to school together, or eaten dinner at the same table, or discussed baseball, bullies or masturbation. And yet, even without words, it was obvious that they were bound by Mila's blood.

The Holocaust was a killer, and a displacer. But now these brothers were no longer yet another installment of some postwar, post-Communist lost and found miracle—the lead story for the six o'clock news. Mila's sons were real, and related.

"We don't have to speak," the older brother began, cautiously. "Nothing we say will give meaning to how we became separated from the start. That we will never know. And words are not the way to learn the answers. All we can do is feel, which is maybe even more important than to understand. But I am happy to finally have a brother."

Isaac then stepped toward Duncan, held out his hand, then changed his mind and embraced his younger brother, barely reaching Duncan's chest. Duncan, tentatively, brought his arms around Isaac, but without really touching him, as though suspended by a force field.

"This is unbelievable, like some sick Mengele experiment," Duncan said. "Do you have any idea how much you look like her?"

"No," Isaac replied shyly, but flattered. "The only picture I have is when she was very young. She was no older than a teenager."

"Well, I knew her when she was the age you are now," Duncan said. His eyes, serious but disbelieving, continued to stare at his brother. He shook his head. "I don't know what to say. You are a carbon copy. You are her twin. A clone. This is too weird. Can we put some more light on in here?"

"You are afraid of the dark?"

"I'm not afraid of anything," Duncan said defensively. "It's all a little too much, that's all." Duncan stepped back to get his mohair coat, which was now bundled on the floor like a bearskin rug. He pulled out the Donnatal and began to drink without regard to dosage. Isaac looked on with interest.

"You have a condition?" Isaac asked.

"No, I am in perfect health."

"What is it then?"

"I travel all the way to Poland to see a phantom brother," Duncan said, wiping his mouth with his sleeve, "and when I get here, I find you."

"You are disappointed?"

"No, amazed. We look nothing alike; we probably *are* nothing alike."

"This is true," Isaac said ruefully. "I was told by Mr. Silver that you were some American football player. I see he was right; you are a big one, like Arnold." Isaac then eased into a front double-biceps pose, which made him look ridiculous. "He told me other things about you, too."

"Like what? I never met the guy."

"That you are blocked. Nothing is flowing inside; I can see it from here."

"You can see inside souls?" Duncan asked.

"Yes, I can."

"Quite a trick."

"No trick, I just can do it."

While staring, Duncan started to wonder whether Mila would have approved of yoga. It wasn't exactly a warrior's sport. What a field day the Poles must have had with this dumpy, defenseless, four-eyed Jewish kid. The replay of a pogrom. Motherless. Muscle-less. What possible good could come from seeing inside souls?

Isaac said, "So, you must look like your father."

Duncan thought about it and then answered, "I don't really resemble either of them."

He stood almost a foot taller than his parents. Although there were some dim features that the family could point to in common, overall Duncan was an anomaly, a genetic mutation, a giant among the broken-down remains of Auschwitz alumni. Mila had wanted a golem for a son, and she got one. She had molded Duncan her way, without relying on the kabbalah manual. There was no riverbank mud, no mystical chanting or gematria. She spent all her numbers on Isaac, and then gave birth to an ignoble savage, an American Frankenstein.

The brothers were nothing alike even as half-brothers go. One was human, gifted with vision; the other, more machinelike and out of warranty.

Yet Duncan was right to marvel at nature's way of compensating for human error. Mila abandoned Isaac, but she left him with so many different imprints to find his way back. All he had to do was look at his own reflection. Mother and son had the same height and shape, the same fleshy lips, the round face, the reddish hair, the wide gap between their front teeth. And there was more.

During their first dinner together, Duncan observed, "She liked chicken livers, too."

"My favorite food," Isaac laughed.

And that, perhaps, was the biggest difference of all. Unlike Mila, Isaac laughed. In fact, he hardly ever stopped laughing. Isaac found something funny in everything in saw.

"I've only known you for two days," Duncan observed, "and you've already laughed more than I have my entire life."

"What makes you laugh, brother?" Isaac wondered. "God put laughter into each of his creations. Surely there is something."

"Some of us he left out."

"Not true," Isaac replied. "You can love, and Mr. Silver tells me that you were trained to kill. Both are human. And so too is to laugh, and to dance, and to express joy."

As proof, Isaac laughed once again.

"I think what you're talking about is what they call gallows humor, but gallows and gas chambers don't make me laugh. After Auschwitz, nothing is funny."

Duncan stayed in Isaac's apartment, a large room with a high ceiling above the yoga studio. The room was spare and unassuming; the wood furniture of breakaway consistency like props for a barroom brawl. The floors were rugless. The walls were covered with pencil sketches of yoga postures. A mustard-colored, uncurtained bathtub anchored the center like a fountain in a town square.

The next morning, Isaac, trying to be a gracious host, asked his brother, "So what do you want to do while you are here?"

"We find out about our pasts," Duncan replied quickly, "and take back our birthrights."

"What do you mean?" He did not yet understand his younger brother's concept of what it meant to be a tourist in Poland.

"This is our country." Duncan's voice filled the room. "It belongs to us. Wasn't our great-grandfather the chief rabbi of Warsaw?"

"Yes, his synagogue was the Nozyk, not far from here."

"We should start with that."

"You want to take over the synagogue?"

"Yes, and then we'll find the house he lived in. After that, the house where our mother lived. By the end of the day we should have two houses. Then we'll start repossessing other things in the morning."

"Are you serious?" Isaac said, then laughed, but with a trace of fear.

"Yes, why not? We are standing on the ground of the greatest archeological site on earth," Duncan continued. "The Dead Sea Scrolls can't compare to all this buried Jewish life."

"But . . . taking over the synagogue?"

"I know it's just a start, and a small one," Duncan's voice animating with each syllable. "But then we'll make a list of other places to liberate."

"We are brothers, but also strangers," Isaac conceded. "I don't know you well enough to know when you are making a joke."

"It's no joke; I'm dead serious. If we don't do it, who will? Mila would have wanted it this way. Honor your mother, Isaac."

"So what do you propose?"

"We clean this country up, make it safe for Jews to come live here again. We rebuild. Start life all over. They did it in Jerusalem with settlements. Why not here? Judea and Samaria may have once been the biblical homeland, but this is the medieval one. Long ago these people invited us to come live in Poland because they didn't know how to do anything on their own. And how did they repay us? A few hundred years later, this country was overridden with concentration camps."

"The Germans put them here."

"Hey, I have no fondness for Germans, either. But the Poles built the camps; then they took over Jewish homes and property while the

Jews themselves became fuel for the biggest bonfire of human flesh on earth. It's time to even the score. There aren't that many Jews who live here now, but you and I can start our own revolution."

"What you have in mind is not Solidarity."

"That's right. I'm talking Jewish vengeance. When we get through with this place, *aliyah* will take on a whole different meaning. Poland as the new Holy Land. Imagine . . . Warsaw, Kraków, and Lublin once again overrun with Jews."

"And I thought you came to Poland to find a brother," Isaac said, sounding wounded.

"You want to know your mother, Isaac? Follow me, I know the way to her heart."

Looking into the flaming eyes of his long-lost brother, Isaac wondered for the first time whether, in not knowing Mila, he had somehow been better off after all.

JUST AS HE had feared, Duncan wasn't acclimating to Poland so easily. For one thing, he was having a hard time finding food that he could eat. Due to his lifelong battle with a fragile stomach, Duncan was primarily a vegetarian. But in Poland, he would have had an easier time eating kosher than healthily. There didn't seem to be a single health-food store or restaurant in all of Warsaw. The people survived largely on meat, borscht, and herring, while Duncan desperately craved seitan and soba noodles. And it wasn't just the food. As far as Western music was concerned, the Poles were just getting around to listening to Elvis Presley, while Duncan had to rush off to the Opel to slip in a tape of Elvis Costello.

But worst of all, there was no suitable gym in all of Warsaw. How could he possibly reclaim Poland without staying in fighting shape?

"What am I going to do for workouts?" he complained well into the first week, pacing around Isaac's studio while Isaac went through his morning meditation exercises. Students were soon scheduled to arrive for their yoga class. Snow was falling outside unevenly, gathering on the lip of the window but not sticking to the ground. "I've been to three gyms already, but they weren't even gyms, just gymnastic studios for girls. Then I found a place, but the weights were rusted, the bars bent and unbalanced. But they had these stupid rubber ropes that everyone was pulling on . . . And there were no machines to speak of. How did you people train for the Olympics? I didn't even see one decent treadmill."

Sitting in the lotus position with his back straight and up against the wall, his eyes closed and his stomach hanging over his belt, filling out his sweatshirt like an overstuffed laundry bag, Isaac said, "We have Levi's and McDonald's. Jane Fonda exercise tapes can't be too far behind."

Duncan tossed him a look of frustration. Then he said, "Does that work?"

"Does what work?"

"You know . . . what you're doing over there. Sitting like that . . . I can hear you breathing all the way from the other side of the room. What muscle group does that benefit?"

Isaac's chest expanded; then he exhaled. "You have much to learn, little brother, but you are lucky. People come from all over Poland to see me and learn about yoga and life. You are already here. Imagine what could happen to you if you let go and let me teach you something?"

Duncan thought quickly; then he replied, "Nobody is going to be intimidated by two deep-breathing brothers. That's not the way to instill fear in our enemies. We need some iron to pump. How else do you kick ass?"

"What enemies are you speaking of?" Isaac asked, his eyes opening for just a moment, then closing again.

"How can you ask that?" Duncan snapped back. "We're in Poland, for God's sake. These people are born anti-Semites; it's the only thing they do well."

"The only hatred I see right now is in you."

"Wait a minute, let me get this straight. You've lived here in Poland—the mecca of Jewish martyrdom—all your life, and you have no bitterness, no rage toward these people? Whose side are you on?"

A few students reached the top of the stairs, removed their scarves and coats, and entered the studio quietly, not wishing to disturb their yogi in the process of enlightening his brother.

"I may work in a cemetery, but I don't live with demons," Isaac replied. "That is not a use of positive energy, not the way to stay centered. If I have rage, I express it through my spiritual life. Fists and anger are not the way."

"That all sounds great," Duncan said, annoyed, ignitable, "this kind of New Age, feel-good exoticism. We have it in America, too. The end of the century is leading people to all kinds of millennial non-sense—magic rocks, wind chimes, biofeedback, soy milk, positive thinking. But all this nonsense assumes that we inhabit a just world, that everything works out for the best."

"It does," Isaac replied with certainty, "even if it sometimes doesn't leave us feeling totally satisfied. There are plans; it is just that we don't make them, and we don't know them in advance."

"You know, the problem with people like you is that you forget that there are bad guys out there who aren't thinking the same way. They have other plans, and none of it concerns their inner spiritual life or what's best for you or all the people on the planet."

"That is true. But like you, they too can learn. They don't have to be that way, either."

"My God, where are you getting your news? I think you need CNN. You're obviously missing what the world is about. Where have you been all these years?"

"Right here, in Poland."

"Then this is truly a holy place. Mila escaped to the wrong country after all; she would have been better off here, with you."

"Yes, perhaps that is true. We journey seeking peace, but often the same journey can be better made without moving a step. Mila should have never left; America sounds angry."

Some of the students had now taken their mats and brought them-selves closer to the center of the room where Duncan was walking in circles, while Isaac held his ground, and his posture, like a round, fleshy statue.

"Where's your pride, Isaac? What are the lessons of the Holocaust if not to show that Jews can't be murdered without retribution? Ob-viously, you learned much about Buddha, but nothing about Babi Yar."

Isaac rose, used his open palm to readjust his neck, and then ap-proached his brother slowly and said, "I'm not going to lash out and fight back. I could do that. I have reasons to, just like you—actually, I have more reasons than you. But if I do that, I will be spending my life energy for nothing other than to fight back and cry out, and it will go into the void like everything else. But instead, I will surrender my rage and anger, and let it open up into a higher energy, something more deeply spiritual and life-affirming."

Duncan looked disgusted, but Isaac continued speaking. "Yes, I work at a cemetery, but I want to reach up out of the grave. I can feel the ghosts around me every day, but they don't call out my name; they don't wish me the same fate. I am not in exile, and I won't live in darkness. That's why I tell all of my students to live a spiritual life—to stay grounded and in this world."

Isaac then said something in Polish so that all of his students could hear. Sockless, stretching on mats with their ears tuned in to their teacher, they all nodded in Duncan's direction, as if to say, "Listen carefully; this is what you came to Poland for."

A thin young woman with cheeks that were pink and an alpine nose that remained red from the outside cold, looked at Duncan with dark, droopy eyes. Not exactly Minskoff material. Duncan noticed that she had a Snoopy tattoo on her left arm, in the same spot where a vaccine would ordinarily go.

Isaac walked around the room and addressed his students. Duncan watched their faces, which were all flushed as though their blood was about to burst through their skin. Isaac then translated for his brother. "Yoga is all preparation for death. The moment of death is the most important, because how you leave determines where you go. Life is all preparation. It's best not to be caught by fear, panic, or anger. These are all distractions. You want to keep breathing no matter what."

The entire room was now focused on Duncan. There was silence and telescopic stares. And of course, the sound of his own uneven breath.

WITHIN DAYS, ISAAC had Duncan on the mat in the first of many life lessons that took the strangulated form of yoga postures.

"Concentrate during your meditation work," Isaac said. "Where is your mind?"

"What kind of an athlete is so stiff?" Isaac wondered aloud. "It's like trying to stretch stone."

His brother was right: Duncan arrived in Poland like a cargo of petrified rock, his meridians and pressure points so ossified and clogged with muscle and tension that his spiritual energy—if there was any—was hopelessly stuck in traffic. On the outside, Duncan looked like an Adonis; on the inside, he was a car wreck. But as the days and sessions continued, Duncan's body began to loosen up. His toes suddenly became touchable, his spine eased into accordion movements, his neck allowed his head to scan the world in more supple directions.

Duncan even began to sit in on Isaac's classes. It became apparent that his brother's students came not just for yoga. Isaac was more than just a teacher. His students were seekers, and he was their compass. A chubby Polish Jew was going to lead the way. Messianic madness all over again. Jesus Christ succeeded. Yet there were so many other charismatic and, in some cases, holy Jews—from Shabbatai Zvi to Vladimir Jabotinsky to the Lubavitcher Schneerson—who were not so lucky. And now Isaac Borowski, Mila's abandoned son, was making his own bid to close out the millennium. With Duncan, she had hoped for a Jewish avenger, but it was the son she left behind who was somehow better equipped for the task. Isaac was both prophet and savior without the credentials of a lunatic. And he had followers. What was it that they saw in him? What did Mila leave behind that couldn't be passed on to Duncan, as well?

The bonding—mother to child, brother to brother—that had nothing to grab onto so many years earlier finally hit on some traction. The brothers took long walks. Isaac spoke in almost a whisper; Duncan learned to listen.

"The murdered ones are still with us," Isaac said. "Their souls did not disappear. You can still feel their presence, but there is no need to worry. They ask nothing of us, only that we be kind to ourselves."

Every so often—and sometimes for no apparent reason at all— Isaac let out a stream of gushing laughter. Howls spilled from his mouth as though his speech had all the moderation of a drunk. Each outburst took his brother by surprise. But Duncan got used to it, and slowly, hesitantly at first, he learned to laugh, too.

They strolled through the center of the Old Town Square. The streets were cobbled, the cracks filled with snow in the mold of toothpaste. There was a fountain without water. The surrounding buildings were steepled, gabled, and domed, their facades freshly painted, oddly enough, in pastels. Rising above them was a loud army plane, a post-historic creature that drowned out the conversation of two tipsy men arguing in guttural Polish, standing underneath the canopied entrance to a restaurant. Meanwhile, a cutting wind hissed through alleyways and pushed the brothers along.

In the old Jewish District near Isaac's studio, they entered a park off Grzybowski Street. Some children were playing soccer with a brown, beat-up ball that skidded on the snow; the children haplessly slipped after it. Near the edge of the park was a fenced-in section that housed the long stilted poles of a swing set. The chains were unworkably rusted, yet Duncan noticed that each basket was moving forward and backward—noisily, unrhythmically, and unoccupied. Twelve empty swings rocking all by themselves.

"Something amazing, no? It happens this way every day, no matter the season," Isaac said, pointing at the phenomenon. "But only in this park. This is where all the Jewish children used to live and play."

"You must have some pretty strong winds in this neighborhood." Duncan said.

"Do you feel any wind right now?"

"No." Duncan's voice dropped.

"It's not the wind," Isaac said, and then bit his lip as if to stop himself from saying anything further.

"What is it then?"

Isaac didn't answer; he just continued walking. Duncan tried to swallow, but his saliva bubbled in his throat like a carbonated drink. He couldn't move. He was cold, and his face felt as though it was getting larger. Or was it just his anger that was swelling? The blended sounds of the squeaking swings and the trampling feet settled down, and Duncan started to hear the melody and Polish lyrics of one of Chopin's lullabies.

The soccer ball now skidded in Duncan's direction. At first he was startled; then he picked it up with his hands as though the rules of the game didn't matter—at least not in Poland. A blond-haired boy wearing a knit cap and earmuffs ran after the ball, nearly crashing into Duncan. The boy's cheeks were stoplight red, and his breath misted in front of his face. Politely, shyly, almost in a whisper, he murmured a request to have the ball returned. Duncan looked back at the rocking swings and winced at the wailing, screeching chorus of chains.

Desperate for guidance, he searched for his brother. Where should the ball go? Duncan didn't know. Isaac, cloaked in a puffy blue parka, was already back on Grzybowski Street. Duncan leaned back and heaved the soccer ball as far as he could throw it. All the children followed the ball's path as it sailed over their heads and landed inside the pen. A few bounces later it rolled against the fence and came to a stop, while the swings continued to sway back and forth, rocking the ghosts of Jewish children at unfinished play.

Chapter Fourteen

Rock. Rock. Rock.

There was a hitch in the movement of the swings as the whole line of them reached for the open, blue sky. Snapping like whips, they eventually doubled back the other way. The lulling route: up and down, back and forth. Despite a brisk winter morning, the sun still warmed the faces of the children. Tiny voices chattered and laughed. At picnic tables, mothers, nannies, and snacks were all waiting for a recess.

Milan knew how to kick her feet forward, propelling the swing as though it were a carriage to the clouds. She was more courageous than the other kids, even the older ones. Her swing seemed to resent the confinement that came from the chains. Duncan had taught Milan to be fearless, as he had been taught—the Katz concession with fun. But one can't escape when the only getaway is a pendulum.

"I won't let you fall," he would say.

"I know, Tatty," she would reply.

But with Sharon doing the pushing, the swing was more restrained, the flight less ambitious. And Milan also seemed less interested. On this day, she was wearing the long face of a child lost in thought.

"What's wrong, Milan?" Sharon asked.

"Where is Tatty now?"

"Were you just thinking about him?"

"Yes." Milan's upper lip pouted with an extreme overbite. "He used to take me here."

"I know."

"So where is he?"

"He's on an adventure."

"Finding his brother?"

"Yes."

"In Poland?"

"Yes."

"Where is that, Mommy?"

"Far away, far, far away, Milan."

"I think he needs us. We should go get him."

Sharon wondered how her husband was faring with his real-life brother. And what about all those once-dead ghosts, rising up to welcome home a native, prodigal son? For Duncan, Poland should have been paradise. But she knew better. What he wanted was a live family, not some reconstituted, haunted replacement.

"Mommy," Milan continued, "he needs us. I can feel it. I had a dream about Tatty. He is lonely and sad. We should go bring him back and make him feel better. He should live with us on Yuma Street."

This conversation had happened before. The child wanted what she wanted. A family belongs together. The modern adult world might revel in the narcissism of individual autonomy and human perfectability, but children come from wombs—they know who they want sitting in the nest beside them.

"There is nothing to worry about," Sharon reassured her daughter, now pushing the swing more forcefully to offset the fact that Milan had stopped kicking. "Your father is great at survival; he knows how to live alone."

"Why should he have to?"

A pair of regal-looking swans glided along the water in a nearby duck pond. Earlier in the morning Milan had fed them the whole wheat portion of a tuna sandwich. Were they mates? Sharon wondered. She watched her daughter bravely extend her little hand over the water, nearly touching the long, elegant broomstick necks of the swans. The swans had returned again, and Milan was ready to get off the swing.

"Can Tatty come home?" she asked as she hopped back to the ground.

Sharon was silent. She came from a world of silence. The hushed music of a childhood spent in the wooded forests of North Carolina. Emotions never registered as emotions; they went somewhere else. The trees didn't speak; why should the people? Duncan always feared that

Sharon would never be able to overcome this perfected stillness, and that she would pass it on to Milan. But he would never have assumed that the proper remedy for his fears would have been to shatter the family and isolate the child from her mother.

Meanwhile, Milan's father was indeed in Poland. No longer anchored to Yuma Street, no longer with his wife and daughter, there was nothing to keep him away from the magical allure of Warsaw, and Isaac, and those demons that would now appear even more lifelike than before. A sad but ultimately true Katz paradox was that abandonment ran in the family. They feared separation and yet they also came to expect it, and sometimes they even helped it along.

Duncan's separation from his family had become unbearable. Sharon knew that. She had consigned a Jewish boy to a biblical exile, banished him from Eden all over again. For a year, Duncan had lived in New York like a Macy's Thanksgiving Day balloon, hovering above the island, relying on clowns not to let go of the line. But all he saw was an empty island, receding and getting smaller, and no clowns. With an existence so weightless, the ground so shifting, why not try Poland? He could never replace what was now gone, but he could find the place where the accident occurred, the fork in the road that led to that fateful detour where all the Katzes were destined to become lost.

"I want Tatty to come home!" Milan threatened to throw a tantrum.

"Tatty will be okay," Sharon said quietly. "We'll all be okay."

"No, I want him!"

Father and daughter were connected by loose-fitting dreams. They came at night, like Morse-code flashes, like Yankee's typewriter tapping in their heads.

HIS GREAT-GRANDCHILDREN STOOD beside the tomb of Rabbi Chaim Lewinstein. Snow covered most of the graves, the crumbling headstones, the overgrown pathways. During this time of year, it was hard to tell that this was even a cemetery. The screeching wind helped. So too did the chalky grayness of the sky. And of course the weeping willows—sorrowful, bent over, disgraced, no matter what the season.

"So this where he is?" Duncan asked.

"Yes, he was a great man," Isaac replied.

"It's a pretty big tomb for a rabbi."

"In Poland, rabbis were gods, like rock stars today. Lewinstein was one of them. I read in a book that all the Jews of Warsaw—and many gentiles—went to his funeral. This place was filled with thousands of people. Many believed he had mystical powers."

"Maybe that's where you got it from. Larry Breitbart told me that people now believe the same thing about you."

"I am not a religious man."

"That's not what I said. I've seen the way your students look at you—like you're some kind of messiah."

"I am just a yoga teacher, and a caretaker of dead Jewish souls—nobody special."

Isaac then stepped away from Lewinstein's grave site, giving Duncan some time alone. Duncan caressed the tomb, running his hand over the coarse stone. He then rested his forehead on the headstone itself. An old man wandered into the cemetery. He was carrying a camera, which he pointed at Duncan and fired. Despite the surrounding flash, which momentarily turned the stone from a toilet-water brown to a neon beige, Duncan didn't notice the light or the photographer. But Isaac did. He raised his finger into the air, about to call out. But the photographer had disappeared darting off through the gate and then around the corner, skidding on the ice.

Isaac returned to his brother.

"This is our playground," Duncan announced. "Cemeteries. What else does our family know? We are undertakers, by profession and family practice. I buried my parents too soon. And you, you never knew your parents. But you virtually live here."

"There is more you should know," Isaac said hesitantly, trying to protect his brother. "My wife is buried here, too."

"What? You were married?"

"Yes. Not for long, just five years."

"When?"

"I was a young man."

"What was her name?"

"Masha."

"What happened to her?"

"She killed herself."

"Jesus. Wow, what . . . ?"

"Life in Poland was hard—I understand why our mother left this country. It didn't get better. Masha was a troubled woman. I thought I could rescue her, to save her. And I was selfish, too; I didn't want another woman in my life to leave me. But she was sick, and she took her own life. A drug overdose."

"What is it with this family? We're cursed; we weren't meant for happiness. The Nazis killed most of us and then stuck pins inside the heads of voodoo dolls to take care of the rest."

Duncan didn't expect an answer, and Isaac wouldn't even try.

"And you . . . you are divorced?" Isaac asked.

"Not yet, but getting there."

"Mr. Silver told me."

"Silver didn't leave out much."

"And you have a daughter, he says."

"Yes, Milan."

"Good, you named her for our mother."

"Well, I put in an extra letter, let her pretend she's Italian. Our family is good with disguises."

"Yes, I know. Duncan is not a very Jewish name, either."

Isaac locked up the cemetery, and the brothers exited through the gate. Duncan would have left flowers on Lewinstein's grave, but there were none to be found.

"Flowers should not be allowed to come in here, I suppose," Duncan said, raising the collar on his mohair coat.

"Beauty belongs everywhere," Isaac replied, "particularly where there has been so much ugliness."

The next stop of the day was going to be the home where Rabbi Lewinstein had once lived and where Mila, in fact, had been raised. The building was on Tlomackie Street near Warsaw's downtown. But that whole block, which included Lewinstein's home and the Great Synagogue, had been razed flat by the Nazis. Now in its place stood the Sony skyscraper, a rocket ship of green glass, the tallest building in all of Poland.

When Isaac brought Duncan to the foot of the Sony Tower, Duncan tilted his neck back, looked up, and grinned.

"Did you bring a padlock?" Duncan asked.

"Why do you ask?"

"I said I wanted to take back what was once ours. This will do—

a nice piece of real estate, don't you think? Good location, right downtown. Spectacular views . . ."

"It belongs to the Japanese," Isaac said. "They had nothing to do with the Holocaust."

"Right now they're on our land, and they fought on Hitler's side. What more do you want?"

"A sane brother."

"I think I'll take the penthouse for myself. Which floor do you want?"

Onward they went, toward the Jewish District, in the direction of the Nozyk Synagogue where Rabbi Lewinstein had once presided. Along the way they passed the beaten-down, pancake-white faces of chubby Poles returning home from work. No one was in a hurry. The end of Communism didn't exactly lead to a world without grimness. The streets were dirty. Clotheslines were arranged with zigzag imprecision, linking the gray, Eastern bloc buildings. Unheated streetcars, pathetic relics of the 1950s, rocked from side-to-side as though too large for the tracks. At Chielma Street, across from the tall monument known as Stalin's gift to the Polish people, Isaac and Duncan strolled through a tacky outdoor shopping mall. The merchants were selling jeans and scarves and coats that were already well on their way to becoming vintage.

Duncan and Isaac arrived at the Nozyk Synagogue in time for Friday night Shabbat services. They hadn't planned on becoming part of a *minyan*. The brothers didn't even realize what day of the week it was. Neither of them was religious, although strangely Isaac wore a yarmulke on his head wherever he went. He stood out as a Jew in Poland, while the scant leftovers who had remained were hiding underneath more than mere skullcaps. It still didn't seem safe to come out. It never would for a Jew in Poland. Duncan observed that his brother was revered and admired by almost everyone who greeted him, as if he were the prime minister or, better yet, the pope. And yet he chose not to conceal the worst scar of all—the covered head of a prideful Jew.

The brothers entered through a side door of the Nozyk Synagogue. The building was white, adorned with a Star of David and adjoining tablets bearing the Ten Commandments. The front of the synagogue had been defaced in red with anti-Semitic graffiti. All around were skeletal trees. A few old men had already gathered in the sanctuary. There was an empty balcony. Several overhead windows were stingy in permitting light to enter from a hanging full moon. A cracked chandelier with blown-out bulbs wobbled above the pulpit. The seats were terribly worn, the red velvet skinned to the hide. The ark was ancient, uncurtained, as though ransacked and left for dead. A Salvation Army Torah sat alone, too old to remove and unscroll, the Hebrew words lying on the sheepskin like dust.

Some tourists entered the synagogue. Many were young students on winter break. They were Jews carrying cameras. Duncan noticed that some of the old men approached the youngsters.

"Dollarin, dollarin?" the men asked.

They wanted dollars.

The students reached uncomfortably into their pockets.

Worse than the threadbare accouterments was the rabbi. There was none. Isaac said that a group in Israel was in the process of sending one over, as though it would take nothing short of a Marshall Plan airlift to bring Judaism back to Poland. Where was Israel going to find a rabbi who spoke Polish—and who was a master of self-defense? Duncan wondered. Without a rabbi, the old men, like a class without a teacher, had for years led their own services, alternating among themselves. Most of Lewinstein's former congregation had gone up in smoke. These were the ones who had made it back . . . well, sort of. Sitting in the last row, Duncan stared out into the near-empty synagogue. Was a mass, reverse exodus back to Poland even possible? This was a land where Pharaoh's heart could never become unhardened, a country that had seen worse than mere plagues, where the seas were unpartable. Duncan turned to his brother and said, "This is too depressing. Let's leave."

THE STRIPED, CANDY-CANE beach chairs would have sagged under the weight of their ample bottoms—except for Mila's. Wraithlike, Mila no longer carried enough flesh to make a difference. Cynthia and her patient lifted their faces toward the midday sun.

"This is nice, don't you think, Mila?" Cynthia asked. "Fresh Miami air. Warm sun."

A balcony on the eleventh floor of Mount Sinai Hospital overlooked Biscayne Bay. There was no shade. The western sun took no pity on the tile floors and concrete walls. The breezes were rare, and the cars speeding along the Julia Tuttle Causeway didn't make the most ideal background music for recuperating patients. But occasionally, when Mila felt up to it, the nurses would bring her out onto the balcony to rest, and nap, and think, and endure the searing sun. Mila was never interested in a tan, just the burn.

"I think it's time for the big secret," she announced to her matinee audience.

The nurses always knew that this day was going to come. Mila had spoken from the very beginning about her gravest secret of all, her deepest shame, the reason why, no matter what else happened to her in life, she was consigned to hell—a place even worse than the one she had survived in Auschwitz. The candle that measured her life had been burning at both ends, and now the wax was running perilously thin, the flames sizzling toward one another.

Abandoning Isaac was not the entire story. It was worse than that. The most sordid aspects of her motherhood were about to be revealed. Cancer's time clock was ticking. If she didn't tell the nurses soon, then the secret would be buried with her and lost forever. The nurses couldn't pardon her; they didn't have the power. No one did, not even God. But they could unburden her of the story, the one that no one else knew, the tale she had carried with her out of Warsaw, the only thing that the border patrol had allowed her to take. Maybe it was the story itself that had caused her T cells to go bad in the first place.

"Call the others," Mila said. "I want them to hear, too."

Anxiously, but also excitedly, Cynthia stood tall in her white uniform. She was about to run off to the hallway pay phone when Mila doubled over in her own lap. The patient moaned and began to shake.

"What is it?" Cynthia, now kneeling, asked urgently.

"Too much pain."

"Where?"

"Stomach . . . where the stitches are."

Cynthia opened Mila's robe, disentangled her arms, and pushed her back against the chair so she could get a better look at Mila's stomach.

"The stitches are healing just fine. I'll run and get you some more pain medicine."

"No, it's the stitches. It feels like they are opening. Ach!" she screamed.

"Don't be silly," Cynthia reassured her. "It's not the stitches; they're shut real good. There's hardly even going to be a scar. You can still wear a bikini. I'm going to get a doctor. Be right back."

Mila was now alone on the balcony, her robe still open, the sun beaming against the brown and blue swollen incision on her stomach. That's where the heat was. The scar caused by the fire, the fire in her belly.

It was dark in the restaurant in the Nowe Miasto section of Warsaw. Red carpet. Wood walls. No windows. The tables a lopsided mahogany. A battleship for a bar, anchored with Polish and Russian liquor bottles, paperweight shot glasses, and a wide mirror against the wall. Across from the bar, a large stuffed fish looked trapped, as though caught in a net. It smelled as if the taxidermist had been called away before completing the job. There was the sound of American jazz—Charlie Parker—swinging from a three-person ensemble. The men were playing on a one-step, elevated stage. All three wore skinny black ties and cream-colored shirts, as if the Kingston Trio were still touring Poland. At a corner table a man wearing a white panama hat gestured wildly with a cigarette in his hand, ashes falling with each stroke, the cigarette like an usher's flashlight.

There was a rumor that all the restaurants in Warsaw had closed down for the night, refusing to serve anyone. Presumably they were protesting the government, which had virtually surrendered to the profitable shakedown operations run by the Polish and Russian Mafia. The restaurants had finally had enough. It was time for Lech Walesa to show who was in charge of the country: was it the new government or the new gangsters?

But this restaurant had decided to remain open, largely because it catered to the mob itself. Russian and Polish hoodlums had to eat, even if the rest of Warsaw had been placed on a forced hunger strike.

At one table several men were playing cards. Duncan and Isaac sat nearby. The brothers signaled for their waitress, a stump of a woman wearing high heels that looked like they had been sliced sideways with an ax. The restaurant specialized in fish, and the menu boasted over twenty varieties: sea bass in German white wine, salmon from the Caspian, and carp and trout from the Baltic. But this was Poland. Shortages were as likely as delays on the trolley. The waitress apologized that there was indeed no fish—neither fresh nor frozen—so the brothers ordered borscht and cold herring, the Polish equivalent of a Big Mac and fries.

"So tell me about our mother." Isaac turned to Duncan, sliding the useless menu onto his lap.

"No, you tell me."

"How would I know? She left me when I was a baby."

"You still knew her better."

"Duncan," Isaac said desperately. He removed his glasses; his eyes were dark and somber. "What was she like?"

His younger brother gazed in the direction of the cardplayers. Duncan could tell that they were playing poker.

"That's all you have to know," Duncan said, pointing at a hand in progress. "It's right there, in that game. Do you play?"

"No, why?"

"Hard to believe. Neither of Mila's sons play cards, not even the one who looks just like her."

"She played?"

"Did she play?" Duncan snickered. "She was a shark."

"A shark?"

"A big fish that eats up all the other fish. It's on the menu, Isaac."

A man standing behind Isaac spoke. "Excuse me, may we join you?"

It was Nathan Silver, the panama now placed on his head, and three of his associates. Two gorillas and an older, dapper gentleman who looked harmless but no more innocent than the others. An old Argus camera hung from his neck like an oversized locket. Isaac stood, pirouetted around, and recognized his American patron.

"Ah, this is Mr. Silver," Isaac said to Duncan gleefully. "I've been telling you about him."

Duncan had already figured it out. He could spot a "made man" from any distance. These people were the baby-sitters from his youth, the confidantes of his parents. There was no incognito for them, not even in Poland.

"Let us buy you a beer," Silver said, removing his panama and ramming half a cigarette into an ashtray. The cigarette folded into itself like lightning. "They serve great German lagers in this place."

"No lagers!" Duncan said emphatically as Silver and his men pulled up chairs.

"Why not?" Silver asked.

Laughing, Isaac answered, "Because *lager* was what they used to call the concentration camps."

Silver examined the label on the bottle that he had brought over with him. "This beer wasn't made in Auschwitz; it's not a concentration-camp brew."

It didn't matter to Duncan.

"Okay, suit yourself," Silver said. "What will you have then?"

"They have seltzer here?"

"Come on!" Silver squawked. "Why don't you just go ahead and order stuffed cabbage and a blintz?"

The goons at the table—a couple of rock'em sock'em robots dressed in baggy black pants and thin black turtlenecks—laughed along with their boss. Duncan didn't find anything about Poland funny, particularly not the food that was once eaten there. But just then, the music coming from the stage changed from one form of jazz to another—Jewish jazz. All eyes at Duncan's table scanned the ensemble, trying to confirm what their ears were picking up. It was klezmer, the mother music of Polish Jewry, now being played by Polish Catholics.

"Do you hear what I hear?" Silver asked.

His men nodded. Duncan cringed. Isaac laughed.

"Jewish folk music is now popular among Polish people," Isaac said. "So is Jewish food. You might be able to order stuffed cabbage and a blintz here."

"I'm getting sick," Duncan said. He reached inside his coat for the Donnatal and took a swig without any seltzer to chase it down.

"I think we should dance," Silver said.

His men nodded in agreement. Isaac had already skipped off to the makeshift dance floor, which was nothing more than a worn-down red carpet in front of the stage. The others followed, and the men joined hands, dancing the hora. Isaac was particularly graceful in his movements—the twisted grapevine where legs cross over and kick, arms swing back and forth, and bodies dip and spin. The band seemed pleased by the presence of dancers. The Poles loved the music, but hadn't quite yet gotten the hang of the choreography. You need Jewish rhythm for that. The cardplayers looked on impassively. The bartender, grooving with the sounds coming from the stage, rapped a heavy cognac glass against the dull wood finish of the bar. In the corner, an undersized, fashionably dressed man was playing a pinball machine, his hips gyrating, his face contorted as if engaged in some Chinese sex act. The front of the machine had a picture of a mermaid and sailors lost at sea. Isaac motioned to his brother to join the circle. But for Duncan, the music, the dance, this place, were all blasphemy.

"Your brother's such a stiff," Silver said as he whirled past Isaac, "like the dead people you deal with everyday."

"I am working on him," Isaac said.

"Good luck. Is there any hope?" Silver asked, the perspiration bleeding from his creased white suit.

"With human beings there is always hope."

Then, surprisingly, Duncan walked over—no, he actually closed in as if he were about to tackle somebody—and joined the hora circle. Perhaps he had gotten lonely. Or perhaps he wanted to make a statement that despite the confiscated homes and the menace of Japanese skyscrapers, the true heritage, the folklore, could still be reclaimed.

Isaac smiled at his brother as they locked arms and danced. The clarinet whined, the cymbals shivered, the violin sent sounds into the air that traveled underneath the skin.

"You see, the music of this country can return without force," Isaac said, shouting above the jazz.

"And also without Jews," Duncan replied.

When the music stopped, the thin clarinet player announced that the band would be taking a break. He nodded at the visitors who had danced not knowing that they were Jews, merely assuming that they were gangsters.

When the dancers returned to the table, Duncan asked Silver, "So tell me, why are you here? You've already reunited me with my brother. What more is left for you here in Poland?"

"Nostalgia," Silver replied. He snapped his finger. The man at the pinball machine pulled away from the flippers, and the silvery ball slid down into its hole without touching a bumper.

"What do you mean?"

"What do you think, you brothers are the only ones with claims to this country? You know, even Jewish criminals have to come from someplace."

"Duncan, you have found your first customer," Isaac laughed. "Mr. Silver is going to stay in Poland?"

"No, I'm not moving back, just taking care of business."

"And what business is that?" Duncan asked.

A tall waitress with straight, thin blond hair and dark smiling teeth brought more lagers, to the table. "For you pretty men," she said. Silver's goons squirmed. The bottles chimed against one another as she removed them from the tray.

"We have things in common with the new captains of Polish industry," Silver said.

"Like murder?"

"No, like Brighton Beach. The Russian Mafia that operates out of Brooklyn works closely with your uncle Larry. And these American Russians, who are also Jews, have business interests in Poland. It's a strange thing: two crime families in New York, both led by Jewish capos."

"Don't say that in front of me," Duncan said angrily.

"What did I say this time?"

Isaac was getting the hang, and hang-ups, of his younger sibling. "*Capo* has a very different association for my brother than what I think you mean when you say it."

"Why else are you here in Poland?" Duncan asked.

"Larry wanted us to stick around and keep an eye out for the two of you. The boss says you're an accident waiting to happen."

"I don't need protection. I don't fear gangsters."

"It's not the Russian mob I'm talking about. We know those guys; we'll always be able to watch over you. What I'm worried about are the anti-Semites. They're still here. I heard that there are German neo-Nazis in Poland right now trying to recruit new members."

Duncan seemed pleased by this piece of news.

"Neo-Nazis?" he asked, as though Silver had just brought out a birthday cake. "Here, in Poland?"

"That's the word on the street," Nathan Silver said. Scratching his head, he added, "You know, I never understood what they mean by *neo*-Nazis. What's so new about them? The way I see it, you either are one or you're not."

As the undisputed expert at the table, Duncan explained, "The only difference is that the neo-Nazis are proud of what the original Nazis did, even though they deny that the concentration camps ever existed or that anyone was killed."

"I'm lost," Silver confessed.

"So are they," Duncan said.

"So are you," Isaac added.

"Anyway," Silver continued, "Larry's worried about the damage you might cause—particularly with all the trouble they already got around here."

"Why does he care so much?'

"Because it's bad for business. He told me to keep you out of disaster, and if I can't do that, at least to clean up after you. He said you have pretty good muscle, that you would have made a good hit man. But you never know, when you're not fighting on your own turf, things can go wrong, even for the son of Mila Katz. I hear your mother taught a whole bunch of guys, including Larry, how to fight; that she could match scars with anyone. It was her idea to take out the Lorenzo family. Did she ever tell you about that one?"

"No, and please don't say anymore. I don't want to know."

"I do," Isaac said. "Please tell me."

"She was quite a lady . . ."

"Stop!" Duncan interrupted. "Not another word. My brother is a virgin."

Isaac began to wonder what kind of men these people were, and why his mother would choose to abandon him in order to befriend them.

The older gentleman, the one with the camera around his neck, leaned over toward Duncan and said, "I saw you fall."

"Excuse me?"

"At your *bris*, a long time ago. I was there. I saw you fall out of Breitbart's arms. I got it all on film."

Duncan nodded, as though he recognized not the man, but his

work, the eyes that once looked through a lens and framed a vertigo that never reached ground.

"I've seen the reel," Duncan said. "It's a fancy piece of filmmaking, especially for a *bris*. I have it at home. In my family, your eight millimeter work is like the Zapruder film. I play it all the time."

"Your mother had great hands," Carlo Costello said, "like a gold-glove shortstop."

"That was the first and last time she ever held me."

Carlo Costello looked at Duncan somberly. It was his recollection that Mila hadn't held Duncan even then. After the catch, and the rescue, she had returned her son to Breitbart's lap.

Isaac had heard enough. With the band now sitting at the bar, he walked over to the musical instruments, which were all leaning up against the wall like kickstands. He sat down at the piano, spinning the stool downward to adjust the height. He then looked over at the pianist and gestured, asking if he could play. The man raised a glass in salute, and Isaac cracked his stubby fingers and slid his glasses closer to the tip of his nose. Slowly he began to play. Notes and chords lifted from the piano; the restaurant became filled with the music of George Gershwin. Isaac was playing "Someone to Watch over Me." His face was serious and mournful. What he lacked in technique, he made up in melody—the refrain that had been the anthem of his childhood. Hearing the music, Duncan rose as if being summoned by a primal beating of the drums. The Katz family theme song. Duncan had never learned to play, nor did he ever remember hearing it while growing up, and yet he had hummed this very song to Milan.

What would Mila have thought of her son? Not the street fighter, but the man at the piano, playing her instrument. Some women from the bar, probably Polish prostitutes, with spiky hair and borderless makeup smeared outside the lines of the face, moved toward Isaac and flirtatiously rested their drinks—screwdrivers—on the piano. The cardplayers stopped in the middle of a hand, their cards lying on the table like an uneaten meal. Everyone in the restaurant was being serenaded, but none more so than the American whose fists and spine and heart were opening with each tap of a musical key.

. . .

No one would have been brave enough to say it out loud, but Duncan was indeed changing. Ever so slowly, but observably true. What was once an inexhaustible fountain of anger—feeding on itself, continually recycling, replenishing, overflowing, making any hope for containment impossible—was starting to break, like a fever succumbing to aspirin.

Duncan had taken a number of his brother's yoga classes. He had practiced the bent-over and sustained movements, the loud-breathing, the posing in the quest for spiritual peace.

"Keep breathing," Isaac chanted. "Hold the position, stay centered, concentrate . . ."

Duncan listened carefully to Isaac's words and focused on his meditation exercises. But Duncan was at best a long-term project. Whatever forces guided him would take time to dissipate, like a volcano that had to smoke up the sky before running out of lava.

They had breakfast at a small café near the university in Warsaw. There were many bookstores along Nowy Swiat, on the same block as the café. Duncan stopped in one of the stores. He was interested in Bruno Schulz, the Polish novelist who was shot dead by a Gestapo officer in 1942. It was yet another crime against the Jews that could never be remedied, because there is no way of knowing what the world had lost by having Schulz's voice silenced. Duncan bought copies of *Cinnamon Shops* and *Sanitorium under the Sign of the Hourglass* in their original Polish. After a meal of eggs, hard rolls, and a strange-looking fish that Duncan refused to touch, the brothers took a *doroski* to another section of the city. Isaac said he wanted to buy something for Milan.

"I have an idea," he said proudly, "a present no other girl in America could have."

They walked into a small shop that had a porthole for a window on a crooked side street. Isaac obviously had been there before. The owner welcomed him warmly, but kept a respectful distance. Excitedly holding Duncan's arm, Isaac walked his brother over to several wide shelves near the back of the store.

"You see, this is what I had in mind for her."

Isaac pointed to a lineup of wood-carved dolls. But these weren't just any dolls. They were carvings indigenous to Poland, *shtetl* life sculpted out of wood. The faces were of Jews. Pious rabbis. A bride

and groom trembling underneath a *huppa*. Hasidic fiddlers dancing
with barn animals. A three-dimensional world that would have impressed even Chagall.

"So, what do you think?" Isaac asked with a self-satisfied smile.
"Milan would like this, no? How about this one?" He reached for the
wedding couple.

"Who makes these?" Duncan asked.

"Some old man in a nearby village. Very talented . . ."

"Is he Jewish?"

"No, I don't think so."

"And who buys them?"

"I don't know. Mainly American tourists. They don't sell many."

"This is a disgrace! How dare they make and sell this Jewish kitsch?
These things are false idols. There's no remorse here, just cheap, commercial tourist schlock. They're mocking all that they helped to de-
stroy. Why don't they just put the faces of dead Jews on T-shirts?"

Cautiously, Isaac said, "I'll buy this and you decide later if you
want to bring it back to Milan."

"I'm not taking this back to America! In fact, nobody is going to
buy any of these anymore . . ."

Isaac darted off to the counter to pay for the doll. He was so
nervous about leaving Duncan alone with the other trinkets that his
zlotys fell out of his wallet like tea leaves. There was a loud noise.
Isaac hesitated, then squirmed; finally, he worked up enough courage
to glance back at his brother. Duncan had windmilled his large forearm, splitting a stack of shelves as if he were back on the *Tonight Show*
amusing Johnny Carson. He then took each wood carving and, without the aid of a knee, broke them in half like breadsticks.

The proprietor, a small man with a round face and white tufts of
hair on the tops of his ears, ran outside, flapped his arms, and tried
to wave down a policeman. He found one walking his beat on the
other side of Malachowskiego. The proprietor hurried the officer into
the store just as Duncan finished destroying the last of the nostalgic
stock.

"Breathe deep, young brother," Isaac said, his hands clamping down
on Duncan's shoulders as though trying to prevent him from becoming airborne. Duncan was already breathing heavily, and his eyes were
wide open.

"Stop telling me to keep breathing!" Duncan replied. "I've been breathing since they cut the umbilical cord. You breathe deep; I know what I'm doing!"

The officer, as solid as an Eastern bloc condominium, grabbed Duncan from behind, but Duncan had little trouble hurling him backward. The policeman tripped over the painted wood carvings that now littered the floor like sawdust.

"Isaac, tell them there's a new sheriff in town."

Isaac didn't translate, but he was just about to say something to the officer when Duncan screamed, "Come on! You want a Jew, you got him! Welcome to the new world of the fighting Jews. We don't go down as easy. We take on all anti-Semites. We're not just trained for Talmud and the SAT's."

"Duncan, don't . . ." Isaac pleaded. "This is not the way."

The proprietor ducked underneath the counter, afraid that more property damage was about to take place. Isaac stepped to the side, realizing that his brother was once again operating under the influence of a consciousness that could not be controlled, largely because it didn't even belong to him.

Other policemen followed, but they were met with the same fate—stumbling sideways or having their arms twisted backward, forced into a backflip. Finally, one of them took out a gun. Duncan raised his arms in the air, but nobody assumed that it was as an act of surrender. To prevent a bloodbath, Isaac stepped in. He too raised his arms and then spoke to the officers in almost a whisper. Until that moment, they hadn't noticed that Isaac Borowski was in the store with them. Seconds later the guns were returned to their holsters. The police seemed embarrassed. Duncan had no idea what his brother had told them, but those few words and Isaac's face had set him free. Duncan went from being a vandal and a disturber of the peace to a sympathetic tourist. It was innocence by association. The police spoke to the proprietor and then exited the store. The owner left as well, departing into the back room, as if leaving the brothers alone.

"Who are you?" Duncan asked Isaac, pleadingly. "What do these people see in you? What are they afraid of? What makes you so special?"

Chapter Fifteen

HE CRIB WAS crowded with stuffed animals. Their colorful limbs stuck through the slats as though they were preparing to break loose from the cage. The baby was sleeping beside them. His little chest rose and then fell with each breath. His arms tossed off to his sides. His head was flopping over; his cheeks were red and lined from the warm sheets.

Mila's brown leather satchel was packed. But she still had one final good-bye before leaving Poland.

Earlier in the day she had gone to Keller's jewelry shop, knowing that he wasn't there. It was a shoe box of a business—one glass counter, several tiny file-cabinet drawers against the wall. She needed the device, the souvenir he had taken from the camps. Keller Borowski had been a jeweler's apprentice before the Nazis invaded Poland. But even before that he always prided himself on his penmanship. Letters on paper were good, but he was even better with gold and silver. He loved engraving, printing names and initials onto the backs of watches and bracelets and inside the smooth loops of wedding rings. His hands were steady; his inscriptions, carved with sweeping elegance. And so when the Russians finally came to liberate the camp, Keller bolted not for the front gate, but for the barrack where all new inmates had first been processed. It was there where he claimed his reparation.

Mila knew that he kept the instrument inside a drawer in the back of the jewelry shop, near a rack filled with cheap, thirdhand watches. She had seen him use it before. He filled the top of the rotary machine with the blue dye, plugged it into the wall socket, and watched the needles pivot up and down, pushing ink into the skin of those who now wanted a fresh tattoo. Years earlier the customers were prisoners in a concentration camp, the Nazis were doing the engraving, and nobody wanted to be jabbed by the device. Keller had been one of those prisoners. And their tattoos were neither elaborate nor fashionable. Just random blue numbers—without a name or picture.

Keller provided this service for only a few customers. None of them knew that the machine was a genuine article from the camps, standard issue of the SS. These select customers wanted to have the name of a girlfriend painted onto their arms beside a swelling heart or an anchor dragging down their biceps. Keller managed all right with these requests. But what interested him even more was the irony of turning the signature pen of the Nazis onto the Poles themselves. During the war, so many Poles had pretended not to notice the barbed-wire fortresses; they had reveled in the fact that they stood on the safe side of the death factory, far away from the assembly line of mass murder. These were the kind of people who wouldn't look you in the eye, even if you stared right at them. They were the guilty ones, the avoidant, with their "please go away" personas.

Mila took the machine and left, making sure that the top was loaded with enough ink to do the job.

She placed her hand on Isaac's face and then stroked his head, which was lightly carpeted with red peach fuzz. There was nothing to reconsider; she had already made up her mind. She reached inside a cupboard to find a bottle of wine left over from a recent Passover. The holiday had passed her by without ceremony. Freed from bondage less than two years earlier, she no longer regarded the Exodus from Egypt as a red-letter day on her calendar.

She filled the cap from the bottle and then brought it to Isaac's lips, which she opened by tempting him with her nipple. Mila then refilled the same cap two more times, and Isaac drank. She waited a few minutes, then removed the baby from his crib and placed him on her bed, surrounding him with pillows. She made sure that his left arm was close to where she was kneeling.

Now it was time for Keller's instrument. It looked like a large pen or a pointer with a bulb on the top, like the *yad*, which is used when reading from the Torah to make sure that the reader doesn't accidentally place human flesh against sheepskin. But Keller's tool had a far different purpose: it was in fact an instrument for breaking skin—of the human kind.

The digits came slowly. Even though Isaac was by now totally drunk, no amount of anesthesia could freeze his pudgy, baby-soft forearm from the sting of Mila's brand. The needles jetted back and forth like pistons, digging inside his skin, releasing the blue ink below the surface, seeping through like blood. He wailed with his mouth wide open and his eyes clenched tightly, the little tears collecting on his cheeks. Mila kept her own wrist steady, even while the rest of her shook like a rattle.

She began with the number one. An easy stroke. She wanted to be precise. There couldn't be any mistakes. There would be no way to fix an error, no erasure for such things. She had shut the door to the bedroom and stuffed towels underneath the space between the door and the hard floor. The same thing was done with the front door. She feared that to the neighbors—and most certainly to God—Isaac's cries wouldn't sound like they belonged to an infant who was hungry or whose diaper needed changing. This was a different kind of distress. In order to make a getaway once the numbers were completed, she couldn't call attention to herself or her son.

Then came a zero. It was much harder to engrave. Isaac's tiny arm throbbed while Mila held him down by his wrist.

"Shah, shah," Mila cried. "Mommy has you . . . Mommy is holding you . . . Mommy is watching you."

There were small traces of blood. Mila must have been jamming the stippling needles in too deep. Isaac's feet kicked wildly, circling as if on a bicycle, but unable to pedal away from his own mother.

Mila's face was soaked. She stopped for a moment, put the instrument down beside the bed, wiped her brow, and tried to comfort her son.

"Shsh, shsh, shsh . . . I am sorry, baby, little *pupzik*."

She placed her head against his chest, then his mouth. His free hand plunged into his mother's hair, getting tangled inside. She removed his fingers, looked away for an instant with her eyes shut, and then went back to work.

Next came another number one, followed by a six. Only two more digits remained. She bit her lip; Isaac was losing consciousness, protecting himself from his mother's violent betrayal. The wine mixed with the intense screams had produced its own anesthetic. Whimpers turned to silence. It was as though he had gotten used to the fire. The flesh hardened; the pain became familiar.

There was an eight, the complicated reversal of looping direction, followed by a two.

101682. The enduring password. These were her numbers, tattooed onto her own left forearm when she was a young teenager. For almost two years they had replaced her real name. Now it was a permanent scar. And this was what she chose to give her son as a farewell, something to remember her by. The digits were now his, too. They would share this in common—the family brand, in case the cattle got away.

How else could she ensure that he would know something of the nightmare? The numbers were all that he needed to know.

"Sorry, Isaac, my *pupzik*, my little survivor . . ."

And these numbers might someday allow her to find him, if she ever chose to look. It was the only trail back, a homing device, a fingerprint right on the forearm. As long as he was alive, the tattoo would be there. She could find him no matter what he looked like.

Mila gave Isaac yet another bottle cap of wine. She then removed the tear-soaked sheets. Finally, she lifted her son into her arms, brought him over to a rocking chair, and gave him her breast. He gurgled and closed his eyes, which were not clenched as tightly as before.

Rock. Rock. Rock. The movement and music soothed him. The mother's milk. The fateful kiss of second hand smoke. Isaac fell asleep just as Mila hummed the final refrain of "Someone to Watch over Me," only to awaken a short while later.

The nurses had sunk far too deep into their chairs on the open balcony at Mount Sinai Hospital. The sun was lowering. Some clouds drifted off the ocean and settled themselves over the bay. The air was still humid; there was no jolting breeze to splash against the terrified faces of the three black women.

There was also no more mystery. Mila had finally spilled it all. The eyes of the nurses were watery but unblinking. Mila stared off into the spreading horizon. None of the four women could look at one another. The knowledge that was now known and shared among them was also forbidden. There was nothing left to say. Silence became its own conversation as the three nurses clutched their own forearms.

IT HAPPENED IN the showers. That's where Duncan first noticed it.

The afternoon yoga class was over. The students bowed to their teacher. Contrary to all that Isaac had just said about preserving the essence and energy of the concluding meditation, Duncan went about the frenetic business of driving himself up and down as he blew through two hundred pushups.

"Are you through?" Isaac asked with a scowl on his face. "This is not the way to find internal peace."

"I know, master," Duncan replied mockingly but still in rhythm, "but you see, I had a much more forceful *sensei* than you when I was a child, and she passed along bad habits."

"Yes, this I see, but these bad habits . . . they have done you no good. What happened at the store in Warsaw . . . something comes over you, a large wave that smothers you, and then you turn the wave back on the world. I don't even know whether you see it, but when it happens, it's already too late. You react like an animal who fears being attacked and so decides to always strike first. But your first strike is usually lethal, and unnecessary. You must break these habits; otherwise, they will continue to keep you prisoner."

"What will make me free?"

"You need to be exhumed . . . unburied."

"Your area of expertise, Mr. Undertaker. Do you think such things are possible?"

"I leave the dead alone. I just tend to their graves. But for those who are alive, anything is possible. Polish winds can do strange things when they blow in your direction."

The brothers decided that they would shower in the studio before going out for dinner. The locker room was small, with just three shower heads all lined up in a row, with no partition. Men and women generally went in at separate times. The brothers were alone; all the students had already gone.

The water dripped through the shower heads sparingly, the pressure weak, the water itself unclear, probably impure. And the soap that Isaac had provided for his students was not of the lathering kind; it smeared itself on the body like greasepaint. Until then, Duncan had not seen his brother naked. In fact, whether in the studio or in the flat or outside on the streets of Warsaw, Isaac almost always wore oversized, long-sleeved, loose-fitting clothing. Unlike Duncan, whose torso was lined and chiseled, each piece of his body sculpted like stone, Isaac was not exactly a pretty picture of human form. Duncan's physique was all geometric angles, while Isaac's body was a dense, heavyset block of long addition.

Duncan cleared the water from his face, rubbed his eyes like a child who had been prematurely awakened from a nap, and stepped toward Isaac. "What is that?" Duncan asked.

"What?"

"Right there . . . What's on your arm?"

"Numbers."

"Numbers?"

"Yes, from the concentration camp."

The showers still released their sputter of lazy water. Duncan took Isaac's arm, rotated it to its underside, and examined the brand.

"Jesus Christ, blue numbers . . . I don't get it."

"That's what they did to us in the camps."

"I know what the Nazis did," Duncan said, amazed. "But when did they do it to you?"

"I don't know," Isaac said defensively. Then after a pause, he added, "In the camps, when I was born."

"You were born in a concentration camp?"

"Yes, in Birkenau, that's where our mother was. Right next to Auschwitz."

"I know my geography," Duncan seethed. "I just didn't know you were in a camp."

The studio was cold, and the water was not nearly hot enough to fog up the shower. Goose bumps riddled the men like imploding bullets.

"I thought you knew."

"How could I know?" Duncan asked dumbfoundedly. "And besides . . . babies didn't survive the camps."

"But I did."

Duncan's face, even in profile, was a portrait in horror.

"Now you know why the Polish people treat me the way they do," Isaac continued. "It's not really the yoga, or the Zen teachings. They see me as a holy survivor. A Christ child. A baby who survived the camps; the only baby who ever lived through the fire. Many people know of me. When I was small, there were articles in the newspapers. Some people thought I had special powers, that I am a healer . . ."

Duncan had not yet released his older brother's arm. He examined it once more, as though it were more artifact than limb. Finally, the branded puzzle piece came together like lock and key.

These weren't Isaac's numbers; they were Mila's. Duncan had seen these digits before; hell, he had seen this arm before. Like the rest of his body and his face, Isaac had inherited all that was Mila.

When he was a child, Duncan had memorized this row of numbers: 101682. As much as he wanted to escape from them and from what they represented in the incalculable math of his family's history, he was also tantalized, as well. He had dreamed of these numbers in his sleep. They became his ATM and E-mail passwords, as well as the pick-six combinations in Lotto. He had been both tortured and strengthened by their presence in his life. The power they had, the unwashable mystery contained in that row of blue! Miami was always so heated and humid that Mila didn't conceal her forearm under her sleeve. Nor was the scorching sun able to tan or burn or erase the blue dye. The tattoo wasn't leaving, which made Duncan believe that the numbers were worth knowing. They were so special that they turned him into an amateur kabbalist. Only through those numbers might he one day be able to understand the legacy that Mila had sealed underneath and invisible inside his own skin.

And what about Isaac and his numbers? How did he actually get them, and what did they mean? Duncan shuffled the cards in his head, trying to sort it out. The Poles treated Isaac as though he had survived the camps. But that wasn't possible. The Nazis wouldn't have used the same number twice. They were too meticulous for that. If Isaac had been in a camp, he would have been burned like the others, not branded like an adult bound for a rock pile. The Nazis wouldn't have wasted a tattoo on an infant. Even older children, useless as slaves, were gassed.

The Poles were either too stupid or superstitious to put it all together. Isaac was no survivor, at least not of Birkenau. The Polish people had confused a savior with a survivor. Because that's what they wanted most of all—to be saved. The end of Communism cried out for a new messiah, another Christlike Jew. The Immaculate Inscription. The virgin birth on the baby's arm. The Poles wanted to grab hold of Isaac's forearm as if they were climbing aboard a life raft. Only then could they be saved.

He wasn't going to be treated just like any other Jew. Isaac had been given the miracle of survival. He had slipped right past death when death was looking the other way, and he had the numbers to prove it. Even during the mass pogroms of the late 1940s, Isaac—and Keller Borowski—were untouchable and protected. Maybe that's why Isaac had no animosity toward these people. Or maybe it was something else entirely.

But how did Isaac get branded? Duncan wondered. Who would have put those numbers there? And why would they have been the same as his mother's?

Duncan let go of Isaac's arm and then shut off both showers, clamping down hard against the levers. He leaned his body up against the stone wall, his cheek digging into the concrete, his eyelashes entwined with each other. He finally understood. There had been child abuse on two continents. Permanent scarring. With Duncan it had been rammed down his throat; with Isaac it had been sandblasted onto his arm.

Duncan pitied his brother for his cheerful ignorance. Should Isaac know the truth? Isaac obviously had never questioned his own age, but despite the numbers on his arm, he was two years younger than the Poles had believed. And his birth certificate would have proved it, if there ever was such a thing, and even if there was, whether it could have been found amidst the unfiled paper trail of Poland's communist beginnings. But Isaac never doubted that he was a child of Birkenau. The numbers were enough for him. Duncan decided to let his brother continue with the fantasy. Let the arm remain a miracle, and a mystery.

"You are upset by the numbers?" Isaac asked tenderly.

"Yes."

"Don't worry," he said, "it does not hurt. I've had it all my life. We both have things that the Nazis gave us."

"Not just the Nazis," Duncan replied.

. . .

THE BROTHERS STEPPED on the wooden boards and stone gravel of the
railroad tracks leading to the main transport section of Birkenau. Duncan wanted to see the death camp where Mila had been imprisoned.
Isaac wanted to go back to the place where he believed he had been
born.

But Auschwitz-Birkenau was not near Warsaw. One had to
travel south and then west. It would be a day's trip to the town of
Oświecim, an hour's drive outside of Kraków. Along the highway
they passed endless forests of spotted tree trunks, like packs of
Dalmations. During the war these trees had been witness to so
many acts against nature. German convoys had seared bald spots
into the earth where nothing would ever grow back. The forests,
soiled and defiled, had been turned into unceremonial, improvised
graveyards.

Isaac and Duncan planned to stay overnight in Kraków, and then
return to Warsaw the next day. There was no way to visit Birkenau
without stopping at Auschwitz, as well. The camps were separated by
only a mile. And Auschwitz was the unofficial ninth wonder of the
world. Like the Pyramids, it was a phenomenon that couldn't have
happened without the participation of Jews. Yet the brothers never
got through the gates where *Arbeit Macht Frei*. It was at the parking
lot where the trouble first began.

"He wants zlotys," Isaac explained.

There was a middle-aged man with curly black hair, sagging eyelids, pockmarks on his face, and an open palm awaiting the brothers
as they stepped out of the white Opel.

"What?" Duncan asked.

"This man here," Isaac continued, "he wants zlotys."

Since Duncan was the driver of the vehicle, the parking attendant
had approached him for the fee. Duncan hadn't used the Opel much
since his arrival in Warsaw. Isaac had put the car in a friend's garage.
Car thefts were common in Poland, and German cars were in particularly high demand. And so parking lots charged for security—even
at Auschwitz.

"I don't understand," Duncan said.

"Polish money."

"What, the shrines of the Master Race don't take MasterCard? What's going on here?"

"He wants us to pay, you know . . . to park the car."

"In Auschwitz?"

"Yes, there is a charge. Look, the lot is full."

"No way. This is a death camp, not an amusement park. We are not at the Magic Kingdom; we didn't come to have a good time. Tell him we've already paid. We have a lifetime membership to all the major concentration-camp attractions."

The attendant was impatient. Other cars had just angled into their spots, and he needed to collect from them, as well. He said something brusquely in Polish.

"He doesn't care," Isaac said. "He's just doing his job. I'll pay him . . ."

"No you won't! Tell him he can have it one of two ways: either he lets us park here for free, or I go in and gas up the ovens. I'll let him keep his hair and his gold teeth because I'm in a good mood, but the rest of him is going in for a shower . . ."

Isaac didn't translate, but he did try to explain to the man what was causing the delay. Just as Isaac reached his left hand into his back pocket to find some zlotys, Duncan yanked out his brother's arm, rolled down the sleeve, and showed the attendant the forearm.

The man gasped after realizing that the arm belonged not to just any ordinary survivor, but to Isaac Borowski. He started jabbering away apologetically, smiling shyly, unable to look at Isaac or his brother.

Duncan hurled his brother's forearm into the man's face. "This is our ticket to get in, and don't stamp it because it has already been done. Our mother also graduated from this institution with very high marks—on her forearm, just like this."

The attendant stepped backward, picked up his pace, and waddled away to collect the hourly rate from those with less storied credentials to the camp.

"I must warn you," Isaac said, "they also charge to go inside."

"I won't pay." Pausing, Duncan said, "Let's just go to Birkenau before something bad happens here."

"Good idea," Isaac said, relieved. "You wouldn't like Auschwitz, anyway. They made it look pretty. You would be offended, and the Carmelite nuns will be in danger with you so close."

Duncan kicked up some of the surrounding gravel, and the brothers got back into the car. Isaac waved at the attendant as Duncan muscled the steering wheel and shifted the gear into second. The Opel rolled out into the town of Oświecim, which would barely exist if not for the twin camps. It was a company town, except that the company once manufactured death. One mile later, they came to a stop at Birkenau.

There was no parking lot, just a stretch of mud and patchy grass with some tire marks planted into the soil. Most tourists were back at Auschwitz, the more notorious of the two camps. Duncan soon realized why this was true: Auschwitz was more museum than death camp. The brick barracks had been cleaned up and converted into gallery spaces. Gravel-paved walkways made the camp look spiffy, rather than spooky.

Birkenau, however, didn't fool anybody. It looked like a place with a deep memory for murder. There had been no renovations. No sprucing up. No landscaping. No special exhibits. No cinemas to screen documentary footage. Not even an admission fee. Simply a hard-core Holocaust vista, a raw combination of silence and the haunted memorabilia of what the prisoners themselves once saw.

Wooden barracks, most without foundations. The same old bunks, empty of skeletons. The open fields were swamps in disguise. Watchtowers orbited the barbed-wire fence like satellites. A train track split the camp down the middle. There was a ramp siding where the men of Canada[1] had once stripped inmates of everything they owned. The gas chamber was near the back of the camp, surrounded by a surprisingly lush forest. The camouflage no doubt helped the local population ignore the forest fire taking place inside. Now a monument separated the pines from the crematorium.

There was a light snow on the ground that in this muck of swampland had turned to ice. The skies were especially gray, as though Birkenau were perpetually folded inside a tunnel. Large crows soared

---

[1] Author's note: *Canada* was the name given to the barrack where Jewish possessions were confiscated upon arrival in the camps.

overhead. A hard wind hissed in between the barracks. It would soon be dark, although it was only early afternoon. The brothers stood on the train tracks that now went nowhere.

"Einsteigen, bitte. Schnell, schnell! Sie Mussen jetzt einstergen. Schnell!"

They walked on the rails, riding invisible cattle cars, their feet sliding over gravel and pebbles as though stepping on dry cornflakes. Since childhood, Duncan had feared trains. He had never owned a train set. It wasn't the Katz way.

"Toys are for sissies," Mila said.

"And trains have not been good to us," Yankee reminded them all.

Duncan never argued. He just never argued, and he gave up trying to understand. He knew the answers to some questions, and the rest he simply chose not to ask. For his parents, trains whistled menace; the tracks could lead to nowhere other than death.

The silence at Birkenau was interrupted by a biblical trumpet. Duncan thought he was hearing an oncoming train, so he hopped off the tracks and ran in a panic. But there was no train. It was only his brother, standing on the rails, looking tall for a short man, a curved shofar coiling from his mouth. Isaac—Mila's musical prodigy—could play the shofar, too. Duncan brought Donnatal for the Auschwitz occasion but Isaac was armed with the mood-making music.

"You scared the shit out of me!" Duncan said.

Isaac continued to blow neither Gershwin, nor anything suitable for the High Holy Days, yet something mournful—*Kol Nidre* by Bruch. The music wasn't meant for *simchas* or dancing. In fact, it wasn't really a song at all—but a wail.

"Why are you doing this?" Duncan asked. "The crows are going crazy up there. All the dogs and cats of Oświecim will be here any minute." His brother couldn't hear him.

When Isaac was through, his face red and swollen like a blowfish, a wisp of heat smoking from his lips, he said laughingly, "I play the shofar whenever I come here."

"Why?"

"It is the music of our people. I play for the dead, and for God."

"If you're playing for God, then you should make him buy a ticket. I think he's had enough free entertainment at this place."

Isaac laughed at his younger brother's spirit; he then wiped the mouthpiece of the shofar on his coat. After that, he said, "Nothing in life is without meaning. God had a purpose for Birkenau."

"No he didn't. There is no purpose for a place like this. Ask the crows. Ask the ghosts. Figure out a way to speak to our mother; she'll tell you."

Isaac blew into the shofar once again. This time the music was louder, more piercing than before.

But at this performance, there was a new audience.

"Stop blowing into that thing!" Duncan shouted. Isaac yanked the shofar out of his own mouth. "What's that over there?" Duncan pointed.

"Where?"

"Way back there, near the forest, off to the side where the gas chamber is."

Duncan grabbed his brother and pulled him away from the railroad tracks. Sprinting behind a barrack, they ducked down and looked out toward the forest and the crematorium.

"Do you see what I see?" Duncan asked.

"It can't be," Isaac replied, his eyes stuck in a squint.

"It is."

Spread out like a mirage, neo-Nazis were going through the motions of paramilitary drills. Young goons, some dressed in brown, some in jungle green. Bundeswehr parachutist boots on their feet, or high-laced Doc Martens. Muscled but mindless, running around with rifles headed by knives, bayoneting strawmen dressed up to look like Hasidim and Wall Street investment bankers.

Still crouched in a squat position, Duncan recalled his appearance on the *Molly Rubin Show* with the young Arthur Schweigert. And he also thought about his visits with Maloney. It had been over a year since he had worked at the OSI, and yet recent events had strangely brought him closer to Nazis and their progeny than he had been when he was working with the government.

"Let's kick some ass," Duncan announced.

Isaac had grown accustomed to this refrain.

"How will that help you?"

"It's not about me—it's about us. This is what we were put on this earth to do."

"There is more on this earth than Auschwitz."

Duncan tried to hold his tongue, but it unloaded like a slingshot.

"Auschwitz is everything! Don't ruin this for me. This is our chance. This is the first street fight in my life that actually makes sense. I've been practicing for years on completely innocent people. You don't get it; strawmen were never enough for Mila. She wanted real bodies and bleeding victims. There were no Nazis in Miami Beach when I was growing up. But here they are; it's like a dream come true."

"You need better dreams."

"And you need some nightmares. You sleep too well. So, are we ready?"

"For what?"

"To make our mother proud."

"This is foolish," Isaac said. "I am forty-seven years old. I never knew my mother. I don't care if she is proud of me, if this is what I have to do. Children don't have to satisfy the wishes of insane parents. Look out there," Isaac pointed at the field. "There are too many of them, and I bet their parents were insane, too."

"There are not that many," Duncan replied. "I count no more than twenty."

"But we are only two," Isaac said incredulously.

"What are you worried about? If they need more men, we'll give them time to call in reinforcements."

"You *are* crazy."

"No, you were right before: our mother was crazy; I'm only a casualty."

"This is not all Mila; some of your own work is here, too."

Isaac slipped in and out of a simple yoga pose. Then he straightened his back as if he were about to leave.

"Have it your way," Duncan said, "but let's at least introduce these clowns to a few good Jews."

"We have no chance."

"You haven't really seen me in action. What I did to those policemen back in Warsaw was nothing."

"You have a nervous stomach, but also a heart that looks for too much trouble," Isaac observed.

That was the last lingering thought for the both of them. Two skinheads rammed rifle butts into the back of Isaac's and Duncan's heads. Isaac's yarmulke had become a bull's-eye; Duncan's shaggy blond locks absorbed the blow, and he went down hard on the ice with a bloodied lip. Even at a half-century's remove, the watchtowers looming overhead had not been empty. Someone had indeed been watching over Mila's boys.

SO MUCH FOR the hair. Duncan and Isaac were still unconscious with swollen bumps on their heads, when a shearing machine mowed off their hair one track at a time. The captors and their victims now shared the same hairstyle, as though lice removal were on everyone's mind.

The brothers stood, in stripes. All around them were bunks layered and jammed with prewar shoes, clothes, eyeglasses, teeth, hair, prosthetics. Duncan's once-wild hair now littered the floor like snakes, and Isaac's red locks formed a little puddle on the ground, taking up about the same size as his former bald spot. Their clothes had been removed and stored elsewhere. The brothers were now in uniform. Imprisoned in the barracks of Birkenau, they had both become zebras.

Duncan grabbed the side of his shirt as if he were missing something, his hand brushing against the stitching of the six-pointed yellow star.

"Were you looking for this?" A young man walked through a tight path between two sets of bunks. His smile was bright but sinister. He was carrying a small bottle.

"Give me that!" Duncan shouted. A rifle then dug itself into the center of his spine.

The young man came closer to Duncan, uncapped the Donnatal, and spilled it onto the floor.

"No!"

"You won't be needing this, Mr. Katz."

Duncan watched as a stream of stomach relaxant splattered around him, staining what was already a soiled uniform.

Then the neo-Nazi tossed the *pysanka* at Duncan, who caught it with one hand.

"I found this in your coat, too. What is it, Mr. Katz, a lucky charm?"

"No, just a gift from a friend."

"I will let you keep it, but it will do you no good."

"How do you know my name?" Duncan asked tentatively.

"We know who you are," the German voice said in English. "We know the Jews who give us trouble—particularly the Jews who don't look like Jews. If you had lived in Germany, we would have already taken care of you. Your car would have a bomb in it. Or your mail would be a danger to you and your family. The American neo-Nazi organization doesn't know how to take care of its enemies. It was our luck that this time you came directly to us," he said, as one of his lieutenants, a young man with a bulbous shaved head, rifled through Duncan's passport and identification papers. "And we didn't even have to bring you here by cattle car . . ."

The skinheads laughed on cue. Duncan noticed that the room was full of them. They stood around the barracks, like matching furniture. Tall and thin bodies with straight arms ideal for saluting. Blue-eyed delinquents. Symbols of the reunification of a country that did not quite take hold.

But the leader of this pack looked oddly familiar to Duncan. He had a narrow fairway of a receding hairline and long, compensating sideburns. On his left bicep was a barbed-wire, crown-of-thorns tattoo.

"Schweigert?"

"My name is Meinthaler."

"Unbelievable . . . you look just like an American I know . . . he's in the same line of work as you." Duncan glanced back at Isaac and then asked, "Do you have a half-brother you don't know about?"

"We are all over the world, Mr. Katz. The Fourth Reich is coming, but you might not live to see it. What a pity . . . So who is your friend, this mesomorph of a Jew?"

Isaac's reputation obviously had not yet spread outside Poland. These prenatal Nazis would have never tried to get away with this kind of thing had they been Poles. Yes, they were lucky—they had not only accidentally captured a former Nazi hunter, but a Polish messiah also got caught in their net.

"This is my brother, Isaac."

"I like his tattoo," Meinthaler said, rolling up Isaac's sleeve. "We noticed this when we dressed you. So you have survivor envy?"

"It's not fake," Isaac said. "It's real. The Nazis put it on my arm."

"Hmmm." Meinthaler seemed impressed, and nodded to his men. "So you have come back for more? The first time was not enough? What we have here is a tough Jew. Well, at least now we won't have to give you a new number."

More laughter came from the pack of slack-jawed skinheads, the sounds more like the cackles of boys pretending to be men.

"No, I had enough forty-seven years ago," Isaac replied. "Now let us leave."

"We'll see about that. And who does this belong to?" Meinthaler asked, holding up the ram's horn as though he had just bagged a big-game trophy.

"The shofar belongs to me," Isaac replied.

"Blow if you want," Meinthaler said, returning the shofar. "It won't do you any good. The world is deaf, and so is your fucking God."

The bump on Duncan's head was now becoming an afterthought; there was no time for the headache to go away. And Duncan's stomach cramps would have to wait as well. He had work to do.

"Let us go, and I'll let you all live," Duncan said. He was mindful of the gun behind him, and yet his threat was serious.

Meinthaler's brow creased, and he cracked a smile. Some of his comrades looked concerned despite their numerical advantage. "Ah, Mr. Katz, how very brave of you. But as you can see, you are very much outnumbered. We have weapons, and you have nothing—no guns, no medicine, just anger. But anger alone is never enough. So if I were you, I wouldn't speak so disrespectfully. You have been fighting imaginary ghosts for a long time. But *we* are real. We are living and breathing Nazis. And we are well trained. You may have prepared your whole life for this, but that won't help. You are finally here, and you will see that you are no different from the Jewish vermin we exterminated before. You have wasted your time. That body of yours will burn just as easily as the Six Million."

"What are you planning to do with us?" Isaac asked.

"What do you think? This is a Nazi death camp, and you are Jews. We are not playing cards."

"You have much in common with my brother," Isaac said defeatedly. "You are not really on opposite sides."

"Yes, we know he likes Nazis," Meinthaler said.

A tall albino with a hidden smile, spindly yellow teeth, and a brown shirt that was too short for his long arms, added, "I bet he likes having sex with people dressed like Nazis—whips and chains, handcuffs, a fist up his ass. What do you say, Katz?"

Duncan sensed the invitation for his first move.

"Yes, you are right, whips and chains . . . Untie me and give me a whip and a chain, and I'll show you what I can do with it." Duncan squared around to face his captor. "It doesn't take any courage to put a gun to somebody's back."

The skinhead handed his rifle to one of his friends, and then said to Duncan, "Come on Jew, I'm waiting. Take your best shot."

Duncan threw a punch that started off like a bazooka but landed with the lazy thud of a docking blimp. The skinhead caught Duncan's fist in his own hand, and then squeezed hard and watched Duncan drop to his knees, the bones in his collapsed fist congealing like burned wax.

Isaac knelt down to reclaim his brother, bringing him back to his feet.

"Are you hurt?" Isaac asked.

"Christ, that's never happened before," Duncan replied groggily.

"You see, Mr. Katz, your worst dreams are now real," Meinthaler said. "You and your brother will stay here until we come back for you. But rest assured, we will be back. You can use this time to think about how you wound up here. Think of it as your last rites," Meinthaler added smugly.

The platoon of gangly arms and demented minds filed out of the barracks, following their führer in lock, goose step. The brothers then heard a thick wood latch slide into place, barricading the door.

Isaac stood by the only window in the barracks. It was caked with layers of dirt and decay—a no-way mirror. Moonlight dripped from the sky, scratching but not penetrating the window. Isaac couldn't see his captors folding out into the Polish darkness.

Duncan recovered from his earlier defeat. He took a running start, channeled the steam like a locomotive, and then rammed himself against the bolted door as though he were once again a charging Bulldog, locking in on a quarterback who was standing too tall in the pocket. Isaac cringed as his brother's shoulder seemed to separate like a hanging scarf. The door was unmoved, while Duncan's naked head and broken body wilted and slowly slipped down to the ground.

"How are we going to get out of here?" Duncan wondered aloud. He was sitting on the floor, legs spread apart like a wishbone. Isaac was surprised, but also pleased.

"I don't know," Isaac replied. "I thought I would leave it up to you. Fighting back is your department, not mine."

"Okay then . . . well, the obvious answer is that we'll wait for the people who take care of the camp to come find us. It's not exactly my first choice. I'd rather beat the shit out of these punks and bury them alive under the crematorium, but without guns, it may be the only way."

"Except that nobody takes care of this camp," Isaac said. "This isn't like Auschwitz down the road. Nobody watches over Birkenau. That's why these neo-Nazis came here to practice their drills."

"Well . . . then I guess we'll have to wait for Silver to come get us out."

"Why would he do that? How would he know we are here?"

"Because that's why he's in Poland—to watch over us. I'll never be able to live this down with Breitbart. Imagine, his men had to come rescue me. It's a good thing Mila's dead; she would have killed me—and you, too—for not being able to take care of this on our own." Duncan's skin started to turn a little flushed, and a hint of cold sweat appeared on his brow. "I bet Carlo Costello has been taking a video of this whole thing since we got here," he said disdainfully.

But if that were true, where was Silver and his men? Duncan and Isaac had already been locked away in Birkenau for six hours. The men of the Mafia usually mobilized much faster than that.

Duncan glanced at his brother, all dressed up in the home jersey of Auschwitz, embroidered with the yellow Star of David—the team logo. Mila's sons had reached bottom. More than anything else she wanted them to know the nightmare. And here they were, having entered the grainy nooks of her sleep as though they had accidentally stumbled into one of her bad dreams. Trapped worse than they were before. Who could wake Mila up and free her children? Perhaps there are indeed nightmares from which there is no escape.

Chapter Sixteen

A FEW HOURS before Mila died, there seemed to be a break in the cancer. Not quite a remission, but more like an intermission, as though the disease was toying with her, the unblinking eye of a hurricane in hiding. This unexpected reprieve gave the nurses an idea.

"It's time to get you out of this ugly gown and put a nice dress on you," Louise, always the most assertive one, said.

"I don't mind this smock," Mila replied weakly. "It's better than looking like a zebra."

"No, you should have some fun and look like a lady again," Cynthia said. "What do you say?"

"Why don't we all get out of our uniforms and go out on the town?" Judy suggested.

"Yeah, do the kind of things you like to do," Louise said.

"I don't know . . . ," Mila said shyly.

"Yes you do," Cynthia said.

At the hospital, at around six in the evening, when the shifts were changing, the nurses put a new sleeveless, floral dress on their stick-figured patient; painted her face with rouge, blush, and mascara; gave her a wide-brimmed straw beach hat that seemed to swallow up her entire body; and then snuck her down the stairwell and out into the parking lot off Alton Road. Like a group of high-school girls heading out to their Saturday-night hangout, they piled into Cynthia's brown station wagon, which soon clanked along the Julia Tuttle Causeway, spitting exhaust and dropping a trail of metal parts.

The fronton was jammed with bettors. Mila hadn't been to jai alai in many months—certainly not since she had become sick. This was, however, the nurses' first time. In fact, as they entered the fronton, they noticed that there were only a few black people watching from the grandstand. Through the net cage they saw the jai-alai players warming up, dressed in their white milkman pants, pastel shirts, and Martian helmets. Odd-looking creatures, the nurses thought. But what was most unusual of all was the straw basket that seemed to grow out of each player's hands, the banana-like gear that hurled a hard pelota with all the thrust of a Cape Canaveral liftoff.

"What do we do now?" Judy asked.

"We get a program and we bet," Mila explained.

The nurses were all dressed elegantly, not as caregivers, but as though they were going to church. Tonight they were putting themselves in Mila's hands. The feverish atmosphere of the fronton had energized their patient. Mila was more alive out of the hospital than in it. The nurses may have risked their jobs by bringing Mila here, but maybe it was an act of mercy that might actually save her life. Where chemotherapy and radiation were bound to fail, the fronton and the dog track held out at least the possibility of a cure.

Mila excitedly tried to explain the difference between a quiniela, perfecta, and trifecta.

"We can bet three numbers, but all we need to win is for two of these players to either win or come in second," Mila said. "It's just a six-dollar bet." The nurses still seemed confused.

The eight players lined up for the first game of singles for the night. Joey and Asis were playing. Joey was Mila's favorite player, and he was in the first group.

"Chula! Chula!" she yelled as Joey's throw found the perpendicular crack where the ball simply dies and cannot be returned.

The nurses started to get into the game: the balletic athleticism of the players scaling the walls to snare the pelota, the betting frenzy of the fans, the dark smoky atmosphere of the grandstand, and, of course, the best part: having Mila Katz around meant that you could turn an otherwise random bet into a sure thing.

"You are amazing, Mila," Louise said as she returned from the betting window with yet another wrinkled brick of cash. "I can't believe you came up with that idea to wheel the six."

The nurses were not natural gamblers. Unused to the stakes, and particularly to the winnings, they were uncool about their good fortune. Soon they tripled their salaries for the week, which only made their excitement even harder to contain. And there were still three more games to go before the night would come to an end.

Those who surrounded them now began to eye Mila suspiciously. The nurses and their patient made for a curious sight—an older, frail white woman escorted by three black women who doubled as Mila's bag ladies. The nurses felt the cold, leering stares that are always directed toward people who are considered to be out of place.

"Do you think they think we're cheating?" Judy asked coyly, her neck retracting deeper into her shoulder blades.

"We *are* cheating," Louise replied, glancing at her hot-handed patient. "We brought a ringer with us. That's not really fair . . ."

But it didn't stop them, either. The nurses quickly became accustomed to the killing they were making, and so they decided on further plans for Mila. With bulging pocketbooks and full-moon eyes, they headed off to Biscayne Dog Track. Mila slept in the backseat of Cynthia's station wagon, the seat belt too loose to strap her in snugly. The lights from I-95 seeped through the blue-veined scrim of her eyelids. She was quiet and content.

"Do you want to go back to the hospital?" asked Judy, who was sitting beside her.

"No, I am your prisoner," Mila replied sleepily. Her body slumped back into the deep creases of vinyl like loose change, her head resting limply on her right shoulder. "I will go freely. Take me to the next adventure."

Judy seemed concerned, but the other two nurses knew that a parimutuel marathon was just what the doctor ordered. Mila was never an ordinary patient; another dosage of this unconventional treatment couldn't harm her.

It was already the ninth race by the time they arrived at the dog track. They found seats in the grandstand. Mila felt cold even though it was as warm and humid as ever on this Miami summer night. Green lizards changed color and wandered off onto the track, only to be chased away by sprinting greyhounds. The moon was set way back in the darkened sky, hanging over the ocean like a luminous pearl. A fog of cigarette smoke loitered above the grandstand, commingling with the smell of hot dogs and the citrus-scented tropical breeze. Louise put her sweater over her patient's shoulders, while Mila searched through her handbag for reading glasses. She scanned the betting program up and down, checking odds, lane positions — and then squinted at the condition of the track. The names of the dogs were as familiar as friends: Donny Boy, The Seven G's, Ephulogy, Body Bodzin, Dauer's Dowry, Sunshine Siggy, Nes Paradise, Puppy Poland.

Mila pointed to Puppy Poland, number eight, and said, "Bet to win."

"How much?" Cynthia asked.

"Bet it all."

"Are you sure?" Judy asked timidly. "This is too rich for my blood. I won't be able to watch," and then she put her hands over her face.

Mila closed her eyes, not from fear, but fatigue. Cynthia darted off to the betting window before it closed.

The bell sounded, and the greyhounds virtually leaped out of their stalls and chased after Rusty, the mechanical rabbit. The nurses watched fitfully as the stretching, lunging dogs circled the track, their muscles moving like gears. The greyhounds seemed terribly lean, gaunt, and underfed, which made them look less curious to the nurses than the often overweight jai-alai players who had entertained them earlier.

Mila was bone tired. She never opened her eyes to see Puppy Poland break out in front, maintain the lead, expand the number of lengths, and then cross the finish line with an enraged pack of dogs barking up behind her tail. It was the last race of the night. All the dogs were tired. Mila had collapsed in her seat.

The hospital records showed that she died in the middle of the night, in her sleep, so drugged up on painkillers that it was no longer certain that cancer could take credit for her death. There was nothing in her file to indicate that her son had come to see her a few minutes earlier. Judy had nervously stayed in the bathroom the entire time, afraid to come out and face Duncan. Nor did the report mention that Mila had spent the last night of her life at the fronton and the dog track. Nobody bothered to write down any-thing about her winnings, or to note that a betting milieu provided the last scent that she was able to breathe in without the assistance of those choking tubes.

ISAAC WAS IN the *sirshasana* position, standing on his head, his legs plopped up against the wall of the barracks as though hanging from a hook.

"What are you doing up there?" Duncan asked, annoyed and impatient. He was pacing around the barracks with fury, weaving in between bunk beds, trying to think of a way out.

"Even in a time like this, I want my blood to flow through me, not to boil like yours," Isaac replied. Then he gracefully wheeled his feet backward and returned to the ground, falling seamlessly into the lotus position. He closed his eyes and began to meditate. Duncan looked on with disgust.

"You should sit with me," Isaac said. "I have taught you how to meditate. Now is a good time; it will help you with your fears."

"I don't have fears!" Duncan shouted. "I just need my medicine."

Isaac opened his eyes and asked, "What is it that you suffer from?"

"It's nothing . . . just a stomach condition."

"It's not about your stomach," Isaac explained. "It starts somewhere else, and then travels to the stomach, which is where all the energy and traumas of life come together. What you have my brother is a problem of the mind. Mila gave you the body, but not the nerve."

Duncan felt embarrassed. Quietly, defeatedly, he said, "Yes, it's true. It's been getting worse over the years. After each crisis, I become more of a prisoner to my bowels."

"You have been to a doctor?"

"Yes."

"What did he tell you?"

"That I have abandonment anxiety," Duncan said. Then he began to pace all over again.

"What is this?"

He paused, sighed heavily, then said, "The fear of being left alone in the world."

Duncan moved further away from his meditating, evenly tempered older brother. He stopped at a bunk cluttered with shoes, prewar overcoats, and leather suitcases mildewed from a half century of not going anywhere. It reminded him of when Mila died. The day after the funeral, he returned to the apartment to pack up all of her belongings—the clothing and furniture, the Rosenthal china, Yankee's typewriter—all of which he put into storage. He went in and out very quickly, not knowing what to discard, what to give to Goodwill, or what to keep for himself. He was trained to travel light, but lightness is the enemy of sentiment, and Duncan always vanquished his enemies.

"Everyone fears being alone," Isaac said. "This is what the modern world has given us: overcrowding and also alienation. The people who have too much also feel empty."

"But I was raised to avoid the modern world, to resist it with suspicion. To be Mila's son means to be alone, to do without. But look at me now. I am paralyzed by the fear of being abandoned. Even my insides know it. My intestines are strangling each other."

"But you *were* abandoned," Isaac reminded his younger brother. "Your parents died too soon, and then your wife left you and took your child. Your stomach is not wrong; you just don't know how to live with the grief."

"I am failing my concentration-camp test."

"This isn't the same thing that happened to our mother," Isaac said sternly. "You can never prepare for such a thing, and you can't predict how you would react. And most important of all, you can't live a normal life with images of the Holocaust playing in your head."

Isaac picked himself off the damp ground with a catlike leap and approached his brother.

"I will help you, Duncan. You shouldn't have to live like this. It's time to begin to find your way back home."

"In Birkenau?"

"Yes, here in Birkenau."

"Why don't you have this problem?" Duncan asked. "How were you spared? You've been branded, and yet you're fine."

"Yes, branded, but I can touch these numbers on my arm. I am not afraid of them. You have no numbers, and yet they terrify you. You are hiding from yourself. You are a stranger to yourself. We are locked in this barracks, but you are trapped inside yourself even tighter. You buried yourself alive in your own tomb."

"I had no choice. For me, it's all a dress rehearsal. I'm caught in a time warp, trapped in a cattle car. Everything is about loss. It feels like there is no difference between my life and what happened to our family during the war."

"There is a big difference," Isaac said, and pitied his brother.

"My life is like one big atonement. Everything is Kaddish. *Kristallnacht* all over again, but this time the glass is not from broken storefronts, but families."

"You are very much alive, and so is your family. You didn't have to leave Milan. But whatever made you go, also brought you here . . . And I too am your family," Isaac reassured Duncan.

"No, all I have is this hole in my stomach . . ."

"You put that hole there. You can close it. The worst prisons are the ones without bars."

Duncan wanted to live in his brother's world, but that world was Poland, a place where the nightmares began and where now insomnia ruled. Duncan was becoming totally undone. He had drifted too close to the ovens, the showers and the gas. There was now no turning back.

Their mother had damaged them both, and yet Duncan couldn't recall having ever seen Mila's guilt. A woman abandoned a son in Poland. Was her poker face that good? Or was it that his own grief-masking had made it impossible to notice the tricks perfected by his mother for the same purpose? Had she stayed in Poland, Isaac would have had a mother, and a blank slate for a forearm.

And yet, ironically, even without her, Isaac turned out to be the more resilient brother of the two. His colon functioned as it should. He managed crisis far better. He internalized no bitterness or rage. And he dealt with his pain. Was it Zen, or was it because Mila's singular branding of her son had been a far more enduring parental experience than all those years of tutoring—and torturing—Duncan? Without Mila, Isaac instinctively knew how to get out of the way, while his brother was an unmovable monument to everything that continued to haunt the psyche of survivors.

"You must mourn," Isaac said, "right here, now. The problem is: You never sat *shiva*, you just walked away, carrying it with you."

"To mourn is to forget," Duncan said, his face cringing, the tears piling up, yet unseen. "I don't want to heal this wound; it's my birthright, it's a permanent scar."

"Mila would not have wanted this for you."

"You are wrong; this is exactly what she would have wanted—for both of us! You managed to escape, and yet look where we both ended up—in the same place."

Snow was falling hard all over Birkenau. A winter storm had landed with the intensity of a blizzard. A loud, shattering thunder caused the corroded wood pilings of the barracks to tremble. A long arm of lightning spread its X-ray fingers throughout the room. The mound of shoes, clothes, and eyeglasses seemed to be inching toward the brothers like Birnam Wood. Hypnotic flames from kerosene lamps bobbed and wove in the shrieking wind.

"You must let her go," Isaac said. "I had to, and I have mourned her for years."

"How can you mourn what you never knew?"

"I know her. I know her even better now that I know you. I see what she has done. But rage is all about holding onto something that you don't need but are afraid to let go. You have a life force inside you. It's time to use it for living, and not as a poison."

Duncan sighed like a death-row inmate. "I'll never be able use it for anything other than revenge."

"And this is also why you have a problem with the American government, no? You lost your job?"

"No."

"But Mr. Silver told me . . ."

"Silver is wrong. The guy works for gangsters. He *is* a gangster, and he talks too much. You can't trust him."

"What happened then, with the government?"

Duncan reached into his striped pocket and removed the *pysanka*, tossing it up in the air like a coin and catching it in his palm. It reminded him of the one other time when his head was nearly shaved, back when he first met Maloney. At the time, in 1987, Duncan looked not that much unlike the unemployed German punks who now held him captive. He began to tell Isaac why he was no longer a prosecutor with the OSI, why his Nazi huntings had descended from the once authorized into the lurid, from the virtuous into the bizarre.

In early 1986, when the INS first informed Duncan that there had been a match for a Malyshko who had changed his name to Maloney after entering the country in 1949, Duncan knew that he had found the Butcher of Maidanek. But as a lawyer he also knew that there were proof problems. The witnesses were quite old, in poor health, and in some cases, simply not credible. Their driver's licenses had been revoked because of deteriorating eyesight. Now he was asking them to recognize a mass murderer who had aged just as rapidly as they had over the past forty some odd years.

And Malyshko had changed his name. In the phone book and on his mailbox, he was now unmistakably Irish—even though his accent revealed a voice far more Russian than Celtic. Most distressing of all was that the picture taken of him on his Maidanek identification card—the dark uncaring eyes, the cold muscular face—didn't resemble the heavyset, unthreatening figure he had now become. The collapse of the Soviet Union had unearthed new incriminating papers, but none seemed to turn up anything that linked Malyshko more closely to his crimes.

But Duncan knew that Maloney was not innocent. His past was insufficiently explained. And the witnesses, while it was true that they could no longer make out road signs or traffic lights, weren't about to forget Malyshko no matter how much their eyesight had failed or how much his appearance had changed. Such was the survivor's burden: to compensate for eroded vision, the other senses would inevitably rise to the challenge.

Duncan had an idea: he would create his own evidence. He climbed the stairs of Maloney's five-story walk-up. His laced-up, but not quite worked-in, Doc Martens squeaked with each step. His crew-cut and camouflage fatigues were central casting's nod to the modern-day militia. And he was wearing an elaborate amount of rubber makeup that altered the lines and angles of his face. Even his eyes went from blue to brown with the aid of contact lenses. If not for the fact that he was the prosecuting attorney, he wouldn't have needed any disguise at all. Yankee and Mila had given him a special genetic gift that was perfect for this occasion: with or without makeup, Duncan never looked Jewish. He was specially and naturally outfitted to slip behind the lines of anti-Semitism. He could pass for an Aryan, or a West Texas linebacker, or a Pennsylvania steelworker's kid, or someone right off the Idaho potato farms. He paused at the door, and then knocked.

"What do you want?" Maloney's harsh voice asked, a solo eye enlarged in the round glass of the peephole.

"I am looking for Mr. Maloney."

"Yes, that is me. What do you want?"

"My name is Joseph Kurtz. Can I come in? I'm from Montana, and I've come all this way to see you."

"Why?"

"We need your help."

"I am a furrier, not a farmer."

"Please . . . I'll explain when you let me in. I can't do it from here."

"This is New York, and I am an old man. What do you want?"

"Maidanek, I want to know about Maidanek. I know you were there."

Maloney unlatched the door, unhinged the long pole that served as the police lock, and with suspicion allowed the stranger to enter his modest apartment.

"May I sit down?" Kurtz asked.

"There," Maloney pointed at a hook on the wall, "take your jacket off and hang it."

"No, thank you, I won't be staying long." While Maloney looked elsewhere, Duncan reached inside his camouflage coat to make sure that the wires that connected him to a recording device were not crossed. He was miked for the occasion. "I've never been to New York before," he said, testing, testing. "Never wanted to come, too many Jews—you know what I mean?"

Maloney didn't reply. He hesitated, and then asked again, "What do you want?"

"Information."

"That was a long time ago. How do you know from such things?"

"I'm here on business for the people I work with. We thought you could help us."

"How so?"

"You have experiences, the kind we need."

"I am a furrier, I told you. I work in the garment district, in the Thirties, on Seventh Avenue. If you need a new coat, I can tell you where to go. But I don't think what you want from me is a new coat. So talk."

Duncan wanted it to be the other way around. So he began, hoping Maloney would finally let down his guard and allow Duncan to get what he came for.

"My family's farm went bankrupt last year," Kurtz began. "The bank took it over—foreclosures, you know, by the Jews." Duncan waited for Maloney to bite. While waiting, he surveyed the apartment for signs, hoping that he would discover some memento of Malyshko's Maidanek days. Instead, all he saw was clutter: Ukrainian newspapers piled up high in one corner, cheap tapestries serving as rugs on the floor, empty bottles of vodka assembled like bowling pins, and enough hanging portraits of the Virgin Mary to grant absolution in almost any other home except this one.

"I'm sorry about your farm, but I don't see how I can help you," Maloney said. He rose, walked arthritically over to his kitchen, opened the refrigerator, and yanked out a strange-labeled beer bottle. He didn't bother to offer one to Kurtz.

Duncan said, "I know what you did before you made dresses."

"What are you talking about?" Maloney responded after having taken a long, stalling sip from the bottle.

"You were one of us. A follower of the Führer."

"I am Ukrainian, not German."

"You were a camp guard in that place. We are now fighting a war against the Jews and the United States government. We need men like you—real men, patriots, men who don't fear doing the right thing, especially when it comes to dealing with the Jews."

"How do you know this about me?"

"I said we are fighting a war," Kurtz said, the role-playing too disturbingly easy, "just as you fought a war. The Jews are even more powerful today than they were back then. We need teachers to win this struggle; otherwise, the Jews will run the entire world."

"I wasn't a Nazi; I was a guard, I tell you. I didn't even want to serve. If not for the Germans, I would have never been involved in such things . . ."

"But you killed Jews!" Duncan said as he brought himself and his microphone toward Maloney.

The guard had remained silent for years. "You are a child. What do you know? Everybody killed. That's what happens in war. Some were fighting the British and the French; others were fighting Jews."

"But that's all we care about—that you killed Jews, because the Jew is our enemy."

"I didn't say I killed Jews . . ."

Duncan wanted to strangle Maloney right there, or simply force his head inside an oven. Con Edison's gas was not nearly as efficient as the Zyklon B alternative, but it would have to do. But Duncan wasn't a murderer. All he wanted was a confession, something he could use at trial. So he stayed, and Maloney talked some more.

When the case finally went to court several years later, Duncan's hair had grown back and the rubber makeup had been tossed into an F/X trash bin. But a federal appeals judge eventually ruled that the tape recording was inadmissible because of the method used in obtaining it. And the court also reprimanded Duncan for his actions.

"What were you thinking?" Bernard Ross asked when he first heard how Duncan had gotten the incriminating, but illegal, evidence.

"I didn't think they'd ever find out it was me," Duncan replied. "I looked just like any other neo-Nazi. What could have tipped them off?"

"Come on, Duncan," Bernard said, his arms flailing, the bristles of his mustache sharpened, "you know the rules. Prosecutors can't disguise themselves and pretend to be someone else in order to get information. And prosecutors can't carry concealed microphones, either."

"The guy's a Nazi, for Christ's sake," Duncan said as he leaned up against the standing podium in his office.

"We have to disclose this, Duncan. The defense has already found out, and now we have to come clean."

"And Malyshko walks."

"This is America, Duncan. Even Nazis are entitled to due process. And sons of Holocaust survivors are not above the law. Maloney's crime was special, but you're not."

Duncan turned to face his brother. "That was my trouble with the government," he said.

"I am sorry."

"No need to be. Our mother was a master of disguise; she would have been proud. I did what I had to do. We're all pretending in some way: Malyshko became Maloney; I became a neo-Nazi; it goes on and on . . ."

"But did he tell you that he killed Jews at Maidanek?"

"No, he just admitted to being a guard," Duncan said ruefully, his tone and energy sinking, "but that would have been enough to get him deported."

Duncan squeezed hard on the *pysanka*. Neither the barbed wire, nor the crown of thorns, punctured his palm. He wanted to feel something, but this wasn't the kind of egg that cracked.

Across the ocean, on the American continent, an old man sat by himself in a rent-controlled apartment contemplating what it meant to win his freedom, to have been liberated from exile and a certain death sentence. The United States had protected him. He had kept his citizenship—all because of an ethical infraction, a legal technicality. But what about his soul? Are souls that lenient? Do they easily forget, or do they simply look the other way?

HOURS HAD PASSED, and yet there was still much time before the end of the night. There was a tarred blackness to the sky and, in front of that, several curtains of fog. The kerosene lamps were now without oil, but Isaac found an even better and more appropriate replacement. There was a box of *yohrzeit* candles tucked away underneath a bunk bed, beside a pile of prayer books. Duncan couldn't imagine what they were doing there. Was it prewar wax? He continued to ponder while Isaac lit all of the candles and scattered them around the barracks. Isaac then brought several over to the center of the room, stepping over clumps of curly blond and red hair.

Neither Meinthaler nor any of his loyalists had returned to check on their prisoners. Perhaps they are off trying to get the showers and ovens to work again, Duncan thought. That's what happens with machinery—even German-made—when it lies dormant for so long. It wasn't going to be easy to retrofit Birkenau back to its death-factory days.

The uncertainty of their situation was not having a good effect on Duncan. He was becoming intensely claustrophobic, and not having any Donnatal around was only elevating the anxiety levels that terrorized both his gut and his head.

Isaac continued to meditate, encouraging his brother to join him, but such pleas came to no avail. Duncan was retreating fast from whatever remaining sanity had kept him tethered to Earth. A prisoner of violent moodswings, he moved wildly around the barracks. A whole assortment of tics seized his face and body. He looked terribly unsteady. He paced over the same ground as though trying to lap himself on some kind of track that looped and circled around on a path going nowhere.

Without a toilet nearby, Duncan shit in his pants; the diarrhea ran in little rivulets, soiling the gray stripes. Isaac urinated chula-style against the sidewall of the barrack as though he were spraying lighter fluid.

Panic dropped over Duncan like a net from overhead. His eyes took on a demonic look, having completed a spin cycle in each socket. He began to pound his naked head with his bare fists. But he felt no pain.

"Oh . . . ," Duncan moaned, his stomach having long since surrendered to the spasms of the moment. His mouth remained open in a gasp. His frail nerves had become both tightrope and trampoline. He was breathing backward, stammering, choking on dry air, shaking as if there were chains inside his body that were being rattled for the first time. His body produced a vile smell. His eyes welled up like a clogged fountain.

"I lost my family, and there was nothing I could do," he said. His voice cracked. He was crying, but the tears were dry. "I am the Pawnbroker . . ."

Isaac stared at his brother in horror. Duncan needed sleep; he had gone too long without it. He was without his medicine, but he was already way past the point where medication would have done him any good. Poland had worn him down. There were too many ghosts, even for Duncan.

Isaac moved closer. Duncan was now lying on the floor curled into a yoga posture that was not based on anything yogic, but rather took its inspiration from the fetal womb. "DON'T BRAND ME!" Duncan screamed at his brother. "I DON'T WANT THE NUMBERS! LEAVE MY ARM ALONE! I DON'T WANT YOUR ARM! STAY AWAY!"

Duncan clicked out of reality, his consciousness like a train bar-
reling ahead without a conductor. He saw Sharon's face, glowing in
silhouette as she lit *yohrzeit* candles for Mila and Yankee. Or maybe
the candles were for him? Her face was disfigured, stretching like
the flame itself. The sky was dripping blood, and no sutures or tour-
niquets could stop its gushing flow. A swastika was carved into the
moon, which was spinning like a roulette wheel. Milan's curls formed
dredlocks with his own hair on the ground. And then he saw his
daughter's face—confused, searching, and afraid. She didn't know
which line was for her: the right one or the left? Duncan didn't know
either, and even if he had, he was certain that if he shouted out,
Milan wouldn't be able to hear him. He just wanted her to know
enough to steer clear of both. But who was going to teach her how
to do that?

He closed his eyes in hopes that it would all go away. But the
images wouldn't leave. And there were the noises, so many different
ones: a roaring, smoking train—the Ten Commandments posted on
its engine—clattering on the tracks; commands shouted in languages he couldn't understand; barking Alsatian dogs; guns that
fired loud and rapid bullets; screaming parents; lost and crying children.

"HELP ME!" he yelled at his brother, who he imagined as someone
else. "MILA, HELP ME! SHARON . . . DON'T LEAVE . . . ! THERE IS NO WIFE!"

Duncan placed his palms against his ears and screamed, "STOP IT!
GO AWAY! ANSWER THE FUCKING QUESTION!" A prosecutor roaring like
a wounded lion. A child sitting alone on a roller coaster, the bottom of his stomach dropping out as the car, derailed from the track,
plunged downward. Alone in the icy, desolate valleys of Wyoming,
learning how to camp out in a wilderness without Nazis. He was
preparing for an avalanche, but not for Birkenau. And then the
scene shifted again. This time, he saw Yankee and Mila dancing. He
had no memory of such an event, but there they were, moving
slowly to some torch song, their steps tentative as if they were being watched.

"GET ME OUT OF HERE!" He reached his arms out to Isaac. "I WON'T
SURVIVE! I AM NOT MILA! I AM NOT YOU! I GIVE UP! I AM NOT STRONG!
COME GET ME, MEINTHALER! I AM YOURS! SHOW ME THE GAS!"

Rock. Rock. Rock. Isaac hugged his younger brother, who was

shaking with a frenzy more violent than before. "Shshsh . . . shshsh . . ." Isaac embraced the useless muscles of his brother and then tried to calm him with the soothing, but sadly unsung, family song. Isaac hummed the melody to "Someone to Watch over Me."

"I got you and I won't let you fall," Isaac said.

Exhausted, hollow, tempted by sleep, Duncan replied weakly, "Yes, you will—they always do."

"Not this time. I am your brother; I am not going anywhere."

"Where have you been?"

"Mila made it hard for us to find each other. But there is still time."

"Not for me. I'm finished. There is nothing left."

"There is your daughter, and there is me. There's much work for all of us. And we need you."

Like a hooked fish that had fought hard only to be reeled in, Duncan stopped shouting. His eyes closed, and his body became languid, then limp.

"Mourn, Duncan," Isaac whispered in between the Gershwin chorus. "The fight is over; nobody won. Not you, not Mila. Say goodbye to our mother. You should have done it at her funeral, but it's not too late."

The sleeves on Isaac's uniform barely covered his forearms. Although his arms were short, he still managed to wrap them around his brother. Before falling asleep, Duncan counted the numbers one-oh-one-six-eight-two like sheep, not to the slaughter, but as a lullaby to himself.

THE BROTHERS AWOKE soon after dawn. They slept in a bunk beside one another, wrapped in a moth-eaten blanket that looked like a fishnet. It wasn't a restful sleep, at least not for Duncan. He screamed throughout the night like a man whose blood was being simmered under a low flame. Isaac held onto his brother during these night frights, as if he were in a sibling rodeo. Despite the muscled armature, Isaac began to realize how fragile his brother was. The packaging was impressive indeed, but underneath it all his emotions packed all the punch of a ninety-six-pound weakling.

Duncan sat up with the difficulty of someone who had been drugged. And yet, at the same time, he felt strangely cleansed, as though some purification had taken place without him even knowing it. Tears can do that. So can the kind of dreams that get summoned up from otherwise unreachable places in the soul.

He moved slowly over to the door to see if it was still locked. He leaned his shoulder against the thick wood and pulled on the latch, but the door wouldn't budge.

"What happened to Meinthaler and his gang?" he wondered. "Would they have just left us here like this until morning? Did they go back to Germany? What kind of Nazis are they?"

Just then the door, without any prompting or shoving or even the slightest turn of a knob, popped open. The brothers stood back, but all that entered the barracks was a blinding morning sunlight—Miami style. No neo-Nazis. No employees of Auschwitz or Birkenau. No tourists. Just a sharp, white, radiant sunlight. For three weeks in Poland, Duncan hadn't noticed any sunlight at all—just pollution as dense as crude oil, corduroy gray skies, and clouds heavy with moisture and shame.

"Let's go outside," Isaac suggested.

"Do you think we should?" Duncan asked, his voice doing little to conceal his fear.

"Yes, we should face our tormentors, wherever and whoever they are."

Isaac and Duncan emerged cautiously from the decrepit barracks. At any moment, they could have been shoved into a line that was angling either right or left. Surely there was a Nazi doctor lurking somewhere with a straight back and a pointing stick, armed with the power over life and death. But the blanketing sunlight made it impossible for the brothers to see what was in front of them. For that matter, they couldn't even see each other. They squinted and cupped their hands visorlike along their foreheads.

"Can you see anything?" Duncan asked.

"Too bright," Isaac replied.

They continued walking anyway, retracing their steps back along the railroad tracks, through the gate, and out into the parking lot.

"I think I hear voices over there," Isaac said.

"Me too."

The voices belonged not to neo-Nazis, but rather to Nathan Silver and Carlo Costello. Silver was sitting on the front end of his white

Mercedes. His overstuffed driver was still inside the car, holding a cup of coffee, wisps of heat fogging up the front windshield. Another man was sitting in the backseat, all bundled up, hands in his pockets, a scarf wrapped tightly around his neck and along his mouth as if he were about to get out of the car and rob a bank.

Silver's trademark panama rested on his head, even in the dead of winter. Underneath, a scarf covered his ears and head, making him look like a bedouin. An overbitten toothpick dangled from his mouth.

The light that had made it so hard for Isaac and Duncan to see was partly the sun, and partly the large drums of professional lighting gear that Costello had set up around the front entrance of Birkenau. Costello had always been a thug of little ambition but a filmmaker of great pretension. In this instance he was trying to bring color to a place that was forever trapped in documentary-film gray. A handheld camera was glued to Costello's face like a snout.

"Silver, is that you?" Duncan asked as he and Isaac passed through the gate and stumbled over toward the car. Duncan's Opel was parked right beside the Mercedes. The two white German cars were covered in snow.

"We're over here!" Silver shouted.

"That's good," Costello said, dollying the camera back, on its own little track, "but we need more pain, much more expression in the face. I realize you're not professionals, but reach deep inside and pull your guts out. Think about how Mila must have felt when she was liberated by the Russians. I can do some of the work in postproduction, but you got to show the camera a little more emotion."

"Where were you?" Duncan asked Silver accusingly.

"What do you mean?" he replied.

"We could have been killed."

"By whom?"

"Neo-Nazis."

"Where? When?"

"Right here . . . So I assume you already took care of them?"

"I have no idea what you're talking about."

"Stop messing around with my head. I've had a hard night. Come on, you know, Meinthaler and his Aryan friends—the kids dressed up in brown shirts, doing the paramilitary two-step. You warned me about

these guys when we were in the restaurant the other day in Warsaw . . ."

Costello pulled his face away from the camera, shut off some of
the lights, and looked at Silver curiously.

"I would have loved to film something like that," Carlo Costello
said. "How come you didn't tell me?"

"I didn't know," Silver replied.

"Stop it!" Duncan yelled. "There were neo-Nazis crawling all over
this place yesterday like rats. They held us captive overnight. Just
look at the way we're dressed."

"You look fine to me," Silver said, "a little tired and rumpled, but
okay, I guess."

"Wait a minute . . . ," Duncan said, examining his outfit. "What's
going on here? What happened to the stripes?" Duncan was wearing
his mohair coat and his underclothes from the day before. "How did
I get back in these?" he turned to Isaac and asked, confoundedly. But
while staring at his brother, who was wearing his old clothes, as well,
he also noticed that Isaac's hair—bald spot and all—was back on his
head.

"Your hair . . . your head, it's no longer shaved." Duncan's hands
then grabbed his own head as though trying to stop a hat from flying
off on a windy day. He was surprised to feel his long, thick, wild hair,
clutching it just to make sure it was real.

"Are you telling me there were no Nazis after all, that they were
merely the Nazis of my mind—the same pretend Nazis who have
been with me all my life?"

Isaac shrugged and then laughed. "I don't know what you mean."

"We spent the night in those barracks over there."

"We did?" Isaac replied.

"Of course we did. The neo-Nazis knocked us out. They shaved
our heads and put us in striped uniforms."

"Oh, this is great," Carlo Costello said as the film advanced
frames and the audio recorded. "What a great idea for a movie! Two
children of Holocaust survivors held hostage in a concentration
camp by neo-Nazis. They are put through the same ordeal as their
parents, but almost fifty years later. The same family tortured all
over again, only this time, it's the next generation. What an imagi-

nation you have, Duncan. You should have been a novelist, not a lawyer."

"What day's today?" Duncan asked.

"Saturday," Silver replied.

"I don't get it . . . We got here on Saturday . . . Isaac, help me out here?" Duncan pleaded.

"What do you want me to say?" Isaac asked. "The mind is the ultimate weapon."

Digging for answers, Duncan reached into the left pocket of his mohair coat. Out came the Donnatal; the bottle was full.

"Madness . . . I've totally lost it . . . Okay, if we didn't spend the night in that barracks, then why are you here, Silver?"

"Costello's been recording your entire trip," Silver replied.

"That's true," Costello said from behind the camera, his face humming with the sound of winding celluloid. "How could I not get pictures of the two of you in the camp?"

Then Silver added, "And I didn't like the idea of the Opel parked out here in the countryside. It could have gotten stolen. It's not safe, what with the mob and all. They're animals, you know. You should see the way they act in Brighton Beach . . ."

Silver's mouth continued to move, but Duncan stopped listening. And although Costello's camera kept rolling, Duncan no longer cared. Meinthaler and his men never returned. Even Duncan himself began to wonder whether they had actually ever been there in the first place.

Tough love. An exorcism. An intervention. A test of courage. A survival mission, this time not in Jackson Hole, Wyoming, but where it really mattered most—in a deserted concentration camp in Oświecim, Poland.

The rear door of the Mercedes clicked open and out stepped Larry Breitbart.

"Did I hear somebody say *keller?*" he asked, then crossed his arms and drew the lapels of his coat closer to his shivering body.

"He said my father's name," Isaac said excitedly.

"No! Well, yes, but . . . oh forget it, it's too hard to explain," Duncan said in exhaustion.

"All right, Duncan, it's cold as shit out here," Larry Breitbart announced. "I don't know how anybody can survive in this lousy climate—in or out of a camp. It's time to come home. Your vacation is officially over. Get in the Mercedes. And by the way, the Opel's battery is dead."

Without blinking or thinking, simply pleased to see his godfather in a place where Jews no longer had fathers of any kind, Duncan smiled and said, "I'll drive."

Chapter Seventeen

FOR LARRY BREITBART, Poland could be nothing other than a short trip, but his godson had other plans. At the airport, Larry once more tried to convince Duncan to return to New York with him.

"I can't believe you're staying," Breitbart said as the other passengers began to board the plane. He was standing in the LOT Polish Airlines terminal of the Okecie Airport in Warsaw, surrounded by a few of his men, all of whom were smoking cigarettes and speaking loudly. "Would you keep it down!" Breitbart screamed at his associates, who responded by sliding a few steps to the side. "Now where was I? Oh yeah . . . when can I expect you back?"

"I don't know. I need a few more months," Duncan replied.

"What's gotten into you?" Breitbart asked. "Something must have really spooked you at Birkenau. And whatever it was, now it won't leave you alone. Why anyone would want to stay in Poland longer than they'd have to, I don't know. I've been here for two days, and I've already had enough. Come on, you've seen all the sights; I think it's time for you to come back and be an American Jew again—you know, the ones who don't give a shit about all this history, but at least they drive a nice car."

"Something's happening to me over here, Larry. I feel different; I've been resisting it, but I'm definitely changing. I have to sit with it a little longer before I return."

"So what's the idea: Yoga *Macht Frei?* I have something better for you: try happiness; see if it fits."

"It's not the yoga," Duncan replied, "and I *want* to be happy."

"Then what is it?"

"It's Poland; it's Isaac; it's just everything. I can't explain it. All I know is that I'm not ready to come home yet. New York is like an opium den for someone like me. I need to feel more secure that I've licked the habit before I return to all that temptation."

"What, they don't get mad over here? Let me remind you of something: that neo-Nazi kid is still in Nebraska, and I don't think you'll ever be able to live with that, no matter how long you stick around here."

"Trust me . . . I'll be back in a few months."

"I hope you know what you're doing. You might get stuck here mentally, and you won't leave. And there's a limit to how long I can have Silver tag along after you. I got work for him in New York."

"Let him go. I promise, I'll stay out of trouble."

Larry Breitbart took a moment to consider his options, then said, "Oh, what the heck? I'll leave him here. He's getting used to the place, anyway. I wouldn't be surprised if he winds up taking a job in your brother's cemetery. He'll be like one of those Chabad rabbis setting up an outpost in Poland."

"The Lubavitchers have already arrived, Larry. They're all over Poland."

"Really? Somebody should remind them to hold onto their beards and *payehs*. Anti-Semites have always enjoyed cutting those things off. Maybe that's what I should have Silver do around here: protection work for the Lubavitchers."

Duncan laughed. It was so surprising a facial gesture that Breitbart reacted as though his godson had just awakened from a coma.

"So what can I do for you in the meantime?" Larry asked, pleased by the apparent changes in Duncan.

"Go see Milan. Tell her that Tatty will be home soon."

"I can do that. What else?"

"Tell me something."

"Okay, shoot."

"What was Mila doing with you and all those other gangsters for all those years?"

"How come you didn't ask before?"

"I didn't want to know before. It's not the kind of thing a kid is proud of—that his mother is the mascot for the Jewish Mafia."

"Hey, boss," one of Larry's hoods said, waving from the jetway, "they want us in there. They're taking off . . ."

"Tell them to hold the plane!" Breitbart shouted, and then shot his associate a look that might as well have been fired from a gun. "Can't you see we're having a private moment? What's with you?" Then he turned to Duncan and said, "Sorry, one of my new guys, one of the Russians from little Odessa. . . ."

"Larry, you should go," Duncan said. "You're going to miss your plane."

"Don't worry," Breitbart replied, "the Poles aren't the Germans. Nothing they do runs on time. It'll be a miracle if the plane takes off at all. Besides, they wouldn't dare leave me on the ground. My people virtually own this airline . . . very sophisticated financing we've arranged here, Polish junk bonds. Sounds like an oxymoron. Where was I again? Oh, yeah, Mila and the mob. Well, let's put it this way: she needed us and we needed her. It was a business deal."

"What do you mean?"

"Look, she came to America in 1950, right? The country was in the Cold War. People were naming names. Nobody was talking about the murders in the concentration camps. That didn't come till much later. America was in a fog. Everything was supposed to be nice. We even had a president who was a general. There was a lot of pressure to conform to new rules: happy families, two-car garages, postwar American superiority. Mila wasn't interested in any of that shit. Nothing made sense to her except us. She didn't want to live with rules anymore, so she became attracted to everything that was corrupt, but also free. You know she hated governments, the police, institutions of any kind. I remember a time when we were at the Miami International Airport, and she wouldn't give up her luggage to be checked in, and she wasn't about to have it tagged, either. What a scene. A policeman came over to handle it. I had to walk away in case he recognized me. I was afraid Mila was going to be arrested. There she was, mocking his uniform, tipping his hat over, laughing at the handcuffs, telling him that she could slip out of them before they reached the parking lot."

"Did he arrest her?"

"No, he was too scared. Didn't even know what to say on the report. No way to explain your mother. The truth is: she only felt safe with men like me, and she loved having the feel of dice in her hand. We were the only game in town for her. We were Jews, but we were also going our own way. She was looking to swim against the current, to piss on authority, to live life more dangerously since she had already proven that she could."

"So what kind of things did she do? She didn't shoot anybody, did she?"

"Nah, nothing like that," Larry said reassuringly. "She was there for the ride, mostly the gambling and an occasional strategic tip on what to do about the other crime families. She was the brains, not really the muscle, although she had plenty of that too, as you know. Lansky always went to her first when he needed to take out an enemy."

"She was advising Meyer Lansky?"

"No, Ida Lansky! What the hell other Lansky was there? She was his rabbi; he didn't have one, and he thought that a Holocaust survivor was the perfect confidante for the Jewish mob. God wouldn't dare disapprove of what we were doing with Mila as our mouthpiece and front man. What business did God have judging us or anyone after his no-show at Auschwitz?"

"Larry, you sound just like Rabbi Sheldon Vered."

"Yeah, that Miami Beach mental patient for a rabbi. You know, he had a vicious forehand. Let me tell you something else, Duncan. The ones who seem crazy are often the ones with the most interesting things to say. People are warned to ignore the crazies, but throughout history the lunatics have changed the world and have given us some of our best ideas—not to mention the fact that the kook community has supplied all of our prophets and saviors."

Duncan scanned the terminal to find his brother. Isaac was staring out a large window frosted with ice. He was cheering the takeoffs and landings, his mouth chomping away on a chocolate ice cream bar. Finally, he dug his open palms into the carpet and right-angled his body into a down dog. "And what did she get in return?"

"A world she understood," Breitbart replied, then crouched down to retrieve his attaché case. "You got to remember something about your mother: she was already dead when you were born. She had nothing else to lose."

"Except for a son."

"Which one?"

"Both of us—Isaac and me."

Breitbart glanced over at the gate to check on his nervous-looking goons. "I'll be right there! Duncan, now I got to go. How about if we spend *Pesach* together? Bring your brother. We'll show him a great time."

"Isaac's an innocent, Larry," Duncan said, searching for Isaac once again. "I'll try to bring him back with me, but you can't corrupt him. He's the best thing Mila ever did."

SILVER AND COSTELLO remained in Poland. For several months, Duncan walked the narrow, crooked streets of Warsaw certain that he was being both tailed and filmed. No one in the entire country had better escorts, was subject to tighter surveillance, or received more flattering camera angles.

He attended services regularly at the Nozyk Synagogue. Fridays, Saturdays, weekdays, he became a mainstay of what was always a chancy *minyan*. The old Jewish men of Warsaw stopped hassling Duncan for "dollarin." Duncan caught on quickly to the cantorial melodies; he was, after all, the lineal descendant of the rabbi who once chanted them. Because of his size and his age, on Saturdays he was given the job of the *Hagbah*, who lifts the Torah after it is read. In Duncan's case, he was also the one designated to carry the Torah around the *shul* both before and after the scroll was opened and the relevant portion completed. All of a sudden, just being Jewish, independent of his Holocaust credentials, mattered to Duncan, as well.

At the same time, he never missed one of his brother's yoga classes.

"Good," Isaac remarked, "the chakras and meridians are finally beginning to open up. There is hope for you, after all."

He stayed off Donnatal as if he had licked an addiction. And he spent a great deal of time alone, meditating while walking, his eyes closed, just listening to the sound of his breath, blocking out the surrounding noises from the street. And he gave the push-ups and sit-ups a rest, too.

Duncan wandered the Warsaw alleyways and rode streetcars without any destination in mind, sometimes just sitting in the back, looking out the window, searching for something familiar, waiting for the trolley to head back in the other direction, satisfied that the train—

even in Poland—wasn't about to do him any harm. He sat on park benches for hours at a time with nothing to read, and no one to talk to. The Polish skies turning, opening, always in a gradual state of becoming. He prayed under the cover of weeping willows as though they were prayer shawls. He leaned against the remnants of the Warsaw Ghetto wall as though it were a fallen Jerusalem temple, and then he slipped a note, written for Mila and Milan, inside one of its cracks. He walked into bars, not to pick fights, but simply to order a drink. He stared into the faces of the Polish people, examining each facial nuance as though he were a sketch artist and was going to draw them from memory later on. He played soccer with the children at the park on Grzybowski Street.

"*Prosto, prosto,*" they screamed laughingly at their big American friend who couldn't kick the ball straight, insisted on using his hands, and instinctively tackled every kid who got near the ball.

When the game ended, Duncan led them over to the haunted swings where they watched and listened in silence.

Duncan no longer wanted to be the hostile tourist, the ugly American with the bulging chip on his Jewish shoulder. Instead, he wanted to see how it would feel to just settle into the crowd. Yes, he was an American and not a Pole. But if not for the accident of Auschwitz and yet another detour in the Diaspora road map, he might have been born right here, in Warsaw, with these people as his neighbors.

But how could he separate himself from this country's past, the black sheep on the other side of the barbed-wire fence, the moral eclipse that will always have a dark side? These people now all seemed friendly and innocent enough, but isn't that how it always is? Time erases the dishonorable history. Eventually, shame gets refashioned into something that is more wearable; the scarlet letter becomes an accessory. These people were not model neighbors; they set Olympic records in moral ambivalence. And even now, there was little remorse, and worst, of all, there was still anti-Semitism, even though there were no Jews.

The greatest treasure of Jewish life was extinguished, leaving a nation without Jews. And now the Poles wished to reenter the Western world without even a word about how different they all were without their former neighbors. Polish Jewish folklore had become a mere nostalgic artifact. If it wasn't spoken of, somehow it didn't exist. It was as if the Jews had never actually lived in this country at all.

What does forgiveness mean? And who do you forgive first when the list is so long? It's best if you can forgive oneself. But Duncan couldn't do that, either. His determination to see through the lens of the world without the Holocaust filter was great, but the family conflict was greater. The continuing struggle to draw a line in shifting sand.

He worked with his brother in the Jewish Cemetery and felt a strange peace among the dead. The wind blew through the thicket of trees and calmed Duncan's spirit. He restored tombs, unearthed graves that had been hidden under weeds and brush, planted flowers that would bloom in time for spring, pieced headstones back together, and learned how to engrave Polish and Hebrew letters into old stone and new marble. Duncan spent a lot of time on his knees.

"You want to make sure to rake the soil with your hands like this. Very gently, then pack it in," Isaac demonstrated. "That's it, you're getting good at this," the older brother observed with a cackle. "It must run in the family."

And Duncan prayed. Sometimes under weeping willows and at the Nozyk, and sometimes inside the dimly ornate Catholic churches in and around Warsaw. That's were the Poles were praying. He didn't understand Polish, but Duncan tried to read more into their prayers than what they seemed to be asking from their god. He searched their eyes and sat with his own sadness and silence, drawing deeper, touching the most vulnerable parts of his soul as though bravely throwing himself into an entirely different kind of fire.

And by mid-March, with the Polish snow falling less often, the birds returning, and the trees awaiting spring, he announced, "I want to go back."

"I am happy that you are ready," Isaac said. "You have had a good visit, a homecoming, and I am proud of the spiritual work you have done. It is time for you to go home. You came to Poland to battle ghosts. Now you have to do the same thing in America; they are there, as well."

"I want you to come with me."

Isaac smiled shyly. "That is not possible. I have no reason to go to America. Everything I need and want is right here. I am not repelled by ghosts; they give me life. I breathe them in."

"We have ghosts in New York," Duncan said. "Believe me, you'd be impressed."

"You need to go alone."

"You need to visit your niece, and I have spent a lifetime being alone. In Birkenau you promised not to let me fall, that you would take care of me." Duncan then struggled to recall whether that moment had actually happened, or whether it too had been a Polish mirage. "Well, I'm making you keep your promise. Pack a yoga mat. I have all the *yohrzeit* candles that you'll need. Come on, let's go."

AND SO THE brothers switched worlds, but stayed together. Duncan returned the Opel to a car-rental office in Warsaw. Isaac told his classes that he was going on vacation, an announcement that created a crash in the psychic currency of Zen Poland.

"I am just the teacher," Isaac reminded them. "The fires in your bellies belong to you."

He wished everyone spiritual peace, and then he bowed in farewell, his hands clasped together longer than usual. Some feared that it would be the last time they would ever see Isaac Borowski in Poland. Isaac arranged for someone to look after the cemetery while he was away.

A few days later, Isaac bent over and kissed the Polish tarmac with his forearm. The brothers then boarded a plane.

As they separated from Poland and reached higher and higher into the air, Duncan leaned toward his brother, who was staring at the clouds, and asked, "Have you ever been on a plane before?"

"No, this is the first time. I've never left Poland before, not even by train."

"Are you nervous?"

"Why should I be?"

"Traveling across the ocean, to a new country . . ."

"Our mother did this almost fifty years ago," Isaac noted.

The brothers each tried to imagine what Mila's journey must have been like, but it was useless. She gave neither of her sons a chance to carry her actual memories into the next generation. Imagination and fantasy—poor substitutes for the lived experience—were all that they ever had.

"You're not afraid of anything, are you?"

"No."

"How come?"

"Because it does no good. Life does what it wants—it will bite you on the ass."

This time Duncan laughed. "Is that all I need to know?"

"One more thing: underwear doesn't help."

Nearly a half day later, the plane circled New York. Duncan pointed out the Statue of Liberty and the Empire State Building from the porthole window. The brothers collected their luggage, Isaac smiling to a pretty African American ticket agent. They breezed through customs without any conflict. The brothers had landed in New York in time for spring.

Cherry trees bloomed all around the perimeter of the reservoir in Central Park. Buds popped like confetti. Throughout the rest of the park the grounds were bursting with bleeding hearts, crocuses, and lilacs. Woodpeckers went to work on hollow trees, branches like antlers that would never know spring. The weather allowed ducks to dip their webbed feet into warmer ponds.

There was smog on the Grand Central Parkway as the Indian cabdriver waved his arms furiously, taking his hands off the steering wheel, weaving in and out of lanes, cursing at everyone and everything in his sight with the exception of the Hindu talisman glued to the dashboard. Stimulated by all the energy in Manhattan, Isaac nonetheless still felt lucky to be alive as the rattling yellow taxi doubleparked on West Eighty-seventh Street and the brothers retrieved their suitcases from the trunk.

Duncan fumbled with the keys to his apartment. He had been doing this ever since he had moved to Manhattan. Every time he unlocked the door to his home, he listened for the voices of his family. And when the door opened, he was reminded once again that they were not there.

"Well, this is it," he said. "Sorry, the place is a mess."

"So many books," Isaac observed. "What can you do with so many books? Too many words can hurt your head. You need more space to breathe—in here, and in your mind. Let's throw some of these books out the window right now."

"We can't do that!"

"Why not? People leave so may different things on the street that they no longer have use for in New York. I saw this from the taxi. You should free yourself from these books." Then Isaac noticed that the words *Holocaust* or *genocide* appeared in almost every title. "Maybe *all* of the books should go."

The books remained, but the brothers left. Duncan retired his mo-hair coat and replaced it with his motorcycle jacket.

"Why are you wearing that?" Isaac asked while they walked down Columbus Avenue.

"In America, it's the uniform of rebellion," Duncan replied.

"Only for those who care what they look like on the outside."

They spent days exploring Manhattan. The cobblestones and nar-row streets of SoHo; the zigzag chaos of the West Village; the manic, decadent shopping frenzy on Fifth Avenue. Isaac drew new spiritual energy from the streets. The crowds fascinated him. A lost army uni-formed in business suits, marching separately to the on-call commands of beeping pagers and ringing cellular phones. The competing ac-cents. The soaring smells. The eyesore water towers perched on roof-tops, empty of water. The homeless sprawled over heating vents that looked like waffle irons. People carrying around lit cigarettes like smoking pistols. Isaac watched clouds of exhaust leave the rear ends of MTA buses. He stared at Calvin Klein underwear ads and assumed that Kate Moss and Christy Turlington were very important, albeit immodest, Americans. His head moved from side to side as he tried to read the ticker tape at Times Square. He boarded the Circle Line but kept his eyes closed throughout the entire cruise. He fed carrots to those drugged pathetic mares—their listless heads festooned with silly straw hats—attached to buggies, waiting for passengers on Cen-tral Park South like a merry-go-round in mutiny. He sat on the filthy floor of the Port Authority terminal, surrounded by discarded drug needles and cigarette butts, and he meditated. When he was finished, he went to the Carlyle Hotel, was handed a sport jacket by the maître d', and sat down at a front table near the piano, where Bobby Short played Cole Porter and George Gershwin. Isaac snapped his fingers, pedaled his feet and played an air piano in a duet that only he could hear.

The next day Isaac stood on the observation deck at the Empire State Building, reached his hands into the sky, and screamed the *Sh'ma*. He twirled around with his arms up and away from his sides and his toes on pointe, ready for the downward plié as if auditioning for a ballet company.

The brothers took yoga classes all over the city. Orlando telephoned Duncan and practically begged him to return to the gym.

"You sick or something?" the philosophy professor asked. "You must have the Heidegger blues. How can you stand not training this long? What about your secret desire to transform yourself into the supreme Jewish *übermensch*?"

"It was never a secret," Duncan replied, "and that was the problem. I don't know, I've just lost the need to feel the pump. The gym is all scaffolding, exterior stuff, anyway. I'm trying to learn how to work the inside organs instead of the outside muscles."

There was a pause at the other end. Finally, Orlando asked, "What gym does that?"

Duncan called Sharon to say that he was back and would like to come down to Washington to visit with Milan and introduce her to her uncle.

"How about in a few days, after the Seder?" Duncan suggested.

"Where will you be for Passover?" Sharon asked.

"At Howard Minskoff's," Duncan replied. "Larry Breitbart and some of his friends are coming, too."

"Oh, that should be interesting," Sharon said snidely. "Models and mobsters, exactly what Moses had in mind. You might as well put a golden calf right on the Seder plate."

It was a joke, but its timing wasn't funny enough to shatter the tension. Neither husband nor wife laughed. The atrophy of their relationship had turned intimacy into strangeness. Like an anorexic, their marriage had become starved. The feelings disappeared, as though they were never there in the first place. The old wires were still in place, but no currents could pass through, like a broken cord dangling from a pay phone.

"We'll see you then," Duncan said.

"I really want to hear about Poland," Sharon said.

"Do you?"

"Bye Duncan . . ."

HOWARD MINSKOFF'S GREENWICH Village brownstone was crawling with plagues on the first night of Passover. As a courtesy to Duncan, Howard invited Larry Breitbart, who asked if he could bring some of his men.

"There's not going to be a shoot-out in here, is there?" Howard asked Duncan while the two of them were having lunch at The Coffee Shop. "Do I have to install a metal detector in my own house?"

"I wouldn't worry," Duncan replied. "I'm sure they'll have the good sense to keep their pieces at home."

"So tell me, did you bring me back a Polish cover girl?"

"No, but I brought back my brother."

"Really, what does he look like? Tall and square-jawed like you? Hmmm, I can see the possibilities . . . How's his body?"

"I'll send him over and you can take test pictures. I think he'd be great for Versace."

For the Seder, Howard rented an especially long dining table and had it brought into his home. He seated himself at one end and Larry Breitbart at the other. Sitting next to Larry were some of his Brighton Beach associates, refugee Russians, all of whom were stuffed into slick gray Armani monkey suits with black shirts, their hands studded with diamond pinkie rings. At the other end sat Howard, who surrounded himself with some of his models from Head Turners, none of whom were Jewish. Monica was there, sitting uncomfortably, not sure whether to approach Duncan, who sat beside Isaac near the center of the table.

"I've missed you," she finally said. Her red hair had grown out, no longer banged in the front and shaved in the back. A new look that might distinguish her from the factory-assembled herd. Now she was modeling clothes for older, working professional women. "I'm glad you're back. Maybe we can get together sometime for coffee."

Duncan reminded Monica that he didn't drink coffee, which sort of said it all. What he wanted to do was return to D.C. and visit his daughter. Isaac, on the other hand, seemed very much interested in

Monica, and they set up a date to take a yoga class in Tribeca the next day.

A ceiling fan hacked away at the air. The chatter from different pockets along the table settled down as Howard tried to call the Seder into some kind of order. Murder Incorporated and Airheads R Us were strangely brought together to memorialize the liberation of the Jews from ancient Egypt. The Brighton Beach Russians, who for the most part were Jews, had never been to a Seder before. Many were newly arrived from the former Soviet Union where Seders, like all Jewish practices, had been outlawed for decades.

But this Seder was different, not only from all other nights, but from Seders in general. For one thing, this gathering wasn't going to be much of a showcase for how a Seder was supposed to be conducted. Ritual wasn't a part of the experience. Yes, everyone drank wine, but it wasn't kosher wine—for Passover or otherwise. And they didn't drink at the appointed time, but rather whenever they felt like it, and without the preceding prayer. There was an Elijah cup on the table, but it was filled with a high-priced, specially imported Indian beer that Minskoff had been drinking lately. There were no Haggadahs, just tear sheets from glossy fashion magazines being passed around the table. The mobsters leered at the models—both at their airbrushed pictures and their live made-up faces. The men and women around the table started to get drunk. The Russians jabbered away in their native language, toasting each other, their speech now accented by alcohol. A few tipsy models stumbled over to the other side of the table and began flirting with Larry's men. Howard looked on, horrified, from his unreclined seat.

At one point, Larry Breitbart stood up and slapped his hand on the end of the table for no apparent reason at all, and then he yelled out, "Pesach!" It was punctuated with the commanding hard "ch" sound, as if a shank bone that should have been lying on the Seder plate had instead been lodged inside his throat. Then Larry announced, "Hey everybody, listen up, I have a proposal for the *afikomen*. I'm going to stuff the bag with five hundred bucks." Most people at the table didn't know that the *afikomen*, an embroidered satchel lined with a middle piece of matzo, gets hidden somewhere in the home until one of the children discovers it and then receives a gift. It took a while before Larry's offer sank into the sloshed crowd. Not to be outdone in his own home, Minskoff rose from his seat and matched the offer. The *afikomen*, at this particular Seder, would have a cash value of a thousand dollars.

Larry Breitbart appointed one of his people to be the bag man— a job he had held before—who then went off to hide the unleavened, laundered money. A few minutes later, nearly everyone at the table dashed off to recover the bag. Models and mobsters slithered on Minskoff's floor like mice, peaking underneath sofas and ottomans. They ran their hands along curtains and checked inside drawers. They searched behind an original painting by Willem de Kooning—one of his *woman* series. A Russian gangster successfully cracked a safe hidden behind a retractable bar, but the matzo wasn't in there. Long-legged models still needed to hop on their toes to get a good look at the bookshelves and reached their hands into the open domes of free-standing halogen lamps.

Matzo and money, models and mobsters, Swedes and Slavs, led to its own madness.

Duncan and Isaac, the only two left seated at the table, turned to each other at the same time.

"This is spiritually empty," Isaac observed.

"You think so?"

"Is this how American Jews remember when we were slaves? What will happen to the Holocaust one day?"

At that moment, Duncan missed his daughter more than ever. He just wanted to hold her, and to be held, as well. The brothers made an early exit. No one noticed them leave, except for Elijah, who had been standing on the stoop of Howard Minskoff's brownstone, waiting for the door to open, and who was ashamed to enter now that it had. Isaac and Duncan walked right through him as they headed down the stairs and made their way to the Christopher Street subway station.

THE NEXT MORNING they were on an Amtrak train headed for Washington, D.C.

"The freedom train," Duncan said.

"A nice idea," Isaac said, "your very own Exodus."

"First, we'll go see Milan; then on to Miami."

As soon as they arrived outside the Yuma Street house, Milan ran toward her father. Duncan lifted his daughter into the air and then smothered her against his chest.

"I really missed you, Tatty!"

"Me too, Milan baby."

Tilting his head to one side, Isaac said, "You know . . . this house is falling over."

"Yeah, isn't it great?" Duncan replied. "Milan, this is your Uncle Isaac, my brother." The little girl wasn't shy. It was as though she realized that this family, by sheer necessity, had to bypass many of the conventions of warming up to strangers. After all, there was always the chance that they would eventually be recruited as relatives.

Isaac soon reached inside his bag and gave Milan the gift he had carried with him all the way from Warsaw.

"A doll," she said excitedly.

"It's for you," Isaac announced. "Your father wanted you to have it. It's Polish, and it's a wedding."

"It's pretty," she said, stroking her hands along the grooves of the carved wood, petting the bride and groom.

Milan's father and her uncle took her out for the entire day. Duncan grieved over the lost time. He had been in Europe for nearly three months, and before that, for nearly a year in New York, and during that time he had seen his daughter only a few times. It felt like he had been on a tour of duty in a foreign war. But she was growing up without him; she wasn't about to wait. Soon she would be a pre-teen, sprinting past puberty, picking up a few diplomas along the way. The parents might never reconcile, but the child still needed parents—both of them. The imperfect family for a culture that in all other respects accepts nothing less than perfection.

"You're funny, Uncle Isaac," Milan giggled. "You make me laugh."

Duncan saw what she meant. Isaac was jiggling his big belly and the fire within it, making a hula hoop circle around him as though it were a halo that couldn't stay on top of his head.

Milan wanted Duncan to promise that he would come back home to Yuma Street, but he couldn't. How could he will something to happen that had no will of its own?

"I'm going away for a few more days, but then I'll be back for good," Duncan reassured her as he pushed gently on the swing. "I'm taking Uncle Isaac to Miami Beach . . . you know, where Tatty grew up."

"I want to come, too."

"Next time you'll come and see where your grandparents and I lived."

"Is Uncle Isaac staying here with us when you come back?"

"I don't know," Duncan replied. "Maybe we should tell him to stay, that we need him."

Milan hopped off the swing and ran over toward her uncle, who was sitting by himself on a seesaw. She whispered in his ear. Isaac nodded but said nothing. He then kissed his niece on her head and lifted her up into his arms. This was the only woman in his family, and the list of female casualties was long. And she was named for his mother. Maybe he could get to know at least one of the Milas. He looked at his brother from that distance, and they spoke without speaking.

BEFORE DUNCAN AND Isaac took the train to Miami, Duncan decided that he would drop by Bernard Ross's office at the OSI. Bernard had left messages that he wanted to see him. It had been a long time since Duncan had last entered the building on G Street. The receptionist greeted him awkwardly. Some of the people in the office didn't even recognize him. What with the long hair and the motorcycle jacket and the two-day facial stubble, he was either a narc or a biker with neo-Nazi fantasies. And yet there were those who did realize that the man waiting to see Bernard Ross had once been the OSI's principal deputy director, but they still looked the other way.

"Welcome back, Duncan," Bernard said warmly. He hugged his friend, squeezing hard against the padding of the motorcycle jacket as if Duncan were an inflatable doll. "Please sit down," he said, leading Duncan to the black sofa underneath the concentration-camp map on the wall. "Thanks for coming to see me. How have you been? You look well . . . I guess."

"Nice touch, Bernard, very smooth."

"Let me get right to the point. It's not definite, so I don't want to get your hopes up, but I think I figured out a way to bring you back into the department."

Duncan was silent. He looked around Bernard's office. Nothing had changed. New briefs had replaced the old piles that were stacked around the room, as furniture. The investigations continued. Nazis and camp guards grew older. The OSI was obtaining documents and developing cases. They weren't waiting for Duncan, either.

"Thanks, but I don't want to come back anymore."

"What? You don't want your job back?" Bernard returned to his desk and sat down.

"No, I don't."

"I don't get it . . . how can that be?"

"I've learned that the Nazi business is hazardous to my health. I can't really breathe in this office, and breathing is really the most important thing—aside from family. I've been choking all these years, and I didn't realize it."

"I'm stunned . . . truly, but I guess I'm also happy for you in a way. You know, you were made for this kind of work. Despite all the reservations I had when I first hired you—and believe me, there were plenty—this office was your destiny. Although the way you look now, nobody would know it."

Duncan stood and walked over to a wall decorated with citations— from the Justice Department, members of Congress, Jewish organizations, even several presidents of the United States—all commending the work of the OSI in discovering and deporting Nazis. There was also a picture of Bernard Ross giving an award to Miep Gies, the woman who helped hide Anne Frank and her family in that Amsterdam attic.

Duncan said, "Shit, Miep Gies, what a hero. You know, Bernard, my mother, you never met her, but she made me this way. Without her, I would have been doing something else. I wasn't alone prosecuting all those Nazis."

"So what's next? What are you going to do now?"

"Don't know yet. Take my daughter to the zoo and free the animals. Get a haircut. Write a novel. Learn to play the piano. I'm told it's in my genes—even more so than Nazi hunting. My brother's great at it. You should hear him play."

"You've changed. What about the Holocaust? Where does that fit in now?"

"I'm going to learn to live without it for a while. One day, maybe,

I'll be able to find a place for it, but I'm not there yet. So now I've got to go. But thanks for the offer," Duncan said. He reached his hand out to Bernard and was preparing himself to leave when Bernard pulled him back.

"Before you go," Bernard began hesitantly, "this letter came for you while you were away. It was sent to this office—in care of me." Bernard retrieved the letter from way back inside one of the drawers and handed it across the desk.

Duncan stared at the envelope. "Who's it from?"

"Feodor Malyshko . . . Fred Maloney."

"For me . . . here . . . ? What he's been up to?"

Duncan was about to slide his index finger through the seal and then tear along the top of the envelope when Bernard said, "Before you open it, there's something you should know first."

"It's been laced with explosives? I don't think so. Maloney wasn't a letter-bomb kind of guy."

"It's not that. Security already checked that out."

"What then?"

"Maloney's dead."

"Dead?" Duncan now acted as though the envelope might explode. "I don't believe it . . . how did it happen?"

"Suicide."

Duncan hadn't yet even considered how his post-Poland life could be reconciled with his former visits to Maloney. Would Duncan have seen Maloney again? What relationship could they have possibly had? Duncan realized that he would now never find out.

"Oh, my God. What did he do?"

"Gassed himself. Head-in-the-oven stuff; Con Ed an accessory. It happened a few days before the letter arrived. I think you're holding the suicide note. You may have to turn it over to the NYPD after you've read it. They're looking for answers, and so is the press."

The letter was short. Duncan read it aloud:

I missed our visits. Maybe now we are both free.
Feodor
P.S. Hold on tight to the pysanka. *Eggs bring good luck this time of year.*

Chapter Eighteen

$\mathcal{A}$ LIFEGUARD WITH a creamy white clown's nose waved from his South Beach tower, signaling that he was watching over Duncan. Duncan waved back, a gesture he had become good at. For over a year, each visit with Milan ended with a painful farewell. His daughter's head bobbing up and down as she pulled away in her mother's arms, leaving him to wave as if trying to catch her in his hand.

The brothers strolled quietly along the beach, retracing the footprints of fellow travelers, aimlessly burrowed deep into the sand. So much had been washed onto the beach overnight: algae, seaweed, seashells, and the outer skin of a waterlogged hairy coconut. The ocean lapped the shore and then disappeared like the steps of an escalator.

Isaac had never before been to an ocean. He sat on the mustard-colored sand in the early morning dawn, closed his eyes, and meditated as joggers ran past him, breathing even more deeply than he. A modeling shoot was taking place on Ocean Avenue. Miami Beach had changed since Duncan had last lived there. Twelfth Street was now topless. Lincoln Road was gay. The old people were, for the most part, Cuban *Marielistas*, not Brooklyn Jews. Collins Avenue was all condos packed with wealthy Latin Americans. On Nineteenth Street there was a sculpture of a large hand digging itself out from the ground, numbers on the inside forearm, emaciated bodies climbing up the arm, all trying to escape.

The Jewish Nostra had kept its name, but not the old decor or, for the most part, its former clientele. The wood panels had been replaced by sunny pastels. The tables and chairs were now some high-tech metal; they didn't wobble. The stuffed marlin, a relic of fifties high chic, was taken down, and in its place was a tall rack filled with fashion magazines and international newspapers. Even the menu had been given a facelift. There was goat cheese with mango and hummus and radicchio salads that satisfied the pallets of models and German photographers who modeled themselves after Helmut Newton. They paraded around South Beach with even more bravado and panache than had Meyer Lansky's hoods a generation before.

"Duncan Katz, son of a gun, is that you?" Morty the Mohel said, struggling to get out of his chair. Duncan had been spotted. Amidst the models and the makeup, there were still a few aging gangsters who had once been guests at Duncan's *bris*. These men were territorial; they weren't about to cede Miami Beach without a fight.

"Don't get up, Morty," Duncan said. Morty wasn't that steady on his feet, and so he gratefully sat down again. "How have you been?"

"Can't complain," Morty said. "I got some pains here and there, but you know, I'm eighty-five, *kena hora*. That's old. You're supposed to have things wrong with you at my age."

"Still practicing the holy craft?"

"*Mohel*ing or murdering?"

"The one with the knife."

Morty's eyes blinked.

"The one that God would approve of."

"Oh that, no, afraid not. I'm retired from both the rackets and the *bris* business. I have the shakes. See," he said, holding up his hands like a freshly scrubbed surgeon. His mitts trembled like a July Fourth flag. "Dangerous in my line of work. If you don't have good hands, an accident can happen. There's a fine line between a *bris* and a cas-tration. I've seen it happen with drunken *mohels*. Yeah, hands are im-portant," he continued distractedly. "Hey everyone, remember when Breitbart dropped this kid from his lap?" The men at the table laughed and nodded their heads in acknowledgment. "So Duncan, tell me, how's your pecker?"

"What the hell kind of a question is that to ask?" one of Morty's friends said, slapping Morty across the chest. All the men at the table looked vaguely familiar to Duncan. They were insiders when it came to knowing his story. The *bris* had whetted their appetites. By the time Duncan had left the city, they were already washed-up men of the Mafia, but the Katzes had become part of Miami mythology.

"What are you talking about?" Morty replied defensively. "I clopped off the boy's foreskin forty years ago. It's perfectly natural for me to want to see how my work holds up after all these years."

The former men of Murder Incorporated had become ancient and incontinent. Like stuffed animals they sat there, surrounded by pill bottles that they opened every few hours. Ordered to stay away from the precoronary brisket and stuffed dermas that the Nostra still kept on the menu in nostalgic reverence for Miami Beach's culinary past, the men now noshed on cottage cheese and fruit cups.

"Wait a minute," Morty said. "That guy over there looks just like Mila."

"Oh Christ, it is Mila," one of the other old-timers said.

"That's not Mila, you morons," another jumped in with the most energy he was going to muster for the day. "She's been dead for years."

"Wait a minute . . . it is," a Cuban gentleman said. He removed his glasses and wiped them off on his white shirt. "Hey, Mila, is that you?" He reached for a betting program that was folded on the table like a napkin and said, "Who do you like in the sixth race at Gulfstream?"

These alleged Mila sightings went on almost everywhere that Duncan brought his brother. The city may have changed, but everyone still seemed to know Mila. He took Isaac to the apartment building where the Katzes had lived. Nearly everyone was now either dead or had moved. But there were still some who remembered her, people who took pride in the vanishing art of remembrance. The cardroom, painted salmon with grass wallpaper, had been rededicated in her name. A plaque was on the door. Duncan took Isaac to where the Miami dog tracks once were, and to jai alai and the trotters, which still existed, and the hotels along the strip where Mila never checked in but always cashed out.

And finally, they ended up at Lakeview Memorial where Mila eventually folded.

"You sure you want to do this?" Duncan asked.

"Jewish history is a story of graveyards," Isaac replied. "That is why we must go. Because that's where the Jews are, and that's where we can find our mother."

The sons drove through the gargoyled gate, lions watching over-head. They parked the car beside the pavilion and walked—through Crespi Lane, Tatum Street, Flamingo Court, Fairway Canyon, Polo Boulevard, North Shore Avenue until they reached Parkview Way. They moved with determination, but also in silence, the bright sun-light both alluring and holding them back.

Isaac couldn't believe how flat and open the cemetery was. Based on his experience with the Jewish Cemetery of Warsaw, and the or-deal that each day presented, this place looked so easy to maintain. All that was needed was a big hat to keep the sun out of the eyes and off the head. There was no forestation. No unearthed graves becoming unburied from the roots of angry trees and livid souls. And no crumbling stones.

The afternoon was soon about to turn to dusk. There were no clouds or wind, just endless streaks of violet blue in the air, more background than sky. Duncan and Isaac marched on toward their mother's grave, along Parkview Way. But even from a distance, Dun-can could see that his mother was not alone. He had only been to this cemetery two other times, for the burials of each of his parents. He hadn't attended the unveiling of their gravestones. But yet he could find his parents instinctively. And as he and his brother got closer, Duncan saw the faces of the three women. They were some-what older than they had been when he had noticed them the first time. Now their hair was touched with gray; their bodies a bit more bent and swollen. But it was surely them, the ebony knights still guarding the chalice.

"What's wrong?" Isaac asked, as Duncan stopped walking.

"Those women over there," Duncan replied slowly. "They know things . . . about our mother."

"That's good, no? An unexpected surprise," Isaac said, hooking himself to Duncan's arm and pulling him forward.

The women were laying petunias and peonies at Mila's grave. They were also mumbling words out loud, words that Duncan couldn't hear. The women turned around suddenly and noticed Mila's boys. There was silence before anyone knew how to begin.

"I remember the three of you at the funeral . . . twelve years ago," Duncan said.

The nurses were startled, not just because Mila had other mourners, but because of who they were.

"Yes, that was us," Cynthia said.

"How did you know Mila?" Duncan asked.

The three nurses didn't answer Duncan, because Isaac proved the more captivating of the two men. They knew who he was. Judy's jaw dropped. Mila obviously had given birth to her twin. Cynthia's mouth opened, too, but nothing came out. Judy's face became showered in tears. She always cried when she came to this cemetery, but more so today. Louise dropped to the ground and rested on her knees as though this were one Easter that brought with it a true resurrection.

"You all look at me . . . like you know me somehow," Isaac said guardedly.

"Your mother told us about you," Louise replied. Then she got off the ground.

"She told us everything," Cynthia said. Then awkwardly, she glanced down toward Isaac's arm, which in Miami was sleeveless and fully exposed.

"Why you?" Duncan asked. "How come you know?"

"We were her nurses; we heard everything," Judy answered. "She trusted us. In the end, we were her family." Her eyes began to water again.

"What did she tell you?" Isaac asked.

"That she was sorry," Judy replied.

"She never forgave herself," Louise added. "You should know that."

"And she took it out on Duncan," Cynthia said, now looking at him. "She was sorry about what she did to you, too."

Judy added through the muffled sobs, "She wanted to tell you herself, Duncan, that day you came to the hospital, the night she died. I was in the bathroom. I heard everything. She wasn't making sense, but she was saying that she was sorry."

"It was all too late," Louise said.

"Not enough time," Judy sighed.

"Her luck ran out," Cynthia said. She then turned to Isaac and said, "If she had lived longer, she might have picked up and gone to Poland herself to find you. But her life wasn't a Hollywood movie. There was no happy ending."

"I guess when it's a Holocaust story," Judy reasoned, "even one that comes after, it's got to be sad."

"How did you find each other?" Louise asked Mila's sons.

"We'll tell you later," Duncan said, "but first, what are you all doing here now?"

"We're always here," Cynthia replied.

"We come once a week, all of us, together. We've been doing it for twelve years," Louise said proudly.

"We've missed a couple of times," Judy acknowledged, "but even then, at least one of us comes."

"We bring flowers," Cynthia said. "I thought the peonies would be nice today."

"And we say Kaddish," Louise said, pronouncing it as though it rhymed with *radish*.

"We promised Mila," Judy added.

"Yeah, she didn't think anybody else would do it," Cynthia said.

"It's not that hard to say," Judy insisted, as if trying to tempt Mila's sons into joining.

"I can't believe you've been coming here all this time," Duncan said. "I guess we should be thanking you . . ."

"Don't have to do that," Louise said. "She was special."

"We loved her," Judy said. "And we're nurses; we know her heart was broken."

"She trusted us with the whole story," Cynthia said. "We've been carrying it around for a long time."

"Sounds like a big burden," Duncan said.

"Maybe you should give some of it back to us," Isaac said.

The nurses knew that it was now time to pass the grail on to Mila's children; these men who were born of Mila, even if not loved by her.

Isaac then knelt down and stroked the bronze plate that was his mother's headstone. Duncan crouched beside his brother, and tapped against Yankee's grave, as though knocking on a door. He then removed the *pysanka* and rolled it on Mila's gravestone as though it were a craps table.

The brothers and sons rose and joined in with the nurses. As though they had all done this before, together as a mixed *minyan*, the mourners recited the Kaddish.

יִתְגַּדַּל וְיִתְקַדַּשׁ שְׁמֵהּ רַבָּא בְּעָלְמָא דִּי בְרָא כִרְעוּתֵהּ,

"Yitgadal v'yitkadash sh'mei rabba b'alma divra khee-rute . . ."

With one arm around his brother, Duncan looked down at Mila's grave. He had never seen the unveiled stone before. He didn't even know who had arranged to have it done or what they had written. What would Mila have wanted to say?

יִתְבָּרַךְ וְיִשְׁתַּבַּח וְיִתְפָּאַר וְיִתְרוֹמַם וְיִתְנַשֵּׂא,

"Yitbarack v'yishtaback v'yitpa'ar v'yitromam v'yitnasei . . ."

While continuing on with the prayer, he read the message on the gravestone.

MILA KATZ. WIFE. MOTHER.
SOMEONE TO WATCH OVER THEM.
101682.

עוֹשֶׂה שָׁלוֹם בִּמְרוֹמָיו, הוּא יַעֲשֶׂה שָׁלוֹם עָלֵינוּ וְעַל כָּל־
יִשְׂרָאֵל, וְאִמְרוּ אָמֵן.

"Oseh shalom bimromav, hu ya'aseh shalom aleinu v'al kol Yisrael, v'imru:
Amen."

As the sons and nurses completed the Kaddish, bruised purple storm clouds drifted in from the ocean. The rains, like a warm vaporous shower, came fast and sprayed hard. Thunder pounded the heavens like a warrior's drum, while lightning split the sky in two, separating this world from the other. Because there was no shade, there was nowhere to go. And the mourners weren't ready to leave yet, either. So they huddled in a violent Miami rain, surrounded by tears of atonement and the glare of a flashbulb in twilight. Duncan blinked and then wiped his eyes, which were ineluctably, almost morbidly, drawn to his brother's forearm. Misty streaks of water, as though spiked with acid, were slowly washing away the numbers. Four pebbles and one *pysanka* lined up on Mila's gravestone, silently bearing witness to the memory of the life that stirred within.

$\mathcal{A}$cknowledgments

NOVELS ARE WRITTEN ALONE, but novelists aren't necessarily alone when writing them. With the deepest gratitude to the following people who thin out the proverb that blood is thicker than water.

Robert Weil and Ellen Levine; the Sarnoff Family, Paul and Judy Berkman, Tracey Hughes and David Stern; Thomas Hameline; Sam Dubbin; Keni Fine; Marcie Hershman, Ellen Pall, Eva Fogelman, Myrna Kirkpatrick, Maggie Delmoral, Sarah Sternklar, Irene Speiser, Barbara Nuddle, Annette Insdorf, Aryeh Lev Stollman, John Thomas, Andrew Hartzell, Richard Horowitz and Jodi Schulson; Michael Lerner, Victor Goldberg and Robin Aronson, Esther Rosenbaum and Pearl Rosenbaum Pantone.

Thanks to Andrew Miller at St. Martin's Press. And for allowing me emotional access to the Office of Special Investigations, Eli Rosenbaum.

About the Author

THANE ROSENBAUM was born in New York City, in 1960, the only son of Holocaust survivors. His family later moved to Miami Beach, Florida, where he was raised.

He is the author of the critically-acclaimed, novel-in-stories, *Elijah Visible*, which received the Edward Lewis Wallant Book Award in 1996 for the best book of Jewish-American fiction.

Before becoming a novelist, he was a practicing attorney at the New York law firm of Debevoise & Plimpton. He now teaches human rights at Fordham Law School and creative writing at the New School. He is also the literary editor of *Tikkun* Magazine, and writes reviews, articles and essays for *The New York Times, The Washington Post, The Wall Street Journal, The Miami Herald, Newsday* and the *Forward*.

He lives in New York City with his daughter, Basia Tess.